THE
OUTCAST

A Novel

MICHAEL J. MARTIN

CONTENTS

This Book is dedicated to the British Military, Help for Heroes, Nurses from the NHS and Great Oaks Hospice, Coleford in the Forest of Dean.

Profits from the sale of this book will be donated to the Charities Help for Heroes, at the bequest of the Author and Great Oaks Hospice, for their support during his illness, at the bequest of the family.

PROLOGUE

In the Beginning

In the beginning it had been easy and the rewards had been good. There were undefended villages and towns built near the coast, the people believing the sea was their friend and ally. Most of them relied solely on what the sea gave up for their livelihood. These people had lived beside the sea in peace and relative prosperity for many years now and had grown complacent and lax and had forgotten how to fight and how to defend themselves. But the villagers in the north were a tough and hardy people and it hadn't taken long for the survivors of the raids to relearn their fighting skills and devise ways to defend their meagre possessions, and their very lives, from the wild men who arrived silently from across the cold waters of the Northern Sea.

As they relearned old skills the odds had shifted more in favour of the landsmen. The advantages which the raiders had enjoyed in the beginning had been whittled away until they were left with only the element of surprise, for they usually attacked in the dark hours just before dawn. But even this had been taken from them by the lookouts and the signal fires set up along the coastline.

Only a foolish raider would carry on as usual, and, if Ofleg was anything, he was never foolish. Ofleg had been doing this as long as he could remember, taken under the wing of his mentor Eric One-

Eye, and he had learnt his lessons well. Childhood play with the other children of his settlement had never existed for Ofleg, and when Eric One-Eye passed on years before, he had laid claim to the boat, which no-one dared to challenge, and the men followed him just as they had followed Eric. Now it was time to move on and they were in search for new victims.

So, as the tenth century ground inexorably towards its end, Ofleg set his course southward, seeking new targets where the people had no knowledge of the raiders and were innocent and naive and vulnerable. Sailing long mile after long mile close to the coast of this place they called Angleland, following each headland and inlet, until their course turned to the south-west and the great white cliffs towered above them. Still they sailed on, leaving the white cliffs far behind until, further south and west than he had ever been before, Ofleg found what he was seeking. The soft underbelly. Just as he knew he would.

'Wake up,' the voice hissed as the hand roughly, but not too roughly, shook his shoulder. 'Lights and a fire.'

Ofleg struggled back to full wakefulness. He had been dreaming of home but the dream was instantly forgotten. He emerged onto the deck and knew instantly by the soft murmur of the water on shingle that they were close inshore. It was a moonless night and it was inky black with not even a star to guide the way. At first he could see nothing, for the light that his second-in-command had spotted had been extinguished, but then a log must have shifted in a fire for briefly there was a flare of flame and a shower of sparks. He turned to the man who had awakened him.

'What do you think we have here?' he whispered. Sound carried a long way over water, you could never be too careful in this line of work.

'Maybe a farm or a fishing hamlet. Nothing big enough to worry us.'

'We need to take a look.' Ofleg turned to the men gathered around. 'You two,' he beckoned them over. 'Get over the side.' The men knew the drill, and immediately stripped off their clothes, lowered themselves over the railing and within seconds were lost to view as they silently made their way towards the shore. Ofleg turned to the other men who were gathered around also watching the shore.

'Man the oars,' he ordered, and took the boat a short distance further from the shoreline.

Suddenly the sky lightened slightly and he was able, for a brief moment, to take stock of their position. It became obvious that they were in the mouth of a slowly flowing river, just where it became part of the sea. The estuary was horseshoe shaped and the waters were calm. Perfect.

*

The killing was efficiently brutal and mind-numbing in its swiftness, for it was all over in a few bloody minutes. Old Jobi was crouched in the ditch behind the shabby houses surrounded by the rank smell of ammonia, following his dawn ritual as he did every morning as regular as clockwork, when he heard the first sounds of the carnage up above.

Jobi was the oldest inhabitant of the hamlet. He would shortly reach his fifty-eighth year and had lived here all of his life along with his wife May. In all that time neither of them had ventured more than a dozen miles from home. May had unfortunately been unable to have children of her own, but was everything to the younger women, midwife when required, nurse and comforter, a bottomless well of knowledge and loved as a grandmother by all. Some of the younger women swore that she had the gift of second sight and other dark powers, and they used her name to scare the young children when they misbehaved. Jobi was, well, just 'old Jobi'.

As the screams reached his ears old Jobi, crook-backed from long years of toil on the land, straightened up as best he could to peer over the rim of the ditch, allowing the hem of his nightshirt to fall unnoticed around his ankles. His heart almost stopped with fright as a huge man with a full unkempt beard and even wilder hair, ran towards him between the houses. Thankfully, in the poor early morning light, the man did not see Jobi crouching low, and instead veered to his left and using the double-headed axe he wielded, smashed his way through the rear door of the house in which Jobi lived. Another stranger ran past the end of the alleyway with a sword held high.

Jobi who some considered to be 'a bit slow' but nonetheless a well-loved member of the community, had been a labourer all his life, never a fighting man, and as the screams and cries of terror came from inside the buildings the overbearing fear of being killed took over. Jobi gathered up his nightshirt and scampered crabwise along the ditch, blind to where he was treading, intent on escaping the men attacking his home. He ran headlong across a piece of open ground and scampered into the thick cover of the hedgerow on the far side.

The screams eventually quieted to be replaced by a droning, dismal sobbing. The bedraggled survivors of the attack huddled together, clutching at each other, on the patch of dew-sodden grass in the middle of the ramshackle houses. Seven women, one clutching a young baby to her chest, a few young children and old May were all that remained of what had been, until then, a thriving farming and fishing community. Only one man had survived the ferocity of the attack, but that man was hiding deep in a thicket hundreds of yards away on the far side of the long acre.

A silence, except for the snivelling of one of the young children as it clung to its mother's shift, descended over the sorry group of terrified and confused women as they stood and watched the raiders rampage through each house in turn. The raiders looted whatever they could find, until a pathetically small pile of assorted pots, pans and candlesticks lay close by, each find announced by its finder with a loud shout in a strange guttural language.

Ofleg watched his men as they went about the business of sacking the houses. He knew they would miss nothing. They had done this many times before and were well practised in finding even the smallest little hidey-hole.

The lack of anything of intrinsic value did not surprise the huge man. He had expected as much, but he was here for something of more value than silver or pewter. It was early October and the harvest was in and he knew the storehouses would contain almost enough food to sustain them through the cold winter and the long darkness when they returned home to their families in the land of the fjords. What they could pillage here would supplement nicely their usual diet of dried fish and, the only other protein available in the freezing winters that far north, rabbit.

The raid had come early, before many of the inhabitants of the hamlet had been up and about and the women stood in various states of dress and undress. Whether from shock or the chill air most were shivering violently, but even so were put to work. Full barrels of salt pork, grain, root vegetables, flour, apples and a side or two of fat bacon, all had to be carried down to the tiny beach where Ofleg had grounded his longboat in the darkness of the pre-dawn. The women were made to rob themselves.

The precious cow and its heifer were butchered and they too disappeared into the hold along with the geese and the chickens and the contents of the cheese store, and the fish that had been smoked and laid up for the winter. Ofleg watched closely as the women worked. They were strong and used to hard work and did the job of loading well.

He would have liked to have taken some of the women back home with him. The younger ones would have been welcome assets, bringing a source of new blood to the villages and hamlets in the harsh lands where the winters were long and the ground remained frozen for many months of the year. To cultivate such land was back-breaking work and the women who would not comply or who were not pretty enough were habitually enslaved and forced to do the heavy work. But his boat was already lying deep in the water, dangerously so, and to take even one would have been foolish. No, they would have to take their pleasure here, before they set sail for home.

When Ofleg was satisfied that every scrap of edible food had been loaded aboard, he at last gave his assent and the men turned their full attention to the women. Ofleg gripped the arm of the youngest woman, hardly more than a girl really, and led her towards the house he himself had crashed into when the raid had begun. She had been tucked up in the bed in the corner of the single room. He had seen her as his eyes had made their first urgent sweep of the room, but his attention had been concentrated on the big man who was over by the fire, coaxing the embers into life with some kindling.

Now the girl was too terror-stricken to put up any resistance and went meekly with the big man, even though she knew what was about to happen to her over the next minutes or even hours. This man with the wild blue eyes and the even wilder, filthy and matted blond hair which gave him the look of a mangy old dog, reminded her of the demons from hell she had only seen in religious pictures.

He dragged her into the house, pushed her towards the bed. Crying now, tears rolling down her cheeks, there was nothing for her but to obey if she wanted to live through this ordeal. She had no doubts that the man would kill her without a second thought if she fought against him, and she knew anyway, that she could never win against such a brute of a man.

From her position on the truckle-bed she could look across the tiny room and see the body of her beloved husband, Harold Twelvetrees, and she concentrated on him as her ordeal began. They had married only a few months before and now he was dead.

His body was still on its knees, bent forward so that his forehead rested on the dirt floor where he had slumped after the vicious scything blade had sliced through his body, almost cutting him in two. His hands were still clasped together over his stomach trying unsuccessfully to hold his intestines and vital organs inside his belly cavity, whilst the dirt floor beneath his body turned black with the blood and guts that he had been unable to prevent from escaping through his fingers.

The other women of the hamlet were led away to other houses. Some put up a fight. One woman who had resisted had been knocked to the ground and was now on her back, screaming, being dragged by the arms by two men. Another, lashing out briefly, could only scream loudly as she was grabbed by her hair before being lifted bodily by the helmsman and carried away. Even old May was dragged towards the barn by two men.

*

The survivors gathered together the few scraps of food they could find and then left the hamlet the day after the raid. Even though they were in shock, they knew there was nothing left for them now and they knew that, not only were they were unprotected from the gangs of opportunist thieves and vagabonds who roamed the countryside; they were also in danger of starving in the cold of the looming winter. Old Jobi had plucked up the courage to return to the buildings and all together they worked away at the ground and buried their men in the soft, freshly dug earth of the turnip field. The old man, full of guilt for having run away and unable to meet the eyes of the women, did the work of three men but it could not make amends. The women treated him with the distain he deserved. To them he was now no more than a dog turd.

After bundling up anything useful that they could manage to carry in pieces of cloth, the women took to the track leading inland. Everything else was left behind including Old Jobi and May. They had nowhere else to go and felt too old to start again elsewhere. They would take their chances foraging through the winter and see what awaited them in the spring of the coming year.

The small and bedraggled group of women headed north. Most of them were from local families and had relatives who would shelter them. They made slow progress after their ordeal and the unmade road and the lack of any food to sustain them served to slow them even further. But at least the weather was kind to them and day by day, as first one then another met family and friends who would take them in, the group grew smaller. On the third day and after more than forty miles of walking, Mistress Twelvetrees found herself going on alone. Of course she had family but had no idea where she was or in which direction she should go in order to find them. They could be anywhere.

*

She was from a long line of travellers and horse traders and had met the young Twelvetrees at the horse-fair in Tavistock. In no time at all they had become enthralled and besotted with each other. A few days later, when the family made preparations to move on, she defied her father and insisted on staying.

'He's different to us,' her father had said.

'But I love him.'

'He's a farmer, a dirt shoveller. He smells of pigs and shit.'

'I still love him,' and, as an afterthought, 'anyway, somebody has to grow the food we eat.'

'Don't have to be you, though, do it? Leave that to them fools as was brought up to it, I say.'

There was silence for a few seconds whilst her father thought of more objections.

'And he lives in a house. How can you love a man who lives in a house?' he asked disparagingly.

'I don't know, but I know that I do and I want to stay with him.'

'You'll go crazy staring at the same four walls all day long, I know you will. You know what your like, you'll want to leave within the week. You're used to the open road, think on that.'

'But I do love him, Pa, I know I do.'

'What do you know of love?' her father sneered, but he now had a new argument. 'You are nothing more than a child.'

'I'm old enough. I am older than Ma was when she had me.' There and then he knew he had lost the argument. It was true. His wife had been pregnant before she had reached the age that his daughter was now, although he had hoped that the subject of his daughter's illegitimate birth would not be brought up.

He turned to threats to tie her to one of the horses and carry her away by force, but deep down he knew that wouldn't work either. He knew his daughter, and her stubbornly ways, too well. As her family moved on towards the coast, she was already travelling in another direction with the man she wanted to call husband.

The young couple took their time and followed the road back to Devon at a leisurely pace, falling more and more in love it seemed, with every passing minute. Eventually they arrived back at the hamlet and Twelvetrees proudly showed off the dark-eyed, black-haired beauty who was to be his wife and she was welcomed into the small community with open arms.

*

Eldred, the one-time shepherd, was enjoying the last minutes of heat from the sun. He had eaten his supper and had taken the chair out to the front of the cottage where he often sat these days waiting for darkness and, maybe, for his own death. He felt complete in these surroundings, at one with himself, at one with nature and at one with God.

He had first spotted the woman over an hour before, a mile or more down in the valley, and had idly wondered where she was heading. No-one came this far up onto the moor these days – not for a social call anyway – and there was precious little else to do up here except admire the views. His cottage was the only one still inhabited this far from the village, although there were several nearby, abandoned and decaying. The little-used track that passed by the gate to his garden petered out to nothing a few hundred yards further on.

He slowly and deliberately rose from his seat and stood watching the woman's laboured approach until she eventually reached his gateway. They stood looking at each other in silence. He could hardly see her face for dirt and the hem of her dress was heavy with mud. She appeared to be carrying a bundle of rags.

He studied what he could see of her face. He had never seen eyes so full of hopelessness in all his life. Eventually he turned, lifted the chair, and went to the door of the cottage looking back over his shoulder and beckoning for her to follow him inside.

Goodwife Twelvetrees had no idea where she was but knew that the track she was following was not well used. She had lost all sense of time and distance hours before but knew that she must keep moving. To lie down and rest would be the end. She would die where she lay.

On legs that threatened to turn to water at any moment she followed the man inside. It was more than a day, maybe two, since she had last eaten anything except a few berries and some wild herbs, and the first bowl of mutton pottage disappeared in seconds with hardly, it seemed, the woman taking a breath between mouthfuls. When the second helping had also gone the way of the first they began to talk.

Eldred could see that he was much older than the woman. He was approaching his fifty-second year, and had been living alone up on the moor since his wife had passed away a good many years ago. When she had died he had almost lost the will to live himself. He missed her more than he had ever thought possible and knew exactly what loneliness felt like. As time passed he had neglected himself. He was dirty and he carried with him a disgusting smell, as did his cottage, but under the dirt and grime he was a good man and a god-fearing man. All he needed was someone to care for him and he to care for them. A reason to live.

Despite her strange accent which Eldred found difficulty to decipher, they rapidly reached an agreement. In return for cooking and cleaning and occasional help outside he agreed to give her shelter, food, warmth and a safe place to stay. She was free to leave whenever she wanted but, deep down, Eldred hoped that maybe she would stay for ever.

They finished talking and he filled a cracked bowl with warm water from the pan over the fire. She washed her hands and face, removing the accumulation of days of grime, and only then did he realise how young she really was. She was hardly more than a child. She returned to her place at the table and, without further ado, lowered her head onto her arms and within seconds was asleep.

*

She carried the baby to its full term and in early July the following year, she gave birth to a son. All the while she had clung to the thought that it would be the child of her beloved Harold Twelvetrees. If it turned out not to be his, the choice was a simple one. It was just a case of how she would get rid of the child.

But life is never that easy or simple. The blond, almost white shock of hair and the deep blue eyes on the new born child screamed 'raider' at her and she knew it was the offspring of the wild man who had raped her. But the baby was part of her as well and the bond was too strong. He was her boy as well.

She had planned to call the baby Harold but now found she could not. Instead she named him Eldredson, which pleased Eldred and made him feel proud, but then, she had never told him the full story.

*

Old Jobi and May were alone in the hamlet and had survived through the cold winter months on what little food they could forage. But it seemed the gods had been kind to them and the weather had been unusually mild and dry with hardly any snow or deep frosts. And the good weather and their good fortune had lasted right through the following summer and into the autumn. A year which to old Jobi seemed to have passed in little more than a blink of an eye. Hardly a day had passed without the sun shining and all the fruit and vegetables had matured early. But something was not right with May. It was not often that Jobi worried about May, rather the other way round, but he was worried now.

For weeks she had been preoccupied, had seemed to have retreated into herself and had hardly spoken a word to old Jobi, which was not unusual, however, as she had not spoken much since her ordeal at the hands of the raiders on the day he had shamefully run away, but occasionally he had heard her mumbling to herself as she moved around the cottage.

Some evenings she had been out and about, collecting strange plants and fungi which she finely chopped before mixing them all together in an old bowl. He had recognised some; foxglove and the seeds of the nightshade, hemlock and the evil-smelling fungus Angel's Trumpet and Destroying Angel, but the others were unrecognisable to him.

Then, more than a week ago, he had entered their cottage to find May squatting over the old bowl, urinating. Without a word she had placed the bowl in the nook close by the fire. Old Jobi was too apprehensive to ask what she was doing, perhaps it was better he didn't know. Several days later he had noticed that a nut-stick had appeared in the nook. It was a solid-looking stick and it was leaning against the wall. One end of the stick had been charred in a fire and then whittled into a vicious point. This end stood in the bowl.

Jobi had been out collecting windfall medlars on the day that he died. He had almost filled the basket and was looking forward to tasting the sweet jelly they would make when he heard May urgently calling his name. Thinking something was seriously wrong, he left the fruit and hurried as best he could back to the cottage. May was standing silently staring in the direction of the beach, although the stand of trees obscured her view. She was so still that she could have been carved from stone.

'It is time. They are back. I knew they would come back.'

'Who's back?' Jobi looked fearfully towards the trees but could see no-one. 'It's time for what?'

'It's time to put an end to it. Everything has to have an ending. Fetch the bowl and the stick.'

Jobi knew without being told which bowl and stick she meant and although he had no idea what 'it' was, he did as he was told and returned with the bowl which he placed at her feet.

'What shall I do with this?' he asked, waving the stick around.

'Be careful with that, my lovely. With that stabber you will end it all today. You will be our salvation.'

Old Jobi swivelled his head quickly to look at her. 'My lovely.' Had he heard right? She used to call him that when they were young and he was so much in love with her. But he hadn't heard those words for a long, long while. And the look that she gave him now was the look she used to give him then.

Jobi was totally confused now.

'What do you mean?' he asked. 'I will be our salvation? What's going to happen?'

'You have been my man now for as long as I can remember, my lovely.' There, she had said it again. 'We have lived and worked together, argued and fought, laughed together in the good times and cried together in the bad. But through it all I have always loved you, although it may not have seemed that way at times, and I know that you have loved me in return. Now we are to die and we will be together for ever and ever.'

And then she smiled at him. A radiant smile that lit up her face. The kind of smile she used to smile at him when he wore a younger man's clothes, but the like of which he had not seen for a long, long time. His heart pounded in his chest and he stood as straight as his crook-back would allow.

'I will protect you, May.' And he turned to face the trees, the stick held out in front.

May reached out and laid a soft hand on his arm.

'I know you will, my lovely, but the time has come.'

He turned to look at her again but her attention was on the stand of trees. He turned back and in that tiny space of time when he hadn't been watchful, the man had appeared. Jobi's stomach turned over and his bowels turned to water. The old Jobi had returned and he would have turned and ran had not May taken a firmer grip on his arm.

'Be brave, my lovely, be brave. It will all be over soon.'

A calmness came over Jobi. He stood and faced the huge man with the wild blue eyes and the wild blond hair. He felt good, as though some kind of strength was flowing into him from his woman. He felt young again.

Two more men appeared from the trees on either side of the blond giant, then a third and a fourth, and a fifth and a sixth and soon it seemed to Jobi that there were dozens of men filling the clearing. But he still felt calm. *Maybe, after all,* he thought, *maybe today is a good day to die.*

*

Ofleg had not known what to expect, returning to the hamlet so soon after the raid the year before, and had approached the houses with caution. Perhaps the place would be deserted and derelict but maybe the women were still here. He hoped so. This year he was on the lookout for young women and boys to take back north to be put to work. It had been a harsh winter and many slaves had died.

When he had emerged from the trees he had not expected to see a thin and bent old man and an even thinner old woman, standing together in the centre of the ramshackle buildings, holding hands and facing the trees as though they were expecting him to appear. The old man was gripping a stick in his free hand and trying to look defiant. Trying to look fierce, as though he could frighten them away.

Ofleg laughed out loud. Such a foolish old man to think such a thing. What did he think he could do with a stick? Suddenly Ofleg leaned forward and bellowed his war-cry into the old man's face, so loud it seemed to shake the nearest trees, and he raised his sword high above his head. He expected the old man to run away. It had happened before, when Ofleg had threatened much younger men than this one, but although the old man flinched and his face paled he stood his ground.

They were less than ten feet apart and Ofleg could smell the fear on the man. Enough of this. Ofleg took a long pace forward, close enough now to land a blow on the man, and was amazed when his target also took a step forward and stabbed his stick at him. He felt the sharp pinprick of pain in his lower belly as the point of the stick penetrated his woollen breeches, but the pain was never going to be enough to divert his sword arm and the weapon crashed down onto the old man's unprotected head and smashed him to the ground.

The woman did nothing for what seemed an age, looking down at the body of her husband. Then, slowly, she knelt down and took his bloody head in her arms. She looked up at Ofleg and said something that he could not understand. She turned away from the raider and Ofleg raised his sword once more and brought it savagely down across the woman's shoulders and neck. It was over.

There was nothing useful in the surrounding buildings and they made their way back to the longboat. Ofleg had just made the water's edge when the nausea took him. He retched uncontrollably into the shallow water until his stomach was empty. He climbed aboard, his heart thumping wildly in his chest and sweat beading on his forehead. He swilled the bitter taste from his mouth with some water from the barrel and spat over the side. His spit was bright red.

Before the men had re-floated the boat and pointed her bow out to sea, the vicious stomach cramps that doubled Ofleg over with the pain, had begun. Within the hour his sight was failing but inwardly his mind was full of visions and demons. He took to cursing and ranting like a madman and all the while the pain increased and his body grew hotter and hotter. He felt as though he was being engulfed in flames.

Some of the men were superstitious and were afraid to go near him, fearing he had displeased the gods and had become possessed by demons They were glad when, during the night, he gave up his agonising fight for life and, with relief, they were able to throw his weighted body into the sea.

The year was 987 A.D.

PART I

THE LORD IS MY SHEPHERD

EIGHT HUNDRED YEARS LATER

CHAPTER 1

Nathaniel Leadbitter

Kent
Summer, 1787

Mr Nathaniel Leadbitter was without doubt a very lucky man. He was also a very, very rich man. It was reputed that he was worth in excess of three quarters of a million pounds. A huge fortune.

He stood in his study, between the huge mahogany desk and the bay window which overlooked the well-manicured lawns that stretched all the way down to the artificial pond in the small valley. He was neither tall nor short, fat nor thin. Some would describe him as being average if they discounted the special something, a distinguished air, which set him apart from other men. His brown hair was thinning as he aged and he had taken to wearing the fashionable 'mutton chop' whiskers on his otherwise babyish cheeks. But it was his eyes that people always noticed first and attracted them to him. They were brown and warm and friendly and crinkled at the outer edges as though he was constantly smiling, but they hid a sharp wit and an even sharper intelligence.

He stood with his back to the room, his hands clasped behind his back which served to extenuate the slight paunch that he had recently developed, and watched the group of peacocks (his wife's idea after a recent visit to the stately home of one of his political acquaintances) strutting over the grass. He had to admit that they had the most magnificent plumage but he thought they made the most god-awful noise, and the mess they made was equally as bad.

At this very moment though, he did not feel at all lucky and all the money in the world would not help him. In fact he felt decidedly uncomfortable. He may have had a most astute business brain but he always found the kind of task that he was about to perform difficult in the extreme. Dealing with the servants was usually the responsibility of his wife, and he was more than happy for that state of affairs to continue. Surprisingly, he lived in a kind of awe of the servants and stayed clear of them whenever he could. He had decided years before that all the female servants he would call Lizzie, regardless of their real names, and all the male servants would be called Seth. It made life so much easier, but his wife was away visiting relatives in the North of England and would not be back for several weeks. Unfortunately the matter in hand could not be postponed.

Mr Nathaniel Leadbitter had spent his younger years in Harrogate in the West Riding of Yorkshire, were he had been born, and where his father carried on his trade of Master Tailor in his modest premises in the market square. The business was modest in size only, for his services were highly sought after by the gentry. He was an excellent tailor and his reputation stretched far beyond the county of Yorkshire.

When Nathaniel reached the age of seven his father secured for him a place at the Minster School in York. How his father had done this no-one could fathom, for those places were usually reserved for the children of Bishops, the clergy and the upper classes. The conclusion was reached that he must have paid out a huge sum of money. There was no other explanation.

This was undoubtedly Nathaniel's first slice of good luck, although he did not think so at the time. Although he was only twenty miles or so from his home he may as well have been on the other side of the world for he was only a small boy and was homesick and missed his mother and brothers.

Over the following months he made friends with the other boys and with one boy in particular, whom he simply called Ben, and the homesickness faded away. Ben was short for Benjamin. Benjamin Alderley or Viscount Alderley, was the son and heir of Lord Cartesforth who owned a huge estate at Knaresborough but who lived nearly all the time in London where he carried on his business in the banking world.

*

The elder Leadbitter had fully expected his first-born son to eventually take over the tailoring business when he finished his schooling, just as he had taken over from his father. But the idea of being a tailor did not appeal to his eldest son who was mightily relieved when his brother Jeremiah, two years younger, showed great talent in all aspects of the trade. His father had died knowing that his business was in safe hands.

Nathaniel had the wish to be a Barrister at Law and part of the legacy left by his father paid for him to move to London to train under a renowned lawyer at Lincolns Inn. But after a very short while he found the work to be tedious in the extreme and dealing with felons was not as attractive as he had imagined. If he was honest, he would also admit that he would not have made a good lawyer as he did not have the eye for detail that was required. After a long interview with his sponsor, during which a frank exchange of views took place, a return to Harrogate seemed to be on the cards. But he had not reckoned on his friend Ben.

Benjamin had also moved down to London to join his father in the family banking business and immediately stepped forward to offer his friend a position. 'Just until you find your feet, you understand,' he had said.

This was Nathaniel's second piece of good fortune.

Nathaniel and Benjamin became even firmer friends and spent a lot of their spare time together. They drank together, went to the same parties and frequented the same 'Gentlemen's' club.

They formed a formidable partnership at the game of Bridge, at which they cheated outrageously, having worked out codes to pass messages to each other regarding the cards they both held. They were known as Ben and Nat and the people who knew gave them a wide berth in the card room for they nearly always took the rubber.

*

Nathaniel did not seem to have much work to do at the bank but was notionally in charge of the loans department which provided capital to businessmen who needed money to expand their companies, or who just needed cash in the short-term. After several months he had learned enough to take on some responsibility.

A notation in his appointment book for March 17 1772, a meeting with a Mr D. Watson – inventor and entrepreneur, was to change his life forever. The man arrived exactly at the appointed time of three p.m. with arms full of rolled-up drawings. He put his case for a loan of two hundred pounds that he needed to enable him to develop his newly invented machine that would 'revolutionise the woollen industry'.

Nathaniel had trouble understanding the technical aspects of the machinery but was fascinated by the concept and the obvious exuberance and confidence of the man. If anyone could make the machine work he was sure this was the man. He wrote a positive report for his principle, recommending the loan.

Despite his glowing report, the loan request was turned down without ceremony. Although seemingly a snub to Nathaniel, this was to be the third piece of good luck to come his way. The bank was wary of lending money to inventors with ideas to change the world, having lost money in the past. Besides, what assets did he have for security? None.

That evening, Nathaniel talked to Ben about the inventor and his erstwhile invention over their cheese and port wine. Maybe they were slightly in their cups, or maybe Nathaniel's enthusiasm carried sway but they made the decision to invest in the man and his machine themselves.

Pay back the money within the year, plus five per cent interest, plus twenty-five per cent shares in any profit was the deal they offered when they visited Mr Watson's rented workshop at Rotherhythe on the south side of the River Thames. Mr Watson eagerly accepted the terms, having no other options open to him. The partners, for that was what they now were, filed their drawings and claimed sole ownership of the machine with the London Patents Office. Four months went by before they were granted what they sought, for nearly two dozen patents were pending on almost identical types of machine. It was a time of great uncertainty but with the granting of the patent, the partners had taken the lead. Everything seemed set fair.

Six months later they advanced Mr Watson another hundred pounds under the same terms. The development was taking longer than expected.

The first demonstration of the machine, given to a specially invited group of mill-owners from Bolton in Lancashire raised a huge amount of interest and brought all three a massive profit. The machine did everything Mr Watson had claimed it would, and the mill-owners could see that production times would be reduced by more than half. Two days after the demonstration an offer was made to buy the patent by one of the businessmen hoping to steal a march on his rivals. The offer he made was two thousand pounds cash and after some haggling they settled in the sum of four thousand five hundred pounds.

Mr Watson went back to his next invention which, he said, 'would revolutionise the cotton industry'. Meanwhile the two friends used their share of the money to buy farmland in the foothills of the Pennines in Lancashire, land which was being sold for next to nothing by farmers struggling to make ends meet from food production. They stocked the land with thousands of sheep for they had also made a deal to supply the mill-owner who now owned the patent, with his raw material.

Within a few years their profit from the sale of wool and mutton had reached phenomenal levels and Nathaniel was on the way to becoming a rich man. Some of that profit he was now wisely re-investing in the cotton trade. Mr Watson, who he now counted among his good friends as well as being a business partner, had recently returned from The Americas with news of some great inventions. One, which he called the 'cotton gin', was, he said, a wonderful machine and would be sure to cut the production times, and therefore the cost, of cotton goods. 'Cotton was set to take over from wool,' he said.

Meanwhile, Nathaniel had become a highly eligible and sought after young man and had married the daughter of a mine owner from South Yorkshire. But she had social aspirations and had persuaded him to buy Harcote Hall at Hollingbourne in Kent, on the main London to Channel coast road, within sight of Leeds Castle, where they now resided. Her plan was to become part of the 'county set'.

*

He was awakened from his reverie by the sound of the door to the study opening and as he turned to face the room a young girl and the housekeeper entered. It was obvious to him that the girl had been crying for the skin around her eyes was red and puffy but despite this he was taken aback by the prettiness of the girl. She had wavy black hair spilling down to her waist and which shone in the bright light from the window, and she had black eyes to match, which contrasted vividly with her milky white, and, unusual in a servant, flawless skin. Her facial features were classically fine with high cheekbones and a broad forehead, not at all like the usually dour downstairs maids that his wife preferred to employ. There was no doubt in the mind of Nathaniel that she would grow into a stunningly beautiful woman in the fullness of time.

He was eager to get this business over with.

'I must let you go with immediate effect,' he said, formally and without preamble, to the girl who was now standing in front of him with her head bowed. She sobbed but did not reply. For she was in disgrace and had known that, at the least, she would be dismissed.

It had been Mrs Jackson, the housekeeper, who had first noticed the extra weight and the enlargement around the girl's waist and hips but by that time all other courses of action were ruled out except to give birth to the coming baby. The housekeeper was an old hand and had seen it all before. She had sympathy for the young, vulnerable girls, some as young as twelve years of age, who were forced to leave the safety of their families to enter service in the homes of the rich and powerful and ended up 'in trouble', but there was no sympathy for the wilful ones who refused to listen to the advice offered by the older and wiser staff. It was no wonder some were sent home in disgrace. She wondered at their silliness, but it had been a familiar story in all the great houses where she had held a position. Great houses, where the servants were treated as a commodity the same as any other commodity, to be used and then discarded when their usefulness came to an end. And this was especially true with regard to the female servants.

But it wasn't anyone from the Leadbitter family who had been responsible for getting the girl pregnant, just a lowly apprentice gardener from the estate to the west of the Leadbitters' property. She had confessed to the housekeeper that she had 'walked out' with him several times before he had plucked up the courage to kiss her. She had enjoyed the experience and had enthusiastically kissed him back. Over the following months they had taken pleasure from each other until the inevitable happened. But they were young and inexperienced in sexual matters and had taken no precautions, even if they had known of any. It was subsequently found, that when the young gardener had been summoned to the Hall, he had hurriedly left his employ and had disappeared.

As the girl stood before him sobbing quietly Nathaniel felt his resolve wavering, for he was not an unkind man, and he had been given nothing but good reports by Mrs Jackson, as to the girl's willingness to work hard and her pleasant demeanour. But he had been instructed by his wife that an example had to be made for the sake of the discipline of the other downstairs staff, not to mention their moral guidance.

Before him on the desk he had an assortment of coins; the wages that were owed to the girl, but they seemed to be a pitiful amount and he was touched by her plight. Sliding open a drawer in the desk he produced a five pound note, issued by the newly formed Bank of England, which he handed to the girl along with the few coins.

'To tide you over, my dear,' he said, exercising his usual generosity, 'until you can get back on your feet. Maybe you will get a chance to pay me back sometime in the future.'

It's ironic, he thought, as he was reminded of the words of his friend Ben when he had left his employ at Lincoln's Inn.

'Contact Mrs Jackson,' he indicated the housekeeper, 'if you need to return to work after the birth, and she will see if you can be of use to us again.'

The girl left the Hall shortly after and Nathaniel watched her from an upstairs window as she trudged down the driveway, walking the mile or so to the main Dover road where she could take a ride with one of the scheduled coaches which plied between the capital and the coast. She carried everything she owned in a canvas bag which looked much too heavy for such a small girl.

He wondered what would become of her and often thought of her over the next few weeks, but gradually she faded from his memory and he thought no more of her.

But, as she had walked away from the Hall, she had stopped crying and she felt a lot better. She was feeling rich. She had never even seen a five pound note before let alone owned one and five pounds was as much as she normally earned in half a year.

*

The girl returned to her parents' house in Dover, a small two-up, one-down with a lean-to at the back with the copper boiler in the corner, and a small yard surrounded by a tall stone wall, containing the privy. A gate gave access to a back lane that ran the length of the street behind the row of houses.

They took her back with few recriminations. She was, after all, their daughter and their only child.

When the baby was born he was called Joshua and took his mother's surname, Deschamps, for her grandfather had been a French immigrant. No-one knew what baby Joshua Deschamps owed to the miscreant young man who was his father, but it certainly wasn't his looks. Just like his mother Louisa he had black hair and black eyes, fine features, and the same pale-coloured skin. Everyone said that he was the most beautiful baby they had ever seen.

CHAPTER 2

North Somerset
June 1819

Goodwife Luffscombe, known to all her friends and neighbours by her given name Eliza and called affectionately Bess by her husband, crossed the room again to the only window in the dark but warm and comfortable parlour and looked out. It was a tiny window and didn't give much of a view of the countryside even at this time of year. The farm cottage had been built years before nearly a mile from the nearest hamlet, in the lea of the only hill for miles. It was almost surrounded by Silver Birch and Italian Alder planted closely together to give the cottage some protection from the winds which, in the winter with nothing to hinder their progress, constantly swept across the Somerset Levels all the way from the Bristol Channel.

Eliza had bitten the nails on the first two fingers of her right hand almost down to the quick, as she was prone to do when she was worried, ever since she had been a young girl. Now she was worried about her daughter Emily, who she had allowed out to see her friends in the hamlet after she had finished the little jobs around the house that she had to do every day. She had never been this late home, ever. In another hour or so it would be dark out.

Eliza Luffscombe had produced six sons and, at the age of forty-four and thinking her time for having children had already passed, had almost given up all hope of ever having a daughter. But then, much to her surprise and joy, she had conceived and given birth to baby Emily, named after her husband's mother, as was the tradition in her family.

The youngest of her six sons had been almost eight years old on the evening of the Harvest Thanksgiving supper in the hamlet. There had been plenty of good food and music and dancing and one of the local farmers, famous in this area of Somerset for his cider and perry, had given several barrels of the new year's potent brew to help proceedings along. The evening had been perfect, the weather had been balmy and the moon had shone brightly. Eliza and her husband, slightly tipsy, had dallied along the river bank on the long walk home, and, at their favourite spot, had lain down and had made love as they used to do when they were a young couple walking out together before they were married.

As early as the following day, Eliza knew that she was with child. She just knew somehow, as only a woman can know. She felt pregnant.

Traditionally, each Sunday, the family, in common with most other families, would put on their very best clothes and walk smartly down to the chapel in the village. Besides praying to God and being reminded of their moral responsibilities, attending chapel was a chance for everyone to socialise on a more or less equal footing, even with the gentry and the landowners. Just as important, it was a chance for the women to show off any new clothes or any second-hand items of clothing they may have been sent from a daughter in service. But sadly for Eliza, having no daughters in service, it was mostly just chapel and praising God.

Since the Harvest Thanksgiving, each and every Sunday Eliza had prayed fervently for the baby to be a girl, as did her husband, her sons and each and every one of the small congregation.

Emily was born the following June and she was everything that Eliza had ever wanted. She paraded with the baby girl and took every opportunity to show her off. She never tired of talking about her beautiful daughter as though she was the first and only girl ever born in the village.

Everyone who had prayed for Eliza to have a daughter now prayed for her to return to her old self. Eventually, many months later, her excitement at having a new daughter calmed and things returned to what passed for normal in the Luffscombe household.

But Eliza enjoyed having a daughter. She enjoyed dressing her up in ribbons and bows and pretty dresses. She spent much of her time sewing, making dresses and petticoats as the girl grew. And Emily was a good baby, she never cried much except when she was teething.

As she grew older, her mother spent lots of time telling her stories of the old times and teaching her things around the home. Her father would sit her on his lap of an evening and snuggle her up until she fell asleep and her brothers, normally rough and ready, suddenly became very gentle and protective around her.

Now, in just two weeks' time it would be her daughter's birthday. Eliza found it difficult to believe that she would be seven already. Where had the time gone to? But today, unusually, she was late home. Eliza knew that she should be getting supper ready for her husband and the five sons who still lived with them in the tied cottage, but she could not settle to the task. She was not usually superstitious, but she had a horribly strange feeling that her daughter could be in danger – and now it was almost dark.

*

The man had pulled the cart thirty or forty yards off the track into a thick copse of trees which would hide it from the eyes of anyone passing by. He mounted a small grassy knoll and surveyed the immediate surroundings. He could see nothing; no people; no houses nor any farm buildings. It was getting dark and the fields were deserted. He stood on the top of the bank, unbuttoned his trousers and took out his cock. He peed mightily on the ground. A Stag-horn beetle, caught in the stream of warm liquid, searched frantically for cover in the undergrowth. He finished peeing and, whilst he re-buttoned his trousers, took a final look around. The countryside was still empty of human life. He looked down, deliberately covered the Stag-horn with the sole of his boot and heard the satisfying crunch as he applied his full weight.

Returning to the cart he clambered up onto the back and approached what would naturally be taken for a large tool chest. He took a key from his trouser pocket and inserted it into the lock.

The lid opened easily on well-oiled hinges despite the weight of the wadding which lined it. Another lid was revealed underneath for this tool chest had another box within it, surrounded by wadding, making the whole thing sound-proof. The inner box was big enough to hide a small child.

He took away the metal bar that held the inner lid shut and pulled the lid open. The air inside smelt fetid but he expected this. He knew from experience that the box contained enough air to keep a child alive for about three hours and it had only been just over half an hour since he had snatched the girl. She was curled into a ball and she blinked rapidly in the sudden light that to her was blindingly bright after the pitch blackness of the box. The man reached down and his large hand grasped her by the shoulder and lifted her bodily up. She squealed like a frightened piglet as the pain in her arm lanced through her. He had heard the bone snap as she had earlier fought against him as he had forced her down into the box.

'Shut up,' he hissed venomously, his face pushed up to within inches of hers, 'or else.' She could smell the onion that he had eaten earlier, on his breath.

He rose and, pulling his trousers up to his waist, he crossed to the cart. He took a deep draught from the flagon of cider that was wedged tightly into the left-hand corner. He took another deep draught as his breathing gradually returned to normal. A loud fart escaped him.

He wiped his mouth with the back of his hand and crossed back to the girl. He looked down at her and noted the smear of blood at the top of her thighs. She was quiet now. He knelt and put his hand on her chest. He felt her under-formed nipple under his hand and under that, the beat of her heart. It was rapid but strong enough.

'Good. You're not going to die on me then?' he said. 'I haven't finished with you yet.' He intended to keep her for a day or two. She would spend her time in the box and he would take her out and 'play' with her whenever the urges overcame him. Until she died or until he tired of her — either way the result would be the same.

*

A little over five miles from the place where the man held Emily, her mother, sitting at the kitchen table, felt a cold shiver pass down her spine and she knew that something terrible was happening to her beautiful daughter. She lowered her head onto her arms and began to make a pitiful keening sound. The sound would continue through the rooms of the small cottage for hours until it would cease as suddenly as it began, to be followed by a dreadful silence.

Emily's father and brothers searched the route that she would have taken to reach home and when daylight came the next day, neighbours from miles around retraced the route once again, hoping against hope that the men had missed something in the dark. No clue as to the fate of the girl was found.

It was more than three weeks before Eliza Luffscombe felt able to leave the confines of the small cottage. She dressed in her Sunday-best frock and her special-occasion shoes and walked to the village. It was just before midday but she met no-one on the road or in the village as she entered the chapel. Inside the bright sunlight streamed through the plain glass windows, for it was a beautiful late Autumn day, and she could see the disturbed dust floating in the sunbeams, but the air was cool and she stood straight and tall in the short aisle. She didn't stay inside for long... just long enough to quietly mutter her curse at the cross depicting the crucifixion of the Lord Jesus that adorned the simple altar.

She left the chapel and walked towards the cemetery, passing the few shops on her way. In the hardware store Mister Barridge, the proprietor, looked up from his paperwork as her shadow moved across his open doorway. He rounded the counter and stood in the doorway and watched her as she passed through the ornate cemetery gates. He couldn't help thinking that she was a fine figure of a woman, despite her recent troubles.

She passed from his sight as she wound her way between the graves, picking up small stones as she went and putting them in the deep pockets of her dress. He went back to his work whilst she walked until she reached the spot at the side of the river where she had conceived her daughter those few short years ago. When she reached the spot her step did not falter and she continued to walk into the water until it was deep enough to cover her and the stones in her pockets held her down and her overwhelming sadness was ended.

CHAPTER 3

Gaston Portier

1793

For months now, members of the British Government, and all those people who were not members of the government but who were in the know, had talked about nothing else. For them it was the main, if not the only, topic of conversation. There was no doubt that there would be a war with France and with it would come the chance to make a lot of money for those who had their fingers in the government pie.

The interests of the two countries were diametrically opposed and no amount of discussion or diplomacy could close the gap between the two sides. Napoleon Bonaparte was setting out to subdue the whole of Europe, intending to build a French Empire that would surpass that of Great Britain and which would eventually lead to the downfall of its arch enemy. Britain, for its part, was determined to protect itself and its interests abroad, especially the trade routes which passed through the Low Countries to the countries further to the east of Europe.

Gaston Portier, on the day that war was formally announced, saw it as the perfect opportunity for revenge.

*

Damon Portier, the father of Gaston, had arrived in England many years before, at the tender age of twenty-two. A position as a secretary in the Corps Diplomatique had been secured for him by his father, a doctor at the royal courts in Paris. After several years, during which he had worked hard, Damon had been rewarded with a posting to the Court of Saint James in London, every Frenchman's dream. Although only a lowly secretary, he was invited to many formal Embassy gatherings and parties. At one such party he had been introduced to Lucy Johnson and had danced with her and monopolised her company for most of the remainder of the evening, much to the chagrin of the other single men present. He was besotted with her and during the following months he had wooed her as only a young Frenchman in love can. He had used all his natural charm to break down her family's reservations concerning his nationality, helped by her declaration of her love for him, and they had married nineteen months later. She had promptly delivered a son and heir. They had named him Gaston simply because they both liked the name.

Nine years later, having been recognised once again for his diligence in his work, Damon had been promoted to Vice Consul and the family moved to the French consulate in Amsterdam. By this time Gaston had a sister, Amelia, four years younger. Whilst their parents struggled to learn the new language, within no time at all the two children were so fluent they could have been taken for Dutch children. When Damon was recalled back to Paris after only three years, he accepted the recall with stoicism and secret relief, still unable to converse easily to the Dutch officials in their own language, definitely seen as a diplomatic shortcoming.

With his highly sought-after new post of adviser to the royal household he was allocated an apartment in one of the wings of the Palace of Versailles. It was an exciting time for Damon and his wife and the children settled into their new life as easily as children usually do. Gaston and Amelia now spent several hours every day with their private tutors but the rest of the time they spent exploring the huge palace and the estate gardens or playing with the children of the other staff. Within months they were fluent in the French language. Both children were very bright and the tutors were large in their praise of the children to their father. Gaston was growing up fast and his father had high hopes of him for a future career in the service of

France, but secretly, Amelia was her father's favourite and could twist him around her tiny girly fingers.

Life for the Portier family went on, it seemed, without a care, but the storm clouds were gathering as unrest grew among the French lower classes. Unrest that had its origins amongst the people in the towns and cities, especially the capital, Paris, but was quickly sweeping across the whole country. There was growing anger in the population at the lack of work and the low wages paid to the few who were lucky enough to find any employment at all.

Taxation had risen sharply as the King continued to increase spending abroad in support of rebel organisations seeking to undermine the rule of law in far-flung British colonies, whilst at home most people were finding it difficult to obtain enough food to stay alive. There were mutterings that the Royal Family were deaf to the concerns of their subjects, or maybe they just did not care. In one of the most radical and outspoken pamphlets it was written that the Queen had stated that the common people should eat cake if they hadn't enough bread, proving how out of touch she was with the plight of most of the populace.

Rabble rousers had their day and at their meetings they shouted aloud that the only way to put things right was through revolution and the overthrow of the monarchy. Members of the clergy, usually on the side of the ruling classes, saw the way that the tide was turning against them and even preached revolution from the pulpit. For once, they were unafraid of the weak authorities and what they could do.

Damon tried to use his small amount of influence as adviser to the King to illicit a change of policy, as did many others who also recognised the growing danger to the order of things. But it was all to no avail. The Royal Family, in their arrogance, considered themselves indestructible, they were, after all, a dynasty, and wasn't it true that they were the representatives of God on Earth and immune to the trouble ahead?

The militancy among the population finally erupted into violent action when Gaston had just passed the date of his fourteenth birthday in 1787. The violence started in a small, unorganised way, but as the rioters saw the impotency of the rulers they became bolder and more organised. The violence culminated in the storming of the Bastille in the heart of Paris, and the organisers of the mobs took full control. For the upper classes worse was to rapidly follow. Anyone associated with, or thought to be a supporter of the King, was arrested by the revolutionaries and thrown into prison. As they became even bolder and even more organised the revolutionaries set up 'revolutionary courts' and the prisoners were brought before them on charges ranging from 'treason against the state' to 'supporting a decadent regime'. Each carried the death penalty if found guilty. Few of those charged with such 'crimes' escaped with their lives.

Damon Portier and his whole family were arrested within two days of the fall of the Bastille, along with everyone else present at the Palace of Versailles, including the servants. The family were imprisoned, firstly in their apartment and then, several days later, transferred to a gaol on the outskirts of the city. Damon was charged with being 'an enemy of the state' and was brought before the self-styled Committee For Public Safety, although who they were protecting was debatable, and put on trial. Found guilty as charged, he was summarily sentenced to death on the insistence of the 'prosecutor', who had previously worked as a gardener at the palace and whose children had regularly played with Gaston and Emilia.

Surprisingly, Lucy and the children were released and allowed to return to their apartment. It had been thoroughly ransacked and everything of value had been taken. They were left with a few broken pieces of furniture and china and not much else. Anything that the vandals could not easily carry away had been smashed.

The pillagers had been brutal in their search of the rooms but they had not been clever. Had they been clever, they may have been able to find the hiding place where Lucy Portier had hidden the box containing all her jewellery and cash. Had they found the box, they would have been much richer than they were for Damon had invested heavily in the diamond markets whilst in Amsterdam, and the box contained a small fortune in uncut stones.

Two days after being set free from the gaol, Lucy and the children were once again forcefully taken to the island in the River Seine on which stood the Cathedral of Notre-Dame and there in the open space before the entrance to the holy building they were made to watch as Damon, wearing a label which denounced him as a traitor, was 'introduced to Madame Guillotine'. His death warrant had been signed by none other than Robespierre himself.

They were made to look into the basket which held his severed head before it and his body were hauled away to be thrown into a huge pit, which had been excavated for the purpose, on the outskirts of the city.

Lucy and her devastated children returned to their apartment and cowered there, bewildered in their sorrow, whilst the executions continued unabated. For some unapparent reason Lucy and Amelia had not been molested by the guards at the women's prison but had been made to watch many times as other women were repeatedly raped and brutalised. The effect on them had been catastrophic, especially on the child. But Lucy was also at her wits' end. She found it impossible to think straight. Alone now, in a country which was not her own, with two children to protect and care for.

They huddled together in the forbidding and uncomfortable apartment which had become their new prison and awaited their fate. But the happenings of the last few months, culminating in the savage death of his father, had triggered a huge change in Gaston. He was no longer a boy. He was no longer a boy whose only thoughts were on playing games and eating and sleeping. He was now the man of the family with the responsibility for the safety of his mother and his sister now resting squarely on his small shoulders, and he took those responsibilities seriously.

Eventually, when the revolutionaries started to re-arrest the wives and children of the hundreds of men who had been put to death and the executions started all over again, he decided to take charge of the situation. He sat down with his mother and sister and discussed the plan of action he had devised. They should make their escape now whilst they could. They had the diamonds, more valuable than any paper money, and they still had some friends, and not everyone in France was in agreement with the ideals of the revolution.

Paris was swiftly emptying of people as those who believed they were in danger of arrest tried to escape. But most headed for the Channel coast, this being the shortest route out of France. Some had carriages, some rode on horseback but the majority were on foot. Very few got beyond the city outskirts before they were intercepted by the patrols of revolutionaries and were brought back in chains. But still people tried to escape even though fleeing the city was considered by the courts to be an admission of guilt. The patrols were kept busy day and night. Security to the south and east of Paris was lax, and Gaston, using the simple logic of someone who was not much more than a child, could not understand why everyone headed north.

His plan was that they should find someone who possessed the means to transport the family but was opposed to the aims of the revolution and, with the help of the diamonds, bribe them to take them and their meagre possessions eastwards, deeper into France. When they reached the border, if they reached the border, they could then turn south into the heart of Italy, or northward into Germany, cross into Belgium and then into Holland. Either way they could buy passage on a ship to England.

As Gaston revealed his plan his mother listened intently but had nothing to add. She had never envisaged herself in a situation such as this and had no experience on which to draw. She left everything in the hands of her young son. His sister sat with her head bowed and was silent the whole time except for a sob which she sometimes allowed to escape from her lips. Sobs which signalled the deep shock into which the recent catastrophic events had sent her tumbling.

Even with the diamonds, finding transport was not as easy as Gaston had thought and had cost four times what they had planned for. But three days later, three days in which every minute they feared the knock on the door, they left Paris with no possessions and no baggage. It was just after dawn.

Eight long, hard weeks later Gaston had stood on the stern of the small ship. It was loaded to the gunwales with cheeses and butter but was taking them to England and safety. He had looked back as the coast of Holland gradually receded into the haze and had been relieved to be leaving Europe, as he believed, forever. For the last several weeks, once they knew they were safe from persecution, they had had time to grieve their loss. His mother had withdrawn into herself and had taken ill. She said nothing unless cajoled into speaking. Gaston feared she was dying as well and would leave him to take care of his sister, who cried all the time now and had terrible nightmares, all alone. Gaston had grown into a man in the last four months. He had grown much taller and somehow looked tougher and harder. His jaw had a firm line to it and he looked everyone squarely in the eye. He was a proud young man and he felt subservient to no-one. Deep inside him was a huge and festering hatred of France and for the people of France for what they had done to his family.

*

Now, five years later he was joining his first Royal Navy ship. He had changed his name to George Porter to save any awkward questions about his nationality and had volunteered. He was nineteen years of age, and he felt invincible and he was looking for a fight. He hoped that the fight would be against Frenchmen. The ship lay at anchor in the estuary. It was a handsome ship and looked like it could take on the world, and win. He read again the name emblazoned on the stern, H.M.S. *Indestructible*.

Once aboard he rapidly settled into the ship's routine. Two days later the ship had set sail for the Mediterranean Station based in Gibraltar but by this time George Porter, fooling no-one, had already been nicknamed 'Frenchie', and Gaston took his place on the lower decks.

CHAPTER 4

The Family Deschamps

Dover, Kent
1788-1799

Even as a newborn baby and through the first few months of his life, his mother Louisa could not find it in her heart to give Joshua the love that he needed. Maybe she was too immature at the age of fourteen to recover from the enormity of the events that had overtaken her. Maybe she had no love in her to give. But it made no matter.

Joshua's grandparents took on the responsibility of his upbringing and they treated him like the son they had prayed for but had never had. During the birth of their daughter something bad had happened inside Louisa's mother's body. Blood vessels burst and tissue tore and it was destined that she would never conceive again.

Joshua called his grandparents Mum and Dad and they were able to give him all the love and affection he needed to grow into a well behaved and bright young lad.

After his birth Louisa stayed at home for a few short months, during which time the money that she had been given by Mr Leadbitter dwindled away to almost nothing. She had then written to Mrs Jackson the housekeeper at the Hall and had received a written reply confirming that she could return and take up her duties again as a downstairs maid. The letter stressed that everything that had happened in the past would be forgotten and she would start with a clean slate. She moved back to the Hall and moved out of Joshua's life for the next few years save for a few brief visits when she was given time off.

During those years his mother changed her employment several times, each time for a better position. It was during one of her infrequent visits home that the family sat down together and Joshua was told the truth about his parentage. He was eight years of age but, at that age, the circumstances of his birth made no difference to him at all and things carried on as they were before. But then his grandparents passed away and everything changed.

His grandmother had been the first to die, followed only days later by her husband. The disease that had caused her death had been festering for a long, long time. It had started, minutely, on the day that their daughter was born and had continued to grow inexorably ever since. In the latter years no-one took any notice of the thickening of the waist and the pot-belly that she had developed, putting everything down to the advancing years. But the signs were there if anyone had cared to take note: the irregularity of her monthly cycle: the heartburn and the indigestion, and later the lack of appetite and the weight loss. Eventually people sat up and took notice as she literally started to waste away, that is, all except for her belly which seemed to swell even more, but that could have just been that the rest of her was getting smaller.

And then the pain started. Not much at first and easily bearable but becoming more and more acute over the weeks until she could be heard groaning out in the street and then she started to scream. Her neighbours helped as best they could but they had never seen a disease that caused such pain. They tried all the remedies they thought would help and, in desperation, a few they had no faith in whatsoever. But nothing seemed to help their friend.

The doctor, who demanded payment up front, had been called as a last resort and he had tried his best to save her but he did not have the knowledge needed to treat the disease effectively and she deteriorated day by day. He tried pills and potions. He tried herbs and blood-letting, even burning incense. It was all to no avail. It took only another five days to succumb and to pass away, but for her they were five long days of agony.

Most of the people who knew Joshua's grandfather believed that the old man had died of a broken heart, for he had loved his wife dearly and they had been a devoted couple. He had sat and watched her die, not in dignity but in terrible pain, feverish, curled into a tight ball, screaming, and begging for the Lord Jesus to take her and put an end her suffering. And he could to nothing to help this woman who he had loved for as long as he could remember.

On the day that she had died she had become calm and almost like her old self. She had smiled at her husband and his heart had leapt within his chest. They say that hope springs eternal.

Following her death, his wife had been laid out by her friends in her best clothes and for three days she lay in a beautifully made coffin in the parlour, without a lid, as was the custom. Everyone who knew her would have the opportunity to say goodbye before the body was taken for burial.

Her husband died on the evening of the second day sat in a chair alongside the coffin.

Louisa had returned home from her latest employ in Canterbury to care for her parents and for the two days after her mother's death constantly heard her father talking to what had been her mother, but was now just a shell. She heard him once reminiscing about their courtship and how shy he had been, how they had discovered each other and their love. Another time she heard him asking if she remembered the day they were married and how beautiful she had been and how fearful they had been the first night they were together. Sometimes he would pause as though hearing an answer. For the first time in her life Louisa cried for someone besides herself. She cried for her father's sadness for she loved him as much as he loved her.

Her mother and father were buried together in the same grave in the graveyard alongside the church they had attended since their marriage thirty-four years before.

*

Joshua was a lost soul after the death of his grandparents. His grandma had always made him hearty meals and made sure that his clothes were mended and clean, things his mother neglected. His grandma had also taught him to read and write. It was the tradition in her family for the mothers to pass the skills on to the children. Her family had been able to read for generations.

But he especially missed his granddad, now that he was growing into a man. He needed to discuss things that could only be discussed between men. Several months after his grandparents had passed away he had awoken one morning to find his cock protruding stiffly from his nightshirt. He had touched the stiffness and found that it was sensitive to his touch and produced very pleasant sensations that he had never felt before. He had lain back on his rough bedding and stroked it gently with his hand enjoying the feelings but when an almost colourless fluid had spurted from it, he had thought that he had injured himself gravely and he was afraid that he would certainly die. But he hadn't died and, over the next few months, it had happened more and more frequently. He was also starting to grow hair where before there had been none. He wished his granddad was there to answer the many questions that he could never ask his mother.

Louisa had inherited the house and the furniture and a meagre sum of money amounting to seven pounds, three shillings and a few pennies, which was the total of her parents' wealth. The money that had been left to her did not last for very long without an income, for Louisa was a frivolous woman and had grown accustomed to spending all of her wages on the best clothes that she could afford and treating herself to small luxuries.

Eventually, when the money was all spent Louisa pawned everything of value including the few good pieces of furniture and, heartbreakingly, her mother's wedding ring. When there was nothing of value left she took to borrowing, believing that she could pay the money back easily when she found a new position. She borrowed only small sums; a shilling here, two shillings there, but before she knew what had happened, the total she owed added up to a considerable amount. She was surprised to find that the money she owed to the money-lender amounted to almost as much as she could earn in a year and the interest charged meant that the total increased day by day. She found herself in danger of having the house taken and being carted off herself to 'the debtors' prison'.

She took out her frustrations with her situation on her son. Her nagging was constant and she would beat him with the boiler stick for no reason that Joshua could understand. She would beat him one day for doing something that the next day went unpunished or even unnoticed. He was a thoroughly confused boy, it seemed he could do no right for doing wrong, and it made no difference for she would beat him for wrong or right. And he tried so hard to please her; he wanted her to like him. He was so in need of a friend.

She blamed him because she couldn't seem to find a husband to take care of her, conveniently ignoring the fact that many men had tried to get close to her, attracted by her beauty, but had soon backed away when they had observed her lack of affection for anyone but herself.

'What decent man would want to take me as a wife with a brat like you tied to my apron strings?' she would say to him and he would wonder why God had allowed him to be born at all. Sometimes, at bedtime, he would pray to God that his mother could find a kind gentleman and he would care for them both and they would live happily together forever and his mother would be happy and the beatings would stop.

Besides not finding a 'good' man, Louisa found that she couldn't get employment either. There were always more people looking for work than there was jobs and having a son 'tied to her apron strings' didn't help. Being a servant was the only work she had ever done, but such employment situations at any of the big houses in the area, were all live-in positions. The employers wanted the servants to be at their beck and call and available whenever they demanded. There were countless girls looking for positions in service so the idea that an employer would consider offering a place to a servant with a child was impossible.

As time passed Louisa sank further and further into debt and her desperation to earn money grew. She skivvied for neighbours and took in washing but the meagre amount of money that she was able to earn from menial tasks such as these was hardly enough to feed them both, and left nothing over with which to pay off the capital she owed. She was at her wits' end as to how she would survive.

But then the day arrived which was to change her life forever.

*

She had written a letter of application for a position as a shop assistant at the milliners at the end of the street, having heard there was a vacancy there from a friend. Wanting to make a good impression she had taken great care with her handwriting and had checked all the spelling several times. The letter must have had the desired effect for, despite her lack of experience, she had been summoned for interview. The hand-delivered message summoning her to the shop had been sent by Mistress Bouchon, as she liked to be known, the wife of the owner of the shop and also the chairwoman of the Townswomen's Guild.

The day had dawned bright and clear and the temperature had risen into the high fifties by the time that Louisa set off for the interview with the Bouchons. It was turning out to be a beautiful spring day. She had pinned her luscious hair up high onto her head and put on her best frock. She knew that she looked good for the thin cotton frock and the hairstyle accentuated the smooth skin of her shoulders, her long slim neck and her dainty ears.

Louisa thought that she had answered all their questions well and had the feeling that both of the Bouchons liked her. She was becoming more and more confident that she would be successful in gaining employment this time until she was asked about her personal circumstances. The atmosphere suddenly changed and Louisa knew that her chance had gone. Mistress Bouchon made it all too clear that they, although her husband said nothing, disapproved of the fact that she had had a child out of wedlock; a mistake that had been compounded and even made worse by her not marrying the father of the child. In no circumstances whatsoever could an important member of the Townswomen's Guild employ such a woman and, besides which, she was much too pretty to have around her husband.

She found herself back in the street after suffering the humiliation of a lecture on her loose morals. She turned for home close to tears. As she turned into the lane at the back of the row of houses she was too distraught to even notice the two men standing together in the doorway of one of the other buildings, talking in subdued voices.

*

Mr Jeremiah Knowles the Debt Collector, was deep in conversation with his principal, The Money Lender. Mr Knowles was a huge bull of a man and was well able to take care of himself in any rough-house situation. But he was also a callous bully and he most enjoyed that part of his job which involved issuing threats to bad payers for, although he would not admit to it, he became sexually aroused from seeing the fear in people's eyes. He always carried with him, secreted in his trousers, a stout stick with a carved handle and a lead knob which he would use when called upon to give a beating to persistent defaulters. He called his stick 'the nobbler' and was known locally as 'Nobbler' Knowles. He would have liked to use the cudgel more often than he did but The Money Lender only issued the order for a beating as a last resort for, as he said, a debtor with broken arms or legs could not earn money with which to pay his debt.

But he did get some opportunities and always took full advantage when he did. Only two days before he had used 'the nobbler' to beat a man to the flagstones in his own parlour, whilst his children cowered, terrified and snivelling in the corner of the room and his hysterical wife grasped frantically at his jacket beseeching him to stop. But Knowles wasn't about to stop until he had taught them a real lesson. He drove his hob-nailed boot into his victim's body and heard the satisfying crack of his ribs and the whoosh as the air was forced from his lungs. The woman screamed as though it had been her who had been kicked. He turned his attention to her.

'Tell me where you've hidden your stash,' he said in his most reasonable tone, 'and all the pain will stop.'

'We haven't any money, Mr Knowles, sir. Please don't hurt him anymore.' She sobbed loudly. 'If I had any money I would tell you, anything to get you to spare my Seb.'

'Don't lie to me, you bitch.' Knowles was unmoved by her tears and not so reasonable now. 'I know he's had work this week at the bakery, he must have been paid. Where's the money?'

'It was only a few pence, sir, and I had to buy food for them.' She indicated the crying children in the corner. 'It's all been spent.'

Knowles turned to the cringeing man, who had half rolled away from him just regaining some breath, and kicked him in the spine. The man convulsed and screamed in agony.

'You shouldn't have been so foolish as to waste your money on food for your brats. You knew the payment was overdue again. You get what you deserve if you cross me. Now, tell me quickly. Where's the money you have left over? Where is it hidden?'

The woman was beaten and knew it. She couldn't afford to have her man crippled up. He couldn't get any work if he was crippled up. If she gave in now, she knew that they would survive this. She led the Debt Collector up to the room above and withdrew a small cloth bag from among the bed-clothes and passed it to the man. He shook the coins out into the palm of his hand; one shilling and ten pennies.

'Is this all?'

'That's all the money we have in the world. Seb hasn't been able to find regular work for months. Times is terrible hard, as you know, sir." Her sobs, which had become quieter, increased in volume again.

Knowles studied her face. She was telling the truth, he was sure. He shoved the coins into his leather satchel.

'Please, sir, don't take all of it. Leave something for us to live on, please sir, please.' She crumpled to the floor and gripped him about the ankles, crying loudly again. He looked down at her. The mixture of adrenaline and her submissiveness had stirred him. She was quite comely even though her face had been ravaged by tears. He felt the hardness in his trousers. *Why should The Money Lender have all the fun?* he thought. There should be some compensations for doing all his dirty work.

'Get up,' he said and pulled her to her feet. He swiftly unbuttoned his trousers and moved closer to her, took her hand and inserted it into the opening.

She had small hands but they were large enough and swift enough to deliver a hefty slap. He was taken completely by surprise by the blow from her other hand and he staggered backwards.

'You filthy sod,' she spat out, 'you dirty bugg—' It was as far as she got as he instinctively lashed out and, seeing the blow coming, the woman raised her arms to protect her head. His closed fist caught her on the side of the forehead and even though her arms took some of the brute force of the blow, it was still powerful enough to smash her backwards onto the bed.

He stood back and looked at her, gingerly touching his hot and rapidly reddening cheek, considering whether to lay into her some more. But he resisted the temptation and instead he re-fastened his trousers over his now flaccid flesh. The surprise of the slap had dissipated his urges but undoubtedly there would be another day for that. He turned to leave the room and, as he did so, he took a penny out of the satchel and flicked it with his thumb onto the bed alongside the prostrate figure.

'Buy your young-uns a pastry each and tell them it's a present from their kind Uncle Nobbler.' He sneered. She heard him descend the stairs and speak to her man.

'I'll be back next week and you had better have something for me and a darn sight more than a paltry shilling or two, or maybe I'll break a leg or two on that bitch upstairs. Perhaps that will teach you I mean business here.'

Knowles went out through the back door and was gone. Upstairs the woman rose from the bed and crossed to the washstand. Just in time she bent over the basin as the yellow bile spewed from her mouth. She was shaking with fright for she knew that she may have made a fearful mistake. Nobbler Knowles was not a man you would want for an enemy.

*

The Money Lender was listening intently to the Debt Collector as he made his report but the man suddenly stopped speaking and pointed at Louisa as she passed by them and entered the lane.

'That's her, sir,' he said. 'That's the woman… Louisa Deschamps.'

The Money Lender's eyes followed Louisa's progress until she was lost to sight as she entered the yard of her house. His employee had described her as a young lady worthy of his personal attention, but he was not prepared for what he had just seen. She was beautiful, that was the only word he knew that was adequate to describe her.

'Be back here in five hours,' was all he said.

*

Louisa had been back in the small, dark cottage for what seemed like only a few minutes after her humiliating experience with the Bouchons when the soft knock sounded on the front door. Her first reaction was one of gut wrenching fear for she knew that Jeremiah Knowles would be calling today in search of a payment towards her debt, which she knew amounted now to over twenty-two pounds, a huge sum that she could see no way of clearing. She knew of others who had suffered a severe beating at the hands of the thug or, even worse, had been thrown into the street for lesser amounts.

But she knew Jeremiah Knowles always called at the back doors of the houses that he needed to visit, for on dry, warm days the doors were usually open and he could be into the house before anyone knew he was about, and today was one of those warm days. In this way he had caught many debtors before they had had time to hide their money.

Although she did not think it was the Debt Collector she wasn't sure and she ducked down below the level of the window anyway, for he was a cunning man and she knew he was capable of any trickery. She cautiously raised herself so that she was able to peep out through the thick glass. The man standing there was certainly not the Debt Collector. To Louisa's untrained eye he appeared to be in his late thirties. He was a tall man, over six feet she guessed, and was dressed in a black frock coat that was buttoned from high on his chest to just below his waist and was then allowed to fall smoothly to knee level. It was tailored to fit to perfection and was made of what, to Louisa's eyes, looked like a very fine material indeed. A black hat sat, at a slightly rakish angle, on his head, atop a fine head of straight dark brown hair. He carried a black lacquered cane. This man looked like a rich businessman, which indeed he was.

The Money Lender had taken the book from his henchman, as Jeremiah Knowles knew he would. Jeremiah may have been a thug and a bully but he understood his employer perfectly. As callous and uncaring as the Debt Collector was, he suspected that the Money Lender was into something altogether more sophisticatedly cruel than he could ever imagine.

The ledger, with the columns of figures detailing all the people who owed money, the amounts owed, and payments made against those debts, was safely concealed in the deep pocket of the Money Lender's black frock coat. He stood back in the road and studied the badly maintained front of the house. It had taken him but one glance to value the house and he had already concluded that the value was enough to clear the woman's debt and provide a healthy profit.

Property rental was buoyant, as it had been for the last few years. Thousands of people were moving from the countryside into the towns looking for work around the docks or in the factories that were springing up almost daily and, as they mistakenly believed, to make their fortune. And they all needed accommodation. But the work in the factories was hard and the hours were long and the wages were only marginally above the wages of agricultural workers. There were rich pickings to be had for the likes of the Money Lender who preyed on the unwary.

He had seen the face briefly appear at the window but had made no sign that he had. It was the face of the woman that he now sought. He waited for a few more seconds and then, using his cane, knocked again, not too loudly but loud enough to demand answer. The door opened a few inches and a face appeared. The Money Lender was immediately struck by the similarity of this young face with that of the woman he had seen earlier but this face sported an ugly green-black bruise close under the left eye.

'Yes?' asked a voice. It was the voice of a young boy.

'I wish to speak to Louisa Deschamps. Is she at home?' The voice was cultured without an accent of any kind.

Louisa stayed carefully out of sight behind the door. She was surprised that the man knew her name and was curious as to who he could be. Was he about to offer her employment? Was he a lawyer? Had she been left money by a rich aunt? She knew the answer to that question, she had no rich aunts.

'Ask him what he wants,' she whispered so quietly that even Joshua could hardly hear her.

'What do you want with my mother?' he asked as he was instructed.

'I have some good news for her, and a business proposition which will, undoubtedly, be to her advantage.' The Money Lender knew how to bait the hook when people were desperate, and Louisa was very desperate, as he knew. Louisa took the bait and opened the door wide.

'I am Louisa Deschamps, sir. Welcome to my home.' And she stood aside for him to enter the house.

The Money Lender removed his hat as he entered and placed it and his cane on the scrubbed table. He unbuttoned his coat as his eyes swept swiftly round the room, quickly putting a value to everything he saw. It was only a cursory glance but it was enough to confirm what his man had told him. The room was almost bare of the normal things you would expect in a home. There was hardly any furniture, just the scrubbed table and a few hard chairs, a padded chair next to the fire, a washstand with a cheap china jug and basin and a dresser with some bits and pieces of china, plates and mugs. A rag rug lay on the stone floor. There were no ornaments or pictures or decoration of any kind. Nothing that he could see was of any monetary value whatsoever. He had been in houses like this many times and he was relieved that at least this house was well cleaned and tidy. Some houses he had visited were not much better than cattle sheds. He wondered how people could live in such squalor.

His eyes alighted back on Louisa and she blushed under his gaze. She looked even prettier close to than she had seemed at a distance, and his pulse raced at what he was about to propose.

He became aware that the young boy was still standing close to the door and he beckoned him over. He reached into his waistcoat pocket and produced two pennies, which he passed to Joshua.

'Go to the nearest inn and bring us a jug of weak beer, and don't dawdle, or else.'

Joshua took a china jug from the dresser and, clutching it tightly to his chest, ran all the way to the inn. He walked carefully back to the house terrified of spilling even a drop of the beer and incurring the wrath of his mother, or the wrath of this strange man who, with just a look, somehow frightened him. He had been hardly a minute but the man was already sitting in the best chair in his waistcoat. He had removed his frock coat and draped it over one of the hard chairs for the room was warm what with the fire and the unseasonable warm weather outside. His mother was busy by the washstand wiping two mugs that she had just washed. They were the two best mugs in the house, mugs that were seldom used. She wanted to create the right impression.

Joshua put the jug on the table together with the halfpenny change, and retreated towards the stairs never taking his eyes off the man. The man caught his eye and beckoned him back to where he was sitting.

'Come here and bring the money with you,' he said. Joshua picked up the coin, rounded the table to stand close to the man and handed the coin over. The man studied the coin for a while as though unsure as to its value then turned his attention to the boy as he stood before him, as though considering a vital decision. The boy became more anxious with every passing second.

'Hold out your hand,' he said eventually. He placed the coin into the palm of the boy's hand and pressed his fingers tightly closed around it.

'I can see that you are a good boy,' he said. 'The halfpenny is yours if you do exactly as I say.' The boy glanced quickly across at his mother but her back was turned to him. He looked again at the man.

'I want you to leave us now and not to return until dark. If you can do that the money is yours to keep.' Joshua glanced at his mother again as he headed for the back door but she was still looking the other way. He closed the door behind him, went out into the lane and ran to find his best friend Sam Hargreaves. It was always easy to stay out till dark.

Louisa was intrigued by the man. He had not said a word to her since he had entered the house and he had taken off his coat and sat himself in the best chair without a 'by your leave'. He gave off the air of a man who was used to getting his own way. She had been relieved when he had sent her son to get beer for she had nothing for refreshment in the house to offer a guest. Now she poured some beer into each mug, handed one to the man, and perched herself on one of the hard chairs by the table. He turned to her and raised his mug.

'To a long and fruitful life,' he toasted and took a gulp of the frothy liquid, swallowing with obvious relish. Louisa took a long drink from her mug. It had been some time since she had had the luxury of beer to drink. He stood, crossed the small space to the table, picked up the jug and refilled their mugs.

'Drink up,' he said, 'you and me, we have much to talk about.'

*

It had been dark for a little while and Joshua thought that it was probably safe to return home. He entered the house from the back lane and crept silently through the lean-to wash house and stood outside the back door listening. He couldn't hear anything, the house was silent. Cautiously he pushed open the door. The parlour smelt of stale beer and was lit by a single tallow wick placed on the table. Even by its weak light he could see that the coat belonging to the man was no longer hanging on the chair.

The two mugs and the jug in which he had fetched the beer from the inn were still on the table. Crossing swiftly to the table Joshua looked into the jug. It was empty. He looked into each of the mugs. One of them still contained about an inch of the dark fluid. He had never tasted beer before and he put the mug to his mouth and cautiously took a sip. He gagged on the bitter taste and had to spit the beer back into the mug before he was sick.

Replacing the mug and treading carefully, he mounted the stairs. His mother's bedroom door was ajar and he could see the room was empty. He went into his own tiny room and sat on the ramshackle bed. His jaw ached but he still felt good. He had bought a huge bag of treacle toffee and, together with Sam his friend, had been chewing manfully all afternoon.

Sleep was slowly overtaking him when he heard an unfamiliar noise from the floor below. It was the sound of his mother singing. He had not heard his mother sing for what seemed like years.

'Josh, are you home yet?' she called. 'Come and see what I've got for us.'

He bounded down the stairs to see his mother busy lighting candles and placing them all around the room. They were made from proper wax and gave off a light which made the room bright unlike the tallow candles they usually had which seemed to just fill the house with smoke.

'I do believe all our troubles are over, see, I've got plenty of food for us tonight.'

*

When the Money Lender had first produced the ledger from his coat, all her optimistic curiosity had evaporated immediately. It had been replaced by fear, which hadn't been allayed when he started to question her closely. But he knew what he was about. He had done the same thing many times before. He asked her how and when she intended to pay off her debt, which, with this week's interest added, had risen to twenty-four pounds; as much as she could earn in two years and more, in service. Of course, the Money Lender, knowing her circumstances, had known the answer before he had asked. She could not pay.

He had toyed with her emotions. He had threatened to take

everything of value from her and, when he had done that, finally evict her from the house that had belonged to her father. He left her in no doubt that he could, and would, do these things if he had the mind to. He had put the fear of God into her, reduced her to desperation and she had cried.

But then he had changed and showed some sympathy for her plight and eventually, when he thought the time was right had suggested a way out of her situation. She had listened to him and she had been, at first fearful and then, hopeful again.

Little more than three hours later he had risen from her bed leaving her lying there. He had washed his body, dressed and left the house. She had lain quietly there for nearly an hour, her head in turmoil as she felt a mixture of elation and shame.

Elation that he had reduced her debt by a full two pounds and that he had also given her five shillings to buy food for the boy and herself. But she felt shame as she remembered the ways in which he had used her body, and shame because of the willingness she had shown to do all the things that he had asked of her. He had told her how to use her hands and her mouth and her tongue. She had found it impossible to say no to his demands and he had explored her body with his hands and then he had entered her in all other ways.

And slowly, as the shadows in the room lengthened, it dawned upon her that, far from being distressed, she had enjoyed what he had done to her, and as the idea that he had put to her grew and took firm hold in her mind, she rose from the bed, poured clean water into the basin and washed away the smell of her sex. She dressed once again in her best frock and went shopping.

She felt elated and was wearing a smile as she went from shop to shop. She reserved her biggest smile for Mistress Bouchon as she was obliged to wait on Louisa as she tried each and every bonnet before deciding on a petite fluster of taffeta and lace which cost three quarters of the money the Money Lender had given her to buy food. She wore the hat from the shop and flounced across the street, swaying her hips in a way that only young woman can, knowing that the shop-keeper would be enviously watching her every move.

*

As they sat and ate their supper they did something that Joshua had missed since his grandparents had died. They just sat and chatted together. To the boy it was like old times and he was happy. He told her how he and his friend Sam had gone down to the quayside and he had bought the treacle toffee and how they had chewed and chewed and chewed all afternoon whilst they watched the boats plying to and fro.

'I've saved you a piece,' he said, proudly digging deeply into the pocket in his breeches. He produced a fair sized lump of the sticky sweet and passed it to her.

'Why, thank you, a present. That is kind of you,' she said as she placed the toffee on the table and briefly grasped his hand He beamed with pride for he so longed to be his mother's friend. They talked together for a little will longer and then she got up from the table.

'Time you were abed, I think, young man,' she said and she pointed towards the rickety stairs. He stood and hesitantly reached out his arms to her as he used to after his supper when his grandmother was alive. His grandmother used to return his cuddle fourfold and he would go to bed content. Sometimes his grandfather would come up to his room when he had got into bed, and he would tell him the same story, with a few embellishments, that he had told him for years.

His mother turned away towards the table and started collecting up the few plates and utensils they had used.

Joshua's heart sank. He turned around and with his head bowed he climbed the stairs and went to bed. His mother smiled again as she cleared the table and, as she did, she started singing tunelessly:

'I'm going to be rich.

'I'm going to be the richest woman in Dover.'

*

She picked up the piece of toffee which Joshua had saved for her, turned it over in her hand and threw it into the fire.

CHAPTER 5

**Berkeley, Gloucestershire
1820**

The boy curled himself up into a small ball, as he always did when he was in his bed on freezing cold nights. He curled up into the smallest ball he could possibly make. His knees were drawn up tight, right up under his chin, and he clasped his arms tightly around them. He was as small, as small, as he could be. He also kept very quiet, quieter than he had ever been in his short life. No shouting now. No laughter. Not even a whisper.

He had tried not to cry. Hadn't his dad always told him that big men didn't cry, and didn't his dad tousle his hair and call him his 'little big man'? Wasn't he big enough now to struggle with the big bucket of slop down to the pigsty and wasn't he big enough now to have his own patch of garden in which to grow his own carrots and the peas that he loved to pick and eat, even before they were ready? And wasn't he big enough, that when the time came, he was allowed to watch the pig being stuck with the spike, and wasn't he big enough to hold the bucket to catch the pumping blood that would be used to make the black pudding that his father liked so much?

He was certainly big enough for these things but he was not as big as the man. Not by a long way. The man may as well have been a giant. And the man was strong too. The boy had tried his best, as his dad had always told him to, but the man was too strong and had hurt him. If I keep very still and very quiet maybe the man will forget I am here, *he thought.*

But the man wouldn't forget that he was there. The man never forgot. He had not finished with the boy yet. But it pleased him that the boy was being quiet and still, cowering under the cart. He needed some time to eat and drink and he wanted to take some time to savour the moments which had gone before.

The boy had been a delight to him after all this time. He had been all that the man had hoped he would be. It had been several long months now and the man had been willing to take a risk or two, but it had been more than worth it. His pleasure had been great.

As he ate, he lay back on the rough blanket and relaxed. He studied the boy, who, it seemed to the man, had fallen asleep.

*

When the boy had been born he had been a skinny baby, all skinny arms and legs. If he had been a pig himself, he would have been the runt of the litter. It was with God's grace that he just survived the first year of his life. Infection had followed infection for he had been a sickly child, but he was all the more precious to his mam and dad for all that. Gradually he had put on a bit of weight and had gained in strength and he was a good boy and was the apple of his dad's eye. He was now lying very still and breathing slowly and deeply.

It would be almost a shame to awaken him again, but of course the man would. He felt the familiar urge in his loins slowly returning as he finished eating and he raised himself up from the ground. As he walked stiffly over to the cart the boy must have heard him approaching because he opened his eyes. They became wide with fear and he tried to scramble away from the man and get further into safety under the cart. He had been afraid when left alone in the dark ever since he could remember. Even as a small child as he lay in his bed at night, he imagined all manner of demons and monsters lurked in the dark corners of his tiny space under the eaves of the cottage, waiting to envelope him if he shut his eyes for one second. His mother always left a small light burning for him and he would listen to the reassuring sound of voices from the room below until he fell asleep. But now he craved the darkness of the box. The darkness had been nothing compared to the reality of the light when the man had dragged him out of the box and played his games. And when the man had laid the knife on his skin it had been icy cold.

The man grasped the thin rope tether tied to the boy's leg and pulled him inexorably towards him until he could grasp it, his large hand easily able to encircle the thin and bony ankle. The heady feeling of his power over the boy washed over and through the man. If they fought against him it was all the better, it increased his pleasure, and if they fought he always took his time before he eventually overpowered them and tamed them to his ways.

The boy kicked out frantically with his free leg but the strength of the man was much too much for a small boy and he was slowly but surely dragged out into the open. Once in the open he lost the urge to resist, knowing that he could not fight the man. The man would only hurt him again.

The man reached out and tenderly and gently touched the boy's face with his fingertips. He stroked the boy's cheek and felt the familiar feeling of the soft young skin. His hand slowly traced a path down the boy's throat and across his shoulder. The man's tongue licked his suddenly dry lips.

The 'little big man' couldn't help himself. Despite what his father had told him, he started to cry again.

CHAPTER 6

Joshua and Louisa Deschamps

Dover, Kent
June 1799

Several months had gone by since the first visit of the Money Lender to the house and life had improved for Joshua. There was money to spend, plenty of food to eat and his mother had even bought him a new pair of smart leather boots. He didn't really care how or why life had suddenly taken a turn for the better; he just enjoyed the feeling of a full belly. His mother seemed in a better temper these days and the beatings with the boiler stick had almost ceased, but not altogether. She largely ignored what he was doing and allowed him to run free, to get on as best he could, but to Joshua it was a lot better than the constant nagging and the beatings that she to used give him before.

A feeling in the pit of his stomach though, told him that the newfound happiness in his life could not last, life was not that easy and, as the months went by, he was proved right.

In the weeks after his first visit the Money Lender came to the house frequently and on each occasion Joshua was given a halfpenny to spend and was sent from the house until dark. He didn't understand why he had to leave the house, but accepted the money gleefully, for he had never had so much money in his life before, and did as he was told. He and his friend Sam had never had as many sweets and toffee as they enjoyed now. In some ways Joshua looked forward to the days when the Money Lender visited the house, even though the man still scared him, for he had always left the house by the time Joshua returned after dark and he always seemed to leave his mother in a good mood, chatting to him about nothing in particular and, more often than not, singing.

Then, as the time went by, the length of his stays at the house became shorter and the Money Lender began to bring other men to the house. Men, who like him, were smartly dressed in good quality clothing and had the appearance of being businessmen. Eventually Joshua seemed to be spending most of every day out of the house. To her son, Louisa seemed very popular and had made many new friends and did a lot of entertaining. But to his relief, the visits of the Money Lender, who he was still fearful of, had become fewer with longer gaps between them.

One morning, to get out of the house early, Joshua walked over to the next street to see his best friend Sam. They had been best friends ever since he could remember. Sam was in the back yard of his house, when he arrived. Sam looked crestfallen as he told Joshua that he could no longer be his best friend. His father had threatened to give him the buckle end of his broad leather belt if he found out he had even spoken to 'that son of a whore' Joshua. Sam didn't even know what a whore was, but he realised that it couldn't be anything good.

Joshua slowly came to the realisation that all of the boys around the streets, who he had called his friends, no longer wanted to play or be seen with him. They shunned him and turned their backs as he approached. He didn't know why but perhaps they were under the same threat as his friend Sam.

The young girls who weren't old enough to be in service and who were still living in their family home, were much crueller to him than the boys. They went much further in their tormenting of Joshua and openly jeered at him about his 'slut' of a mother and the 'dirty' house he lived in. Even the rhymes they chanted as they skipped with the long rope between the rows of houses referred to the family Deschamps and the lice and fleas and other bugs that abounded in their house and especially their beds.

But they were only repeating the gossip which they had heard from their mothers and fathers, and repeated amongst themselves.

He became a very confused and lonely boy. He did not know what he had done wrong or why they were picking on him. No amount of food or new boots could replace the friends who no longer wanted to even speak to him leave along play with him, or go exploring, as they used to do. He hid from them in the house, hiding in the tiny space where he slept, or went for long, lonely walks along the coast paths on his own.

Then, as with all things in this world, the day arrived that would shape the rest of his life, when the truth fell into place and all became clear to him.

He had been sent by his mother to empty the shit-bucket from the privy, a job which he hated and which would normally take him well over an hour because he had to walk the mile or so to the pit on the edge of town, provided for those people who lived in the close confines of the town, without access to gardens or grounds of their own. He had made sure that the lid was secure and walked slowly and carefully to avoid spilling the stinking contents of the bucket, but he needed to rest every few minutes, for the bucket was full and heavy and made his arms ache. Progress was slow. But today, as sometimes happened, he was in luck. He had hardly reached halfway to the pit and was making his way through an area where the cottages were spaced further apart and boasted large gardens. The gardens were mostly laid down to vegetables and he looked in awe at the rows of carrots and turnips and potatoes and things he couldn't name but knew were good to eat. He set the bucket down to take one of his many rests and leant against a low stone wall which bordered the track. A weather-beaten old man was working on a patch of newly turned ground on the other side. He stopped work and approached the boy, sniffing the air.

'What yer got there, lad, ith that yer thit bucket I can thmell?' He had no teeth left in his mouth and lisped badly.

'Yes, mister.' He pointed in the general direction in which he had been walking. 'I'm on my way down to the shit pit.'

'You've thill a ways to go. What would it be wuth to yer if I could thave yer the bother?' the man asked.

'I don't know, mister.' Joshua was wary now, not knowing what was coming next.

'Would it be wuth a ha'penny to yer?' the man carried on regardless of the expression on the boy's face.

'I haven't got a ha'penny, mister.' He turned his trouser pockets inside out to prove the point. 'I had better get going now.'

'I were teathing yer, lad. Yer could tip yer bucket in me rhubarb trench and wath it in the water tub over yonder. Do me a thervice and thave yer thelf a walk at the thame time.'

Joshua didn't need asking twice and within minutes the bucket was clean and he began retracing his steps. The old man watched him go for a minute or two, maybe remembering when he was Joshua's age and had to do the same stinking chore. With a sigh he turned his back and began to backfill the trench.

Joshua had been gone from the house less than half the time it usually took him to reach the pit and return home and had arrived at the end of his narrow street when he spotted a group of girls. The group included Sarah Huckle, a big girl for her age and a bully with a nasty streak running right through her. She was his chief tormentor. The girls were playing Hopscotch, and thankfully had not spotted him yet. Joshua had grown tall and strong in the last few months as he became a man, but he was no match for a bunch of girls and their venomous tongues and jibes.

Dreading having to face them he quickly turned into the back lane, ran the short distance to his house and, thankful that he hadn't been seen by the girls, turned into his walled yard. He replaced the bucket in the privy, went through the lean-to and opened the door into the parlour. No-one was in the room but he heard voices, or at least one voice, a deep male voice from upstairs.

He climbed the stairs. Usually the door to his mother's room was tightly shut but for some reason, today it was open. Not open fully, but open wide enough for him to see nearly all of the room. Curiosity got the better of him and he crept closer to the opening.

The room had only a tiny window and was dark even on the brightest day and two candles were alight, one on the dressing table, the dressing table with the flimsy upholstered stool which his mother had recently purchased, and the other on the washstand. A man was standing near the dressing table, half turned away from him, and even in the dim light he recognised the tall thin frame of the man and knew straight away who it was. It was George Hargreaves, the father of Sam who used to be his best friend. The memory of the day when Sam had told him that his father had threatened to beat him if he as much as spoke to Joshua, that he could not be his friend anymore, flashed through his mind and he felt the hurt all over again. He was confused. Now George Hargreaves was in his house, with his mother, in her bedroom.

Joshua could not see his mother but knew that she must have been in the room because George Hargreaves was speaking quietly to someone, although the words did not make sense to him, and his voice sounded different to how he remembered it.

'Don't stop now. Go on. Don't stop. Yes, yes, that's it, don't stop now, go on,' and he groaned, and his breathing was fast and shallow.

He thought that his mother must be on the other side of the room out of his line of sight. But then, Hargreaves moved slightly so that he could lean back against the dressing table and now Joshua could see that his mother was kneeling in front of him and his trousers were unbuttoned. She was doing something with her mouth. Her head was moving slowly to and fro, in a rhythmical fashion, and his hand was at the back of her head grasping a handful of her luscious hair.

'That's it. Do it. Go on, do it faster,' he said, his voice now louder and becoming more husky. Her movements became more urgent.

Joshua could see that his mother's bodice was pulled down to her slim waist and her shoulders, arms and back were bare. He suddenly realised what she was doing. Her mouth was wrapped around his cock and she was sucking it and he could see it moving in and out between her lips. Despite himself, Joshua found that the sight made him feel strangely excited.

Joshua was spellbound by the scene which was unfolding before his very eyes. Not fully understanding what he was witnessing but somehow knowing that it was wrong for him to be watching. Then, to his embarrassment, he felt the tightness of his trousers and realised that his own cock had become erect and hard and was pressing against the tight and rough material. He felt his face reddening.

'Now. Now. Yes,' followed by a long, drawn out, 'yessssss, go on, yesssss.' Then all that could be heard was the man's breathing.

Hargreaves was looking down at his mother's face, relishing the sight for she was stunningly pretty when compared to his own downtrodden wife. His hand was still in her hair, pulling her forward, urging her to continue what she was doing for as long as possible, even after he had climaxed.

She stayed in the same position for a few more seconds, her mouth nuzzling against his diminishing penis and then she got to her feet. She crossed to the washstand, cleared her throat deeply and spat into the slop bucket she kept underneath. She turned and pulled her bodice back up over her shoulders and slipped her arms through the dainty straps. Hargreaves stepped across to her and slipped his hand inside the flimsy material and felt again her erect nipple.

'You've had your money's worth for today, mister. Anything more means more money.' She pulled away from him and slowly re-buttoned the bodice but not before Joshua had seen her milky white breasts with the dark protruding nipples.

Hargreaves straightened his trousers and finished buckling the belt around his breeches. He reached into his coat pocket and produced a few copper coins which he placed on the dressing table behind him. He turned to go, for he was in a hurry to leave now that it was over.

'Same time next week?' suggested Louisa. 'Isn't it about time you tasted the other pleasures I have on offer?'

'I'll let you know. If I can find the money, I'll come round about the same time,' he promised.

'You'll be back,' stated Louisa confidently, knowing from the gossip that his wife denied him any rights in bed since the difficult birth of their one and only child, 'but it'll cost you more to see and taste the rest.'

'What if I can't find any more money? My wife takes all my wages. She says she needs it to feed me and the lad and to keep the roof over our heads,' he was on the verge of pleading. What a pitiful fool he was, she thought, but he was a regular customer and paid good money and was easy to please. His money was as good as anyone else's and money was what she wanted most. She needed fools like him.

'You'll find the money from somewhere, and when you do I promise I'll be worth every penny.' She paused and her tongue flitted across her lips. 'Why not borrow a few pennies from the Money Lender?' She and the Money Lender had an 'understanding'. 'But if you can't find the money, don't come around again,' she added coldly, and he knew she meant what she said. He knew that nothing in this house would be for free, and he was already trying to think of ways to keep his hard-earned money out of his wife's hands. He turned away towards the door to the stairs when he suddenly saw the boy.

'What's he doing here?' he demanded. 'Is he spying on us? You said you had sent him to the pit and he wouldn't be back for hours yet. You need to deal with him, or do you want me to give him a leathering?'

He was angry but also fearful that he had been caught out and the need to get out of the house was uppermost in his mind. He scowled at the boy as he pushed roughly past, and he could be heard hurrying down the stairs. He went out through the wash-house, crossed the yard, and after looking both ways along the lane, went through the gate and turned left.

'What are you doing back?' she asked the boy, but before he could say anything Louisa noticed the bulge in his breeches despite his trying to hide it with his hands.

'You dirty little sod,' she said venomously, 'you worthless little bugger, you've been spying on me and now look at you.' She pointed to the bulge in his breeches. 'I'll teach you not to spy on me again. I've seen you playing with yourself in bed, you disgusting sod. Get down into the parlour you filthy bugger, you worthless little turd.'

She pushed him roughly down the rickety stairs and followed close behind. She immediately went out into the wash-house and Joshua knew that he was about to receive another beating. He thought about fleeing from the house but when he tried to open the door leading into the street it was locked and bolted.

She crossed to the copper boiler and lifted the short, thick stick that she normally used to agitate and remove the washing. Joshua was cowering in the corner next to the grate when she came back into the parlour for he knew from other days that if he crammed himself far enough into the niche she had difficulty taking a full swing of the arm which held the stick, although the shortened swing still hurt. She raised her arm high and the first vicious blow caught him squarely across the shoulders and he cried out as the pain sliced through him. The next blow took him across the shins and was more painful than the first. She beat him with the stick and she uttered the words 'filthy bugger' or 'filthy sod' with each blow, until she had used up all her remaining energy, and her anger had burned out.

She slowly climbed the stairs back up to her bedroom, breathing heavily, and when she reached the top step she looked back at the pitiful shape in the corner that was her son. Her anger had now been replaced by the fear that maybe she had seriously injured the boy, but no matter, what's done is done, and he deserved the beating anyway.

She crossed to the dressing table and retrieved the coins. Ten minutes later she was ready to go out to the inn. *There may be some business there*, she thought, *and if not, I can still have a good drink, I deserve a good drink*. She retraced her steps down to the parlour and crossed to the dresser that held her few pieces of china. The dresser had been built by her father and had a secret compartment that only the family knew of. She opened the bottom drawer, reached in her hand and pulled the small catch that enabled her to slide the drawer completely out of the carcase to reveal the secret space behind. From the space she took a tin box, decorated with brightly coloured flowers.

The box rattled as she set it down on the scrubbed table and she opened the lid to reveal a small wad of banknotes and many silver and copper coins. She put all but two of the coins that Hargreaves had left behind into the box and replaced the lid. Within seconds the box and the drawer were back in place.

Joshua watched his mother go out through the door into the yard with eyes almost glued shut with dried blood, and he heard the gate to the back lane shut. He stayed where he was in the corner until it was dark in the house and the pain in his bladder became unbearable and he knew he had to use the privy or burst. He dragged his battered body out to the yard. Sitting over the newly cleaned bucket he decided what he must do. There was only the one answer to his plight.

Racked with pain in his back and shins he slept fitfully in the corner next to the long-dead fire. He heard his mother return to the house and felt her looking at him. He lay still and gave no indication that he knew she was there. She climbed the stairs and he heard the floorboards creaking above his head.

During the night he dreamed and once he awoke to the sound of someone sobbing, and realised in his sorry state that it was he, himself. Something happened to him then. Something inside him changed forever. He would never be the same again.

His mother, throughout her service days, had always been an early riser. But early in the morning, not long after dawn had broken, when his mother came down the stairs into the parlour, he was not there. She went back up the stairs and looked in the tiny room where he usually slept but he was not there either. She was puzzled. She went down to the parlour again and went out through the wash house into the back yard to see if he was there. She opened the gate and looked into the lane. She walked back through the parlour and opened the front door leading to the street, but he was nowhere in sight.

If she had walked the few yards to the end of the next street she may have been in time to see her son talking quietly to Sam Hargreaves and his agitated mother. The hopelessness that had settled deep in Joshua's very soul in the hours following the beating he had received the day before had been replaced during the dark night by a cold and venomous rage. A cold anger such as he had never known before, and he was filled with the desire to lash out and hurt those around him. And if he couldn't hurt his mother then there were other people who he had loved who he could hurt. Those so-called friends who had cut him deeply. Those so-called friends who had abandoned him and who could now share some of the hurt he was feeling.

Sam Hargreaves' mother suddenly turned from him and rushed back into her house and the conversation between the three of them ended. Joshua stood silently looking at Sam and then turned his back on the boy who used to be his best friend, the boy who had been his best friend for years, and slowly walked away as raised voices emanated from inside the house.

It took him almost an hour to walk to the edge of town. He had briefly stopped at the graveyard, standing silently, staring intently at the patch of earth under which his grandparents were buried. He started the long climb up the road that would take him onto The Downs and eventually all the way to London, he did not once look back, there was nothing there for him now. He trudged slowly on his way. Each and every step caused a stab of pain to shoot through his legs and back but he hardly noticed. For, worse than the pain in his body, Joshua Deschamps had the pain of a broken heart.

The day turned out to be one of the best summer days so far that year, sunny and warm and with a cooling breeze coming in off the English Channel, but the day was ruined for Louisa Deschamp several hours later that morning when she realised that the brightly coloured tin box containing the bank notes and the coins had gone from its secret place in the dresser. She knew straight away who had taken it.

But she would never see her son or the prettily decorated tin box again.

CHAPTER 7

John Harkin

Exton, Devon
18 August 1799

Great Britain had been at war with Napoleon Bonaparte's France for more than six years when the men of the Royal Navy first made their appearance in the small town of Exton, in the southern part of the County of Devon, near to where John Harkin lived with his father, mother and older sister.

In the years between 1770 and 1793, when Britain had begun hostilities with France, successive British governments had allowed the fighting capability of the Navy and the Army to decline to pitiful levels. Manpower and equipment were diminished in the cause of saving money under the mistaken belief that the present stability between the nations of Europe would be enjoyed for years and years to come.

Not heeding the lessons to be learnt from the revolution in France and the ousting of the monarchy in that country, the government in London complacently believed that the turmoil across the narrow strip of water which separated the two countries would have minimal effect on Britain, and the political malaise continued.

The Army had been allowed to reduce in size to a paltry twenty thousand enlisted men and the Royal Navy was desperately short of seaworthy fighting ships, and the crews to man them. In September of 1793, shortly after the outbreak of hostilities, the French army had easily defeated the British forces at the battle of Hondschoote. The British were in disarray and Napoleon Bonaparte immediately massed his army, totalling more than one hundred and fifty thousand well trained and well fed soldiers, in Northern France, in preparation for the invasion of England. There were two obstacles to the invasion... The English Channel and the weakened, but determined, Royal Navy.

The government hoped that the combination of the two would buy them enough time to reorganise the Army and bring it and the Royal Navy up to strength. They were right. The obstacles were insurmountable to the French and the invasion failed to materialise. Enlistment into the British Army and the Royal Navy continued to increase year on year, both voluntary and by conscription, well into the new century.

In the meantime a state of stalemate ensured between the two countries: the French Armies superior on land and the Royal Navy holding the advantage at sea, but it would be many years before the British and her allies would be able to match the might of France on land, and break the deadlock.

*

He heard the sound of the drum beating time, long before the small party of naval ratings marched into the square in the centre of the town. They numbered eleven in all and, at first glance, appeared to be a shoddy bunch, but they were in step and marched along jauntily as only sailors can. None of the men were in full uniform (the navy was still woefully short on equipment) but somehow still managed to make an impressive sight – at least in the eyes of young John Harkin.

A tall man wearing a blue tunic and white trousers led the way, followed by the sailors. On his head he wore a round black hat with a narrow brim. He had a weather-beaten face and, to John, looked very fierce. Two marines, resplendent in their bright red jackets, brought up the rear. Each carried a musket at shoulder arms, and long bayonets bounced in scabbards on their belts. A younger man, not much more than a boy, with a snare drum, marched in front of the marines beating time.

A wagon, pulled by two horses and driven by another marine, followed a short distance behind. Seated in the cart were three men, none of whom were wearing anything that resembled an article of military uniform. One of the men was smiling and looking around with interest whilst the others looked miserable and kept their eyes downcast. They kept their hands low so that the manacles and chains they wore could not readily be seen. They had been residents of Exeter prison until the previous day.

John Harkin felt his heartbeat increase with excitement and he watched with fascination as the party of men made their way to The Raven's Head Tavern, which sat next to the chapel and was the largest public house in the town. He had not seen a sight of this sort before. Like all young boys he was intrigued by all things military.

The party of men halted outside the inn and the drum beat ceased. The leader barked the order which stood the men down and disappeared through the open door into the dark interior. All of the men, except those in chains in the back of the wagon, sauntered slowly over to the horse trough, with its supply of fresh running water. It seemed to John that they walked with a strange gait – they walked with their legs slightly apart, as though they expected the ground to shift from under them at any time. Whilst a few splashed water over their heads, others drank deeply from cupped hands. It was mid-summer and baking hot and the men had been on the road since early that morning. A fair sized crowd of the townspeople had gathered in the street to see what the commotion was all about. The sailors stared balefully back at their curious looks, they had seen it all before, it was as expected, nothing here to cause them concern.

Soon the leader emerged from the inn and ordered the men to gather around him. He swiftly detailed them off, and several of the men entered the inn, whilst those left outside paired up and strolled off in different directions. He shouted to the driver of the cart and he drove the cart through the arched gateway into the yard belonging to the inn, followed by the two marines. Minutes later the gate slammed shut.

This was the Extons' first, but not last, experience of the 'Naval Press Gang'.

John Harkin stepped aside to allow the two sailors to pass him as he stood impatiently outside the shop. He had been waiting for what seemed like hours since his sister Lizzie had gone into the shop to buy a length of printed cotton. Their mother had sent them into town for the material and told them not to loiter as she urgently needed to make a pinafore for the girl. She was off into service in Exmouth and had outgrown what few clothes she had and her mother couldn't send her off looking like the family couldn't afford any decent clothes. She was due to leave home at the end of the following week and mother wanted her tidy before then.

If you asked John if he had a good life he would not know how to answer for he had never known any other life and therefore had nothing with which to compare it. He did know, however, that he was bored at home. He also knew that there was a huge world out there and he craved excitement. Despite living in the country he was reasonably well read. His mother had made sure that both her children could read and write from an early age and there had always been books and pamphlets in the house.

He had no friends to get into any mischief with. Their cottage was three miles from Exton and was tied to the farm on which his father worked. The main farmhouse was only a quarter of a mile from the cottage but only the farmer, his wife and their grown-up daughter lived there. John's sister, two years older than him at fourteen seemed to have lost all interest recently in scouting around with him or fishing in the river or climbing in the old quarry, and doing such things wasn't much fun on your own. Even though rough digging the garden for his father was a chore he liked to eat the vegetables that were grown there and at least the heavy work gave him a well-developed body, with a surprising amount of strength for a young boy.

His father had worked on the farm all his life, as had his grandfather. His father loved his work with the animals on the farm and took great pride in the condition of the herd of cows and, on the higher ground, the huge flock of sheep, bred exclusively for their wool. His father told him time and time again that the future prosperity of the country lay in the land and the people who worked it, for there would always be a demand for food and clothing. And he said, according to every article he read, it was obvious that the population of Britain was increasing year on year. But John was not convinced and found it difficult to see any evidence of this in the empty countryside. But despite his scepticism it was taken for granted by his parents and the farmer that he would eventually follow in his father's footsteps.

When James Harkin had married Elizabeth Parsons, a girl he had known all his life, his employer had provided him with the tied cottage where they now lived. Lizzie and John arrived quite quickly after the marriage, but it was a mystery why no more children followed. When John had made his appearance his father had asked the farmer for, and had been given, an increase in wages, but the increase came in the form of an extra allowance of bread, cheese and beer. The farmer swore that profits were down and that he could not afford to pay extra money.

But the Harkins were content and had no desire to change anything, even if their son was not. They lived a simple life that suited them. The only time Elizabeth left the cottage was on infrequent trips to the market in Exton where she would sell as much of their surplus from the garden as she and the children could carry. Some of the vegetables would be bartered for other goods, but some would raise a few pennies. She used the money to buy small necessities for her home and children and would always purchase the latest news-sheet for her husband.

Each Sunday, come hail or shine, all the family, father, mother and the two children would put on their best clothes and would walk together the three miles to the town, to the service in the chapel there, as did nearly everyone else. The children would attend Sunday instruction, where they would learn about the scriptures, whilst the grown-ups would take part in the main service. Regularly there would be travelling preachers who would give sermons and lectures and the congregation would listen with rapt attention for this was an important link with the big wide world and the people loved to hear of new ideas and thinking. This was the highlight of the week for most people, including the Harkins.

*

The two sailors had stopped despite his moving out of the way.

'What's your name, lad?' the taller of the two sailors said.

'John Harkin, sir.' He was in awe of the men, and maybe a little afraid of them, and answered with his eyes looking at the ground.

'Stand up straight, lad.' The man had a strange accent but his tone was kindly enough. 'Do you live hereabouts?'

'Yes, sir,' was all he could manage in reply, forgetting to mention that the cottage was a least three miles outside the town.

'Nothing much to do in a small place like this, eh?' the sailor persisted.

'No,' he answered, although he thought that there was more to do in the town than out in the middle of nowhere where he lived.

The sailors were under strict orders. Recruit as many men as possible for the cause by whatever means. The second sailor thought he had recognised something of himself in the boy and took the initiative. He haunched down, looked the boy in the eye and lowered his voice to almost a whisper.

'When I was a young man, about the same age as you,' he said conspiratorially, as though telling John a state secret, 'my father wanted me to follow him into the bakery trade. But baking bread was not for me. Do I look like a baker to you? I wanted something more than just being a baker, I wanted some excitement. I left home and joined the King's Navy, and I have seen lands that ordinary people can only dream about. I have had wonderful adventures and the King, God bless Him, paid me handsomely for the privilege. How would a life like that suit a likely young man such as yourself, eh?'

The first sailor was determined not to be outdone by his companion. 'If you are man enough and want a life full of excitement and adventure it's yours for the taking. Step into the inn and swear allegiance to His Majesty and accept the shilling. I promise you, if you don't you'll live to regret it.'

The sailors studied the boy and tried to see if their words had had the desired effect but his head was still down and there was no way of knowing what he was thinking. John had heard every syllable of every word and had felt something stir deep inside his being. He suddenly realised that his heart was pounding and his mouth was as dry as tinder and for some unknown reason he felt the need to pee.

The sailors moved on for they had been ordered to try their luck in several streets, and if they had not stirred the heart of the young boy already then it would not be stirred.

'We are billeted at the inn until midday tomorrow,' one of them called back over his shoulder.

When Lizzie came out of the shop carrying a small bundle, her brother was nowhere to be seen. She looked around, her temper rising, for he was always disappearing when he shouldn't. She spotted him across the road looking through the window of the inn, his face pressed tight against the glass. She stalked angrily over to him.

'Come away,' she ordered, as only older sisters can, 'we need to get back home.'

On the long road home, they walked along leisurely for it was hot and the sun beat down remorselessly. Lizzie carried the bundle of material and walked in the centre of the lane while her brother picked up stones and threw them down the lane in front, challenging her to try to throw further. But she was too old and ladylike now to indulge in such childish activity. Eventually he grew tired of throwing and after cutting a stick from the hedge took to beating down the cow-parsley and flowers that grew in the grass verge instead.

As Lizzie watched her brother thrashing about with the stick, she was struck again by the differences between them. However had her parents managed to have two children who were so different? She asked herself, not for the first time. Temperamentally they were as different as it is possible to be, so much so that she wondered sometimes if he was her brother at all. But she did love him so.

They had enjoyed pretending to have great adventures together but as she had grown older she had begun to spend more and more time around the house learning all the skills of womanhood from her mother. She could clean house and cook as well as her mother although she had a way to go before she would be as adept with a sewing needle. John spent very little time in the cottage during the day, sometimes even missing meals, which was surprising considering how much he ate when he did sit down to his meal. He was adventurous and inquisitive and was blind to any danger. When they were younger and they had spent more time playing together, some of his exploits had so scared her that she would run home and hide, fearful that he would turn up dead. Even so, Lizzie knew that her brother was her mother's favourite.

Now, in the evenings after supper, if the weather was fair, he would disappear outside until it grew dark whereas she enjoyed sitting quietly with her parents. She would sit by her father and they would read the *Exton Gazette* or any other pamphlet that they had, and they would discuss the issues of the day. She tried to make sense of the news and the happenings in the wider world and would listen to her father and to some extent her mother, for her mother could read and had opinions of her own, and so her grasp of the affairs of the world was much more developed than that of her brother.

Their parents were both dark-haired and had brown eyes, her mother having particularly thick dark chestnut coloured hair with a slight curl, which she kept long but wore ordinarily tucked up under a lace cap. Sometimes in the evenings, she would set her hair free from the confines of the cap, which particularly pleased her husband, who said that, with her hair down, she reminded him of how she looked on the day they had married.. Lizzie's hair was a shade or two lighter than her mother's, but with the same thickness and curl, and she had also inherited the same dark eyes. The upper part of her body was slim and shapely but she had her mother's hips which were on the heavy side and, she thought, her feet were too big.

Physically John was, not unexpectedly, much bigger than his sister. He was already taller and broader, and had the kind of build that promised well for the future. Now, even at such a young age, the muscles in his chest and upper arms were well defined. But what really set them apart was the colouring. His hair was blond, turning almost white in the summer months, as some of the colour was bleached out by the sun. His eyes, instead of the brown of his parents, were a beautiful deep blue, and were big and round with blond eyebrows that were almost invisible except when you were able to look really closely. No-one was able to remember anyone in the family with the same hair and eye colouring as him. His mother was often teased about the fairness of the boy, but the banter was always in good fun. His features, his nose, his chin and his cheekbones, were more finely defined than those of his sister or his mother. *He will break a few hearts when he is older,* thought Lizzie.

Looking at her brother now, Lizzie was concerned. He seemed to be preoccupied as though he was considering something of importance. He was subdued and quiet which was not like him at all, for he usually breezed through life seemingly without a care. If he did worry about something it was usually forgotten or pushed aside in no time.

He sat quietly through their evening meal and picked at his food and as soon as he was given permission he was back outside. Later, when she went outside to wash the pots in the bucket beside the back door, she could see him sitting down by the river. Strangely, he seemed to be talking quietly but intently to his father's two working dogs which were sat beside him and watching his face intently.

During the night she was awakened several times by his tossing and turning, for they slept in the same small room separated by a curtain, which stretched down the middle of the room, hanging from hooks in the ceiling.

Just before the dawn arrived she heard him get out of bed and there was the sound of him dressing.

'What's the matter?' she quietly asked, raising herself up on the pillow.

'Nothing,' he whispered back. There came the sound of him lacing his boots.

'Something must be wrong,' she persisted. 'You've had me awake most of the night with your tossing and turning. What is it? John, you can tell me.'

He parted the curtain and came into her side of the room.

'I'll tell you if you promise to keep it a secret until tonight.' And he looked to see her nod in agreement. Over the years they had had many secrets, which they had kept from their parents, and he knew that he could trust her to say nothing until the time was right.

'I'm going to join the Navy, I'm going into Exton to sign up.' He waited for her reaction.

Her first instinct was to tell him he was too young to leave home and that he was only a boy and that the Navy would not have him anyway for he was only twelve, but she knew that this would be the wrong thing to say to her stubborn brother. She looked into his face and could see the determination in the set of his jaw.

'But we're at war,' she tried instead, 'you could be killed.'

'I know,' he said slowly, and he looked directly into her eyes. 'I can't stay around here. I can't look forward to working on the farm, like Father. There has to be more in this world for me.'

This was the first time she had heard her brother speak so candidly on the subject, but she had known for a little while that he had been restless and had seemed to be retreating into himself. Maybe he needed something more than a cottage in the country.

By the dim light that was now creeping through the tiny window under the eaves she could see the gleam in those beautiful, blue eyes and she knew that his mind was made up and there was nothing she could say to dissuade him, for she knew full well how stubborn and headstrong he could be.

'Please sis, do this last thing for me. Don't tell mother and father until it's too late and I have gone far enough away that they can't find me and so can't bring me back.'

She knew then that she loved this brother of hers and would miss him terribly, but she herself was leaving in a week's time. Was it fair that she should try to stop him?

'Let me walk with you so far,' she said, making to get out of bed.

'Please don't, sis,' he begged. He took her hand. 'Let's say goodbye here.'

She reached out for him and the tears came to her eyes. 'I will pray for you every day, and I will ask Jesus to look out for you and to keep you safe until you come back.'

They clung to each other for several minutes. Then John got up from her bed, parted the curtain and reached through to his bed. He picked up a small bundle and a piece of paper.

'Will you give this to Mother and Father at the supper table this evening?' he asked, passing the piece of folded paper to her.

'What is it?' she asked, taking the paper from his hand.

'It is just a note.' He turned and crossed to the door and quietly pulled it open. He looked back at his sister and softly said, 'I will never forget you, sis, I'll think of you every day.' The door closed quietly behind him, and he was gone.

She could see very little from the tiny bedroom window but she did get a fleeting sight of him climbing the wall and jumping into the lane, as she had seen him do since he had been able to climb. Her father's dogs, maybe thinking this was another of the boy's games, came running from the barn and jumped the wall as well, tails at full mast and ears flying in the slipstream, only to be curtly sent back. They slunk back into the barn, looking back over their shoulders, as though knowing that he was going away and wanting to catch a last glimpse of the boy they thought of as their friend.

*

The sailor in charge sat self-importantly at the best table in the inn, as he had been since early morning. In front of him, placed exactly in the centre of the table lay a large leather-bound book, a bundle of important-looking papers was to his left and a small strongbox to his right. He looked again at the lad standing in front of him.

'So, you want to join us?' It was more a statement than a question, for why else would the boy be in the inn?

'Yes please, sir.'

'How old are you, lad?' the sailor asked.

'Fifteen, sir,' the lad lied, but his eyes gave him away.

The sailor studied him for several minutes, absent-mindedly twirling the gold ring in his right ear. More like thirteen, he thought, but a well-built thirteen nonetheless, with plenty of muscle on him. Still too young, he thought, but wasn't the great Commodore Nelson only twelve when he joined the Navy as a midshipman? And besides, powder monkeys were as valuable on a fighting ship as anyone. But even so he still hesitated, taking time to gauge what the reaction of the First Lieutenant would be when they went back aboard ship.

The silence and the delay were making John feel more nervous than he had before. *Don't send me home,* he thought silently. *I won't let you send me home.* And he stood straight and tried to be as tall as he could. The sailor noticed the way that the lad had drawn himself up and puffed out his chest and was impressed. But it was the lad's eyes that held his gaze. Those eyes were as deep and as blue as the deepest South Seas, but seemed to have more than a touch of steel about them as well, he thought.

'Right,' he said. He had made his decision.

The sailor moved in his chair. He reached forward and opened the leather-bound book. The page he selected had several columns and he wrote something in the first column. It was the date, August 19, 1799.

'Name?' he asked without looking up.

'John Harkin, sir,' said the lad proudly and with relief, for he knew that he was about to become a sailor, like the man before him. The sailor wrote the name in the next column. He turned the book towards John and pointed to the space alongside his name.

'If you can write, sign your name there,' he instructed. 'If you can't write, put your mark.'

John signed his name and it was duly witnessed. An entry was made in the final column; the book was closed and straightened on the table. The sailor pulled the strongbox towards him and, opening the top, withdrew a shiny new coin which he passed across the table to the new recruit. John picked up the coin and held it tight in his fist. He could not remember having seen a shilling before, let alone owning one.

The sailor spoke. His tone seemed to John to have changed and had become less fatherly, more businesslike.

'Right, you have accepted the King's Shilling and you're now an ordinary seaman. You will abide by King's Regulations and will answer to the Naval Code of Discipline, starting now. Get out into the yard to the cart; we'll be leaving within the hour.'

'Yes, sir.' John made for the door, taking his bundle with him. He was halted at the door by the sound of the voice behind him.

'Lesson number one,' said the sailor, 'I am not an officer of the King's Navy. I am the Master-at-Arms on board His Majesty's Ship *Relentless*, and I am responsible for the discipline of the crew, aboard ship and on land. In future you will always address me as Master. The title 'sir' is reserved for officers and others who think they deserve it and that is how you will address them,' he paused, 'now, get outside and report yourself to Able Seaman Williams, he will tell you where to stow your gear.'

CHAPTER 8

James Macdonald

Wexford, Ireland
19 August 1799

James MacDonald could do nothing except stand with the gathering crowd and watch his workshop burn. He had been roused from his bed by a loud and insistent thumping on the door of his house and even in his sleep-drugged state had known immediately what the commotion was all about. The reflection of the flames from across the lane, dancing on the bedroom wall, told their own story.

Already the watchers had been forced by the fierce heat to move back several yards and now as the roof began to collapse they moved away further still. Nothing could be done to save the wooden building. The tinder-dry structure was well alight and it would not take many more minutes for it to be completely consumed by the flames.

There could be no doubt in any of the watchers' minds that the fire had been set deliberately. The words 'UNITED CATHOLICS' had been roughly daubed in black pitch on the front wall of the building and, even now, some of the letters could still be recognised through the smoke and the flames. Even as the crowd watched there was fresh intensity to the flames as first the roof and then one of the side walls collapsed into the fire.

Half an hour later there was nothing left except the smouldering remains of what had been a thriving business.

His neighbours clapped him on the back and offered lots of sympathy but after a while even they drifted back to their beds, for tomorrow was another day and life had to go on.

James had been half expecting an attack of this nature, but had hoped and prayed that it would not happen. The burning of his business premises was not the first or even the second or third incident in the town. There had been five attacks in the last few weeks, all on business properties owned by Protestant families. Several unfortunate people, who lived in accommodation over or adjoining the premises, had been burned to death, at least he had been spared that.

James was the grandson of Ross MacDonald, a Scottish immigrant who had arrived in Ireland sixty-two years before from his native Fife on the west coast of Scotland. He had found work, courted and married an Irish Protestant girl, and settled down to raise a family. He had fathered seven children, two boys and five girls. One of the boys had been christened Robert.

Robbie, as Robert had been called by everyone, had followed in his father's footsteps and became a carpenter. Eventually Robbie had also married and fathered two sons, James and Tam, both with thick red hair just like their grandfather.

James MacDonald had also become a carpenter whilst his brother Tam had been apprenticed to a blacksmith in Waterford. As soon as Tam had finished his apprenticeship, and had his indentures, he had decided that he would look for work and better wages over in England. He had been gone for nearly three years.

Their grandfather Ross MacDonald was a devout Christian and was a practising lay preacher in the local Anglican Church of Ireland. He had brought up his children and his grandchildren strictly in the Protestant tradition.

At that time eight out of ten ethnic Irish were of the Catholic faith but, despite this, the government in London decreed that the Anglican Church was the official church of all Ireland. This sorry state of affairs had been the norm in Ireland for nearly one hundred and fifty years since Oliver Cromwell had defeated the Irish Royalist supporters during the Civil Wars. As a punishment he had confiscated much of the land owned by the Irish farmers and given it to his own supporters, predominantly English and Scottish Protestants. Catholics were also barred from voting in local, council and government elections. The small minority of Protestants wielded all the power.

But Catholic unrest was spreading throughout the country and secret dissident groups and organisations were springing up all over Ireland, especially in the South and West, and these groups were willing to fight for their political and civil rights. One group, in the Wexford area, had taken to burning protestant owned businesses as a way of showing their dissent.

Even before the events of this night, James had been fully aware and fearful of the growing danger and had been considering taking his wife Rachel, and newborn daughter Mary, to England.

Several months after his brother Tam had left Wexford a letter had arrived from him with news. He had laboriously written about the journey over to England, the sights he had seen and the new people he had met. Few letters followed but one letter had described the opportunities that abounded for skilled artisans in the larger and more affluent towns. He himself had travelled south from Liverpool and passed through Chester and Shrewsbury and eventually had arrived in the city of Hereford, where, on the very same day, he had secured a job working for a house builder. He had been staggered to have been offered the wage of fourteen shillings a week, more than twice as much as the maximum wage paid to the equivalent skilled workers in Ireland.

He had described how the whole city seemed to be one huge building site as more and more poorly paid agricultural workers moved into the city from the countryside. The demand for any kind of living accommodation was so high that it could not be met by the builders, and there was lots of work on the new factories and mills which were creating all the new jobs.

*

Now that the business was burned and gone forever, the decision had been made for him. There was nothing to stand in the way of James leaving Ireland and making a fresh start somewhere else. They talked through the rest of the night and by morning he and his wife had decided to make the break and go somewhere new. They had talked of The Americas, now called the United States of America since the ending of the War of Independence between the British and the colonialists in 1783. Many Irish people were abandoning their country and making the long journey across the Atlantic Ocean, but that country seemed a long, long way from home and, being a conservative man, James felt that the risk, with a wife and child to support, was too great for him to take. The decision had been made to travel to England and seek out his brother.

Most of their furniture they were able to sell, for it was of better quality than most of the people living around them owned, but it did not realise much money. What possessions they would be able to take with them were packed, and in a matter of days they had left County Wexford forever.

Two days later they had reached the fair city of Dublin and James had gone down the coast to the tiny port of Dun Laoghaire. There he had booked a passage for himself and his family on a small ship carrying potatoes to Liverpool. Even though Irish men, women and children were dying of hunger, the merchants still sent the essential produce of the country to where the profits were highest.

The ship sailed early next morning and as they stood on the deck and looked back at the coast of Ireland they were struck by the enormity of what they had done and Rachel clutched her baby tightly and sobbed quietly, for she had left her mother, father and sisters behind and knew that she would probably never set eyes on them again. James put his arm tenderly around his wife, but was thinking excitedly of the new life ahead.

CHAPTER 9

H.M.S. *Relentless*

Topsham, Devon
19 August 1799

The men had taken turn and turn about riding in the cart or walking along behind, and the party had covered in good time the twenty-two miles to Topsham, the furthest point up the River Exe that a ship of the tonnage of H.M.S. *Relentless* could safely navigate. The Master-at-Arms had pulled rank and had ridden all the way back to the ship, up next to the driver, and had set a fast pace, but no-one would have dared to object. Every few miles he did allow the small column to come to a stop, enabling the men to rest for a short while and to drink from the water barrel, but he had orders to return to the ship by 1700 hours and devil take them if they were late. He knew the ship sailed on the afternoon tide and he intended to be on board when it did.

The quayside was a hubbub of feverish activity when they arrived at their destination. The last of the supplies were hurriedly being swung aboard or carried up the gangway which spanned the six feet of water between the wall and the ship. Two other ships, cargo vessels both, were due to sail on the afternoon tide, as well as H.M.S. *Relentless*. The Captain was adamant that *Relentless* would be first away.

The new arrivals boarded and stood on the main deck looking around them in utter amazement at the feverish activity. The chained

men, there were five of them now for another shore party had
reported back at the same time, were led forward and taken down
below decks. The sailors who had formed the shore party which had
visited Exton returned to the jetty and set-to helping with the
loading. The Master-at-Arms seemed to have vanished. Crewmen
scurried here and there obeying the shouted orders from the few
officers, easily recognisable by the difference in uniform, and sacks,
barrels and baskets disappeared below decks at an impressive rate,
until only crates of chickens were left on the deck in the open air.

Another officer appeared on deck from a hatchway at the stern of
the ship accompanied by the Master-at-Arms. He was obviously
more senior, rapidly took command and started issuing orders. The
new recruits, including John Harkin, were led to the deck below and
shown where they would billet.

The decks were eventually cleared, the gangway jettisoned, and the
ship was pulled slowly into the current of the river by four longboats.
As the ship took the current, lines were cast and she gathered pace
under one small sail, heading downriver to the English Channel. Off
the small port of Exmouth, the civilian pilot was put ashore and the
coxswain was ordered, by the Officer of the Watch, to steer a course
which would take the ship westwards towards the wide Atlantic
Ocean. All sail was set and the ship pushed her stem into the swell
and increased speed. Her next landfall would be the island of
Trinidad in the West Indies.

*

That evening, sitting together around the big table in the
downstairs room, Lizzie gave her parents the folded note and told
them her secret. They had not seen their son all day, but that was not
unusual, although John missing supper was. They read the note in
stunned silence and then there was a barrage of frantic questions
followed by tears from both her mother and her father, for they
knew that their son had gone from them and they had not even said
goodbye to him.

When the tears had dried they sat in silence for what seemed like
hours to Lizzie, each lost in their own thoughts. Then, for there was
nothing left to say, they clasped hands and prayed together and
begged their God to keep the boy safe and to bring him back home
to them, sometime.

Eventually they even exhausted their prayers and fell silent. Only now did Lizzie pick up the note and read it. There were tear stains on the paper and her brother had written:

Dearest Mother and Father,

By the time you read this letter I will be many miles away on a ship at sea.

I hope that you will not be angry with me for leaving without saying goodbye but I was afraid that you would stop me leaving.

I know that I shall miss you both, and Lizzie too, but this is something I have to do.

I shall think of you each day and I shall pray for you.

I hope that in the future I can make you proud of me.

Thank you for all that you have done for me.

Take care of each other. I love both of you with all my heart.

Your loving son,

John

CHAPTER 10

Herefordshire

1820

He knew he had taken a wrong turn. He wasn't familiar with this corner of the county but his instincts told him he was heading in the wrong direction. All the signs backed up this feeling. Since he had passed the lonely cottage over half a mile back he had seen no other signs of habitation, and the lane was getting narrower with each passing yard. The lane looked unused and uncared for and weeds and grass had sprouted into a thick band down the centre. It was too narrow now to enable him to turn the cart and retrace his steps, unless he could find a gateway into a field.

As luck would have it he spotted the gateway into the wheat-field at exactly the same time as the girl came into view. The gate was off its hinges and leaning in the hedge. It looked like it had been in the hedge for some time. He pulled the cart just past the entrance to the field and stopped.

The girl drew closer to him, approaching without a care. He guessed she was about ten or eleven and was dressed in the usual clothes for a weekday in the country: a cotton print dress which reached down to halfway between her knees and her ankles, covered with a pinafore. On her feet was a pair of stout boots. Her dark brown hair was pulled tightly back into a thick plait which hung nearly to her waist and swung from side to side as she walked jauntily along. A wickerwork basket, which appeared to contain something quite heavy, was carried over her right arm.

He climbed down from the driver's seat and stood in her path.

'Good day to you, mister,' she said politely, just as she had been instructed since she had been a very young child. Her voice had the faint burr common in these parts.

'Tell me child, where will this lane lead me to?' He noticed her eyes were also dark brown and had long lashes.

'If you follow the lane,' she turned and pointed back the way that she had come, 'you will come upon the main road, and then if you turn that way,' she pointed to her right, 'you will come to the town.'

He noticed the slightly tanned skin on her arms as she pointed, and the way the dress pulled tightly across her chest.

'Can I get through with the cart?' His voice was thick with emotion. 'The lane is getting narrower and seems not to be used over much.' He followed the line of her jaw and could almost taste the flesh of her throat where it disappeared into her dress.

'Yes mister. It's narrow but you can easily get through. Nothing comes this way anymore since they built the tram road from the pit down to the coal yard in the town. It cuts off a good distance.' She had a funny feeling in the pit of her stomach. She didn't like the way the man looked at her. She ought to be getting home.

He noticed for the first time the fullness of her lips. Before he knew what he was doing he was reaching out to touch her cheek. She recoiled and took a step back. He stepped forward and reached out again, his lust for her taking him over.

She knew now that she should get away from him but he was blocking her path. She turned and ran into the field, panicking now. Anything to get away. She was young and fit and fast. But she was wearing her heavy boots and they slowed her. He followed her, drawing the cudgel from his belt, the cudgel he had taken to carrying to protect him from robbers.

She turned to her right and followed the line of the hedge, knowing that further along there was a gap that she could use to get back into the lane. She ran as fast as she could but she wasn't fast enough. The cudgel caught her on the right side of her head with a resounding crack. She went down in an ungainly heap, all legs and arms and the wickerwork basket spilled the huge leg of pork she had bought from the butchers in town. He was on her in a flash, tearing at her clothes. But he had no need to hurry. She was not able to run anymore.

He waited for her to recover consciousness. She was naked now and he ran his hands over her body, feeling the smoothness of her young skin, his lust growing out of control. He took off his trousers and spread her upon the ground, but she still did not move or cry out or struggle. He slapped her face and slapped her again. He was disappointed and angry. He liked them to struggle for a while before they were subdued.

*

Joe found her under the Silver Birch tree that grew in among the hawthorn of the hedge. She could have been asleep, lay like that, on her side with her legs pulled up. But something about her looked unnatural, broken somehow. Joe was afraid. He didn't go near, instead he called out.

'She's over here. I've found her. She's over here. She's in the field.' He went on shouting, almost hysterically, until more men came running.

When they saw her they all stopped short. Most of the group of men that had assembled at the cottage and had set out to search for the girl were farm labourers. They could slaughter a cow or butcher a pig but the body of a young girl was different. They stood, not knowing what they should do.

Another group had started searching from the town, following the path the girl would have taken. They arrived within minutes. Among them, riding on a cart with a wooden box in the back (just in case) rode the undertaker, who also doubled up as the doctor, the dentist and the town barber. Shaves and haircuts would need to wait today. He came through the gateway at a fast walk, almost a trot, and pushed his way through the group of men. He carried with him a white cotton sheet that he had used many times to cover corpses.

He knelt down by the girl, seeing the head wound and the dried blood in her hair. He reached out with the sheet to cover her nakedness. His hand was halted in mid-air. Had she just moved? He was sure that her eyelids had fluttered. He gently placed his fingers on her throat and felt for a pulse. Yes. There it was, faint and slow, but definitely a pulse.

'She's still alive. Good Lord, she's still alive. Quick, give me the sheet.' He once again reached out and used the sheet to cover her. 'Joseph, you're strong, pick her up and carry her to my cart. We need to get her into shelter and warmth.'

Joseph bent to lift the girl, relieved now that it was not a dead body that he had to touch. He lifted her easily; she was no weight for his young muscles.

'Gently now, don't jolt her head. Henry, try to hold her head steady. Thomas, go and turn my cart. We need to get her back to town quickly.' The undertaker organised the men. The other searchers stood and silently watched.

Before they reached the gateway they were interrupted by a shout and the girl's father ran full tilt from the lane into the field. The undertaker, doctor, dentist and barber stepped into his path and clasped him in his arms.

'She's alive. We need to get her back to town. Quickly now, jump up into the back of the cart.' The girl's father was used to taking orders and did as he was told. Joseph reached up and placed the girl on her father's lap. He grasped her to his chest and, when he looked at her face, tears rolled down his cheeks.

They made good speed to town but the roughness of the track and the jolting of the wagon restarted the bleeding in her poor cracked head. By chance, they halted the cart in the exact place in the square where the man had stopped the day before to take a drink and to ask directions. He had not stayed long before moving on.

*

And as the man moved on along the road, within the hour the girl moved on also, but from this world to the next.

CHAPTER 11

H.M.S. Relentless

Mid-Atlantic
10 September 1799

The Master-at-Arms left his post beside the binnacle and fell in alongside the Captain as he emerged from his day cabin onto the quarterdeck. It was his duty, or that of the First Lieutenant, also known as 'Jimmy the One' or simply 'The Jimmy', to accompany their commanding officer whenever he inspected the ship. Today it was down to him. Jimmy the One had the forenoon deck watch and was busy with the business of sailing the ship as it followed a course to the south-west.

Captain John 'Chalky' White (a nickname given to him by the lower deck ratings, a nickname never used in his presence, however) made it a priority of inspecting the ship from stem to stern each and every day. It was said among the crew, not without good reason, that the Captain had the capacity to see more with one glance than ordinary people would see if they looked all day.

The Captain's eyes at this very moment were looking upward, noting the men working aloft and the lookouts. The state of the rigging and the trim of the sails. He unconsciously felt the strength and direction of the wind, the temperature of the air and the formation of the high clouds. He could taste the familiarity of salt in the air. He used all the signs to gauge the coming weather. To him, and he was very rarely wrong, all seemed set fair.

At eight o'clock that forenoon, as he did each and every day, the Captain held a meeting in his cabin with all his officers. All officers, no matter what their rank, were obliged to attend except those who were on duty. At the briefing this morning the navigator had given his usual report on the progress of the ship during the previous twenty-four hours and the position of the ship after twenty-two days at sea. He reported that, in the main, the elements had been favourable and, combined with the natural agility of the ship in good seas, they had made excellent speed. He was confident that the noon sightings would confirm that the ship was at least one hundred and twenty miles ahead of where they had planned to be.

During the three weeks that they had sailed south and west they had sighted ships of all shapes and sizes but only one had been worthy of interception and further investigation. She could have been an enemy ship but disappointingly she was out of Bristol, bound for Gibraltar with provisions for the garrison there.

'Good morning, Captain.' The Jimmy, who had walked across from the conning position to join them, saluted with the flat of his hand held stiffly across his lower brow. Both men were wearing their uniform hats and therefore tradition had it that salutes should be exchanged, a show of respect that was rarely used or needed on a ship at sea.

'Estimated speed four knots. Twelve more minutes before we alter course onto the north-west leg,' he reported formally, for even if the men were the best of friends in their private lives, any show of familiarity was frowned upon in front of the lower ranks. 'All else is as it should be, sir.'

'Very well, Mr Armitage. The Master and I are about to commence our inspection starting below on the gun deck. We will be no more than an hour, all being well. Then as we discussed in my cabin earlier, I intend to stop the ship immediately after 'up spirits' and give the men a chance for a swim and some relaxation. It will also give them some time to clean ship and to 'make and mend'. Have Midshipman Johnson select four men to man the longboat and make it ready to launch at thirteen hundred hours and detail your best men for lookout duty. I do not want to be caught still in the water by a Frenchman or a Spaniard.'

'Aye-aye, sir. I'll see to it immediately. Is there anything else?'

'Yes. Could you join me in my cabin as soon as you are relieved at twelve hundred hours? We will take lunch together. Today seems an ideal time for all the officers to meet and be made aware of the orders from the Admiralty. We need a plan of action.'

'Yes, sir.' The Jimmy was relieved. He had been curious for weeks. Now he would learn what was in the thick packet which had arrived on board the day they had sailed from Topsham.

'Use the bosun's mate to pass the word to all the other officers, would you? My cabin at twelve hundred hours sharp.'

'Aye-aye, sir.'

'That's all. Carry on, Mr Armitage.' They briefly saluted each other once more and the Jimmy turned away.

The Captain watched him as he strode back to his position alongside the coxswain. The Jimmy leaned over and checked the binnacle and exchanged a few words with the man at the wheel, but the Captain could not hear what was said. Checking the ship's heading, he assumed, as he would expect all his officers to. The Captain turned away from the steering position and faced forward towards the bows of the ship.

'Let's get on, Master,' he said, and with the Master-at-Arms trailing one step to the rear, he descended the ladder from the quarter deck to the main deck and then down another hatchway to the deck below.

They descended into the space on the port side between the ranks of cannon and the wardroom, the officers' quarters where they ate, drank and slept. The space they had entered, partitioned off for privacy, was known as the heads, the main privy for the crew. Nothing fancy about this area. The heads consisted of a plank which hung out over the sea with three large holes cut through it. The men sat on the plank and their waste dropped straight into the water below. There were hatches behind the plank primarily for ventilation but which also allowed light into the space. The hatches could be closed during bad weather, making the space almost watertight. Two buckets full of clean sea water were kept in the space for the men to clean themselves.

This morning the space was spotlessly clean, as it always was. The Captain was pleased. After all, wasn't cleanliness next to Godliness? Wasn't a clean ship a happy ship? John White had served on a ship which had been gripped by an outbreak of dysentery. He knew first-hand how the disease could decimate a crew and leave a ship totally defenceless. He had no intention of such a thing happening aboard *Relentless*.

On the starboard side of the ship there was a space identical in size to the heads but this time housing the capstans which were used to raise and lower the stern anchors.

They moved on, working their way through the gun deck, and descended to the next deck before heading into the most forward part of the ship. As they descended the ladder they heard the faint sounds of shouting from above followed by the sound of running footsteps and they felt the ship heel over as the ship came around to begin the northerly leg of their zigzag course.

Here it was dark and smelled of tar and damp Hessian rope. Even after all these years of service aboard ship the smells and movement still made the Captain feel sick. They were below the water line and the sound of rushing water was all around them. In the darkness they could hear the sound of small, clawed feet. They climbed over the cross braces and quickly checked for leaks, in a hurry to be out of this place. They found none, the ship was tight. Relieved, they climbed the ladder to the deck above.

*

They ascended to the main deck and emerged into the sunlight. The sunlight was bright after the gloom of the lower decks and both men had to shade their eyes. They had emerged within yards of Leading Seaman 'Frenchie' Porter and the young lad with the amazing blue eyes. Frenchie was teaching the lad to take soundings with the length of knotted rope. He was giving his instructions in French.

'Mr Porter, sir,' the Master-at-Arms immediately challenged Frenchie. 'Why are you using that dago language on board this ship? Lest you have forgotten, this is a British Navy ship, and we happen to be at war with that country, sir. Can you not speak in the good King's English? Are you trying to teach the lad bad ways? I'll have no sedition aboard my ship, sir.' He had spoken in his 'official' voice, clipped and terse, standing rigidly to attention as he did so. But he suddenly realised that he had gone too far, he was after all in the presence of his commanding officer.

'Begging your pardon, sir.' He had turned to the Captain. 'I do of course, mean your ship.' But he needed to reassert his authority. He turned back to Frenchie and the boy.

'Stand to attention in the presence of your Captain. Show your respect.' Frenchie hardly moved but John stood ramrod straight, overawed.

The Captain had stood aside and watched the exchange with almost a smile on his face. He knew both men well. They had served with him since his first day aboard and he knew they were excellent men to have as part of his crew, even though he knew that Frenchie was indeed half French. He also knew that Frenchie, for a reason that he did not know, had no love for that country. But there could be no familiarity. There could be no humour between the upper and lower deck.

'Answer the Master, Mister Porter. Are you preaching sedition aboard my ship, sir? Are you leading this young man astray?'

'Indeed not, sir.' Frenchie touched his forelock as though in subservience, but did not fool anyone. 'I was merely teaching the boy a new language, something useful, something he may use when the war is over.' And he added, 'Something which could be more useful to him than trying to make sense of the language of the men from up north or the language of the men from Liverpool.' He knew that the Master-at-Arms had been born and bred in the port of Liverpool.

The Captain caught the slight but unmistakable narrowing of the eyes of the man next to him and decided not to pursue the subject further. Instead he changed the subject.

'Pass the word among the gun crews that I have allowed a 'make and mend' during the afternoon and first dog watches, starting after 'up spirits'. Scrambling nets are to be lowered and I want everyone who can swim to take to the water at least once, except those ratings who are on special duties. Those who can't swim can be scrubbed down on the upper deck. The rest of the time is theirs to do as they wish but I leave it to you and the other leading hands to ensure that they should use it wisely. I do not expect to see rips and tears in any of the men's clothes after today.'

'Aye-aye, sir. Swimming it is until we are all lily white and smelling of roses.'

The Captain saw the Jimmy watching him from his position by the quarterdeck ladder and suddenly remembered their meeting. It would be bad form to be late.

He turned to walk away but seemed to suddenly have a thought and he turned back.

'Proceder à la leçon, si vous la voulez, Mister Porter.' He turned away again. He hoped he had spoken the words correctly. It had been years since he had spoken the language to anyone. His French was definitely rusty.

As they walked away the Master-at-Arms thought about what the Captain had said to Frenchie. In all his years in the Royal Navy he had learnt how to order beer in eleven different languages, but he had never learnt to speak a word of French.

CHAPTER 12

Captain John White

H.M.S. Relentless

John White, unlike his subordinate Lieutenant Armitage, had never had the chance to serve as a First Lieutenant during his rise to the exalted rank of Captain R.N. He did know. however, just how incredibly lucky he had been to progress in the service as far as he had. Born in Witney in Oxfordshire, he was the second son of a shop owner. Craving adventure and excitement, he had pestered his father until he had given in and allowed his son to join the Royal Navy as a lowly Midshipman in 1769, at the age of sixteen years and two days. By the year 1774 he had been promoted to the rank of Lieutenant, but by then he had come to realise that this was the highest rank that he could ever aspire to.

The peacetime Navy was run down and under resourced and the opportunities for promotion were few and far between. He had neither the social connections nor the wealth needed to buy his way into the higher echelons. However being an officer, albeit a low level one, in the Royal Navy was not a bad situation to find oneself in, and any rank brought with it advantages all of its own. Not least of these advantages were the opportunities to visit foreign lands and, of course, the attraction of military men to the opposite sex. And, on the whole, he enjoyed life aboard ship, as hard and as basic as it could be.

He had served time on several frigates, usually as the Gunnery Officer, and on one Ship of the Line, as the Victualar. He had served in the Mediterranean Fleet based at Gibraltar, and had sailed as far as the Bosporus and into the Black Sea. He had served in the Home Fleet based at Plymouth and had patrolled the coast of Europe from Portugal to the Baltic. He had spent some years on the Barbary Coast and had travelled as far south as the Horn of Africa and visited everywhere in between, all in the name of protecting 'British interests'. But there was never any hint of promotion.

His luck changed for the better when he was posted to the Navy squadron based at Gibraltar and commanded by a charismatic young officer by the name of Horatio Nelson. Ostensibly there to prevent the French fleet, based at Toulon, from breaking out of the Mediterranean and sailing north to support the invasion troops gathered in Northern France, Nelson also used his ships to blockade the Spanish fleet at Cadiz. Although Britain was not yet officially at war with Spain, he considered Spanish ships legitimate targets as the French and Spanish governments had aligned themselves together and had signed a pact of 'mutual support'. Commodore Nelson also had his ships patrolling the sea-lanes from the West Indies as they neared mainland Europe, operating under the guise of the protection of British trade routes. He actively encouraged the officers under his command to pursue and sink or capture any Spanish bullion ships sailing home from the Spanish colonies in Central America. A lucrative business and one which in other more peaceful times, would have been labelled piracy.

During one such pursuit, a Spanish ship had been chased into Santa Cruz, a port on the Island of Tenerife, in the Canary Islands. The Spanish officers and their crew believed themselves to be safe from attack, anchored at the centre of this friendly stronghold which they considered to be impregnable from the sea, but had made a fatal error of judgement. This was no ordinary man they were dealing with. Commodore Nelson developed a plan to capture the Spanish ship with a full frontal assault from the sea, combined with a daring overland sortie from the other side of the island. The ship was to be taken and a prize crew would sail her to Plymouth for stripping and subsequent sale to the highest bidder.

The plan to take the ship had been both audacious and full of risk, but with the element of surprise he believed it had every chance of success. It was unheard of previously for an officer of his seniority to take such risks, but Commodore Nelson had insisted on leading the landing party himself. His officers, fearful for his well-being, had put forward many arguments against this but he would not be swayed. Lieutenant White, acting as the Gunnery Officer on the flagship, was chosen to accompany his commanding officer as second in command of the raiding party, and to command the prize crew for the transfer of the ship back to England after they had taken her.

Early on in the fighting Nelson had taken a fearful musket ball wound in his upper arm and shoulder and the assault had faltered and been driven back. After Nelson's injury, White had taken command of the raiding party and, showing great panache and courage, had led his men in fighting the rear-guard action that allowed the British to withdraw with the minimum of casualties.

Captain Nelson had been transferred swiftly back to the flagship but, even with the best of care from the ship's surgeon, within days his wound had turned gangrenous. In order to save the man's life the surgeon had to take the knife to his badly infected arm and remove it completely.

It was almost another year before White left Gibraltar and went home, on half pay, to his wife and five children. They were growing up rapidly and, after nearly three years at sea, were almost strangers to him. At first he even had a problem remembering their names in the right order but gradually he got the hang of it again.

He had been at home at the modest town house in Cheltenham for nine weeks, and was growing weary of the social round, when his sailing orders arrived from the Admiralty in London, by courier:

You are requested to report to the Royal Dockyard at Harwich Kent on, or by, 18 September 1795.

There you will take command of His Majesty's Ship number 39.

We are assured that the ship will be ready for sea trials on that date. You will inform us when you consider she has been worked up to full operational status. We do not expect however, that this will be later than 20 October.

You will receive detailed operational orders before that date.

Usually the signature above the Admiralty seal was that of an anonymous clerk but this time the name was unmistakably that of Commodore Sir Horatio Nelson, R.N. There was also a postscript:

I have every faith that you will discharge your duty to your country in the manner that I have come to expect from you.

You have sir, the attributes and the panache to be the type of sailor I need in my navy and I trust you will not let me down.

I will leave the naming of the ship to you: choose her name well.

Congratulations on your promotion, <u>Captain</u> White.

Horatio

He had arrived at Harwich on 15 September, well ahead of schedule and full of both excitement and trepidation in equal measure. He had been escorted down to the dockside by the Port Authority Superintendent and they had both stood and looked at the new ship. Ship No. 39 was like no other warship he had ever seen.

He crossed the strip of water between the ship and the quay via the after gangway and asked the Officer of the Day for permission to come aboard. The officer, who had not been expecting his Captain for several more days yet, had asked him his business and had rapidly thrown him a smart salute, even though he was in civilian clothes, when informed that this man was in fact, his new commanding officer.

The promotion to Captain, doubtless at Commodore Nelson's insistence, had come to him like a bolt from the blue, and even after a few weeks, he still found difficulty in accepting his new status. He was shown to his cabin and his sea chest was carried aboard. He made arrangements for the Naval Architect to call upon him the following day, and then made a cursory inspection of the ship accompanied by the young officer who had greeted him on the quarter deck.

The meeting with the Architect, who had arrived aboard early the next morning laden down with drawings and a box of correspondence between himself and the Admiralty, went well. They had walked the ship and every few minutes the man would produce the relevant drawing and would explain the special design features, and there were many, which gave the ship her unique look. Everywhere they went they were greeted by the sounds of hammering and sawing and the shouts of the shipwrights as the builders strived to finish the job on time.

That evening, alone in his sparse cabin, he studied the drawings again and read his way through the pile of letters and notes which had passed between the ship builders and the Admiralty over a period of months and gradually he began to understand. The original concept had come from none other than Horatio Nelson himself. She was to be the first of a new breed of ship built specifically to chase and capture or destroy the armed merchantmen which the French and the Spanish favoured on the voyages to the West Indies. She was built for speed and agility but was armed with enough firepower to effectively outgun the enemy. She would never be used against the huge 'ships of the line' which would be able to blow her out of the water before she got within range of them with her smaller guns. Her only weapon against them would be her speed.

The next few days were hectic as deadline day approached but when it did arrive they were ready. They put to sea with a reduced crew but a full complement of shipwrights and carpenters who scurried this way and that, checking bulkheads and decks, listening to the groans of the timbers as they took the strains and searching for burst seams and leaks. They need not have worried. She was well designed and even better built. She sailed like the thoroughbred she looked. Each day they piled on more sail until finally she was under full canvas. It was a fine, clear day and there was a fresh breeze blowing and all the men on board were stunned with amazement as she accelerated past ten knots, then twelve knots and then fourteen. She rode the water as steady as a rock.

Satisfied with the seaworthiness of the ship, it was then the turn of the gun crews to be put through their paces. Three days of intensive drills and live firings and the Gunnery Officer was able to report to the Captain that his crews were ready for action. The Captain, who had watched everything with a critical eye, concurred.

The final day of sea-trials arrived and the official speed trial over the 'measured mile'. With all sail set, the ship gained speed and entered the measured course. The ship seemed to know what was required and fairly skipped over the waves. One of the midshipmen, standing near the rail on the quarterdeck, was overheard to say excitedly, 'She is as fast as one of the King's greyhounds.' He had been taken to Windsor by his father and had witnessed at first hand a hare coursing event organised by the Royal Court. 'And they are relentless in the pursuit.'

John White heard the words and he now knew the new name of his ship. She would also be relentless in the pursuit.

The King's dogs always won, of course.

*

On the 12 October 1795 the Admiralty allowed Captain John White to officially sign his new ship over from the shipbuilders and to take full responsibility for her. They had received his report on the readiness of the ship and crew two days earlier.

They also approved his choice of name for the ship. As of that day she would be H.M.S. *Relentless*.

On the 13 October 1795 H.M.S. *Relentless* had sailed out of the dockyard at Harwich on her maiden voyage. She was fully stored and had a full complement of men. The pennants were hoisted to the very top of the mainmast and the orders were given. The helmsman turned her bows south toward the English Channel.

CHAPTER 13

John Harkin

10 September 1799

'What's a 'make and mend'?' he asked Frenchie as soon as the Captain was out of earshot. There were so many things he did not know.

'Some would say it's a way of rewarding the crew for their hard work, partly a way to relieve the boredom of weeks at sea and partly to allow the crew time to relax,' Frenchie explained. 'But others would say it's to allow the Captain and the officers to feel good about themselves. To show how good they are to the ratings on the lower deck.' Frenchie had cultivated the healthy cynicism of the lower deck, believing that officers did nothing if there was not some direct benefit to them.

*

Since coming aboard *Relentless* the days and weeks had passed in a whirlwind of activity for young John Harkin. There were so many new things to learn. His education began with the 'de-licing', which always took place during the first day back at sea. The old hands of course took it in their stride. This was part of the routine which happened after any length of time ashore. Most of the men had been through the indignity so many times that they came to regard it as an essential part of life aboard a Royal Navy ship, especially Captain John White's ship.

But for John, standing in line before the surgeon, as naked as the day he was born, with the other men of the gun crew, came as a rude shock. He stood, embarrassed, his hands covering his cock and balls and watched as, one by one, the men had their heads, their genitals and their underarms painted with a bright purple liquid. When it was John's turn to have the liquid applied he found that it stank to high heaven and had a sting like horse liniment on his tender flesh. It was rumoured among the crew to not only kill lice and crabs but was an effective treatment for penile warts and mild doses of the pox.

The smell had made the sea-sickness that he was suffering from even worse. Even when some of the crew were taken aside and had their heads shaved John was not interested enough even to ask why. All he wanted to do was to get back up into the fresh air or he was sure he would die.

He had been fortunate that the Master-at-Arms had assigned him as powder monkey to the forward port-side gun crew under the watchful eye of Leading Seaman 'Frenchie' Porter. Frenchie was the gun layer for the port side guns and was recognised as being one of the best gun layers in the whole Navy. The ten cannon under his control very rarely missed their targets. He was also an experienced sailor and was known for his fairness to the men in his team.

But Frenchie was thorough and being sea-sick was no excuse for slacking. He had drilled John until he could have supplied the guns in his sleep. After two weeks John dreamed of carrying the deadly black powder from the watertight, airtight and virtually fireproof powder magazines deep inside the ship up to the huge cannons on the port side.

When Frenchie was satisfied with his performance John was given other duties. His sickness had faded with time but now the fear of what was expected of him had taken its place.

He had been sent aloft to help trim the sails and had been afraid and it was all he could do to hold on for dear life. The other members of the rigging party seemed not to notice John's fear or at least it was never mentioned. Perhaps they could remember their first time aloft.

He had been sent down into the bowels of the ship and heard, for the first time, the rushing of the water all around him, just the other side of the bulkhead, and again he had been afraid.

He had heard for the first time the practice firing of the big guns and had been terrified by the noise and the dust and the smoke and the shockwaves that seemed to pass right through his body. And he had been terrified and thrilled by the sea stories told by the old hands.

But he was learning all the time. He spent time with the sail-maker and the shipwright and the helmsman and he had learnt to tie half hitches and bowlines and sheepshanks and reef knots and numerous other knots and bends.

He had taken a turn in the sea boat when the bosun had practised launch and rescue routines, and had tried manfully to row in time with the others. He had returned to the ship needing treatment on his blistered hands.

He had spent days with the armourer and learnt how to handle the muskets, usually secured in their racks alongside the racks of fearsome cutlasses, and he had learnt how to judge the quality of the steel in the officer's swords. He had learnt how to put a fine cutting edge on the swords and cutlasses using the whetstone.

He was coming to understand and use naval terms, some of which made perfect sense, and some which seemed to bear no relationship to the English language as he knew it. He heard terms like 'handsomely, now lads', dog watches, eight bells, tiddly bows, some knots were not knots at all but bends, and he learnt that a painter was in fact a rope, and without realising it, he slowly and naturally began to use these terms himself.

He now understood the hierarchy aboard ship from the Captain down through the officers and ratings, right down to where he stood himself. He understood that he was lowest of the low, being the newest crew member, an ordinary seaman and a junior at that. It seemed to him that he had to take orders from just about everyone, and to be quick about it.

There were so many new things to learn. His head buzzed. But he had never been this happy in all of his short life.

And today he had been swimming in the ocean. He had stripped off his skivvies, no longer shy or embarrassed at showing his body, and had dived into the blue water with the other naked men. He was a good swimmer, thanks to all the time he had spent down by the river at home, and had enjoyed himself until he had started to tire. At least he was thoroughly clean for a change. Now he was back onboard and was heading down to the gun deck. He felt good. He had dried off in the sun and felt warm and relaxed.

Able Seaman Davies of the starboard-side guns stood at the bottom of the forward ladder. John had the feeling that Davies was waiting for him. As soon as he stepped down onto the deck Davies spoke.

'Leading Seaman Thomas wants you down below. He needs help on the bilge pump.' John hesitated; he had not had dealings before with the starboard crews. 'Hurry up, shift yourself, he wants you down there now. Follow me, I'll show you where to go.'

John followed Davies down the ladder to the next deck then down one more. They turned towards the bows. Down here it was dark but John could just make out the bulkheads in the pathetic glow of a single lantern up ahead. He could also make out the shape of a man. He sniffed the fetid smell of the chill, damp air and knew that they were well below the water line. He wished he had taken the time to put on a shirt. He thought he heard the scuttling of several rats but could not be sure.

John ducked under one of the crossbeams that were designed to help the forward bulkheads withstand the pounding of the waves. Leading Seaman Thomas Thomas was there, sitting on what looked like a bale of canvas. John couldn't help wandering what his parents were thinking of when they gave him his name.

'You took your time,' he said to Davies. 'Come over here, young Harkin.'

John looked around but couldn't see anything that looked like a bilge pump, even if he could recognise a bilge pump. But he had expected to see other sailors. Surely he wasn't expected to pump the ship dry on his own, was he?

'Where is everyone?' he asked.

'There is only you, me, and Davies here.' Thomas stood. John looked around again, suspecting that something was not as it should be.

'Where is the pump? The bilge pump that you want me to help you with?'

'There is no pump. I have something else in mind for you and Davies does too. We have been watching you.' He glanced across at Davies. 'We think you are too soft and pretty to man a pump.' He reached forward and grasped John's bicep. 'Just as I thought,' he gripped tightly, 'arms like a girl.' His other hand grasped a handful of John's blond hair. 'And hair to match.'

He pulled John against him and John could smell his rancid breath.

'Are you with us or against us? I don't want to hurt you but Davies here likes to rough people up a bit,' he threatened. He was hoping that John would resist, even slightly.

John felt the panic rising. Something was wrong. More than wrong. Something terrible was about to happen but he didn't know what. He knew that he should get away. Get back up top. Get back where there were other sailors. Get back up into the open air out of this dismal place. He tried to pull away but Thomas still had a grip on his hair.

'Let me go, please, I need to get back up top.' His voice rising, shrill, panicky, girl-like.

Thomas pulled him tight against his chest in a bear hug, releasing the hold on his hair.

'Get him, quick.' There was no need to hurry. The leading seaman was a big man and strong after years of hard work aboard ship. He easily held the boy.

Davies used his bandana as a gag before John had time to shout out. It was doubtful if anyone would have heard him anyway but Thomas was not taking a chance on being discovered. The gag was tied tight and John felt the rope encircle his wrists, tying them together. Illogically, even in his panicky state he recognised the knot that they had used, a simple reef knot.

He was thrust, face down, over one of the crossbeams. Davies ducked underneath to hold him from the other side. Thomas untied the drawstring at the waist of John's skivvies and eased them down over his hips. Even though the lad was kicking out it was easy for him to pull them off him completely. Then the pain and the humiliation began.

They took it in turns to sodomise him. The tears ran from his eyes as, first one then the other, brutally thrust into him, grunting their vile noises in their lust, their fingers digging into his tender flesh. John closed his beautiful blue eyes and prayed for the end to arrive quickly. And then they changed places to do it again and again, until their lust was spent and they had finished with him. They cut the rope that tied his wrists and Davies took back his bandana. It didn't matter now if he shouted.

Through his agony and his tears John had only one thought: Davies' bald head was still stained slightly purple.

*

Sitting comfortably in the Captain's cabin the Jimmy thought that yes, it was exactly as he had suspected. They were to patrol as before. Why change a winning formula? Any French or Spanish ship that they encountered was to be captured or, as a last resort, sunk, as was any suspicious ship carrying no flags. No quarter was to be given or, indeed, expected. This time though, the patrol was to extend much further north than usual. Fewer treasure ships had been intercepted in the last year and Naval Intelligence had surmised that the Spaniards were taking a route which followed the coast of the State of Florida and north of the island of Bermuda before setting out on the hazardous northerly route across the Atlantic, to escape the British patrols. Time would tell and it would make a change from the patrols of last year.

On the gun deck Frenchie had mustered his men for inspection and had checked them over. Smelling of roses they weren't but they were all clean and their uniforms were in good repair. But his mind was elsewhere. John Harkin was missing from the muster. Where could the lad be? He hadn't drowned, that was for sure. Frenchie himself had seen the lad come aboard and go below. If he was skiving then he would be on a charge before the evening watch and no mistake, lad or no lad.

Frenchie dismissed the men and went below in search of the missing boy. He found him in the heads. All thoughts of putting the lad on a charge were forgotten in an instant. The lad wasn't himself. It was obvious that something horrific had taken place.

*

Frenchie Porter was nowhere near old enough to be John's father but he had taken to him as just that. The boy reminded him so much of himself when he was the same age, always happy and eager to learn.

Now they were sitting close together in the prow of the ship, as far forward as they were able to get. They spoke quietly in the French language. Not for practice but for secrecy. It was late, almost the end of the first watch, and everyone else except the deck watch were in their hammocks. It was the time of the new moon and the sliver of light low down on the horizon served to make the stars appear even brighter in the black vault of the sky.

With gentle persuasion Frenchie had managed to get the truth from John in his faltering French. He had needed to tell part of the story in English, not knowing the foreign words for some of the things that they had done to him.

The story had appalled Frenchie and he had become silent, needing to take some time to digest what he had heard. He had seen women and girls endure some terrible things during the troubles in France but that had been at a time of mob rule, a time of anger and frustration, a time of great upheaval and the breakdown of the order of things. It had been a time of mass hysteria when the rules which govern civilised societies were abandoned. A time when there may have been some excuse for the actions of the mob.

But what had happened to John was planned. What had happened was in cold blood. The assault had been against a fellow crew member and a mere boy at that. There could be no excuses for that.

They sat in the dark. The sails were full and the ship cut its way through the calm ocean with just a gentle roll. The deck watch went about their duties and took no notice of the man and the boy sat up forward in the bows. The ship was in darkness, its navigation and deck lights extinguished, the lookouts on high alert. If they came upon another ship the Captain wanted the surprise element to be with them.

Eventually Frenchie spoke.

'What do you intend to do about it, John?'

'I don't know.' The reply was spoken quietly, almost inaudible against the noises made by the water and the creaking of the timbers.

They sat silently for a few more minutes before Frenchie spoke again.

'When you left your home and your mam and dad and your sister you left the security of your family behind. But you joined another family. A family of men. A family of fighting men, of violent men, of men who earn their living waging war and killing the enemy. This family has different values to the one you left behind. Different, but no less honourable in their own way. Your mam and dad and sister loved you regardless of what you did because you were part of them.'

Another pause.

'In this family, you forego that. In this family each and every man of us has to earn the allegiance of those around us. We need to earn their respect and their loyalty, for in the moments of danger, and there will be many, we need to know that we can rely on them and they can rely on us. That each man will support the man next to them regardless. That if necessary, every member of the crew will perish together. There has to be that trust between us.'

A long, long pause. Seconds turned into minutes but eventually John spoke. His voice low but steady.

'I understand all that you have said and I do want to be a trusted member of the crew, I want to do my bit. But I feel so ashamed. I did not fight hard enough, I let it happen. They hurt me, but that hurt has gone away. Now it is my pride that needs mending. I cannot look my friends in the eye anymore. I don't know what to do.'

More silence.

'Help me, Frenchie. Please. What would you do?'

'What is good for me may not be best for you,' Frenchie answered quickly. 'Each of us must make up our own minds. Each of us must take time to consider and then take responsibility for our actions, whatever they may be.'

'But I am at a loss. I don't know what to do to put things right again, to make myself feel clean.' He turned to look at his friend and even in the darkness Frenchie could see the hurt and the anguish in those blue eyes which, up until days ago, had been vibrant and full of life. 'Should I go and report to the Master?'

'Remember what I said about trust. If you report to the Master he will pursue the men but it will be your word against theirs and if they deny the charges then nothing can happen. There were no witnesses to back up your story. Even if they admit to what they did it is not a capital offence. They will feel the lash of the cat but they will still be aboard and surely looking for a way to get even. But what is worse is that everyone on board will know that you were raped. Is that what you desire? And you will have lost the trust of the men. They will take sides. There will be those who will say that you must have asked to be raped and there will be those who will say that Thomas and Davies should be cut. But either way you will be seen as the one who runs and tells tales and you can no longer be trusted, you have become a squealer, an establishment man.'

'What else can I do?

'You could try to forget about what they did to you. You could close your mind and hope that time will fade the memories and heal the hurt that you are feeling. I know that you believe in the presence of God. You could ask Him for help. Perhaps your forgiveness of the men is the way forward for you.'

'I don't think I am a good enough Christian. I don't think that my heart is big enough.'

Once again silence descended on the man and the boy. The ship sailed on and the men of the deck watch, coming to the end of their watch, were handing over to their reliefs. The silence stretched into minutes.

The man turned to the boy.

'Of course there is another way,' he said.

CHAPTER 14

Leading Seaman Thomas Thomas

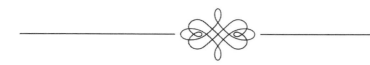

H.M.S. Relentless
1799

Leading Seaman Thomas Thomas was feeling distinctly tetchy. In fact his mood was worse than tetchy, it was foul. And when he was in a foul mood his men had learnt to keep well away from him. He hadn't had a good shit for the last three days and he always felt tetchy if he didn't shit at least once a day. He was normally as regular as clockwork. Usually within minutes of eating his breakfast porridge and drinking the mug of strong black tea, he would feel the rumblings start deep in his belly and he would know it was time to go below. But he hadn't had that feeling for days now. It wasn't the first time either. On every long voyage there came a time when the food ran low and hardtack biscuits and salt pork became the staple diet. Salt pork always had the same effect on the digestive system of Thomas Thomas. There was something about salt pork that served to bung him up.

He had been to see the surgeon to get a dose of his magic potion and had stood in line with the others. He had tried to decide which of the men were genuine and which were malingering. In his foul mood he had decided that all the men who stood in line were 'swinging the lead', except himself of course. Luckily, none of the men in the line were in his watch, otherwise he would have had their guts for garters. The surgeon had dosed him with the evil-looking brown liquid that was so bitter on the tongue that it made him retch, and now he was waiting for it to take effect.

He was staring morosely out over the starboard side, looking at nothing in particular. It didn't help his mood that the ship was making slow headway. There was just a hint of a breeze blowing across the deck but the sails flapped emptily and the ocean was so calm that the water looked more like oil. And it was hot. There was not a cloud in the sky and the sun beat down remorselessly. It had been like this for almost a week.

At this rate it will take forever to reach land, he thought. More than a month at sea and boredom was settling over the crew. Petty arguments were more often than not turning into fully fledged fights and were becoming more frequent. The Master-at-Arms was being kept busy maintaining discipline. But even he was taking a more lax attitude than he normally would. He knew that when progress was slow it did strange things to the nerves.

Then he felt it, deep in his gut. Was that a twinge? Yes, there it was again. Definitely the start of a rumble. He waited a few more minutes and there it was again, but stronger now. A few more minutes and he knew it was time to go below. He descended the after ladder and passed through the partition into the heads. All the gun ports and the hatches in the heads were wide open to allow any breeze to circulate through the ship and down here, out of the sun, it was appreciably cooler.

He dropped his skivvies and, choosing the middle hole where there was the most air, he sat on the well-scrubbed plank. He felt his stomach muscles cramp again and gave a tentative push. He felt something move deep inside and knew that relief was near.

As he gathered his internal muscles to push again he heard someone approaching and young John Harkin appeared around the partition. He was carrying one of the four-foot-long handles that were used to wind the capstan. In two swift strides John crossed the space that separated the two and, using the handle like a battering ram, smashed it with all his might into the face of Thomas Thomas.

Thomas Thomas had seen the look in the eyes of the lad as he had approached and had recognised it for what it was. He tried to move but wasn't anywhere quick enough to avoid the blow. The piece of oak, four inches square and seasoned as hard as iron, caught him on the right side of his face, smashing his cheekbone and his eye socket. A fine mist of bright blood spattered the bulkhead. He rocked backward, dazed. Another blow smashed into his face, this time destroying his nose and mashing his lips to pulp. Although only just conscious, he tried again to rise but his skivvies were around his ankles and suddenly all the strength seemed to have left his body. Once again the piece of oak smashed into his head and this time he was knocked backwards totally off balance and, despite trying to find a hand hold, he went out through the open ventilation hatch and fell head over heels into the sea below.

Although barely conscious he felt himself falling and knew in his heart that he was finished and in his fear he felt his bowels let go.

The stern lookout heard the splash as the body hit the water and rushed to look over the side.

'Man overboard, man overboard!' His shout was taken up all over the main deck and the 'man overboard' drill, which the crew had practised day after day, began. The sea boat was rapidly launched with its complement of eight oarsmen and with strong strokes the small boat moved away from the ships side. The coxswain turned the ship a few degrees to take her out of the little breeze that there was. The officer of the watch was at the stern rail trying to keep a fix on the body as it drifted slowly but inexorably away.

Everyone who saw the body knew that this had been no unfortunate accident, not with the kind of injuries that were evident on the head and face. But the crew of the sea boat managed to recover the body, for it was just a body by the time they reached it, and return it to the ship.

The Master-at-Arms launched his enquiry and listed the incident as a murder in the ship's log for that day. He interviewed all the members of the crew who he considered to be likely candidates to have carried out such an attack. But of course no-one had seen or heard anything. He had to report to the Captain later that evening that he had got nowhere and had no known motive or suspects. The two men agreed that the enquiry should be ended.

Among the gun crews everyone knew, or could guess, what had happened to Leading Seaman Thomas Thomas.

*

It had been three weeks since the death and burial at sea of Leading Seaman Thomas. His body had been stitched into a piece of sail cloth and it had disappeared below the surface of the Atlantic Ocean weighted down with some rusty chain, accompanied by a brief prayer from the surgeon, who had assumed the role of chaplain for the day. There were few regrets at his passing and Thomas Thomas had already been forgotten by most of the crew. But he had not been forgotten by Able Seaman George Davies. Thomas and Davies, both being from the same region of the Principality, had formed a natural attachment from day one. John Harkin was not the first young lad they had raped but the other two instances had not ended like this.

He still remembered vividly the damage done to the face and head of his accomplice and knew without a shadow of a doubt that it had been either John Harkin or, more likely, his friend Frenchie Porter who had exacted his terrible revenge. He wondered when it would be his turn to die, and where and how it would happen. The lad had a look about him these days that scared the living daylights out of him. He could feel the boy watching his every move. He lived in constant fear and tried to keep away from the pair but in such a confined space as a ship at sea there was nowhere to hide. He had determined that as soon as the ship reached Trinidad he would request a transfer to another ship, or failing that, to desert the Navy and disappear. But they had to make Trinidad first and in the meantime he kept his head down, kept out of the way, and watched his back at every turn.

The pilot's reckoning put them at one hundred and thirty miles out of Trinidad when the ship ran into the leading edge of the storm. The black clouds appeared on the horizon to the south and bore down upon them faster than they could run, typical of the kind of storms encountered in the tropics. They barely had time to reef the sails, and batten down all the hatches before the storm hit. Everyone except the upper deck watch was confined below deck and those on the upper deck wore safety harness and were tied to safety lines rigged across the deck.

Off-watch men were detailed to man the bilge pumps deep inside the ship and there was feverish activity as everything that was movable was lashed down. Then they waited for the worst.

The helmsman, helped by a spare hand, fought to keep the prow facing into the wind as the battering began and waves began to break over the main deck.

*

The ship had been riding out the storm for what seemed to the crew to be hours but all seemed well. The pumps were keeping the levels constant in the bilges and nowhere had the bulkheads sprung any major leaks. The ship was well designed to withstand this kind of treatment from the elements. It would need more than such a storm to get the better of her.

The Captain ordered the watches to be changed, not wanting anyone to spend too much time out in the wind and the rain. It had grown dark and the storm clouds obscured the stars. It was pitch black on deck.

The wind howled through the rigging and the sea raged across the exposed upper deck looking to carry the ship down. But she withstood everything the storm could throw at her.

The pounding went on for hours but slowly, to the men on the deck, the storm seemed to be abating. The clouds did not seem as black now and stars could be glimpsed in a few clear patches that were appearing. The tired helmsman with the aching arms let his concentration slip for only a second. He allowed the ship to veer just a few degrees to starboard and the next wave broke over the port bow and swept across the deck. Thousands of gallons of salt water scoured the deck and carried away everything in its path that wasn't secured, including Able Seaman George Davies. He was swept over the rail but felt his safety rope halt his headlong plunge and he was left dangling above the waves, but quite safe.

He knew that his watchmates would soon haul him back aboard. He might even get an extra ration of rum out of his escapade. A head appeared above him and he opened his mouth to shout out, although he doubted if he would be heard above the sound of the wind. His mouth stayed open but no sound came as he made out the shape of the knife and he recognised the face of the boy holding it. He knew then that the time had come. He dangled there for what seemed like an age but which could not have been more than a second or two, whilst the boy looked down at him. The boy's mouth moved as he said something but the words were lost in the violence of the storm.

George Davies was not a religious man and hadn't attended any denomination of church in years, but suddenly he found God and he began to pray.

The knife described a small arc and easily parted the thin safety line. George Davies dropped into the sea. His last coherent thought was how warm the sea was before the undertow dragged him under the keel and the barnacles and other shelled creatures attached to the hull tore, first his clothes and then his flesh, to shreds.

John Harkin returned to his allotted station on the gun deck carrying the sick bucket that he had been sent to empty and which he had left in the after heads. The gun ports had been tightly sealed shut and the air was full of the stench of vomit. The shadows swung from side to side in the light from the few lanterns as the ship corkscrewed wildly accompanied by the thunderous crashing of the waves breaking over and around the ship.

If anyone noticed that John was soaked to the skin they made no comment. No-one even noticed the tears in those huge blue eyes.

CHAPTER 15

The Master-at-Arms

Trinidad
1799

The Captain was deep in conversation with the Port Superintendent and so the Master-at-Arms waited patiently for his chance to speak to his commanding officer. Although he stood several yards away he could hear every word which passed between the two men. He found their conversation totally uninteresting. He had more important matters on his mind. He was about to give the Captain his report into the death of Leading Seaman Thomas and the disappearance of Able Seaman Davies. He was full of trepidation for he had nothing of consequence to report.

The Port Superintendent was full of curiosity as to the purpose of the strange devices, shaped like dinner plates but measuring over four feet in diameter, adorning the hawsers securing *Relentless* to the quay. He was interested to hear that they were the idea of the shipwright aboard the ship and were designed to prevent rats from entering the ship by crossing the watery divide along the thick ropes. As Captain White said, 'British rats were one thing. Tropical rats, carrying all manner of diseases were quite another.'

The two men had ostensibly been surveying the ship from the quayside, assessing the damage brought about by the fury of the storm, but the Captain's mind was not really on the job. He had more pressing and important questions to answer. The loss of a crewman under such dubious circumstances as had occurred aboard his ship, was bad. To lose two crewmen was infinitely worse, and could, in some circles, be interpreted as a lack of leadership and discipline. He knew that the Master was waiting to make his report and, as quickly as possible, bid his goodbyes to the Crown's representative in Trinidad.

The Master-at-Arms stepped forward immediately and saluted his commanding officer. Captain White briefly returned the salute and indicated for the Master to follow him to a secluded area of the quay.

'Well? Have you finished your investigation? Have you anything to tell me that will shed light on the whole sorry episode?'

'I only wish that I had something positive to report, sir.' He looked like a man whose reputation was about to be blown away.

'Tell me the worst then. Hold nothing back even if it puts us in a bad light. The log has to be completed tonight and I need to persuade the Admiralty that we have done everything in our power to solve the mystery.'

'I have carried out the most extensive investigation, as is my way, sir.' He had drawn himself up to his full height and was standing rigidly to attention as he began his formal report. 'I have spoken to every single man aboard, some I have spoken to more than once. I have tried to be nice to some. I have cajoled others and I have threatened the ones that I thought capable of inflicting the grave injuries that Thomas sustained, and all the while I have looked for the usual signs of guilt. I have looked for the blushing and the stammering and the refusal to look me in the eye. I have tried to catch them out in a lie. I have asked the same question twice or even three times, seeking contradiction. I have to report, sir, that I have made no headway. I am completely at a loss as to who the guilty person might be.' He looked down at the ground. 'I am completely baffled and defeated by the whole thing.'

The Captain had expected as much. In his experience, crewmen always closed ranks in such situations.

'So what do you think happened, Master?' Not unkindly. It was obvious that the man had tried his best, and was not enjoying the feeling of failure. 'Could you help me here? Could you use your experience of such things to hazard a guess?'

'In my considered judgement, sir, it was someone with a grudge who did this terrible thing. We know that Thomas could be a bully and Davies could be led into all manner of things. I have seen crewmen killed aboard other ships but there always seemed to be an obvious reason, jealousy over a woman or more usually cheating at cards, but what they could have done to warrant such revenge I cannot hazard a guess. I have heard none of the usual rumours of card games or, for that matter, fights over women. It is outside my comprehension, sir.'

'I had assumed as much myself.' The Captain changed tack suddenly. 'Have you noticed the change in young Harkin these last weeks?' he asked.

'I have indeed, sir, he seems to have lost his innocence and naivety very quickly. Do you think that the young man is somehow mixed up in the murder and disappearance of Davies? Do you think, sir, that a mere boy could have done such things?'

'I do not know, Master, but the boy doesn't smile as he did before. He belies his age. In the two months we have been away from England he has grown tall and strong and is almost a man. But would he be capable of murder? That is a question we can ask but we cannot know the answer to without witnesses. You questioned him closely, I presume?'

'As I did all the others, sir. Perhaps I should speak to him again?'

The Captain considered what to do. He was in a hurry to get out on patrol. It didn't take many days in port for the restlessness to return. The matters they were discussing, as important as they were, were a distraction from the real purpose of their being here in the first place. He made his decision.

'I will write up your findings tonight and send a report to the Admiralty on the first available package returning to Britain. I thank you for your diligence in this matter. Let us close the matter now and get on.' He was eager to drawn a very firm line under the events of the last few weeks.

They saluted each other stiffly. The matter was closed.

CHAPTER 16

James Macdonald

Hereford
December 1799

The last three months had passed in a whirl of activity with hardly time to draw breath, and now Christmas would be with them in just a few days' time. James could hardly believe his good fortune. Leaving Ireland and his well-established reputation as a craftsman had been a huge gamble, especially with a wife and new baby to care and provide for, but taking that gamble seemed to have been worthwhile.

They had landed on English soil without mishap and had travelled south to the city of Hereford and had sought out his brother Tam. Accommodation was at a premium in the city but Tam was able to put them up temporarily in his meagre lodgings. The next day, whilst Tam and Rachel scoured the city looking for a house or a cottage or rooms, James went looking for work.

James had been more successful in his quest than his wife and brother, landing a prestigious position as a carpenter at the cathedral. The church was not renowned for its generosity to its workforce but, even so, James would be earning more than three times the amount that he was used to. That evening they celebrated his good fortune with Tam and some of his friends and they met the girl that Tam, although he hadn't asked for her hand as yet, planned to marry.

The weeks had rolled by. James and Rachel and baby Mary, now showing the same red hair as her father, moved from Tam's lodgings into a house they could afford in Widemarsh Street. The work at the cathedral wasn't hard work, but what the estates manager required was work of the highest quality, which suited James and allowed him to show off his considerable skills.

James was well and happy. Rachel was well and happy and not missing Ireland too badly and the baby was growing strong and healthy. They were cosy in their new home. And now Christmas was upon them.

He left his workshop and made his way home. It was dark and there was a light dusting of snow on the ground. The snow had been falling gently for most of the day and by the time he arrived at his house his red hair sported a cap of white. The windows were aglow with light and when he reached the front door he shook his head and stamped the snow from his boots. He was smiling broadly as he crossed the threshold and went inside.

CHAPTER 17

Louisa Deschamps

Dover
1802

The new house was much better suited to her needs than the squalid little cottage she had left behind. Better by far. A house on a wide street, lined with trees, wide enough for carriages to pass easily, with large houses set far enough apart to afford a degree of privacy. A house that was large enough for her to entertain her clients properly. A house where they would feel comfortable in the kind of surroundings they were used to. And she deserved such a house. Hadn't she worked hard these last few years to establish herself? And wasn't she the most beautiful prostitute in Dover, if not the whole of England? She disliked the word 'prostitute' intensely, preferring to think of herself as a high-class mistress who dispensed pleasure to gentlemen, but she knew in her heart of hearts that a prostitute was what she was, there was no other way to describe what she did.

The new house on Southdown Road belonged to the Money Lender, doubtless one of his repossessions from some poor soul, and he had rented it to Louisa for the payment of a peppercorn rent of only one penny per year. Of course that was not the full extent of his involvement. He visited the house occasionally himself to be entertained by Louisa. He also took one third of every penny she earned.

But the house was everything Louisa wanted. There were three spacious reception rooms on the ground floor and a huge kitchen. There were three bedrooms on the first floor, and, the first one that Louisa had ever seen, a bathroom with a bath, a washstand and a privy. In the roof space were two servants' rooms, one occupied by her new housekeeper Cissy.

Louisa had interviewed and selected Cissy for the post herself, recognising the advantage of employing an ex-prostitute who knew the ropes but was past the age when she could still entertain men friends. And, most importantly, she knew how to be discreet. Cissy had proved to be a wise choice and was a welcome addition to the business. Strangely enough, she was also an excellent cook and organised the house as efficiently as any housekeeper Louisa had known during her time in service.

*

Louisa was standing in the large bay window of the master bedroom overlooking the street below. Although it was only just before two in the afternoon she was awaiting the arrival of a new gentleman caller. She no longer called her visitors customers or clients, only businessmen or gentlemen visited her these days.

Louisa had no idea who the new gentleman was, not even his name. The 'appointment' had been made by the Money Lender. Most of her gentlemen callers were introduced by, or recommended by, her business partner. She guessed though, that he would be rich and most probably a well-known businessman. All her gentlemen callers now fitted one or both of these descriptions. The ones that had not been introduced by the Money Lender had been introduced by other satisfied gentlemen.

She had left behind the sordid backstreet business she once had. The giving of favours for a few shillings. She was now known as 'the gentle lady who knew, and could cater for, the needs of gentlemen'. And she charged accordingly.

Louisa turned and surveyed the room. The size and scale of the room still took her breath away. She had never expected to live in such a house with such rooms. Some of the furniture had already been in place when she moved in but she had gradually added her own pieces and most of the decoration. She had bought the ostentatious four-poster bed herself and the dressing table, the top of which was almost covered in the perfumes and potions and lotions of her trade and with the highly polished mirrors.

Her eyes rested on the partition that the Money Lender had had built across the end of the room specifically for the use of one gentleman caller who wanted nothing more than to secretly watch Louisa undress, wash herself at the washstand, and get dressed again in outdoor clothes. Louisa found the whole thing strange but he was most generous in his payment. The secret room could only be entered from the adjoining room and was just large enough for two chairs and a small table.

It would be ideal if all her gentlemen were so easy to please. The so-called gentleman who had visited her last evening had been upsetting. The man was the captain of a ship which plied its trade between Dover and various ports, thousands of miles away, in Indonesia and China. He called himself a Master Mariner but to Louisa he was just a sadistic old sod who enjoyed inflicting pain on women.

He had called on her several times over the previous two years and each time his preferred form of performing the sex act had grown stranger. In the beginning all was normal, or what passed for normal in her business. Yesterday, however, had involved the insertion of various objects into her body, and when he had tired of that, culminated in the insertion of his cock into her anus. He had hurt her badly. He had not been gentle, as one or two of her other gentlemen who had a predilection for anal sex were, and who always used ample amounts of the sweet smelling lubrication that was always to hand, but he had been savage, like a man possessed. But worse than the pain, she had felt that she had lost control of the situation and had been demeaned as a woman and had felt that he had meant to degrade her. She felt ashamed. When he had left the premises she had actually cried, something she hadn't done for many years. But then her natural resilience and defiance had taken over from her self-pity and she pulled herself together again. She swore that he would not be allowed to cross the threshold of the house again. She would speak to Cissy about the man.

The sound of a carriage came up from the street and Louisa turned back to the window. As she did so, she caught sight of herself in one of the many mirrors. She studied her reflection for a few seconds. *Yes,* she thought, turning this way and that, *I am beautiful.* And she was right. The crimson silk house coat, buttoned from throat to mid-thigh and allowed to fall gracefully to her ankles, did nothing to hide her full figure and contrasted perfectly with her delicate pale skin and her luscious black hair. But she had no time to admire herself further, business came first.

The plain black carriage of the type common all over Dover town, had stopped in the street directly opposite the steps which led up to the front door of the house. A man alighted but all she could see was the top of his hat and his shoulders. He turned to the driver and a few words were exchanged before he turned toward the house again.

She heard the doorbell ring below and the sound of the street-door opening followed by the sound of voices. Approaching footsteps on the stairs and a quiet knock on the bedroom door. The door opened and Cissy ushered Louisa's new gentleman caller inside. She was already taking a step forward to welcome her guest, her hand held out towards the man. She stopped in amazement, recognising the man immediately.

'Mr Leadbitter, sir, what a pleasant surprise. How very, very nice to meet with you again.'

Several hours later Nathaniel Leadbitter sat alone in the large public room at his club, nursing a large glass of brandy. He had felt in the mood for some light-hearted banter, but none of his friends were present this early. He may have been alone, but he had a huge sloppy grin on his face. When he had left the house on Southdown Road he had felt different somehow. He felt rejuvenated, younger, and strangely proud of himself.

She had enquired as to his preferences and he remembered nervously mumbling something stupid and inane in reply. He blushed at the memory. He had felt like a young boy meeting with a girl for the first time, but then Louisa had gently taken charge and had led him along the path to ecstasy. She had encouraged him to unbutton her housecoat and had loosened his clothing to match. She had inserted her hand into his open trousers and had taken him out.

'You have quite the most handsome cock, sir,' she had said. She knew the words that her men liked to hear, and then she had dropped to her knees and had taken him deeply into her mouth, her tongue writhing against him. He felt his cock grow stiffer, more rigid than he had ever known, and he had groaned deep inside himself.

Later she had continued to use her mouth to excite him and had readied him again. They were undressed now and were lying on the huge bed. She had grasped his erection and called it 'a gun, a veritable cannon', and then she had spread her legs and had sat astride him and he had seen that she had razored her pubic hair and that had excited him even more. She lowered her hips down upon him and had guided him into her most intimate place and began to move slowly and gently against him, all the while whispering encouragement to him, using words that he never expected to hear from a lady. Time and again she took him to the edge but each time stopping her movements at the crucial time and relaxing against him, until she knew he could stand no more teasing. She began to move in earnest.

'You are so hard, I feel you deep inside my cunny.' She had moaned out loud and had feigned ecstasy, and he had caught her rhythm and had pushed up against her. 'Yes, yes,' she had moaned. 'Fuck me harder. Please, harder still. I feel I will burst with the pleasure of it.' She seemed to be begging him now, and he reached up and grasped her breasts and pushed harder and she thrust herself down upon him and he had come, and the ejaculation had indeed felt to him like a cannon firing. He had felt nothing like it in his whole life before.

When it was time to leave the house, Louisa had refused all payment.

'I remember you did me a great kindness once and you were concerned for me and you treated me with fairness, more than I had any right to expect. I am now glad that I can repay you somewhat,' and she had smiled broadly at him and he had found himself smiling back.

'Let us consider the debt repaid and we are now equals,' he had said. He had felt so elated he couldn't just go home and sit alone. He told the cab driver to take him to his club.

Louisa had watched him leave from the bedroom window, just as she had watched him arrive. She felt that something of importance had happened that day, something that may well change her life. There was something genuinely likeable about Nathaniel Leadbitter and already she wished him to be a friend, not just a customer. But what would be, would be.

She helped Cissy re-make the bed and straighten the room and whilst Cissy took the used water from the washstand she brushed her hair and touched up her rouge. She needed to get a move on to compose herself. Her next client was due to arrive at five o'clock, in just a few minutes' time. But all the while she was thinking of her previous caller.

CHAPTER 18

Nathaniel Leadbitter

Dover
1802

Nathaniel Leadbitter still sat alone except for the brandy bottle which was now half empty. The brandy had mellowed his mood and he found himself thinking about his life, his childhood and the times in school, and the friends he had made both then and in later life.

He came to the conclusion that Nathaniel Leadbitter, businessman, intelligent, very rich, owner of property, owner of companies and with shares in many others, had only made one bad decision in his life: his decision to marry the woman who became his wife. But at the time he was still quite young and rash and on the face of it the marriage was made in Heaven. He was a well off young bachelor and she appeared to be the doting young bride.

In the early days of the marriage they had been attentive and caring of each other but as the years went by the running of a business empire took over Nathaniel's life and he, unintentionally and without malice, neglected his wife. She, for her part, had 'done her duty' as a wife and had produced his children. Now she was finished with 'all that' and had settled down to satisfy her ambition to become part of the upper classes. Didn't their great wealth give them privileges? After all, she was aware that they had more money than most of the titled people she knew.

She liked nothing better than organising parties and 'gatherings', and 'evenings' and 'suppers'. She organised balls and charity affairs, all for good causes, and she made sure that each occasion was on the most lavish of scales that money could buy, after all, money was no object in the pursuit of status. She oversaw the guest lists to ensure that invitations were issued to everyone who was anyone in the county. She became well known in the South of England as a hostess. Her 'gatherings' were famous affairs.

Nathaniel always felt uncomfortable on such occasions but even so, and under the strictest of orders, he made a charming and most gracious host, and he did not begrudge her the opportunity to mix with the 'good and the great'.

He much preferred the more informal evenings at the various gentlemen's clubs he frequented in the city or the even more informal drinking sessions at one or other of his business colleagues' houses, where they would sit about after their meal supping port and swapping stories, some true, some not so. These drinking sessions always followed the same pattern. The guests would eat and drink and then the stories would begin. Some men told stories of adventures abroad but most told tales about making money.

His musings brought back memories of one night in particular. Nothing seemed unusual about the drinking session he attended in the spring of 1795.

The men were meeting at the house of his long-time friend Benjamin, Lord Carforth, in Knightsbridge. The group of men were a mixed bunch. There were several that Nathaniel knew well and some who were mere acquaintances. One guest he did not know at all. He was not a tall man but the way that he stood and his general demeanour gave the impression that he was much bigger than he actually was. He looked like a man who was used to being listened to. But he looked also like a man who had been very ill recently. The left sleeve of his immaculate frock coat was empty and pinned up.

Ben introduced Nathaniel to the man.

'Nathaniel, I would like you to meet my new friend and colleague Horatio. Commodore Horatio Nelson of the Royal Navy. Horatio, at this very moment, is working on a special project for the Admiralty.'

He turned to the man. 'Horatio, this is my school chum and long-time friend, Nathaniel. Nathaniel Leadbitter of Yorkshire, but now residing at Hollingbourne in Kent.'

They had dined well, as always, and now they were sitting in the salon with full bellies and full glasses. They were relaxed and comfortable and the lively conversation ranged from subject to subject. Eventually the talk turned, as always, to money. How to make money and, more importantly, how to keep it. The light-hearted talk with the serious undertones went on for a little while before Tom got to his feet and addressed the whole group.

'The real reason I have asked you all here tonight is that I, speaking on behalf of the government, need your help.' There was deathly silence in the room. The men knew that there was only one way in which they could help the government and that was through their wallets. No-one seemed very enthusiastic about that idea.

'As you all know, the war with France is going as well as can reasonably be expected, but, and you know this also, we are in a state of stalemate. We cannot win the war with the resources we have at our command. We need to raise more money for equipment and munitions and, vitally, to arm our allies on the continent. Austria has threatened to leave the alliance which would mean we would probably lose Holland and Russia also. We must, I repeat must, preserve the alliances. We cannot win on our own.'

To the casual observer travelling through London it would be difficult to see what effect the war was having on the population, if any. The shops were full of goods and there was a vibrancy about the markets and bazaars. The new factories and mills had demanded more labour and were running at full production. Menial jobs were plentiful and wages had risen by a substantial amount accordingly. The common people seemed to have money to spend.

However that may seem, the government knew that unrest was bubbling just under the surface. To fund the war the treasury had increased taxation to a level that was virtually unsustainable and the memories of what had happened not many years before in France, were never far from the minds of the ruling classes. The overthrow of the French Royal Family and the disbanding of government, the show trials and the indiscriminate executions, the eviction of the rich from their estates, the pillaging and the looting and the chaos, to be replaced eventually by a dictator, could never be allowed to happen in Britain. And they knew that one more tax rise could be the last straw, could be the catalyst to the very thing that they feared most. But they still needed to raise money. The question was, how?

They needed men of intelligence, expertise and knowledge to guide them through this sticky patch. They needed men with initiative and innovation and finesse. They needed men like Benjamin. Men who had been making money all their lives. Men who could raise money from the rich men and the businessmen. Men who knew how industry and banks worked and spoke the same language.

Official appointments were made. A representative of the government was appointed in each of the regions, charged with the task of fundraising, and the representatives were given the honorary title of 'Special Advisers to The Treasury'. Ben was selected for the Greater London region.

Late in the evening, most of the guests had departed, leaving Nathaniel, Benjamin and the man Nelson chatting quietly together. It had been a good evening's work for Ben. He had elicited generous gifts and investments from all. His report to the treasury next day would be a pleasure for him to give.

Nathaniel himself had invested the sum of one hundred thousand pounds in the new Government War Bond knowing that when the war ended there was a chance that he would get his money back. But he was more interested in Nelson and his special project. The longer the man talked, the more Nathaniel felt himself being drawn into the plan. He was carried away by the enthusiasm of the man and the drive. But he also recognised a good investment when he saw one. The capture and resale of enemy treasure ships in the West Indies looked a sure-fire winner. By the end of the night he had invested an extra fifty thousand pounds. It was to be used to build a special ship, designed for just that purpose. Nathaniel would receive a twenty percent share of any profit made. Later, when they parted, a fledgling friendship had also been forged.

Nathaniel had been a fascinated observer as the shipwrights began the job of laying down the keel of the ship with the number 39. He, his new friend Horatio and Ben had taken time to visit the Royal Dockyard at Harwich for the traditional ceremony which marked the beginnings of the new entity. The government had shown great urgency and determination to get private money to help fund the project. Time was of the essence.

Time was of the essence for Nathaniel's wife also. The three months' notice that she had received was hardly enough time to organise the new clothes and the reception. There were fittings to attend and caterers to consult and invitations to send out and entertainers to hire. There was so much to do but she was in a state of high excitement. She was in her element.

Nathaniel had received the letter from the Lord Chancellor's office in May summoning him to the Palace of Westminster in August. He had knelt before King George as the sword had tapped him lightly on the shoulder and he had been dubbed Sir Nathaniel Leadbitter, Knighted, so the letter said, for 'his services to the war effort'.

A second visit to the dockyard on 1st September to witness the launch of ship number 39 had coincided with the arrival at his home of a second letter from the office of the Lord Chancellor elevating him to the rank of Lord of the Realm, following a further 'donation' to the war effort of a measly (so Nathaniel thought) twenty thousand pounds.

When he returned home and opened the letter his wife was ecstatic. They had arrived, hadn't they? All her dreams had come true. She could hold her head up in any company. She was, after all, Lady Leadbitter, the wife of Lord Nathaniel Leadbitter, well known benefactor, businessman and millionaire.

They had celebrated with his finest wines long into the evening and later he was invited to her bedroom, the first time in years. But she was still the unenthusiastic and unimaginative lover that she had always been and he had returned to his own rooms a disappointed man.

Lady Leadbitter in her excitement, oblivious to his feelings, gleefully set about searching for a new and much grander house. The kind of house that matched their newfound status. The kind of house that a Lord and Lady of the Realm could call home. Her search took her back to Yorkshire. Nathaniel meanwhile, bought a beautifully appointed, but small, townhouse in Dover, a town that he had visited often for the sea air and had grown to like immensely. In essence, he and his wife now lived separate lives.

Nathaniel had received word that the ship he had partly financed had been named *Relentless*. He wondered where the ship was at this very moment. He tried to picture what life aboard her would be like but couldn't. He did know, however, that the life of the sailors would be very different to the pandered life he led.

CHAPTER 19

Evesham
1821

The entire village square could be easily viewed from the bay window of the tavern. The man looked around the square once more; nothing had changed since the last time he had looked. His wagon was where he had left it under the aged Copper Beech tree which cast its huge shadow over the patch of grass around which the village seemed to have been built. There were a few businesses opposite, a general store with its door wide open, a milliners shop, a barber and a building whose windows were covered in words which the man could not read from this distance. An intermittent ringing sound came from an open archway to his left, as a blacksmith struck his anvil. In all the time he had been sitting there, well over an hour now, he had only seen an occasional person entering or leaving the shops and a few more crossing the street, going about their own business. A sleepy village indeed.

He had chosen the seat in the window so that he could stay away from the few old men who were sitting around the unlit fire with their pots of ale. He had no desire to become engaged in conversation with them, although he found himself listening with one ear to their gossip. He understood hardly a word. He didn't even know the name of the village, it just so happened that it stood astride the main road to Gloucester. He would not have stopped here at all except that he had travelled a long way that day and was ready for a rest and the smell of fresh bread issuing from the tavern had made his mouth water and made him realise just how hungry he was.

The cheese that went with the bread had been matured well and was good and tasty once he had scraped away the mould, and the ale had been cellar cool and bitter on the tongue. He had downed two jugs as he had eaten his bread and cheese and now, with his belly full, he was content and relaxed. But it was time he was moving along. He would travel a few more miles before finding a place to bed down for the night.

He rose from his seat but his attention was suddenly drawn to the noise; the giggly chatter of children playing, and two children, a boy and a girl, both aged about eight years, skipped past the window. The boy was bowling a metal hoop and the girl was trying to get in the way of his effort and, at the same time, snatch the short piece of stick from his hand. The hoop careered across the street with the boy and girl in hot pursuit until the hoop ended up crashing into the huge tree and falling on its side. The boy bent to retrieve the hoop and the girl pushed him over onto the grass amid squeals of laughter. The boy got up and chased the girl for a few yards before deciding the hoop was more important and returned to pick it up. The man crossed the room to the door to the street and was in time to see the boy get the hoop in motion once again. The girl made to follow him, but they were stopped in their tracks by a shout from the doorway of the general store. A woman stood there, her arms folded across her chest.

The boy and girl stopped their play and crossed to the woman. A few words were exchanged before the boy made his desultory way to the blacksmith's archway whilst the girl followed the woman inside the shop. The boy disappeared under the arch.

The man shrugged his shoulders, left the inn, and walked across to his wagon. He was about to get underway when the girl and the woman reappeared on the street. The girl carried a small bunch of Sweet Peas. The woman pointed along the street and the man heard the words 'church' and 'hurry'. He turned and looked in the direction that the woman had pointed. Over the top of a stand of trees he could see the crenulations of a tower with a weather vane. The church the woman had indicated, no doubt.

The girl turned and skipped towards the trees and the sight of her awakened the longing again in the man. How long had it been? Too long. The urges grew more insistent with each passing second as he watched the girl disappear into the trees. He needed her. He got the wagon in motion and followed her. All being well he would have her in the box before long. She would be his tonight.

He followed the road around to the right and suddenly emerged from the shade of the trees into an area of wide grass verges and wild flowers. Just a few yards away stood an old lychgate, set into the low stone wall which surrounded the churchyard and the graveyard. He could easily see over the wall. The girl was kneeling on the grass alongside a fairly recent grave. There was nothing to mark the grave except the mould of bare earth on which now rested the bunch of flowers that the girl had been carrying. She had her back to the man and appeared to be talking to someone. He looked quickly up and down the road. No-one was in sight and he was shielded from prying eyes in the village by the stand of trees. It couldn't be better; everything was perfect.

His heartbeat quickened and the blood rushed around his body. The feeling of what was to come was so intense that he was almost swooning with the pleasure of it. He felt that he would burst. He approached the gate and taking a final look around, he pushed it open. It made a groaning sound but the girl could not have heard anything, for she did not move or look around. He had done this many times but the pleasure never diminished, his whole body was trembling with excitement. He was about to take a step toward the girl when he heard the unmistakable sound of the church door opening and a man dressed entirely in black came into view, followed closely by a man in coarse working clothes. They didn't seem to notice the girl or the man standing not far behind her kneeling form.

The man in black pointed to the grass and his hand described an arc of the churchyard. As his hand reached the direction of the gate, the churchyard was empty but for the small girl. It wouldn't have been possible to see it from the road but there was a scythe leaning against the wall of the church porch and the working man lifted it, spat on his open hands before rubbing them briskly together, and made to start work cutting the grass between the graves. The man in black watched for several minutes and then turned back into the church leaving the workman to his task.

Several hundred yards up the road the man's passion had turned to anger. He had her in the palm of his hand. Almost. He could almost taste her she was so close. Bastard churchmen, always poking their noses in where they weren't needed or wanted. He had looked back once he knew he was safe. The girl was standing now and had clasped her hands together in front as she had been taught in Sunday school as the proper way to say a prayer. She looked like an angel and he was enflamed. What was he to do now with the hot blood running?

He had only travelled a few miles but felt that he could go no further and found a place under some trees to spend the night. The ground was damp here where the sun had not penetrated, and he spread the canvas under his cart for shelter in case of more rain during the hours of darkness. He covered it with his thick blanket and then he took the small box from its hiding place and carried it with him as he crawled under the cart, and made himself comfortable. He lifted the lid of the box and, almost with reverence, took out a small boot. He remembered the boy. He had been a bony, scrawny boy but his meat had been sweet for all that.

From the box he took several more small items and turned them in his hands before carefully putting them aside. A piece of scarlet ribbon, another small shoe, a cap and a bonnet, a cheap broach and a bangle, a cloth button and last of all a torn petticoat. The petticoat was his favourite. She had been a strong girl and he had taken her from the box many times over the five days that he held her until eventually he had tired of her and he had made her clean the box with soap and water before he had used his knife on her for the last time. With her strength she had taken a long time to die, as he somehow knew she would, and he had used the knife many times and his pleasure had been great, before he had broken her completely and she had died.

Before replacing the assortment of precious objects back into the box he held the petticoat close to his face so that he could smell the sweet smell of the girl who had worn it.

*

The small girl from the churchyard had gone back to the shop and then had walked home with her mother for tea. It was a special day and together with the girl's father they had fresh bread and salted butter and, the girl's favourite, homemade blackcurrant jam made by the girl's Auntie Maud, who was good at such things.

She had gone to bed happy and had knelt with her mother at the foot of her bed to say her nightly prayers. She prayed that her grandma was happy now and no longer in pain and, being reassured by her prayers, went to bed content. She would never know how lucky she had been that day.

The man uttered the occasional groan as he slept on the bone-hard ground under his wagon. His dream came again and was black and troubled.

CHAPTER 20

The Money Lender

Dover
1804

Louisa and the Money Lender sat comfortably in the drawing room supping tea. They were discussing the idea of finding another girl to help Louisa with the business, as they had been for several months. In the two years since moving to the house on Southdown Road the demands for Louisa's services were such that she had had to turn potential customers away, in fact, she was so busy that she had become tired and worn and was in grave danger of losing her beauty. The Money Lender was not happy. Money was slipping through his fingers. They determined to find a girl to 'help out', but she had to be 'right'. She had to be young and pretty and she had to be from the 'right' social class so that she would fit well with the type of gentlemen who called at the house. Above all else, she had to be willing. They both awaited an opportunity.

*

The Money Lender had disliked Henry Teague intensely from the very moment he had first stepped across the threshold of the Teague house. The house was an imposing building on the outskirts of the town and from the outside looked quite ordinary, but the inside was verging on the bizarre. Each room was lavishly decorated to the extreme and the furniture was obviously very expensive, but nothing matched, in fact, with such a mixture of styles, everything clashed. Mrs Teague had filled the house with a mixture of old and new, traditional and contemporary and had ended up with a style all of her own. And the Money Lender knew that some pieces would fetch a pretty penny when he sold them, for his visit was for the purpose of recovering part of Teague's debt. He determined that the huge mahogany desk which dominated the room in which they stood, the room Teague had grandly called his study, would be the first piece he would take.

Teague had defaulted on his interest payments for the previous two months, despite the threats of the Money Lender's man, 'Nobbler' Knowles, who had hoped that a beating would be the order of the day. It seemed that all of Christendom was to blame for Teague's lack of funds. Never his gambling, or his lavish lifestyle or, indeed, the bad management of his late father's business.

The man was a whinger of the first order. The Money Lender hated whingers above all else. He was much more likely to give a third chance to a genuine citizen who admitted his mistakes. And now the time had come. The Money Lender wanted some money on account.

The Money Lender had been briefly introduced to the man's wife, Dorcas, whom Teague had then swiftly dismissed from the room, but not before the Money Lender had appraised her worth. She was a handsome woman, aged between thirty-five and forty he guessed, with a good figure although slightly wide in the hips. Her eyes were brown but she had the fairest of hair. She was dressed well, wearing a low-cut cotton dress which showed off, to her advantage, the swell of her breasts. Her skin was creamy white. Dorcas saw where he was looking and coquettishly she took a deep breath, which made her breasts more prominent, before turning and leaving the room. *She is flirting with me,* thought the Money Lender, and smiled. *She is much too good for the man.*

How she had ended up married to Teague was a mystery. The man was short and stout and looked a sorry, bedraggled excuse for a man. Even in the middle of the day he smelt of strong drink and had the red bulbous nose of the habitual heavy drinker.

The Money Lender made his demand for a payment and Teague rolled out the excuses he had used with the Debt Collector. As he watched the man snivelling and grovelling in front of him his disgust grew and with his disgust came anger. He felt like kicking the man himself. The Money Lender, in his anger, decided to end their association once and for all. He would demand the return of the debt, the principle sum and all the interest owing. He knew the man could not pay, 'Nobbler' had told him so. He would take the whole house, not just bits of furniture. That would teach him a lesson he would not forget in a hurry.

Before he could put the threat into words the door to the room opened, and a young girl entered the room with a beaming smile on her face, carrying a silver tray laden with a teapot and cups. The Money Lender assumed she was a servant until Teague introduced her as his eldest daughter, Agnes. The Money Lender could not believe what he was hearing. How could an ugly runt of a man like Teague have been the father of such a child? She was beautiful, not classically, but in a childlike way. Tall and slim and the colouring of her hair and eyes she had obviously inherited from her mother.

But more surprises were to follow. Teague was the father of four more children, three of them girls. The children ranging in age from the youngest at eight to Agnes at seventeen. The Money Lender demanded to see them all and they were duly lined up in the parlour. He was astounded. They all had fair hair and brown eyes and each of the girls was as pretty as Agnes.

The Money Lender recognised the opportunities. He saw the potential immediately. The threats could wait for another day. Negotiations began as to repayment of the debt, but now the tone was different and the terms were easier than they would have been only moments before.

*

She had arrived at his house at almost exactly three o'clock as he knew she would, somehow he knew she was the kind of person to be punctual. He had waited three weeks before sending for her and he also knew she would be intrigued by his brief note. She had sent her acceptance back to him with the small boy he had paid to deliver his invitation, written in his best copperplate on his most expensive paper.

He had seated her close to the desk and they had each consumed several cups of weak tea, as they observed the niceties and exchanged small talk, for the Money Lender was well versed in social etiquette. But eventually her curiosity overcame her good manners and her natural reticence.

'Please, sir. You hold me in great suspense. What is the important information that you wrote of? How does it affect the future prosperity and happiness of both myself and my children?'

The Money Lender had made sure that all the paperwork was in order before he sent the small boy around to Teague's house, and it lay neatly before him on the desk. He passed some sheets across the desk. The dozen or so sheets of paper detailed Teague's borrowings with dates and amounts. The last I.O.U. had a notation at the bottom of the page with the total amount borrowed to date. Dorcas Teague picked up the first sheet and began reading.

'But…'

She lifted another sheet and read that, then another and another until she had all twelve sheets gripped in her hand. Only then did she raise her head to look at the man across the desk.

'But I don't understand. This cannot be right. My husband doesn't need to borrow money, he is a successful businessman, he is a chandler and seller of good-quality goods to the Navy.'

'The signatures are genuine, believe me. It seems he has kept his affairs secret from you.' The Money Lender was impassive. It was a common occurrence; he had seen the same many times before.

He picked up another sheet. It was a page from a ledger showing the payments made by Teague to service his debt. The entries on the sheet were meagre and showed that, with the accumulation of interest, the debt had risen, and had been rising, since the beginning of the year. He passed the sheet across to the woman. When she took the sheet from him her hand was shaking. She studied the numbers on the sheet without comprehension until she reached the foot of the page. Then even she, with her limited knowledge of book-keeping could see that the debt had increased to a grossly inflated figure.

'Why hasn't he paid you the money owing? He has money. We live well, we have a lovely house, we have all we need.'

'Your husband hasn't any money. He gives you a few pounds from the money that he borrows and he squanders the rest. Do you know he drinks and gambles heavily?' He paused for effect. 'Do you have any idea where your husband is today?'

'He is in London, on business. He has important meetings with his suppliers.'

He sat, still as a statue, and studied the woman whilst she became ever more nervous under his scrutiny. She wondered why he would ask her such a question. Of course she knew where her husband was, he had told her yesterday as he had set off.

'Your husband is not in London. Not in any meetings. Not with any suppliers, for he has none. His credit is no longer acceptable to anyone. He was forced to declare his business bankrupt weeks ago. He signed it over to me as part payment when I visited you at your house three weeks ago. Your husband now works for me. Today he is at the race meeting at Epsom, probably putting his last few pounds on the 'sure-fire winner' given to him by a friend in the know. He neglected to say that the friend was also in debt to the Money Lender and knew no more about horses than the woman's husband. The King, God bless him, will be there today. I hope that he has more luck than your husband.'

The woman sat in her chair, stunned. Why hadn't her husband told her that he was in dire straits with his finances? He obviously did not want her to know. She felt confused, disoriented, let down, but most of all, hopeless. She had never expected this when she had entered the fine house belonging to the man sitting opposite.

Two more sheets of paper lay on the desk, before the man. He slowly passed the first across. The woman was reluctant to pick it up, knowing that it would not be the bearer of good news. It was, in fact, an evaluation of the value of the Teague house, including an estimate of the value of the furniture contained therein. She could see immediately that the total valuation fell short of the amount owing as shown by the ledger. Realisation began to dawn on her. The nightmare was getting worse.

Stifling a sob, she looked up at the Money Lender.

'But... but you can't. Surely you cannot be thinking of taking my house. It's my house, no-one can take the house from me. No-one would be so cruel as to want to take our house from us. We own the house, it's ours. The furniture is mine, I chose it.' But even as she uttered the words the look on the Money Lender's face told her she was wrong on all counts.

The man said nothing. He savoured the woman's discomfiture, her distress. He would let her stew for a few seconds before driving the final nail into her heart.

The final sheet of paper was folded and the folds were held together with a seal. He slowly broke the seal and passed the heavy document across to her. She had never seen such a document before but knew instinctively what it was. A tear squeezed from her right eye as she lifted the piece of paper and read the imposing heading:

WARRANT OF THE DEBTORS' COURT

'You see for yourself, goodwife Teague; I can if I have the mind to. I can have you and your children on the street this very minute and your worthless husband committed to the debtors' prison, until he can repay the balance. My bailiffs could be there even now, putting your children out with nothing but the clothes they are wearing.'

She was crying openly now.

'But where would we go? What would happen to the children? Please, sir, have a heart. Tell me this is not true.' She was having difficulty speaking through her sobs. 'We have nowhere else. We have no relations who could take us in. What will happen to my babies?'

'Why should I care? What is there for me to gain if I delay?' He was enjoying himself now. 'Every day that passes I am losing money on the amount that you owe.' The afternoon was progressing exactly as he had planned. His heart was racing, the blood coursing through his veins, fuelled by the sensation of the power he now held over this woman. It was almost overwhelming. He had done this many times before with other families, but it never ceased to thrill him. He spoke again, compounding the horror that she was feeling in her head as well as her heart.

'If you are lucky there may be a place for you all in the workhouse where at least you could share a bug-ridden mattress, but of course you would be separated from your boys, you may never see them alive again. If they have no room for you in the workhouse, you could always try begging from the sailors on the docks. Doubtless you have seen the beggars there?'

She had indeed seen the beggars there. Thin, raggedy people, who came up to you with dull eyes, holding out their hands, imploring you to throw them some money. All of them filthy and smelly from sleeping rough among the excrement that littered the narrow streets down there. The very thought of them sent a shudder through her very being. She had also heard tales about the workhouse and what went on inside there. Tales that were too horrible to contemplate.

He rose slowly from his seat. He rounded the desk and perched himself on the corner of the desk, close to her. Her head was lowered and her shoulders were shaking and he could hear the sobs that wracked her body. In her misery, she had shredded the lace handkerchief gripped in her hands.

'Of course,' he said very softly, 'I don't have to put you out on the street. I am not a cruel man, but I am afraid business is business. However, there may be a way for you to save the situation.'

She raised her head slowly and her eyes met his. Her tears had streaked the rouge that she had applied to her cheeks earlier that afternoon but, despite this, she still managed to look attractive to the man, in fact more so now than ever.

'H…how, sir? H…how can I save the day? What is it… what do I need to do?' The shuddering had stopped and her sobbing had quieted somewhat as she grasped at any hope. He knew that now was the time.

'Your eldest daughter Agnes may be your saving grace. I know of a position available to a young lady such as her. I have knowledge of a businesswoman who is looking for an assistant, a young lady willing to learn the ropes. The position has a good yearly salary. The lady is willing to pay up to two hundred pounds a year and all found, for the right person, a most generous sum, I am sure you'll agree. If Agnes is suitable and were to take the position she could help you to pay off the debt and, as an act of good faith I would allow you extra time, in fact as much as you require, and I would cease to charge you interest.' He was speaking softly and gently, the very picture of the magnanimous benefactor. But the salary was a pittance amounting to less than four pounds per week. If he and Louisa were successful, Agnes would earn for them more than four pounds each and every day.

'Oh, sir.' She grasped at the thread of hope that he had just given her. 'I am sure that Agnes would suit the position admirably and, after all, she is seventeen and should be making her way in the world. I will speak to her today. But, if she were to take the post, she must not know the true circumstances in which I find myself.'

'Very well, and the suggestion that she should apply for the post should appear to be your idea, and your idea alone. My name should never be mentioned in connection with the position.'

The woman nodded her head.

'It will be better if I am the one to broach the subject.' Her sobbing had stopped now that she thought that there was a way out. 'May I be so bold as to enquire as to the business that the lady in question is in? Agnes may ask me and it would appear strange if I did not know.'

The man thought for several seconds before answering.

'You may loosely describe her business as being linked to entertainment, but don't worry, I can assure you that Agnes will not be asked to appear on the stage.'

The woman let out her breath in a long, shuddering sigh. Relief was written large on her face, which still showed the ravages of her earlier tears.

'And what about yourself, Mistress Teague? What will you do to ease your situation? You cannot expect Agnes to bear all the burden of her family's misfortune. What will you do to keep your children out of the workhouse?'

'Sir, I will do anything to support my husband, as any good wife would, and to save the children from the workhouse, but I have no skills to offer. I married young and I have been a wife and mother ever since. I even rely on my maids to clean the house. I am afraid, sir, I am useless.'

She was wearing her best Sunday dress. It was made of thin cotton and was buttoned tightly from the narrow waist right up to her throat. He leaned forward the short distance between them and deliberately undid the topmost button exposing a narrow strip of her neck. Her hand came up to his.

'Please, sir. You must desist.' But her voice lacked conviction. This was the part he liked best. The part when they finally succumbed.

'The workhouse is a terrible place, especially for young girls and boys. Have you heard the stories?' He looked directly into her eyes and the threat was explicit. He needed to say no more. Her hand relaxed and her head dropped and he undid four more buttons until he was able to insert his left hand into the opening. His hand slid beneath her chemise, and encircled her breast. Her breasts seemed larger now that they were unrestrained by the dress. His fingers sought out her nipple and gently rolled it between his first finger and thumb and, to her shame, the nipple stiffened and became erect under his caress.

His right hand cupped her chin and lifted it upwards and he bent and kissed her, very slowly and gently, full on the mouth. He pulled back and looked at her face. Her eyes were tightly screwed shut but even so a tear had squeezed from under her right eyelid. He bent to her and kissed her again, more insistent this time, and his tongue pushed between her slightly parted lips, exploring her mouth and seeking and finding her tongue.

They parted and he removed his hand from her breast. Instead he took hold of her right hand and stood, pulling her to her feet.

'We will be more comfortable, my dear Dorcas, in the other room,' he said, leading her towards a connecting door to the next room. She followed meekly. She had not an ounce of resistance left.

He left the papers strewn across the desk.

*

She knew she had been raped, but somehow it felt like she was partly to blame for what had happened to her. She felt as though, somehow, she may have encouraged the man to do what he had done. She was ashamed of herself because eventually she had done everything that the man had asked of her. She had done things that she had not even done with her husband.

He had disregarded her modesty. He had taken away her pride.

She felt she could never face her family and friends again, she was sure all of the world would be able to see what she had become. He had stripped her, not just of her clothes, but of her dignity.

But she knew also that if and when he called for her again she would go to him. She would do exactly as the man wanted for the sake of her children, not for her husband. Not to keep him out of prison. She would do nothing for him, ever again. She had never loved him, even when they married, although over the years a certain amount of affection had grown between them. But that was all finished. The affection had been replaced by loathing, even hatred. After all, he was responsible for their plight. He had lied to her and misled her. He had put her in this position where she had to degrade herself, to please the Money Lender, just to stay in her own home.

She looked around her familiar bedroom, at the furniture, the drapes and the many ornaments she had collected over the years. Everything was precious to her. She loved every piece of china, every piece of silver. She had built this safe haven, this nest for herself and her family. She could not and would not see it taken from her. She would do anything to preserve their way of life. But that did not stop the tears.

*

The Money Lender spent the evening at the house in Southdown Road. He and Louisa talked for a long time before he returned home. The plan was progressing well. He thought about the afternoon he had spent with Dorcas Teague. Such a pretty and obliging woman, he thought. But he knew that he would tire of her soon and then he would have the house. It was only a matter of time and convenience.

CHAPTER 21

Agnes Teague

Dover
1804

Poor Agnes Teague was naive almost to the point of stupidity. It was like leading a lamb to the slaughter now that she was away from the protection of her family. She had yet to understand what her duties were to be in the house or what business Louisa was in. All she knew was that Louisa seemed to know many influential men who constantly called at the house for meetings. But that did not matter to her for she was enjoying the freedom of being away from her parents, and she was enjoying the attentions of the handsome colleague of Louisa's who had called on her several times at the house on South Down road. No matter that he was much older than her. What did age matter when you are in love? Agnes genuinely believed that she was falling in love with the man, and he with her. He was generous and always brought with him a small present when he called, a trinket or some such.

But this morning, as she went down for breakfast, she was troubled. The evening before, when they had been left alone in the salon, the man had kissed her. She had enjoyed the feeling of his lips on hers and had responded. He had kissed her again and she felt his hand touch her on the breast through her dress. She jerked back, confused and a little afraid. She had never been touched in that way before and therefore did not quite know how she should respond. She did what she thought was the right thing, disentangling herself and moving away from him. She had enjoyed the kisses but was fearful of the emotions which they had awakened in her. He seemed disappointed and even angry, and had looked at her long and hard before excusing himself and leaving the room, leaving her alone. She did not know what to do now, had she lost him forever?

Louisa seemed to have been waiting for her as she entered the dining room, as indeed was the case.

'You stupid, stupid girl. What have you done?' Her anger was apparent. Agnes had never seen Louisa like this before. 'You have ruined everything. What will happen to your mother and your brothers and sisters now?'

'What… what do you mean? What about my mother?'

'What about your mother? You ask, "What about my mother?" Do you not realise that the only reason that your family are still in their home is because of the Money Lender's affection for you?'

'The Money Lender? But what has that to do with my family?'

'You silly child. Your father is in debt to the Money Lender. He owes him hundreds of pounds, if not thousands. It is because of his liking for you that he has not foreclosed on your home and thrown your family into the street.'

'But I had no idea. I did not know. He wouldn't do that would he? Throw my family into the street?'

'That, and worse. Your father could also go to jail if the Money Lender said so.' She paused to let the portent of what she had said sink in. 'He could take everything. You would all be ruined.' She paused again, before continuing.

'But the Money Lender did not want to see you or your family distressed. Why do you think I took you in? The Money Lender asked me, as his friend and business partner, to help your family at this difficult time otherwise you would not be here at all. And you have thrown it back into both of our faces.' Louisa strode across to the sideboard, feigning more anger, and retrieved the document lying there, seemingly put there by accident, but carefully placed. 'Do you know what this is? Have you ever seen a repossession warrant before?'

'But I did not know,' was all that Agnes could whisper.

'Here. Read it. See for yourself.'

She handed the document to Agnes. She only needed to see the words 'Debtors' Court' at the top of the sheet and the broken seal, to be convinced. She had no need to read more. She knew that Louisa was telling her the truth. She did not have the intelligence to even wonder why Louisa should be in possession of the warrant in the first place.

'Do you see what you have done? I hope that his anger has calmed this morning and that he will give you another chance otherwise your family could all be evicted by the middle of the day.' Louisa pressed on and Agnes was terrified now as it dawned on her what the repercussions of her abrupt actions the evening before could have. She started to cry and Louisa put her arms around her and hugged her close. As the tears flowed from Agnes a broad smile appeared on Louisa's face. It had gone well.

*

Within three months they considered her to be ready to entertain clients. Just like her mother, her resistance had been brushed easily aside. But what had surprised Louisa and her partner was the enthusiasm shown by Agnes once the initial reluctance and shyness had been overcome. She had a real appetite to learn all the nuances of the job and, as important as all that, the practicalities of using the different potions and creams and the skins and the pig's bladder and the douche bag. She was, in all ways, the perfect student. She would be an asset to the business.

But as Louisa watched the Money Lender and the girl from the secret room, she had a feeling she had not felt before. Could she be jealous that his hands were on the girl instead of caressing her body? Surely not. Hadn't she come to the realisation that she loved Nathaniel Leadbitter with every part of her body? With every breath she took? The anticipation of his every visit leaving her all a-tingle? Of course, but she still felt something. Could it be possible? Could she be in love with two men at the same time? Two men who were obviously so different.

CHAPTER 22

The Money Lender and Dorcas Teague

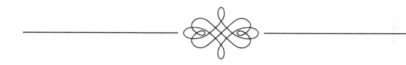

Dover
1804

This was only her third visit to the house. She had expected to be summoned more often and it had been so long between the second and third visit that she had begun to hope that the Money Lender had no more use for her. But then the boy with the note had knocked on the front door once more and dismay had filled her heart again. But she knew she had to answer the summons, there was nothing else for it.

He lay naked on the bed and waited for her to finish at the washstand. She was naked except for her silk stockings and garters. He absent-mindedly watched her movements as she washed, noting the smooth contours of her narrow back and the flair of her hips. She turned and made her way over to the bed and he could not help but compare her to her daughter. Her breasts were much larger and heavier and her belly was slightly rounded, nicely rounded, something he had not noticed before, not flat and firm like that of her daughter, but otherwise she could have been an older sister. The colouring of the two was identical in every way, but they were totally different in the bed. He had difficulty deciding which was best.

She climbed onto the bed and her hands were like butterflies on his body. He closed his eyes and lost himself in the pleasure of her ministrations.

*

Agnes was in great demand at the house in Southdown Road which pleased The Money Lender immensely, and the money was flooding in. The sad men who were her clients were willing to pay over the odds to have a girl so young and, as they believed, so innocent. In the first week alone she had 'lost her virginity' nine times. If she continued to attract men in the way that she was doing he would need to consider setting her up in a house of her own. Maybe the family home would be the place, after he had gotten rid of her father and mother of course. He could then proceed to take on a new girl or maybe two. Her younger sisters maybe, they were reaching an age. He decided that the time was not quite right for such action. It would be a little while yet. She needed more experience under the guidance of his friend Louisa.

CHAPTER 23

Folkestone
September 3, 1805

The old woman quietly closed the door of her house and hurried away across the street. She carried a large wickerwork laundry basket full to the brim with what appeared to be her weekly washing. She turned the corner, walked a dozen or so yards before turning left under the archway. She emerged on the other side into a cobbled yard and spoke to the man there. He pointed to a door and the woman opened the door and passed into the gloomy interior. There was a sound of hammering from within.

She called out a name and a man appeared from behind a screen. The undertaker walked over to the woman and they hugged each other. They were brother and sister as well as business partners, which seemed a strange combination. He helped bodies leave this world; she helped to bring tiny bodies into it. Recognised by the locals as being an authority on childbirth despite having no children of her own, she had been present at the birth of most of the children within a three-mile radius of the street in which she lived.

At this moment she was afraid, the poor woman lying in the bed in her house could be dying. What she had done was illegal but, as usual, nothing would be said as long as the outcome was satisfactory. A death was the worst thing that could happen, but first she needed to dispose of the 'thing' that she carried close to her chest. The birth had been a painful ordeal and the woman had been torn open dreadfully. She had still been bleeding when the old woman had left the house. She should not have left the woman alone but she felt that she had to get rid of the tiny body, she had to get it out of her house.

The woman stretched out on the bed in the upstairs room had been in good health and had several children already. Everything should have been straight forward. She had been adamant that she did not want the baby. She had offered to pay extra if the old lady would rid her of the child; give it away or something; do anything, just so long as she didn't have to take the baby home. The old lady had not been surprised. This was not an uncommon occurrence in Folkestone and she was used to such requests but if she had known she would never have become involved in the birthing.

The waters had broken hours before and, as far as the old woman could tell, the baby's head was properly engaged. Everything should have gone without a hitch, but something was wrong. The old woman could see the baby's head clearly but despite the woman's strong pushing it refused to emerge through the narrow pelvic opening. After several hours of straining and pushing the woman had visibly weakened. The old woman knew from experience that something had to be done if the woman was to survive.

She had used her 'spoons', gripping the head of the baby with the crude instruments. The head had come out of the woman in a rush and a shower of watery blood and mucus, splattering the sheets of the bed and the apron of the old woman. One more push and the baby was free, seemingly eager suddenly to be out into the world.

The old woman gasped and rapidly sucked in a great lungful of air. She could see the baby clearly now. She had seen many things in her long life but she wasn't prepared for this. The head was misshapen, elongated with a huge growth, overhanging the thin neck, at the back. But worse, where the eyes should have been there were only hollows covered in leathery skin and the lump of cartilage, which should have formed the baby's nose, began high on the forehead, hooked viciously downward and ended in a single nostril just above the cleft upper lip which deformed the mouth.

The old woman quickly crossed herself and lifted the slime-covered baby. She carried it across to the wash-stand where the jug of hot water stood ready to wash the newcomer. She put the baby into the bowl and poured the warm water over it. As she washed the baby she was overcome by revulsion. Which, among the childless families that awaited the delivery of one of her unwanted babies, would want such an abomination? Who could love such a creature? This was the devil's work. This was a devil child, she was certain. She was a religious woman and alongside her religion ran the superstitions and stories of the Old Testament. Suddenly she was as certain as she had ever been about anything in her life before. The compulsion overcame her and she did something which went against everything she held dear.

She turned the baby in the bowl until it was face down in the water. She held its head below the surface for what seemed to her to be an eternity, but was no more than a few minutes, before feeling for a heartbeat. There was none. Suddenly she was struck by the enormity of what she had done: she had murdered a newborn and she panicked.

*

The undertaker had two coffins laid out in the corner of the workshop in an area that he grandly called 'the chapel of rest'. One contained a young woman who had died of consumption and was to be buried that afternoon. He had already sealed the coffin but it took him only minutes to remove the lid. The old woman placed the body of the baby, still wrapped in the rags that she had used to cover it in the laundry basket, into the coffin beside the feet of the woman. The lid was screwed back on, very tightly.

Although there was a good turnout for the funeral there was still plenty of room in the pews along the main aisle of the church, but the old woman still chose to sit in the side chapel dedicated to the Virgin Mary. When the funeral procession left the church to make its way to the graveside, the old woman followed. No-one took any notice of her or thought to wonder why she was there. She watched the coffin as it was lowered into the ground and stayed to see the hole refilled. Only then was she satisfied.

She re-entered the empty church and once again took a seat in the side chapel. She sat for a long, long time doing nothing but staring up at the frieze of the Madonna.

*

Dorcas Teague, alone in the upstairs room of the old woman's house, slipped quietly into an exhausted sleep. The bleeding had stopped at last, but she was very weak. Her sleep was disturbed and restless and the dream came again.

She was back in the drawing room of her home. It must have been cold outside because a roaring fire burned in the fireplace. Her children and her husband were there also, sat around her, talking together and laughing. Suddenly, she felt the familiar cold chill on her back, and her eyes were drawn to the fire. There in the leaping flames she could see the face of the Money Lender. The face rose from the flames and floated towards her and gradually acquired the body of a man, and she screamed as she felt his hot hands upon her. His hands were everywhere and she screamed again but no-one in the room seemed to hear her and they continued to laugh and joke among themselves. It was as though she was invisible; as if she had ceased to exist.

The Money Lender drew back and she heard his laugh and, as she watched, his face faded away and then re-materialised into that of a demon, right before her very eyes. It had a wide grin on its face and she could see the sharp pointed teeth and the pair of horns protruding from its forehead, just like the pictures she had seen in the church. She screamed, but once again, no-one in the room took any notice. The demon ran its tongue over its thick lips and reached forward to touch her cheek. It bent to kiss her and she tried desperately to turn her face away and she screamed again, louder than ever.

She awoke with a start and in utter confusion. Where was she? Where was this strange place? Her eyes searched the room for any signs of familiarity. She was terrified and she panicked. And what was that agonising pain she was feeling deep in the pit of her belly? She tried to rise but she was too weak to get out of the bed. Gradually, she gathered her thoughts and the memory of what had happened during the previous hours came flooding back. She shouted out but no-one answered; she was alone in a strange house. Had she been purposely left to die? She didn't want to die alone in this soiled bed.

The tears flowed freely and she fell back against the pillows, exhausted once again. She felt dirty and clammy and her nightdress was soaked with blood and sweat but eventually she drifted back into sleep as she clutched one of the pillows tightly to her breast.

Thankfully the dream did not return.

*

Many miles from Folkestone the body of a man bobbed gently along in the calm waters inside the bay at Lyme Regis, kept afloat by the putrid gases produced by its internal decomposition. The two genteel ladies, out for a fashionable stroll along the Mole to take in some invigorating sea air, succumbed immediately to an attack of the vapours when they spotted the corpse, but recovered enough to shout for help after flopping onto an adjacent bench, where they continued to hug each other tightly. Several fishermen, unloading their catch of crab and a few lobsters, ran to the scene, but none of them wanted to touch the body once they had seen its condition. The local militiamen were sent for.

It had been three weeks since the body had been dropped into the water off the end of the breakwater at Dover, where it had immediately sunk without trace in the deep water. After a week or so, decomposition had started and, in the small hours of the night, the body had bobbed back to the surface and it began its journey.

The bloated body had crossed and re-crossed the English Channel, carried along at the mercy of the tides and currents. It had bumped along the coast of Brittany and had scraped along the sea-cliffs of Hampshire, on each leg of its journey drifting inexorably westward until, eventually, it had entered Lyme Bay and had fetched up in the sheltered waters of the peaceful seaside town, so admired by local people and visitors alike.

And all the time the tenderised flesh had been like a magnet to the scavenger fish and the other sea creatures that fed off dead meat, and they had done their worst. They shredded the flesh and hid the identity of the person perfectly, and hid the fact that the body had received a vicious beating before death. Now, the body was left marooned half in and half out of the water by the rapidly ebbing tide, and the stinking clothing was the only clue to the fact that the body had once been a man. Eventually, and with no great haste, the militia, a sergeant and two men appeared followed by a horse and cart which contained a coffin. The men were ordered to retrieve the body and, with no great enthusiasm, they reluctantly moved forward with an old fishing net. They waved away the bluebottles and greenbottles which, by now, were swarming around the corpse attracted by the smell of the rotting flesh, rolled what was left of the man into the net, and lifted it onto the Mole.

The sergeant made the official and superfluous announcement that he considered the body to be dead and it was loaded, along with the fishing net, into the coffin. The cart moved away followed by the militiamen and the small crowd dispersed. Life went on.

When the small party reached the undertaker's premises he was given the voucher which would enable him to claim his twenty-one shillings from the authorities, for the burial of the body. The sergeant and his men departed and the undertaker called his apprentice to help him transfer the body from the coffin into an old crate which had once contained a dozen muskets, but not before he had drenched a piece of cloth in lavender water to hold over his mouth and nose whilst he searched the body for anything of value. He found nothing; no rings, no watch, no money. None of the things a man would normally have about him. He shrugged. He was philosophical; such was life. Or death.

Later that afternoon, an old man was buried by the undertaker in the municipal graveyard. When the few mourners had left the graveside the cart pulled close to the grave and the old crate was hastily lowered into the hole. The apprentice got busy with a large shovel. No single grave for the washed-up body. What did they expect for a measly twenty-one shillings?

*

Over the following weeks the ground settled and a beautifully carved gravestone was put in place at the head of the grave. Below the pair of entwined cherubs was the simple inscription:

Here lie the mortal remains of

Nehemiah Joseph Green

Revered citizen of this Borough

Born Dec 2 1729 Died Aug 28 1805

May he rest in Eternal Peace.

Of course, there could be no mention of the other body buried in a crate atop the fancy coffin of Nehemiah Joseph Green, but poor Henry Teague would never be an inconvenience or an embarrassment to anyone ever again.

CHAPTER 24

John Harkin

West Indies
1807

John Harkin very slowly and very cautiously raised his head and peered around the rock which concealed him from anyone casually looking in his direction. He took a quick look around. He could see no-one, but his view was partly obscured by a huge outcrop of volcanic rock. Ducking down again he moved crabwise across the ridge for several yards and raised his head again. His view was no longer restricted and he had a good view of most of the bay which lay below him.

The French ship was there, anchored close inshore, a huge tricolour of the Republic flying from the flagstaff in the stem.

They had climbed the steep slope of the headland, skirting around the rocks and the coarse scrub, leaving the lush tropical vegetation a hundred feet below. Up here the soil, what there was of it, was poor and could only sustain the patches of tough grass that seemed to grow everywhere in these islands. The party of five men had climbed with great care for if the French ship was anchored in the bay, as the Captain thought, then they could not afford to be seen. It was almost a certainty that the French Captain would have posted lookouts up here.

This was the second such headland they had scaled that day

looking for the elusive ship. Far off, on the horizon, a bank of white cloud billowed high into the heavens but here there was no shade and they sweated freely as they climbed. But as he climbed and even though he was hot and tired, a part of John had hoped that the bay would be as empty as the other they had searched, that there would be no French ship and no French sailors lying in wait for him, for this was dangerous work.

But there the ship was. John ducked down once more and turned to signal for the Jimmy to come up to join him. As the officer carefully made his way upward, John was able to look past him, down into the bay from which they had climbed and which was almost identical to the one he had just surveyed, except for the five sets of footprints in the sand and his ship, which was anchored in the bay, but much further out than the Frenchman. He knew that on H.M.S. *Relentless* men would be training their telescopes on the small party, watching their every move, waiting for the prearranged signals that would tell the Captain that the ship they had shadowed for much of the previous day had been found.

*

Nine long weeks at sea had yielded nothing. Bermuda had been a welcome distraction at the northernmost point of their patrol, with its English pubs and welcoming women, but they had left that island weeks ago and, despite their vigilance, they had sighted no other ships worthy of their interest, other than a coast-hugger registered to the United States of America. The booty on this trip would amount to nothing and the crew were disgruntled and bored.

The ship was on the homeward leg back to Trinidad, still only marginally south of the known routes usually taken by the Spanish and French ships as they headed for Europe. There was still a chance of an interception, but that chance was diminishing with each passing mile.

The shout of 'sail ho' from the topmast lookout was first heard early on in the morning watch and galvanised the crew into action. They were sailing almost due south and the lookout had been particularly alert to have spotted the tiny patch of white as he looked directly into the rising sun.

'Give us her bearing, mister.'

'Five degrees off the port bow, sir.' The reply was shouted back instantly. All eyes on deck were turned toward that point on the horizon. But from their low vantage point the deck watch could see nothing except the broad expanse of water.

The Captain and the Jimmy arrived on deck, hastily summoned by the Officer of the Watch. Most of the crew were now crowded at the portside rail straining their eyes to catch a glimpse of the ship which could make this patrol a success after all. They could still see nothing but water. The Captain needed confirmation.

'Send the lookout with the best eyes aloft with a telescope, Mr Armitage.'

Within minutes he had his confirmation. The ship was moving away. The stern rail was clearly visible through the telescope. She had two sails for a certainty but may have three, the angle of sight made it difficult to be certain. One thing was certain: she was flying the Tricolour of France from her stern. At last, a chance to get at the enemy.

The Captain quickly ordered the topsails to be lowered, and H.M.S. *Relentless* dropped back below the horizon whilst he considered his options. If his lookouts had been able to see the Frenchman had they themselves been seen? In his experience, lookouts rarely paid as much attention to what was astern as they did to what was possibly ahead, so there was every chance that they had not been spotted, but he needed to be sure. If the ship was a three-master then it would be heavily armed, with more and bigger cannon than *Relentless*. Surprise was the name of the game. It was everything.

If he shadowed the ship during daylight hours and ascertained the course they were following, during the night he could push on and overhaul the ship. It was a period of the new moon with not enough light to see the approach of a ship until it was very close. And at dawn, he calculated, they would be close enough to engage the ship and overwhelm its crew before they had the time to arm themselves and to load the cannon. He had used this tactic before, and each time he had used it, it had proved successful.

They sailed at reduced speed for one hour and then set more sail and tentatively increased speed. Their quarry soon hove into view, following the same course as before which indicated that *Relentless* had not been sighted. They slowly sank back below the horizon again to repeat the process three more times. Each time the ship reappeared exactly where it should have been: same course, same speed. On the fourth occasion the shout of 'ship ho' was followed almost simultaneously by the shout 'land ho'. A small island was coming into view and the French ship was on course to make landfall there.

*

John Harkin and the Jimmy moved further along the ridgeline and then raised their heads above the rocks. From where they were secreted they had a panoramic view into the bay below them. Surprisingly they could not see any French lookouts.

The Jimmy took out his short telescope, scanned the decks of the French ship and then turned his attention to the beach, where men could be seen manhandling what appeared to be water barrels. It took only a few seconds to see what he wanted to see and then they dropped back out of sight. They returned to where the others, two marines and a signalman, were waiting. The Jimmy gave the order and the signalman sent the prearranged signal with his flags. The ship below seemed immediately to be galvanised into frantic activity, even as the signal came back to proceed as planned. Men were seen scurrying to and fro and whilst the company of marines were disembarking into the small boats which already lay alongside in the water, the anchors were being raised and the ship was preparing to get under way.

The plan had been gone over time and time again until no-one could be in any doubt as to the sequence of events. The landing party would disable any lookouts posted up on the headland and, when the time was right, would fire upon any French sailors who were ashore, keeping them pinned down and preventing their return to the ship. *Relentless* would engage the ship from the seaward side, the Captain relying on the element of surprise and his ship's speed and manoeuvrability, to give them success.

Taking John with him, the Jimmy climbed back up to the ridgeline, leaving the others to wait for the reinforcements, with orders to follow on post haste. They both raised their heads again. Still there was nothing to be seen in the immediate vicinity. Drawing his sword the Jimmy rose and eased himself over the top. John took a firmer grip on the cutlass he carried and, without thinking, followed close behind. His mouth had suddenly gone very dry but he could still feel the sweat trickling down his spine.

Both men approached the huge piece of volcanic rock and cautiously stepped around it.

The young French Lieutenant had re-buttoned his trousers and was straightening his tunic when he heard the whisper of the footfall. His reflexes were superb and before he had fully completed his turn he had drawn his sword and his left hand was pulling his ceremonial dagger from its sheath. The Jimmy, although prepared for such an encounter, was taken by surprise at the speed of the man's movement and stood no chance. The Jimmy's reactions were much slower. His sword hardly moved.

Fuelled by the surge of adrenalin coursing through him, the Frenchman lunged forward, arm straight and sword pointing in the classic way, just as his swordsmanship instructor had taught him at the Naval Academy in Toulon. The razor-edged point of the sword deflected off the Jimmy's sternum and pierced him at the base of the throat, passed through his windpipe, nicked the jugular vein, cut clean through the carotid artery and exited through the left side of his neck.

The French officer's instructor would have been proud to see how his hours of tuition had been heeded by his student but he would have been less happy at what followed. The Frenchman withdrew his sword and, in his excitement and the heat of the encounter, made a grave error. He lunged again. His sword penetrated the unprotected belly of the Jimmy but he had no need to stab him twice, the Jimmy was already a dead man, his lifeblood pumping freely from the hole in his neck. Surprise and horror showed clearly on his face and his sword fell from his grasp as he sank to his knees. As he sagged forward he pulled the French officer's sword, still lodged firmly in his intestines, down.

John sprang forward and swung his cutlass in a vicious downward arc. The Frenchman had wasted a precious second and his advantage had gone. He had no defence and took the blow in the right shoulder. The naval cutlass, a heavy slashing weapon, smashed through his collar bone and far into the soft flesh between his neck and his chest. The man screamed in agony as the blade penetrated deeply into his chest cavity. The strength of his swing and the violence of the impact had caused John to lose his footing, and in the spray of the Frenchman's bright blood which covered his face and his upper body, John lost his grip on the handle of his weapon.

Still crying out in agony the Frenchman dropped his sword and fell forward against John who, being off balance himself, fell with the man. Fearful for his own life, he wrestled the injured man onto his back and, feeling the dagger between them; he gripped the man's hand, turned the blade and pressed it with all his strength into the man's chest. The Frenchman gurgled and they lay together, enemies locked in a deadly embrace, both covered in the sticky, already congealing, blood.

John pushed the Frenchman aside and rose to his knees. He knelt over the young French officer. He was shaking violently in the aftermath of the encounter and he felt sick from the sight and the strange metallic smell of fresh blood.

The Frenchman was not moving and John assumed he was dead. He got to his feet and crossed to where the Jimmy was slumped against the rock, in a huge pool of his own blood. He had bled to death in seconds. It hardly seemed possible that such a small wound could kill a man so swiftly.

John heard the wet cough from behind and swung to meet the new threat, his heart pounding in his chest. He suddenly realised that he was unarmed and defenceless. His first instinct told him to run, to find a place of safety. But it was not a new enemy. The French officer sprawled on the ground had opened his eyes and was looking up at him. Painfully he raised his arm a few inches. John found himself kneeling over the young man, there was no danger here.

'Vous avez fait pour moi, monsieur. Vous avez pris ma vie de moi, je suis mort.' The Frenchman's voice was low and he seemed to be speaking to himself. 'Je vais plus jamais voir ma France bien-aimée, ni tenir ma belle Teresa dans mes bras mon fils Phillippe se transformer en un homme.'

John leant closer over the man for his voice was faint as the strength drained from his body with the last of his blood. His face was ashen white but he did not seem to be in any pain.

The enormity of what he had done now overwhelmed John.

'I am sorry sir,' he spoke in French and surprise showed in the other man's face. John found it difficult to speak but continued as the tears began to leak from his eyes, 'I never thought to kill you, sir,' he sobbed, 'but I was afraid. I thought that I would be killed myself.'

'You speak good French for a poxed English matelot, eh.' A smile flitted across his face for a split second. His eyes were still bright but his voice was now barely audible. 'But we are still enemies although we have not met before. We have done no harm to each other and yet we fight because someone has said that we should. Is your friend dead?' His eyes moved in the direction of the Jimmy. 'Have I killed your friend?'

John nodded.

'War is a bastard.' He coughed and a bloody froth appeared at the corner of his mouth but he swallowed to stem the flow. 'It makes murderers of us all.' He shivered even though the sun was beating down on the two men. His blue tunic was stained black with blood but John lifted him and held him close, afraid of missing a single word.

The Frenchman looked into John's eyes and seemed to be considering something he could see there.

'Are you a Christian man? Do you attend a church when you are home with your family?' Not waiting, but seeming to know the answer, he whispered, 'Will you say a prayer with me and ask for my forgiveness so that I may leave this place in peace? I ask only that I am remembered with honour and that I died in the service of my country.' He weakly grasped John's hand. The bloody froth had reappeared at his lips.

John was crying openly now.

'Only if you will forgive me. Only if you say you forgive me.'

'Of course I forgive you. It was a good fight, yes? It is a pity I had to lose.' He closed his eyes and John hesitantly began to recite the only prayer that he knew. It seemed strange to be praying here at the top of the headland:

'Our Father who art in Heaven
Hallowed be thy name...'

'My name is Phillippe Girardeau.' John was hardly able to hear the words even though he put his ear close to the man's mouth, but he could feel the slight pressure against his fingers. 'Please remember Phillip Girardeau of Perpignon.'

'For ever and ever.

Amen.'

*

The man was dead and John held him for a few seconds not really knowing what to do. He dragged his hand across his eyes, wiping away the tears.

'I will remember you forever, Phillippe Girardeau. I will never forget you.'

The man having died in front of him, in his arms, had affected him deeply. But years of discipline and training took over. The warnings of his friend Frenchie and the others came back to him. Always be aware of danger. Danger is often where you least expect it. Stay alert, stay ahead of the enemy. Survival can be a matter of luck, but is more often the result of vigilance.

He gently laid the body down on the baking earth and rose to his feet. It was only then that he noticed the Frenchman's boots. His uniform trousers were neatly tucked into them as they encased his calves, reaching almost to his knees. He had never seen such beautiful boots. Even he could see that they were fashioned from the finest and the supplest of leather. Highly polished, they shone brightly in the afternoon sunlight.

He knelt again and without really thinking why, eased the boots off the feet. He started to rise again, clutching the boots, when he realised that the man's dagger was still embedded deeply in his chest. The handle seemed to be made of silver, nicely tooled and with gems worked into the intricate design. Someone would take it, why not he? He pulled the dagger from the wound and, having nowhere else to put it, dropped it into one of the boots.

*

The two French lookouts had been secreted a hundred yards or so further along the ridge and three or four yards below the skyline, where they had a perfect view out to sea. They had been told to keep alert and to keep their eyes open, but they thought that they had a cushy number, much better than heaving water barrels around the

165

beach in the hot sun.

They heard their officer scream and knew straight away that he was in serious trouble. They knew him well having served under him for more than two years, and they knew that only something really bad would make him scream like that. They left their post and quietly and cautiously made their way toward the place where they thought the sound had originated. They moved slowly, not knowing what could have made their officer scream and fearful of what they would find. They crested a slight rise and understood immediately what they were seeing; a British Navy officer on the ground in a pool of blood with his back against a giant rock, and a British sailor, holding a pair of boots, bending over their officer. Neither officer was moving.

In one single motion, both men raised the muskets they carried. The younger of the two, full of bravery until seconds before, discharged his weapon a split second before his fellow, but he had never been in this kind of action before and his nerves were stretched to the limit, and he was afraid. He had not taken careful aim, but he could not miss a target so large at such a short range.

John's mind was elsewhere and he didn't hear the approach of the Frenchmen. He felt the searing pain as the four ounces of lead, travelling at almost the speed of sound, smashed into him even as he heard the sound of the muskets firing. The first musket ball took him through the left buttock, passed easily through the muscle and, on its downward trajectory, mushroomed as it shattered his thigh bone into several jagged pieces. It continued on its path and passed through more soft tissue before coming to a halt inside his knee joint. The hasty shot undoubtedly saved his life as the impact sent him pitching violently forward over the dead body of the French officer for the older and steadier lookout had taken more care and his aim was true. But when the second shot arrived at its mark, the mark was no longer there, and instead of smashing through John's back and into his lungs and maybe his heart, the ball took him high in the shoulder, missing the shoulder blade and the collarbone, and exited through the soft tissue where the shoulder joins the chest, leaving a hole almost big enough to take a man's fist.

As the blackness descended over him and he felt himself falling, John thought he heard the crackle of more musket fire and, from what seemed a very long, long way away, the deep boom of a cannon firing.

CHAPTER 25

H.M.S. Relentless

West Indies
1807

The surgeon selected the scalpel from among his meagre but vicious-looking array of instruments. He knew that the time he had dreaded had arrived. If he was to save the boy he needed to cut deep and take away the source of the infection. If he didn't act now he doubted that the boy would last many more hours. The boy had been in a delirious state for nearly two days now and, standing next to him as the surgeon was, was akin to standing close to the galley stove. The fever was raging through the body that lay on the sodden sheets which covered the wardroom table.

The surgeon was not confident. He was not a trained medical man. Everything he knew about injuries he had learned through bitter experience during his time in the navy, and what he knew about the anatomy of the human body was negligible. But the lead ball was somewhere inside the leg, probably near the knee joint, he guessed. It needed to be cut out. The die was cast. He was determined that he would not lose another man. He straightened his shoulders, picked up the leather strap, and began to strop the blade. At least the blade would be clean and sharp.

*

They had left a row of nine graves when the two ships had eventually sailed from the tiny island. They had buried the Jimmy, the French officer, the two French lookouts, cut down as they fled from the company of British marines who had suddenly appeared, and five other Frenchmen who had died as the first salvo of grapeshot, fired from *Relentless*, had swept, shrieking, across the main deck of the French ship.

The French captain had made a grave error; he had become complacent. Over the years he had replenished the supply of fresh water many times on the tiny island and had never before seen any indication of other ships. The musket shots high up on the headland had distracted him, and lowered the vigilance of his crew for vital seconds as they all rushed to the rail looking upwards. No-one noticed the British ship entering the bay, portside cannons loaded and rolled out ready to fire. *Relentless* closed swiftly to within three hundred yards before firing a single shot from the upper deck gun. At that range the shot was unmissable and devastating, and within seconds five men had died, cut to ribbons by the grapeshot, and many more had been terribly injured. The French captain was uninjured by the whirlwind of destruction which had swept across the main deck of his ship but immediately recognised the hopelessness of his position; more than half his crew ashore, his ship dead in the water and a British warship, already at action stations, within yards.

He struck his colours and surrendered his ship. He would not be seeing France again for a long, long time.

*

The precisely weighed quantity of molten lead had been deliberately dropped from a great height into the cold-water sump, where it cooled rapidly. As it fell, it formed into an almost perfect sphere. For the next two years it was transported around France along with thousands of other similar spheres, as part of the ammunition stocks for a regiment of French Infantry, until the boxes of shot were commandeered by the French Navy and loaded onto a ship bound for French Guyana. There the consignment was re-assigned and part of it found its way aboard the ship which *Relentless* had now captured.

The box of ammunition had spent months in the hold deep in the bowels of the ship, before the box split open in the damp air and with the constant movement, spilling the lead balls among the cockroaches and the other crawling insects. By this time the musket ball was finely coated in poisonous lead oxide powder which was soon joined by the piss and faeces of the numerous rats and mice which lived in the hold, and all this filth was carried by the ball as it smashed into John Harkin.

*

John Harkin had been placed on his right side and was tied securely with strips of canvas to the table. His leg was almost unrecognisable as human. The skin on the thigh was mottled red and black and tight with the obscene swelling. It looked like it could tear open on its own at any minute, from the pressure within. The surgeon checked the ties on his apron and pulled it higher over his chest. Even then it was still long enough to reach the deck.

The swelling made it impossible to locate the lead shot by touch. Taking a deep breath the surgeon selected a point in the back of the thigh, an inch or so above the knee, and pressed the scalpel into the skin.

Twice now the surgeon had been to the water bucket to wash the stinking pus from his hands and to swill out the cotton wadding he was using to mop up the mess. He had located the flattened lead ball and had been manipulating it for minutes trying to dislodge it from its resting place against the back of the cracked kneecap, with no success. It was wedged tight. He took a firm grip on the scalpel once again and started the business of cutting. As he worked, slicing easily through tendon and sinew and ligament, opening up the wound, in the back of his mind he knew the damage he was doing to the vital parts of the joint but knew of no other way to proceed.

Within the hour the misshapen ball was nestling in a jar and the wound had been cauterised, stitched and thoroughly cleaned using some of the Captain's precious brandy. The surgeon made up a poultice using dried turmeric, which he had learned from an old man in India had great antiseptic and healing properties, and lavishly covered the wound. Now only time would tell whether the boy would live or die.

CHAPTER 26

West Gloucestershire
September, 1821

The girl knelt on the damp earth on the bank of the River Wye and dipped the iron pan that she carried into the water. She would have been naked if she had not had a small piece of woollen material draped around her shoulders. She was tethered to a wagon by a thin cord which was tied tightly to her right ankle, but with enough slack to allow her to reach as far as the water's edge.

During the dark night, when the man had briefly nodded off into sleep, she had tried to untie the knot securing the cord to her leg, but the more she struggled to pull the knot loose, the tighter it became. The knot was unlike any other that she had ever seen. In desperation she had contorted herself so as to be able to use her teeth, which were white and sharp, but to no avail, the cord was tough. The other end of the cord was secured to the wagon by a metal shackle, but the man had made sure that the bolt was tight and there was not enough strength in her small fingers to undo it.

It was early morning, in the minutes just before the dawn, and in the failing moonlight a thin mist could be seen creeping slowly over the surface of the running water. It was cold now but all the signs boded well for the coming day. England was enjoying a late 'Indian Summer' and, as it had been for nearly two weeks, the weather promised to be hot and dry later.

The man had been laying full length on his rough blanket close to the small fire watching the girl as she went about her chore but now he stirred. He yawned deeply and contentedly.

It's time I was on the move again, *he thought, as the girl carried the pan of water back to her place near the fire where she had lain for some of the night.* This is a well-used road. People will be about.

He rose slowly from the blanket and moved stiffly over to the cart, stretching his back and his arms and legs as he went. He walked with great care for he wore only an undershirt and was barefooted. Over his shoulder was draped a thick leather belt.

He reached into the back of the cart and his hand found the joint of bacon which he had purchased the previous day from the butcher in the centre of the town, and who had carefully wrapped the meat in a clean piece of muslin cloth. He took the muslin from around the bacon, and, taking his knife from its sheath attached to the belt draped over his shoulder, he cut two thick rashers. The knife was double edged and he had ground it to a fine point and it was sharp, very sharp: sharp enough for a man to shave with. It easily cut through the thick bacon rind.

He placed the rashers on an enamelled plate which he had also taken from the back of the cart. He almost reverentially wiped his knife on the muslin, checking to make sure that no trace of the bacon remained on it and returned it to its place on the belt. He rewrapped the bacon and placed it carefully back into the cart. The bacon would be called upon to sustain him for another meal or two, at least.. He did not want to stop to buy victuals again until he was many miles away from this place.

He took up the enamelled plate and found a thick china mug among the goods in the cart. He carried both back to the fire.

A large flat stone and a billy-can of water were already placed in the embers of the fire that he had used to bake some potatoes the night before. He placed the rashers of bacon on the stone. Immediately there rose the aroma of bacon frying in its own fat and his mouth watered in anticipation of the taste to come. The girl had taken her place on the other side of the fire and the man noticed her raise her head as she also smelt the bacon. She licked her lips. But bacon would be wasted on her.

By the time he had made a brew of tea with the hot water in the billy-can the bacon was ready. He liked his bacon fat burned black and crispy. He slid the bacon from the stone onto his plate using a twig and sat down on the fallen tree that he had been using the night before as a seat. He waited until the meat had cooled enough for him to pick it up with his fingers. He put the meat to his mouth and began to eat. As he ate he studied the girl who was crouched on the ground on the other side of the fire. She was also watching him intently.

*

He had first sighted the group of children late the previous day in the meadow and he had watched them for a while through the thick Hawthorn hedgerow that separated the meadow from the lane. He loved children. He loved boys and girls almost equally for when they were young, and the younger the better; there was not that much difference between them.

His preference though, was for young girls, like the one that hung back from the others as the group of children made their way home. She seemed to him to be about seven or eight years old. She knelt down in a patch of daisies and orchids that grew everywhere here. She only needed a few more to finish the daisy-chain she was making to take home to her mother. Her friends had gone slowly on their way and left her all alone.

When the girl eventually emerged from the meadow into the lane he was waiting for her. He was well prepared, as always, and in just a few minutes he was on the move again, the girl bundled up and crammed into the blackness that was the box. He was on his way to the Kerne Bridge which spanned the River Wye between Bishopswood and Walford and he knew of a place only a mile from the crossing, surrounded by a thick stand of trees that was perfect for his purposes. No-one would find them there.

It had taken over an hour to reach the place and by then it was dark, the road only lit by pale moonlight, but he knew the place well and could have found it if he had been blindfolded. Memories of the last time he had used this place had come back to him.

Then, the girl he had brought here had been much older. She had been small for her age and he had been fooled into thinking she was younger than she actually was. She had been strong and feisty and had put up more of a fight than he had expected from someone so slight. He had needed to hit her hard to subdue her and she had become unconscious. He had ripped the clothes from her body. He was surprised to see that she had pubic hair between her legs and her breasts were small but well formed: she was well on the way to womanhood.

She had regained her senses faster than he had anticipated and she started fighting him again and screaming. He had been afraid of being discovered and had silenced her forever. He had had no fun then, and even less satisfaction. But he had learned from the encounter and was always careful now to choose younger victims: they were always easier to pacify and manipulate to his ends.

This young victim had stopped crying now but was still making a quiet whimpering sound that seemed to come from deep inside her being, for he had sorely used her body during the night hours. He had liked this one more than most. She was a pretty little thing with fair skin and light brown, almost blonde hair. She was slim, just the way he preferred them to be.

He had finished the bacon now and he threw the rind into the embers where it sizzled loudly and briefly flared into flame before dying back to become just another ember like the ones it lay amongst. He watched the bacon burn before draining his cup of the black bitter tea. His attention turned back to the girl. Once again he experienced the feeling of power as he saw her helplessness and vulnerability.

'Come here, girl,' he said quietly. He only needed to speak softly to her for at the sound of his voice she was filled with fear. She quickly scrambled around the fire to him. He pointed with his finger and she fell to her knees on the ground in front of him. He reached out with his left hand and took a handful of her hair, grasping it tightly. She sobbed out loud. He held her still for a few seconds and then slowly drew her face into his naked groin.

'Suck him,' he whispered. 'Suck him just one more time, and then you are done.'

The scant piece of woollen material slipped from her shoulders and he could plainly see the two huge wheals which criss-crossed her upper back and shoulders, the result of the blows he had given her the previous night with the nut-stick he had cut from the hedge. She hadn't dared disobey him again after the beating.

He had instructed her well and she knew what to do to please him, and at this moment she wanted nothing more than to please him. Even this was better than the things he had submitted her to during the night and she dreaded the pain of the nut-stick across her back.

He would have liked to have put the girl back in the box to use for a few more days but he would make his destination later today and to take her would be impossible. By the time the girl child had brought him to his climax the knife was already gripped in his right hand. He would have liked to have played with her body using the blade; a few cuts here and a few cuts there, but it was getting late and he had no time left. He needed to hurry now.

Skin and young flesh are no match for finely honed steel and the thin blade slid easily between her third and fourth ribs and into her lungs. She tried to shout out but he held her face tightly against his belly for the few seconds it took for her lungs and throat to start to fill with blood. When he slackened his grip she was only able to make a wet gurgling sound.

He lifted her head so that he could see her face in the brightening light as the dawn started to break. He liked to watch their faces. He liked to see their eyes. Especially their eyes. He liked to watch the lights in their eyes go dim and then go out altogether as they breathed for the last time.

A pink froth showed at the corner of her mouth, but the girl had ceased to struggle against his grip as though knowing and accepting her fate. She returned his stare evenly. A frown creased her smooth forehead and puzzlement showed in her already dull eyes.

A small amount of blood oozed from the wound as he tenderly withdrew the blade from her ribs. She winced. He had chosen the spot to stab her well and knew there would be little, if any, bleeding. He selected another spot and very slowly but firmly pushed the knife into her body again, this time the blade went up under her breastbone and into her heart. He knew where to apply the knife for he had done this many times before. Intently he watched her, savouring every moment as she tried to breathe. A sigh escaped from her lips and she shuddered. A huge tear rolled down her cheek and she died.

When he was sure that she was truly dead he withdrew the blade and gently laid her body on the ground next to the fire. Her body seemed even smaller and frailer now. Using his knife he cut the cord from her ankle, taking great care not to mark the skin. He walked to the cart and undid the shackle. Coiling and tying the cord neatly he placed it in the back of the cart alongside his neatly folded jacket and trousers. The girl's clothes were beside his and he picked up her dress and used it to meticulously clean the blade of his knife which he then placed in his belt.

He picked up the rest of the girl's clothes and studied them, running the material between his fingers and lifting them to his face. He picked up her tiny boots. He liked her boots. He pulled the small box from its secret place and placed one of them into it atop the other small items of children's clothing which it already contained. The boot would remind him of the girl on the cold winter nights which lay ahead.

He pulled on his own boots, took a short handled spade and moved off a few yards into the trees. It did not take him long to scrape away a shallow grave. Here the leaf mould was thick and the ground was soft and damp. He returned to the fire and lifted the body of the girl. He placed the body in the shallow grave and when it was covered to his liking he replaced the spade in the cart and removed his boots again.

Taking the girl's clothes he went back to the fire, took up his cup and plate, moved to the water's edge and waded into the shallows. He washed himself, his cup and plate thoroughly and used the girls dress and underskirts to dry himself.

When he was done he tossed the clothes into the water and watched them drift slowly away on the current.

Within minutes he was fully dressed. He poured the pan of water the girl had fetched over the embers and then used his foot to scrape a covering of earth over the blood on the ground where she had died. He picked up the piece of woollen material and tossed it, his cup and plate and the pan into the back of the cart. He took a long, last look around the clearing. At last he was satisfied that he had left no indication that he had ever been there.

*

The brass bell, with its covering of green patina, hung on its piece of frayed rope next to the toll-gate, but he had no need to ring it for the old woman who collected the tolls had already risen and was out and about, feeding her few plump chickens that she kept in the small pen next to the house. They viciously fought each other over every little scrap waste food, cabbage leaf and stale bread that she threw among them.

The woman was approaching her fifty-fourth year and the weathered-looking skin on her hands and face told a tale of a hard life, most of it outdoors. She was a devious woman and told everyone who would listen that she was nearly blind and could hardly move for the pain of the 'screws' in her joints but, even so, she expertly caught the farthing that the man tossed to her and, all in the same movement, it disappeared into the leather satchel which hung around her middle.

She unlocked the gate and pulled it wide for her first customer of the day and he passed through and made his way onto the bridge. He had passed this way many times over the previous dozen years or so but they had never exchanged a single word. She had no idea of his name or where he came from or where he was going. There were words written on the sides of his cart but they meant nothing to her. She had never learned to read and write, although she did know that the words on the cart started with the letter 'J'. That had been the first letter of her husband's name and he had pointed it out to her many times.

She may not have been able to read but she knew a good-looking fellow when she saw one and in her eyes he was certainly the most handsome man she had seen in many a day. Her husband had not been the only young man who had come calling on her when she was a young girl. In fact there had been plenty of male callers and hardly any of them went away disappointed for she was a 'generous' girl. But she had made her choice and had married the man who, she had to admit, had excited her most, but who turned into the drunkard who was to be her husband for the next twenty-three years, until he had fallen into the river as he walked back from the Forge Hammer in the nearby village of Lydbrook one dark night, with a belly full of strong ale. At the time it had been a sort of relief to her that he had drowned. No more drunken rages. No more shouting or rowing and no more slaps and punches. But on occasion she had missed the brute especially on dark winter nights when her bed was cold and empty. She had to admit to being lonely. Sure, there had been a few men, travellers, who she had enticed into her bed, but none wanted to stay for longer than an hour or two and the last had been such a long time ago.

She watched the young man now as he made his way up the incline on the far side of the river that would take him to Goodrich village. On the skyline the ruined medieval castle loomed above him to his right and the steep rise of Coppice Hill was to his left. Both were now bathed in sunshine but it would be at least another hour before the sun's rays would reach the valley floor. There was a curve in the lane and the man passed from view among some trees.

'I'll wager I could teach you a thing or two under the duckdown,' she said out loud, but no-one heard her, only the chickens. 'I reckon I could make you stand up nicely.' She laughed at her own crudity and returned to feeding her chickens.

In the trees the cart crested the rise and, at the meeting of the two lanes there, the man turned to the right onto the road that would take him on to Hereford. He was sobbing now and the salty tears rolled down his cheeks.

CHAPTER 27

John Harkin

Exton, Devon
1807

He just stood there in the opening that led into the garden. He had unlatched the gate but was reluctant to proceed further. Everything looked the same, the cottage and the garden, except there were more weeds than he remembered and generally there was an unkempt air about the place. He was aware that the horse and wagon was still standing in the lane behind him.

There was a sudden commotion and two dogs erupted from the barn to his left. They ran towards him, yelping and barking excitedly, ears and tails flying in the slight breeze. They reached him and skittered around him, bashing into each other, trying to be the one to get closest.

'Easy, boy.' He heard the gentle voice of the wagon driver behind him but was unsure if the words were to calm him or the horse.

He looked up as he heard the door of the cottage opening and a grey-haired woman appeared, wiping her hands on her apron as she stepped into the sunlight, obviously attracted by the noise from the dogs.

*

The ship that had brought him back to England from the West Indies had anchored in Plymouth Sound late in the evening two days before, and had entered the dockyard on the morning tide the next day.

In the eight long months since he had been injured he had lost a lot of weight and his clothes, hanging on his thin frame, looked like he had borrowed them from a much larger man. There weren't any outward signs of the damage caused by the lead shot except a few ragged scars and, of course, the makeshift crutches, knocked up from a few spars by the carpenter aboard *Relentless*.

Inside though, John was on the brink of a black abyss. Two emotions dominated his every waking minute; hopelessness and, at really bad times, total despair, brought on by his physical condition. He had tried many times to walk without the support of the crutches and, no matter how hard he tried, he always ended up grovelling on the floor in agony. He had reached such a low point in his life that he did not care too much whether he lived or died.

And sleep brought him no respite. He dreamed constantly; the same black dream over and over again in which he repeatedly stabbed a man who spoke to him in the French language, but he could not understand a word of what he said, and the man smiled constantly at him as he pushed the knife further and further into his body until his arm disappeared into the man's chest and the blood cascaded from his nose and mouth and they became covered in the sticky substance, and they were bound together and he could not get away. And he would wake up covered in sweat and the pain in his knee throbbed in time with his thundering heartbeat. He dreaded sleep as he dreaded waking.

*

And now he was alone with his demons. In less than an hour after the ship had tied up alongside, John had been put ashore and, without ceremony, the Navy had said goodbye to him forever. He was on his own now. He stood on the quayside and watched the hubbub of activity as the ship replenished and knew that he was no longer a part of all that. He was no longer needed. He was a cripple. The Navy had taken all he had to offer, except his life, and now it was discarding him. He was no longer of any use. He took a deep breath of the familiar salty air and he turned his face away from the ship and hobbled towards the huge gates that marked the limits of the Royal Dockyard.

He took directions to the coach-house and before long he was aboard the carriage which would take him as far as Exeter. His crutches and the canvas bag which contained his meagre belongings, everything he owned in the world, were securely tied to the roof.

They reached Exeter late in the afternoon and he stayed overnight at the coaching inn. He made inquiries but there were no coaches plying between Exeter and Exton, Exton being just a small village on what was virtually a dirt track. There was nothing for it, he would have to walk. Maybe he would be lucky and get a ride on a farm cart or with a local trader returning from the city. He started the long and, for him, almost impossible, walk home.

Painfully slowly he had reached the outskirts of the city when he heard the sound of the wagon coming up behind him. He shuffled as best he could onto the grass at the side of the road, but instead of passing him by, the wagon came to a halt.

'You look like you could do with a ride, lad.' He hadn't heard the accent in years. 'I'm going all the way down to Exmouth, stopping off at Exton, if that's any good to you.'

'Aye for sure, a ride would be most welcome. I'm making for Exton. If you could take me there I would be most grateful. I fear I could not make it all the way on my own but I am afraid, sir, that I cannot climb aboard without some assistance.'

With the driver's help he was soon sitting uncomfortably on the plank that served as a seat, his canvas bag stowed safely in the back of the wagon among the cargo of bales and crates, his crutches at his feet on the running board. The driver took up the reins. The horse, without any urging, took up the strain and they moved off at a leisurely pace.

They had travelled for several hundred yards before the driver spoke.

'Do you live in Exton then, lad?'

'I did when I was a boy but I have been away for a long time.' He thought again of home and the reception that he would get. Would his mother and father still be angry with him for leaving home without their blessing and without even saying goodbye? He had thought of home and his mother and father and Lizzie almost constantly since he had said goodbye to his friends aboard H.M.S. *Relentless*. He missed his friends, the people he had come to trust and rely on, especially Frenchie. He even missed the Master, the old rogue. But that life was now gone, consigned to the past.

The sadness that he felt must have showed. The driver said, not unkindly, 'Something appears to be ailing you, lad? Are you in trouble?'

'Perhaps. I think that I may be in trouble with my parents.' He had not really talked to anyone since he had left Trinidad and, for some reason which he could not understand he felt the need to talk to this man, a perfect stranger. Now that he had started the words came tumbling out.

'You see I left home years ago without really saying goodbye. I was too cowardly to face them and just left a note for them with my sister, and that wasn't fair on her either. I have had no contact with them since that day. And now I don't know if they will welcome me back or tell me to go away again. I don't know what I would do if that happened, I have missed them so and I do love them.' *And I am a cripple now and useless to everyone,* he thought bitterly. They rode on in silence, a silence which was only broken by the sound of the horse's hooves and the creaking of the wagon and the rumbling of the wheels on the uneven hard surface.

'Do I know your parents, lad? I do a lot of business around and about Exton.'

'My father is a stockman and has spent all his working life on the farm at Larkhill.' John hesitated for a second. 'He wanted me to follow in his footsteps.'

'I have delivered to Larkhill often. The only stockman I know there goes by the name James Harkin, a good man. Could that be your father?'

John nodded his head in the affirmative. It seemed that everyone knew everyone in the countryside.

The driver suddenly turned and looked at John.

'I remember now. James Harkin had a son who ran away to join the Navy. He was only a boy. I think his name was John. Are you

John Harkin? Are you the boy who went to fight the French?'

John nodded his head again. 'For my sins. Yes. I am John Harkin.'

'And this is what they did to you?' He shoved the crutches with the toe of his boot.

'Aye. This is what they did to me, and worse for many more like me.'

The rest of the journey went by slowly with little or no conversation between the two men and when they reached the junction with the lane which led to John's parents' cottage, without a word and much to John's surprise, the driver guided the horse into the narrow opening. After a mile or so they halted outside the gateway to his home. The driver jumped to the ground and helped John down. He handed him his bag and crutches, but he hadn't finished. He laid his hand on John's shoulder.

'Have faith in the capacity for people to forgive almost anything of those they love.' He took John's hand and held it for a second or two. 'I am pleased to have met you, John Harkin. May your God watch over you.' He backed away and John turned his attention to the gate.

*

'Who is it? How can I help you?'

The woman took a step or two down the garden path. She didn't altogether recognise the tall young man who stood at the gate, but something about him looked familiar, the way he stood with his head tilted slightly to one side. She took another step, squinting with eyes not as good as they used to be. But she, even with her bad eyesight, could not mistake the shock of badly cut blond hair and the deep blue eyes in the deeply tanned face of her son.

Her hands suddenly flew to her face and she shrieked.

'John? John, is it you? Is it really you?' She took a tentative step forward. 'It is you, isn't it? Please God, let it be my John.' And suddenly she was sure, as sure as only a mother can be. She turned and shouted back through the doorway. 'Dad, quick. It's our John, he's home. He's home from the war. He's come back to us.' She was crying openly now and, abandoning all restraint, she ran down the path and enveloped John in her beefy embrace.

'What have they done to you?' Through her tears he had noticed the crutches at last. 'You are hurt. Dad, come quick, our John's back and he's hurt.'

A man appeared in the doorway and, after a moment of hesitation, he too ran down the path and put his arms around his wife and the grown-up boy he knew instantly to be his son. Tears streamed down his lined face, something that had not happened since the birth of his daughter, years before.

They were all crying and talking at once, and the dogs barked even louder and tried to get closer and nobody noticed the driver climb back aboard the wagon and start on his way. He tipped his cap towards the family; he knew that everything would be alright.

'Yes, I am pleased to have met you, John Harkin,' he said to himself. 'And I am pleased for your family.' He tried to smile but failed as the memories came back again. Once upon a time, a long time ago, before Napoleon Bonaparte, he too had had a son.

CHAPTER 28

Lizzie Harkin

Exton, Devon
1807

John Harkin's father got to his feet as he heard the coach approaching. He stretched and rubbed life back into his backside; the milestone that he had been perched on had been convenient alright, but very hard and unforgiving. This was the third coach today and he hoped it would be the one and his long wait would be over.

The letter in answer to his desperate cry for help, posted over a week ago, had arrived the day before yesterday and said that she would leave London immediately and would arrive today. If anyone could help, she could. He had been waiting since just after dawn, but he was not bored. Suspecting that the wait may be a long one, he had taken with him several pamphlets and a few copies of the *Gazette*.

And there had been no lack of company, during his wait. This was the main road between Exeter and Exmouth and carried all of the traffic which plied between the two. To his eyes, a staggering number of coaches, wagons and carts of all descriptions had passed him as he sat on the milestone or as he occasionally strolled up and down the hedgerows restoring some circulation into his cramped muscles.

Most of the drivers and the occasional passenger acknowledged him with a wave or a shout and several had even stopped and sat with him for a short while, discussing the weather or the state of the country. He heard shouted comments like 'you look like you're waiting for God' or laughingly, 'I hear you were only a boy when you began waiting here?'

He had even been quoted a poem about 'standing and staring and watching the world go by' and one driver had stopped his wagon and had dismounted and shared his bread and cheese. When the bread was finished the man had taken a final swallow from the cider jug and had remounted the wagon. Before the wagon moved off, the man had surprised James by asking how his son was fairing.

'I don't think there is anything which can be done for his leg. We are resigned. We think he will never walk properly again. He will never by fit and strong as he should be. But we are more worried about his mind; we fear that we are losing him. He lives somewhere we cannot reach and he tells us that in that place he is so alone and frightened, and sometimes we know that he thinks about his death and we are afraid he will kill himself.' James had spoken without thinking, without questioning how the man knew his son or of him. The words just spilled out.

The man reached down from the wagon and grasped James' hand.

'As you care for your animals so someone is caring for you and yours. Help is at hand, believe me.' And then he was away, rumbling up the road and out of sight.

James stared after him. Help is at hand? He sat down again.

'I hope so. Good Lord, John needs it.'

*

The coach had hardly stopped when the woman erupted from it, covered the few yards of grass verge like a whirling dervish and thrown herself into the outstretched arms of the waiting man.

'Dad. Dad, it's so good to see you. It's so good to be home. I was afraid you wouldn't be here.'

She hugged him tight and kissed him roundly on the cheek, and then did it again. He was aware of the faces at the windows of the coach and felt the colour rising in his cheeks. He tried to gently restrain her but she promptly kissed him again. He gave in to his emotions and hugged her back. This was his girl. This was his Lizzie.

She had come back.

On the long, long walk back to the cottage her father talked of John. He talked about his physical condition, his weakness, his inability to walk, his lethargy, the lack of appetite, and he warned her about the weight loss and how John now looked; bedraggled and skinny.

But mostly he talked of John's mental state. He talked of the terrible black moods and the silences that would last for weeks, of his retreat into a place they could not reach and of the fear which showed in his eyes. And of the hopelessness that they all felt. He told her of the lack of emotion and his lack of interest in the things he used to love as a boy. And he told her about their fear that John would take his own life, that one day soon he would no longer be with them.

The last few hundred yards they walked in silence, each lost in their own thoughts. Lizzie looked around at the now familiar landscape and felt a feeling of déjà vu, of having done this exact same thing before. She was coming home, and something told her it would be for good.

She reached out and took her father's hand. He turned his hand over and gripped her hand tightly, as though seeking comfort. They looked at each other but neither smiled. There was something strange about her father that she had not seen before, but could not quite put her finger on the change.

If she could have seen inside his head she would have cried for him. He was desolate and was weeping for his boy. Had it been him who, with his insistence that John follow him onto the land, had driven him away and into the Navy? Now his boy was home and desperately needing his help but he was out of his depth and did not know what to do for the best. He felt the full weight of his impotency and he could feel his boy slipping away, and he had been theirs for such a short time.

Despite her father's warnings Lizzie was still not prepared for the changes that had taken place in her brother. She was sure that if he hadn't still got the blond hair and his gorgeous blue eyes, she could have passed him bye and not known him. She had envisioned changes, but nothing like this. She rushed across the kitchen and gathered her brother up in her arms. Through her tears she whispered, 'Oh, John. Oh my little brother. What has happened to you? What have they done to you?'

*

By any means at her disposal Lizzie would get John out of the cottage. Today, being another fine day, she had bullied and cajoled him into the dog-cart and driven him into Exton. He was reluctant to go with her but she was stronger willed than him and eventually he had to give way. It wasn't the first time he had been into town in the past few weeks, this being probably the seventh or eighth time, but it hadn't gotten any easier for him to face the people of the town.

His sister usually sat him on the barrel close to the blacksmith's shop and in full view of everyone on the street. She would go to the inn across the road and buy him a jar of ale, which he would drink disconsolately whilst she went about her business. She usually took her time; dawdling in the few shops, giving ample opportunity for something, anything, to happen, and for John to at least speak to someone. So far he had not.

*

'Mister?' The hesitant voice hardly penetrated the fog in Johns brain. 'Mister?'

He had been in Barbados. He had been enjoying his time ashore with Frenchie, Lefty, and Jug. Now, it seemed, he spent most of his waking hours dreaming of the past, relief from the darkness that constantly filled his days. It was a time when he had been happy and fit and had seemed invincible. Then, he and his friends could do whatever they chose and no-one laughed at them. Then, no-one thought of him as being different, thought of him as a cripple, an oddity. No-one stared at him then.

'Mister?' the voice came again, louder but still not too loud.

The small voice penetrated the fog and John dragged his mind back to the present and he slowly turned to face the voice. The boy, as small as the voice, stood four or five yards away in his oversized hand-me-down coat, his flat cap had managed to become skewed on his head which contrived to give him a rakish look that was out of place on one so young. He was about ten years younger than John, maybe nine or ten years of age.

186

'Mister? Are you Mister John Harkin, mister?'

Something about the small boy touched him deep inside and he felt compelled to answer.

'Yes, lad. I am John Harkin,' he answered very quietly. 'Do I know you?'

'I don't think so, mister, but I've been sent to talk to you by my dad.'

More confident now that John had spoken softly to him.

'Go on then, what is it your dad wants you to say?' What had this boy's dad to do with him?' John was of a mind to dismiss the boy, to return to the past, to better times.

'My dad says that you joined the Navy when you were not much older than I am.'

John said nothing.

'My dad says that you joined the Navy to fight the French.' John nodded silently, not knowing, or really caring, what was coming.

'My dad says that you saved my mum and me from the French invaders.' The boy pressed on.

'My dad says that you protected the country and were shot for your trouble and you have been treated badly ever since.' He seemed to have got to the end of what he had to say, or maybe he was disconcerted by John's silence, for he fell silent himself.

John became aware that the normal sounds of the street and the hammering had stopped. He looked around and people were standing quietly in the street listening. It was as though the whole town had come to a standstill, waiting. A man and a woman arm-in-arm, an old woman with a wicker basket full of what looked like vegetables, a farmhand who had been leading a huge horse, a few shopkeepers, the Shoemaker, a man who stood in the entrance to the inn, the Blacksmith and John's sister, who stood quietly off to one side. All of them had been listening intently. The boy hadn't finished yet. He took a tentative step forward.

'My dad says that you are a bloody hero, and no mistake.' His face reddened as he realised that in his excitement he had repeated the swear word and he pressed on quickly, hoping that no-one would notice.

'My dad says that it would be a – a – a,' he fumbled for the word, "onour if you would take a drink with him.' He looked pleased that he had remembered the words.

The boy stepped forward and for the first time John noticed that the boy carried a pewter pot in his right hand. He held the pot out towards him.

'My dad says that he is sorry, but he only had a farthing left and it would only buy half a pint.'

He looked over towards the inn and the man there raised his own pot in salute. John looked into the half-full pot and raised his eyes back to the inn, but the man was gone back inside. He took the pot from the boy and raised it to his lips. A tear started from his right eye and slowly rolled down his cheek. Soon there were two wet tracks down his face. He hadn't cried for a long, long time but now the floodgates opened and he cried openly for everyone to see. He no longer cared if people laughed at him or not. Let them do their worst.

The boy stepped up close to him and reached out a hand to touch John's arm.

'I want to be a hero like you, mister. Please don't cry.'

'Aye, lad. Don't cry. We all feel the same about what has happened to you. We are all praying that things will come right for you.' The blacksmith had come up behind him and now laid a huge hand on his shoulder and squeezed as gently as he would have squeezed a baby, before turning away and going back to the forge. He blew his nose loudly on a piece of cotton waste.

People in the street began to move again and resumed going about their business. The noise levels rose. The young boy tried a salute and then turned and ran across the road to disappear into the gloomy interior of the inn. Everything returned to what passed for normal, except in John Harkin's self-pitying view of the world.

Some bloody hero, he thought. *I can't even cross the road without falling in a heap. The Navy chucked me out and I am so useless I can't even find any work. And look at me now, blubbing like a baby just because a man showed me some kindness and a boy said something nice to me. What kind of hero is that? I should have listened to Lizzie the morning I left home.*

Lizzie had witnessed the whole scene. With tears streaming down her face she ran over to her beloved brother and hugged him as tight as she could. Together they cried. He spilled his beer down her dress but she didn't care. He had shown some emotion at last. Perhaps now she could help him.

*

Several hours later the Shoemaker was making his way home to his house on the edge of town. He stepped onto the grass bordering the lane as a trap carrying two people came towards him, pulled by a beautiful grey horse. He tipped his cap as the trap passed and the Major and his wife acknowledged him in return with a wave of the hand. He stared long and hard at the trap as it went on its way into town, an idea suddenly forming in his brain.

CHAPTER 29

Dorcas Teague

Dover
1807

Dorcas Teague was ready to die. In fact she wanted the release of death more than anything in the world. It wasn't just the jagged pain deep in her belly or the constant crippling cramps that never seemed to give her any respite. Yes, she was in physical pain but the pain was nowhere near the torture she was feeling from the mental anguish and turmoil she was in. She was broken completely.

She was being used by a man she despised for his own pleasure, and had given birth to a monster by him, a monster that had torn the insides out of her. The man professed to love her but how could she feel anything other than loathing for a man who had done what he had done? He had taken her house and all her property from her, left her penniless and dependent on his handouts, handouts which always seemed to come with a price. A terrible price.

She had allowed him to control her eldest daughter and to put her to work as a whore, there was no other word for it. Her daughter was a whore. She had even condoned his actions in the very beginning when she so wanted to believe that he was their benefactor. Now he was taking her second daughter down the same road and she could not stop it happening. She was powerless, ashamed and distraught.

The family had always enjoyed a certain standing in the town. Her husband had worn the mantle of successful businessman, a man of means, a man not without a little influence. An employer, but she had seen neither hide nor hair of her husband or word of where he might be, for months. He could be dead for all she knew. What a fool she had been. She had lived in a false utopia. She could see that now, now it was too late to do anything about it. She was ashamed of where they had ended up and she felt nothing but disgust.

She had spoken to her daughter, Agnes, but the girl had just laughed everything off. She had taken to the work and was enjoying the life and the finery she could now afford, she neither could nor would ever give the life up, and her mother knew that she was past redemption.

She had to find a way to rid herself of all her cares and worries and as the dark clouds descended over her once again she made up her mind. It would not be too long before she left this world, leaving all behind.

CHAPTER 30

Nathaniel Leadbitter

London
1807

He gazed out of the window and studied the house as the driver of the carriage slowed the pair of chestnut geldings to a walk and then brought them to a halt precisely opposite the steps that led up to the front door. The house had an imposing air and sat well in the quiet street in Knightsbridge. A man-servant had appeared at the top of the steps and Mister Leadbitter waited for him to unfold the step and open the door to the passenger compartment.

He blinked in the sudden bright light that flooded through the open door for he had partially drawn the blinds and dozed most of the way from the overnight stop outside Peterborough. As he got older he found travel becoming more and more tedious with each passing day.

He had daydreamed about the events of the last month or so. The wedding of his eldest daughter, now Mrs Scarsbridge of Scarsbridge House, had been and gone and he was now returning to Dover, to the one place he truly felt at 'home'. And to Louisa, the woman he now knew he loved more than anyone in the world, and, of course, to the girl Agnes, now a regular bed-mate also. He felt content. He had everything; wealth, a comfortable lifestyle, the respect of his peers in the city, good friends in Dover and two beautiful women, although one was not much more than a girl, who catered to his every need. If it hadn't been for the pain from the 'screws' in his joints and the swelling which had appeared recently on his jawbone under his chin, everything would have been perfect.

He would conclude his business here as quickly as he could and be on his way. He had made up his mind to try to reach Dover and the 'girls' this evening if possible.

But the journey north had been important to him and his family. The arrangements had been carefully made and the wedding had passed without a hitch, as he knew it would. His wife and daughter had 'chosen' a much older man, a true member of the gentry, as her husband, and he had been led to the alter like a lamb to the slaughter. Nathaniel felt sorry for the man, though not too much, for he had one less child to worry about and, besides which, he had not taken to the man, finding him uncultured and uncouth to boot. He wondered how his daughter could possibly like such a man much less marry him. But she had made her choice and when you make the bed you cannot complain at the making when you lie in it. At least the five thousand pounds a year allowance he had settled on her, which could not be touched by her new husband, would give her some sort of independence.

His ageing knees and hip joints had stiffened after the long hours of sitting in the swaying coach and he clumsily descended the steps to the pavement with the help of the servant. Just as clumsily he climbed the steps to the house, surprised to note that there was nothing about the house to indicate the nature of the business within. No brass plaques, no name-plates. The house was completely anonymous. He assumed the people calling here did not want their business known. Leaning heavily on his stick, he crossed the small portico and passed through the open doorway. He found himself in a cool and elegantly decorated hallway with a beautiful, highly carved stairway curving up to his left. The servant passed by him and knocked lightly on a door to his right. Not waiting for a reply the man opened the door wide and beckoned Nathaniel to enter the room beyond.

Despite being without a coat and being dressed only in shirt-sleeves, the middle-aged man sitting behind the mahogany desk still managed to look distinguished and businesslike at the same time. As Nathaniel entered the room the man rose swiftly and came round the desk, hand outstretched in greeting.

'My lord, at last we meet, and you are exactly on time.' His voice was moderated low, probably deliberately so, and there was no trace of accent or dialect.

'I should thank my driver for that more than any good judgement on my part, sir. And please, address me by my given name, Nathaniel. After all, the nature of our business is purely personal.'

'Very well then. But only if you will use my given name, Richard.'

CHAPTER 31

Louisa Deschamps

Dover
1807

There was an air of quiet excitement about the house on Southdown Road as there had been ever since the arrival of the letter three days before, informing Louisa of her beloved Nathaniel's return to Dover.

For most of the day, Louisa had scurried to and fro, checking this and checking that. She wanted everything to be perfect.

She had sent Cissy to buy extra food including the best joint of mutton she could find, now stewing nicely on the black lead range.

New bottles of Porter and Sherry stood on the sideboard. The house had been given a spring-clean and the smell of lavender and beeswax hung in the air in every room.

Louisa had made sure that her appointments book was clear for the whole of today and tomorrow and had instructed Agnes to do likewise. She was like a small child and could hardly contain herself in her excitement.

Together with Cissy she had gone through her wardrobe several times before deciding on the turquoise dress, the dress which had no shoulder straps and seemed to be held up by gravity alone. They had chosen the lacy underwear and petticoats, the most seductive she possessed, and the ones that she knew Nathaniel liked above all. They laid the clothing out on the bed and Cissy went off to prepare Louisa's bath. She would be at her best tonight.

Nathaniel was due back in Dover this evening or early tomorrow morning. He had been away for far too long. She could hardly wait in her longing to see him again.

CHAPTER 32

Nathaniel Leadbitter

London
1807

The physical examination had been painstakingly thorough and had taken longer than Nathaniel had anticipated. The doctor, for that was what the man was, had come highly recommended by his friend Ben, Lord Carforth.

'He is the best in England, if not the known world,' was how the doctor had been described by his friend. 'If he can't cure your ailments then they can't be cured at all.'

Nathaniel had sat in the chair clothed only in some kind of cotton smock which revealed more than it concealed. The doctor had started with his toenails and the soles of his feet whilst he had tried not to squirm as the cool hands moved over him, tickling. They moved to his ankles, up his calves and gently but firmly probed his knee joints.

'How long have you had the pain here?' The doctor had one hand behind the left knee whilst his other hand grasped the leg above the ankle.

Nathaniel tried to remain stoical as the joint was flexed left and right, then straightened and the pain washed over him from deep inside the knee.

'Almost five months now, but both knees have become more painful in the last six or seven weeks.'

The doctor rose, crossed to the desk, and made a scribbled note on a pad.

'Is there a history of joint pain in your family? Do you know of anyone else who has or had the same complaint?'

'Not that I can recall, no.'

Another quickly made note.

The hip joints were given the same prodding and probing. Another note. The doctor picked up what looked, to Nathaniel, like a trumpet and moved around behind him and he could feel the instrument pressed against his back. There was a moment of silence. The doctor came around and faced Nathaniel.

'Do you have any difficulty breathing when you walk?'

'No.'

'Do you get breathless climbing stairs, for instance?'

'Doesn't everyone of my age?'

The doctor smiled.

'I wouldn't know.'

Another note on the pad.

The trumpet-shaped object was put back on the desk to be replaced, in the doctor's hand, by a magnifying glass. He leant close and peered through the glass into each of Nathaniel's eyes in turn.

'Has your eyesight worsened lately?'

As he spoke, Nathaniel caught a whiff of his breath. It smelled pleasantly of garden mint.

'I have to admit that I have needed the use of eye-lenses to read for several years and just recently I have had the necessity of using a magnifying glass, such as the one you are using now, to read most of the print on my business letters. But I have attributed this to normal aging.'

The doctor made no comment, turned to his desk and made yet another note. With his back still turned to his patient the doctor asked, in a very quiet voice, almost a whisper, 'And how is your hearing?'

He heard Nathaniel say something to him.

'I'm sorry, I didn't quite catch that.'

He turned. Nathaniel was smiling.

'I said, fine thank you, how is yours?'

'Touché.' And they both burst into laughter.

Once again the doctor's hands were on him, this time busy amongst his hair.

'Your scalp is very dry and flaky, and your hair appears very brittle. Have you noticed hair loss recently?'

'I am sorry to say that I have lost a great deal of hair in a very short time, but once again I attributed this to age.'

'And does your scalp itch most of the time?'

'Yes.'

Another note. The pad was rapidly becoming full of writing. The doctor turned his attention to the small lump under his chin, on the jawbone.

'How is your appetite? Do you eat well?'

His fingers gently traced the outline of the hard nodule.

'I enjoy my food, if that is what you mean? And I eat whatever takes my fancy, although I find it a little difficult to chew at the moment with the swelling. I had similar several years ago with a wisdom tooth. I hope it's not another one.'

'Let me see inside.' He studied the inside of Nathaniel's mouth through the magnifying glass. 'No, I don't think so.' He drew back slightly. 'How is your sense of smell?'

Nathaniel was surprised by the question.

'The same as usual I believe.' Nathaniel remembered the smell of the man's breath. 'Yes, definitely the same as usual.'

The doctor suddenly knelt and laid his hands on Nathaniel's knees again as though he had been struck by a sudden thought. He rose and made another note on the pad.

'Could you stand for me, please?' Nathaniel did as he was asked and the doctor put his hand under the gown and unashamedly grasped his testicles as though he was weighing them. 'Hm. Similar size.' It was as though he was talking to himself.

'You can get dressed now,' he said over his shoulder, as he walked over to the washstand against the far wall.

Nathaniel was dressed by the time he had thoroughly washed and dried his hands. Nathaniel took his seat again and the doctor took his place behind the desk.

'I am almost certain of my diagnosis but I need, if I may, to ask a few more questions before I can be really sure?'

'Of course.'

'Do you suffer from frequent headaches?'

'No.'

'Do you suffer from loses of concentration? Do you forget things easily?'

'No and no.'

'Do you sleep well? Do you dream bad dreams?'

'Yes and no.'

'Are your bowel movements regular?'

'All the clocks in my house are set by them.' Nathaniel tried, and failed, to keep a straight face.

The doctor briefly smiled himself before going back to his notes.

'Does it pain you when you pass water?'

'No.' He kept a serious expression this time.

'Have you ever noticed traces of blood in your pee?'

'No.'

'Are you still sexually active?'

'For modesty's sake I think the answer to that should remain between me and my maker.'

The doctor laid down his pen and steepled his hands on the desk.

'My lord.' He returned to the formal address. 'I do not ask these questions through curiosity or simply for my titivation. I ask them in order to build as perfect a picture of your health as I possibly can. Without that picture I cannot help you as I should. I can assure you that everything that passes between us in this room is sacrosanct. It will go no further than these four walls. It is important that I ask you if you are sexually active. It makes no difference to me if you are or you aren't, or if you have relations with a woman or a man, but for the sake of my diagnosis I need to know the answer.' He picked up his pen again. 'Although I think you have already answered.' He bent over the pad again.

The doctor had been studying his notes for several interminable minutes and seemed to be considering how to proceed. Not a word had passed between the two men. Nathaniel began to feel restless. At last the doctor raised his head to face his patient.

'I have seen and dealt with several cases like yours before and I am as sure as it is possible to be, that I know what ails you. I am afraid that I have no good news to give you.' At the tone of his voice Nathaniel felt his heart begin to pound in his chest.

'To tell me straight is best, I think.'

He tried to appear not overly concerned; after all, he was a rich man who could afford the best and a Peer of the Realm. He was Nathaniel Leadbitter. Nothing could harm him.

'Very well then.' The doctor paused. 'I am afraid that you have a particularly virulent form of syphilis.' The doctor said the words slowly and quietly. Unfortunately it was a part of his professional lot to sometimes be the bearer of bad news and there was never any pleasure at all in the telling.

Nathaniel Leadbitter had been lucky all his life, but just when he needed it most his luck deserted him.

CHAPTER 33

The Blacksmith and the Shoemaker

Exton, Devon
1807

'Do you remember the grey that threw the Major in the ditch that time?'

'How could I ever forget?' The Blacksmith took a sip of his ale. 'He is such a magnificent animal.' He and the Shoemaker had been friends for as long as they could remember and often enjoyed a flagon of cool ale after they had finished work for the day. They fell silent but he knew that the Shoemaker would get to the point in his own good time; he rarely said anything without a purpose.

He had good reason to remember the horse all right. The Major had high hopes of the grey as a point-to-point champion, it could run and jump like no other horse he had ever owned. That is, until the day the horse had put in that fatal, extra half stride and instead of sailing over the drainage ditch they had slid into it. They had got too close and the crumbling edge had given way before they could take off.

The Major was unhurt except for his battered pride but the horse was not as lucky. When they had eventually extricated the horse from the ditch it was lame, and unable to put any weight on its left foreleg. Fearing the worst the head stable lad was sent for, with orders to bring a gun. But he could find no evidence of any broken bones and the horse was reprieved.

The damage to the tendons and ligaments of the leg, however, was worse than they expected and after several months, when the horse had shown no improvement, the Major had taken the heartbreaking decision to send the horse to the knackers' yard. Being a gelding, it was no good for anything else. The Blacksmith had been at the stables at the big house on one of his regular shoeing visits when the decision was made and had asked for permission to take the horse back to town. He had an idea. He had studied the way that the horse walked, how it was reluctant to put any weight on the leg, and if it did put weight down, how the knee joint collapsed inward. And he had seen how the knee joint became swollen and obviously painful after any exercise. He thought he could put things right, or at least he wanted to try.

It took him months but he had succeeded. By trial and error he had designed a shoe for the horse which had a built up area on the inner edge to hold the hoof at a specific angle. A brace was attached to the shoe that stretched upwards and held and strengthened the knee joint. Once he had got the design correct the improvement in the way the horse walked had been astounding. The swelling had disappeared and the heat had gone out of the joint. Over a period of weeks, and with constant exercise, the knee joint became stronger and the brace was eventually removed. In triumph the Blacksmith had returned the horse to the stables, much to everyone's amazement. The horse would never take part in point-to-point ever again, but the Major loved his horses. The Blacksmith had made a friend and ally for life.

*

'Saw the grey again yesterday, trotting as well as any horse I've ever seen.'

'Aye, finally turned out to be a fine animal.'

He hoped the Shoemaker would get to the point soon, but he was preoccupied tasting a mouthful of ale. Eventually the Shoemaker continued, 'It worked well, the contraption.'

'Aye, it turned out to be a fine contraption.'

'Do you think something like it could work for young Harkin?' The Shoemaker turned slightly towards the Blacksmith to gauge his reaction. Now it was the Blacksmith's turn to be silent.

'You mean make a shoe with a brace to fit the lad?' he eventually asked.

'I could make the shoe and you could make the brace. Between us I'm sure we could help him walk again or at least allow him to hobble around better than he can now. I think it's worth a try. We've nothing to lose and neither has the lad.'

He paused, waiting for the Blacksmith to comment. When he remained silent he added, 'I'm sure it will work, will you help me?'

*

And work it did, better than in their wildest dreams. John's initial reluctance had turned into amazement when he first tried the boot, which the Shoemaker had fashioned from his best leather, and the brace made by the Blacksmith from the most delicate forgings he had ever worked. He could put his foot to the ground and stand straight without the agonising pain he usually felt. Of course, there was still some pain but easily bearable after what had gone before.

During what was left of the summer, through the autumn and winter, John continued to exercise his leg, limping around the house and garden and the countryside, mostly alone but sometimes accompanied by his sister, gaining strength and confidence. The Shoemaker himself, learning all the while, improved and refined the support given by the sole of the boot until the day arrived when John was able to discard the brace altogether for long periods of time.

In the late spring, the Sunday arrived when he was able to walk unaided to the chapel with his parents. He still limped badly but that didn't matter and he gave thanks to God for being able to walk unaided again. He offered up a special prayer for the Shoemaker and the Blacksmith, for the precious gift he had received from the two men. He felt that he could walk for miles and miles and miles.

*

He had remembered the boots that he had taken from the French Officer only that morning and had taken them from his canvas bag to present to the Shoemaker.

'Could you do the same to these boots as the ones I am wearing?' he had asked. 'Adapt them, to support me as these do.'

The Shoemaker took the boots from John's hands. He was intrigued. He had never seen boots like it before, boots of this quality. They were fashioned from the finest leather he had seen in many a year. And the style was exquisite. Such fine stitching. They were certainly not English, maybe Spanish or French.

'Where did you get such fine boots as these?' he asked.

'I took them from a French Officer in the West Indies.'

The Shoemaker hawked and spat. 'Bloody Frenchies, the scum of the Earth.'

'Please don't talk of him in that way, mister.' John had bridled at the Shoemaker's tone. Suddenly he felt the need to speak of the man for the first time. To try to make people understand part of what was troubling him. He faced the Shoemaker square on.

'He was just a man, flesh and blood the same as you or me, and I killed him with his own dagger. Three men have perished by my hand. Two I feel no remorse for and I am glad that they are dead. But this one did not deserve to die and as he died he forgave me and begged me, that if I ever had chance, I would let his wife know that he had died honourably and thinking of her and their young son. He was fighting for his country just as I was. He believed that he was on the side of right, just as I did. He was thousands of miles from home and is now buried on a foreign uninhabited island and his wife will never know what happened to him or how he died, she will never hold him again and his son will never know his father.' John paused and then continued in a much softer voice, almost a whisper. The Shoemaker stood silent, stunned by the outburst. 'He had so much to live for, so much more than me, but I took it all away from him. In my darkest hours I often wished it had been me who had died, but those are foolish thoughts. What is done is done. All I can do is keep his memory alive in my mind and learn from what I did to him, and pray that his eternal soul is somewhere better than a dark and miserable hole in the ground.'

John felt himself breaking down and, not wishing the Shoemaker to see, abruptly turned and left the shop. He had some business with the Blacksmith to attend to, anyway.

*

He returned to the shop several hours later. He was contrite and feared what his reception would be. He stepped into the breach.

'I owe you an apology, mister. After all that you have done for me I had no right to speak to you as I did. I value your friendship and would hate to lose it. Will you forgive me, sir?'

'Nay, lad, it is me who should ask your forgiveness. You have taught me a valuable lesson here today. I try to live life in the Christian way but never have I thought of the war or our enemies in the way that you do. I have thought hard and long about what you said of the French Officer and his poor family. I feel humbled.'

The two men smiled at each other and shook hands and the mood was lifted.

The Shoemaker had worked his magic on the boots and they fitted John perfectly. He wore them when he left the shop.

CHAPTER 34

Nathaniel Leadbitter

London
1807

He poured another large measure from the rapidly emptying bottle. It seemed there was no shortage of French brandy at this very select private members' club, even though Britain had been at war with France for what seemed like a lifetime to Nathaniel. It had been in fact only fourteen years, but there seemed to be no end in sight.

He took a sip from the glass and swallowed the smooth neat spirit and felt the heat burn all the way down to his stomach. He had not eaten anything since his early breakfast and the alcohol was having the desired effect. He had set out to get drunk, and was three parts there already. The doctor had discussed the illness with Nathaniel at great length and had set out how he thought the it would progress, although there were so many options that he couldn't be sure of anything.

'We know the disease is rife in some of the countries around the South China Sea, so it is safe to assume that someone who has travelled in that area has brought the disease back with them,' he had said. 'We also know that the disease is passed from one person to another by sexual contact, there is no record of it being passed in any other way.'

That meant he had caught it from either Louisa or Agnes, or both. There was no other answer. They were the only two people he had bedded in the last few years. The girls, his beloved girls, had to be infected themselves. They must have been infected by one of their customers, but which one? Had any travelled to the East Indies and beyond? And if he had caught the disease how many others were now infected?

'Whilst we know where it originates and how it is passed on, we struggle to find an effective treatment.' The doctor had continued, not sparing Nathaniel any details. 'The symptoms, whilst quite striking, are too diverse. The disease affects different people in different ways, sometimes attacking the person's mind and sometimes the symptoms are purely physical. It can affect the respiratory system, the stomach and bowels, the liver and kidneys. It can cause blindness and deafness and sometimes, worst of all, madness.'

He could see that his patient was listening intently as he spoke.

'In your case it appears to be attacking your bones and is causing your skeleton to deform. It is also causing calcium deposits to promote new bone growth as is evident in your knee and hip joints and inside your mouth.'

'So what does the future hold for me?' he had asked. He feared the answer but needed to know.

'I am sorry to be the one to tell you this, it upsets me, but I will try and give you the truth.'

The doctor paused, gathering his thoughts.

'In my experience there is no cure for what ails you, and you will not get any better than you are now. What we do know, however, is this. You will become rapidly more immobile as your joints stiffen until you become totally crippled.'

He paused to see the effect his words were having. He could see that his patient was stunned.

'Your joints will be painful, and the pain will get increasingly worse as the disease progresses, but I can give you ample supplies of laudanum, and when that is no longer effective we have stronger drugs, like opium, for you to manage that pain.'

'How long will that take… the crippling I mean?'

'It seems to be well advanced now. My guess would be a year or at the most two, no more.'

'And then what?'

'You may live on for some time. I cannot tell.'

'You mean I am going to die from this?' It was a question he didn't want to ask.

The doctor nodded his head.

'You see, Nathaniel you already have bone growths in your joints and inside your mouth; and I detect hard swellings at the top of your spine. As these grow bigger you will find that it becomes increasingly difficult to swallow and your throat may close altogether.'

'That means I will be a cripple and I could starve to death?'

The doctor nodded again.

*

The glass was empty again and so was the bottle. He tipped the bottle and held it upside down over the glass and distractedly watched the few droplets that fell. As if by magic another bottle appeared on the low table alongside his favourite deep leather chair. He hadn't noticed the porter's silent approach.

*

As he had left the house in Knightsbridge the doctor had laid a hand on his arm.

'I know that this is has been terrible news for you, but please try also to think of your loved ones, your family, especially the person who has the infection, as you do. As difficult as it may be, they need to be told.'

But all thoughts of returning to Dover had gone from his mind.

*

Back in Dover, Louisa extinguished the last of the candles and made her way into the hallway, leaving the remains of the food on the dining table. Cissy was waiting silently there and was struck again by Louisa's beauty and her graceful movement as she walked across the polished floor towards the stairs.

Louisa had spent the best part of the afternoon preparing for

Nathaniel and looked resplendent in the turquoise dress, but all to no avail, Nathaniel had failed to appear at the house on Southdown Road.

She smiled sadly at her mistress and the smile was returned with a shrug of Louisa's slender shoulders. No words passed between them and Louisa slowly climbed the stairs to spend the night alone.

When Cissy heard the bedroom door softly close she picked up the candleholder with the two candles that were still alight and made her way back to the kitchen. It wasn't like Nathaniel to disappoint anyone; he always kept his word and was usually so punctual.

She liked Nathaniel, maybe she was even in love with him a little bit herself. She hoped that nothing bad had happened to him on the way down from Yorkshire.

CHAPTER 35

John Harkin

Exton, Devon
1808

It had been his sister Lizzie's idea. He had been fretting around the house for weeks on end and she had recognised the familiar signs of John's wanderlust. He needed to get away again. He had been too long in one place already. It had been almost a year since his road to recovery, initiated by the collective inventiveness of the Blacksmith and the Shoemaker, had begun.

He was now as fit as he had ever been, except for the very pronounced limp which would be with him forever. He had regained his appetite, which his mother and sister were more than willing to feed, and with it had come the weight and strength. He had developed an insatiable hunger for walking, as though afraid that the gift may be lost again if not constantly used, or maybe just making up for lost time. And the fear and the darkness had left him, and he had found a faith of some sort.

He had no need of money. When he had left the Navy he had several hundred pounds of prize money and back pay in his money belt. It would last him a while yet, but not forever.

He had paid good money to the Blacksmith, despite his protests, for the foot-driven whetstone and the alterations to the cart and was ready to go. He would travel the country, going where the will would take him, earning a living by sharpening knives and any other implements that required a sharp edge, for anyone who had a few pennies to spare. The skill that he had learned in his first weeks in the Navy could be put to good use. He would be his own man once again, free and independent. But he had learned a valuable lesson and would always remember the debt he owed to his mum and dad and especially his sister, and those others around him who had helped him and had asked for nothing in return.

The time came to say goodbye and there were tears from his mother as she hugged him tightly to her breast. And then he said goodbye again to his sister. They had hugged but said nothing. They had already said their goodbyes down by the river.

They had stood and looked at each other and Lizzie had looked deep into his deep blue eyes and had seen the light and the life that had returned there, and there was no need for words between them. She knew the dark places he had visited and he knew that her strength had been his saviour. There and then he had made a solemn promise to her that he would return.

His father shook his hand formally and then, as an afterthought it seemed, accompanied him down the lane, which led to the main road, insisting on pushing the cart. When they had turned the first corner, and were out of sight of the cottage, his father stopped and said that here was where they would part.

'Son, you know your mam and I wish that you would stay home but I know that you would be restless and unhappy. You have a good heart. Be led by it. You should always do what it tells you is right, to be really happy. But always remember that I love you and I am proud of you.' He suddenly took John into his huge embrace, but almost immediately released him again, embarrassed. 'I will see you again, won't I?' He looked long and deep into John's eyes.

John had never seen his father like this. He was always strong, a man of few words, even stoical.

'I will be back before the winter sets in,' he said. His father sighed, a deep sigh, a look of relief on his face.

'Your mother will like that,' was all he could say.

The two men silently faced each other for a few seconds. They didn't need to say anything more. The invisible bond between them said it all.

They turned away from each other and slowly went their separate ways.

CHAPTER 36

Nathaniel and the Money Lender

Dover, Kent
1809

There was something in the way that the two men sat closely huddled together that would have suggested, to those who knew them well, that their respective worlds had ended that day. Their chairs were pulled up close to the roaring fire and occasionally tiny tendrils of steam could be seen to rise from their damp clothing. If anyone had ventured close enough they would have smelt the dampness in the air, but no-one came near, preferring to leave the two men to themselves, save the waiter who had brought the bottle of ruby Port.

They had hardly uttered more than a few syllables to each other since they had entered the room together almost half an hour before, the older man leaning heavily on the other. In the damp air Nathaniel coughed, a wet cough from deep in his chest, which left him breathless. He took another gulp of Port to clear his throat, and turned painfully to his companion, who continued to stare into the flames seemingly lost in his own thoughts.

Recently Nathaniel had noticed things about the man that previously had not registered in his mind, his rude health, his vitality and energy, his fitness and his dark handsome looks. He seemed to be no older now than he did when he had first met him years before.

They must have been of a similar age, although Nathaniel had never asked, but the difference in them physically was startling, and with every passing year became more noticeable. Nathaniel wondered how he could have escaped the dreadful disease that was ravaging him and their friends and acquaintances.

'She had a child once, you know.'

'Aye I know. She had a boy, a son. I met him several times when he was young. He seemed a good boy.'

The fire claimed their attention for long minutes before the Money Lender spoke again.

'She wasn't a good mother by all accounts. She used to beat the boy for no reason and eventually he ran off. She has never heard from him since that day.'

Nathaniel changed the subject, not wishing to dwell on the subject of parenthood. He had not been a good father himself.

'I shall be leaving Dover by the end of the week.'

There was no sign for almost a minute that his companion had even heard him speak until, without shifting his gaze from the fire, the man replied.

'Aye. I thought you might.'

'There is nothing here for me now.'

'No,' he agreed. 'Not now.'

Nathaniel struggled to reach for the bottle and the Money Lender intervened. He refilled both glasses and handed one to his friend, before leaning forward, elbows on knees and resumed his staring into the flames.

'I am returning to York to be with my wife and children. I think perhaps I owe them more than just returning to die, but it is all I have left except for, of course, the money.'

'Aye, as you say, except for the money. They say it is the root of all evil,' his companion mused.

'What good is money, what consolation can it give when you feel as I do? God, already I miss that woman.'

*

The rapid onslaught and subsequent death of Louisa had left all who knew her stunned. It seemed that one minute she was there, full of life, and the next she was gone. Both men, and her friends Agnes and Cissy, had been with her at the moment of her passing and, in her blindness, she had professed her love for them all. Afterwards they all agreed; it seemed she was, in a way, glad to die. She was at peace with herself and had made herself ready. She had fought against the pain, pain that no amount of opium seemed to ease, for long enough. She was exhausted.

Nathaniel had found a vicar who, for the right price, had been willing to conduct a service and commend her soul. Despite her 'profession' he had even said a few kind words at the graveside. The sadness of the occasion may have affected him after all, and prompted him to offer some succour to the meagre gathering, the four bedraggled people standing before him in the rain. But there wasn't even a crumb of comfort to be had; she was gone forever.

*

'But if you leave what of your project?' The Money Lender suddenly turned to Nathaniel as though waking from a long sleep. 'Surely you cannot abandon the work now?'

'The work is in safe hands, I am sure of it. The trustees have been appointed and I have every confidence in Mister Donaldson. He is one of the most competent architects that I know of and I have every faith in the project manager he has appointed, and I have put ample money in place. The building work can continue without me, the project can now run itself without any help from me.'

*

The idea for the 'project' had first entered Nathaniel's mind many months before, in fact, well over a year before. He had been walking slowly, which was all he could manage now, along the quay in Dover harbour, deep in conversation with a business acquaintance. Absentmindedly he noted that a newly arrived ship was preparing to unload its cargo and, not wishing to be caught up in the hustle as seamen rushed to and fro, they stood aside. Nathaniel, with his usual interest in everything that happened around him, watched with interest as gangways were secured and derricks were swung out amid a great deal of shouting and gesturing, and the business of landing the cargo began.

The quay was soon cluttered with boxes and crates and barrels and then, to Nathaniel's amazement, a line of seamen appeared from below decks carrying crude stretchers between them. Obviously this was also a troop ship carrying the injured home from Spain. They carried the twenty or so stretchers, and the men they contained, ashore and laid them down side by side on the rough cobbles. More walking wounded followed and they also found their own space to lie, until the quay was littered with two or three dozen men who lay silently in the hot sun. Some stared about them at the strange place they had arrived at, fear and trepidation plainly etched on the faces, others lay with their eyes shut… looking for all the world like dead men. All of the injured men were covered in bloody rags, some with the stumps of missing legs and arms plainly visible.

And then Nathaniel noticed the smell. The stench was appalling. The smell of the filth the men had been laying amongst for weeks on end mingled with the putrid smell of rotting flesh. Nathaniel quickly covered his mouth with his linen handkerchief, he felt sick at the sight and the smell, but felt compelled to watch, held there as though by some invisible hand.

Suddenly a woman appeared from the gathered onlookers. The lower part of her face was covered with a pretty coloured scarf and she carried a bucket of water. Without hesitation she knelt by the nearest injured soldier, brushed away some inquisitive flies which had gathered about his soiled bandages, and gently lifted his head before holding a cup to his lips. Most of the water ran down his chin and onto his blue tunic, but he managed a barely audible 'thank you' as she rose to attend to the next man. Another woman stepped from the crowd, and then another and another and another and they passed among the men with cool water and cloths and they gave drinks and cleaned the men as best they could and offered words of encouragement. Several of the soldiers were past any help and died before their very eyes and these were covered with cotton sheets from the shop at the corner of the quay.

A tall man, looking as bedraggled as the wounded men, passed among the stretchers. He was bare-headed but as he came near, Nathaniel recognised the tattered gold braid on his collar that marked him out as an officer. Nathaniel stepped forward and gently reached out to touch the man's arm. The officer slowly turned towards him and surveyed him with eyes which burned feverishly in his thin face, which, despite a deep sun-tan, still managed to look waxy and pale at the same time. Only then did Nathaniel see the bloodstains on the deep blue tunic with the missing buttons, and the blood-soaked filthy bandage wound tightly around his chest.

'Sir, are you in command of these poor men?' Nathaniel asked gently, trying desperately to keep his stomach from heaving his breakfast over the cobbles at the sight and the smell which emanated from the man. He had never been good where blood was concerned. *Thanks be to God,* he thought, *what a sheltered and safe life I have led.*

'Yes sir, you could say that,' he spoke in a low monotone, 'although I am almost ashamed to admit to having let my men get into such a sorry state.' He started to raise his right arm as though to salute but winced in pain and allowed the arm to drop back to his side. 'Captain Aloysius Brookbanks, if you please.' He had a strange accent which Nathaniel failed to place, although he would guess at somewhere in the West Country, possibly Somerset or even as far north as Gloucestershire.

'What happened to you, Captain?'

'We were serving in the army of Lord Blanchette down on the Peninsula and had been there for almost two months without making any contact with the enemy. Most of my enlisted men were new to service but a better and more disciplined company would be hard to find in the whole of the British Army, good men all.'

He turned at the sound of a loud moan, as a man was lifted to sit upright.

'Steady soldier, steady man. You are back in England now, you are in good hands here,' he reassured the man and the moaning stopped as abruptly as it had begun.

'We were ordered forward by Colonel Rodgerson, one of His Lordship's aides, to skirmish with a platoon of French artillery which was blocking our progress across a small river, as the whole regiment advanced. "It will be easy," the Colonel said, "a company of infantry against a few motley Frenchmen, and artillerymen at that." We formed up in platoons and advanced in good order, pressing against the centre of their line. The French fell back and, at first, we made good progress but the Colonel had not told us about the French Cavalry regiment which was also billeted nearby. They did not release the Cavalry until we were well into their trap. The first charge took us by surprise and broke our ranks, we were in disarray, foot-soldiers out in open ground stand no chance against men on horseback. We could do nothing.' As though he needed to explain his failure, he took a deep breath and continued. 'Their second charge drove us onto the big guns and we were cut to ribbons.' He slowly looked around the quay. 'This is all that remains of my men. Out of one hundred and fifty men who left England with me, this is all.'

'What will happen to them now? Where will they go?'

'We have been ordered home, wherever that may be. We are of no use to Lord Wellesley, the Duke of Wellington now. We have served our purpose.'

'But your men need medical help, they need treatment and care.'

He looked around at the men, some weakly waving away the growing swarms of huge flies that had been attracted to the place from miles around by the smell of rotting flesh.

'Even I can see that. You cannot just send them home.'

The Captain looked directly into Nathaniel's eyes.

'And where, sir, do you suggest I take them?' he asked defiantly. 'Are there hospitals in Dover that can take my men and care for them?' He waited for a reply, but none came. 'No, I thought not.'

'Then why did they send you back here? Why not to one of the Naval ports or somewhere where there are facilities for wounded men?'

The officer looked at Nathaniel almost pityingly. He was obviously a good man but how could he be so naive?

'After the French allowed the dead and the wounded to be collected from the field the order was issued for all of us to be transported to the nearest port and sent home. You see, sir, allowing soldiers to see their comrades lying dead and dying is bad for morale and must be avoided at all costs. My men were given their twenty-one shillings and loaded on the first ship out of Gibraltar. It just happened to be coming here, but it could just as well have been going to any other port in the Kingdom. The fact that there are no facilities here, as you put it, was not a consideration. This, I am afraid, is the lot of the common soldier, out of sight, out of mind.'

Nathaniel was aghast.

'But these men have served their country well. Surely they deserve more?'

The young officer said nothing. There was nothing to say. He once again surveyed his men and then turned back to Nathaniel.

'If you will excuse me, sir, I feel the need to be seated myself.' He bent his head to Nathaniel and his friend and walked falteringly away only to slump down in an open space among his men.

That was the moment the idea for the hospital and sanatorium came to him. He had the money, but who could make it happen?

*

'I am also leaving Dover, perhaps in the next day or two.'

The Money Lender broke the silence that had again descended on the two men.

'When did you decide this? You've never said a word about leaving before.'

'It's been in my mind since Louisa passed on, but I must admit I only made my mind up in the last few minutes. Your leaving may have made my mind up for me. What is there left besides more misery?' He turned fully to face Nathaniel. 'I did love her, you know, Dorcas I mean. She meant everything to me but I could not find the words or the deeds to convince her.'

He thought back over the last months and the rapid decline of the health of the woman he now mourned. It was as though she had given up on life, and everyone around her, completely. She had faded away before their very eyes. And when the time came that it was obvious that she could not be saved it was as though a great weight had been lifted from her. She said goodbye to no-one, just closed her eyes and stopped breathing.

Nathaniel studied his friend for several minutes and the thought crossed his mind that if he had truly loved the woman he had a funny way of showing it. He had taken everything from her, including her children and the last remains of her dignity. But what is done is done.

It had been easy to see that the woman hated the very ground that he walked on.

'But where will you go? I always thought of you as a Dover man through and through,' he eventually said.

'I haven't thought that far ahead yet. I may travel for a while, see some of England, I might even go abroad… to The Americas perhaps, before I find the right place to settle down again.'

Nathaniel looked at his friend, because over the years they had become firm friends, seeing his own despair mirrored in the man's expression. He managed to reach out his arm and offered his hand, which the Money Lender grasped in both of his.

'Whatever you do and wherever you end up, I pray that you will eventually find some kind of happiness.'

*

Not much later they left the fireside and parted company at the door, each man to go his own way. From the top of the steps which led up to the front of the club a new building site could be seen high above the town. The beginnings of the new hospital and sanatorium which would bear his name could be clearly seen. He had made provision that, in the future, there would be free medical care and assistance for those who needed it.

Nathaniel looked up to the site of the new building and choked back a sob.

'All well and good, but it's too late. It's all too bloody late.'

CHAPTER 37

Lizzie Harkin

Exton, Devon
1816

Lizzie arrived slightly flushed after the walk home. She usually rode in the trap on workdays but today, being fine and warm, she had decided to leave the pony in the paddock. After all, it was only three miles there and back. She knew how fortunate she had been to gain her position at the timber company. It was unheard of for a woman to gain such a position. Some people called it luck but she knew it was a case of 'who you knew'.

On the day that she had returned from London, in answer to the letter from her parents asking for her help and her father had been waiting for her on the Exmouth turnpike, she knew that she would not leave Exton again. Exton was in her blood and she was Exton through and through.

*

She had entered the world of domestic service only days after John had left home to join the Navy. Although employed as a lowly upstairs maid, her willingness to work hard and her sharpness of mind, together with her ability to read and write and figure, were soon recognised by her employer, the Honourable Timothy Worthington, Liberal Member of Parliament for the Exington ward.

All those years of reading pamphlet after pamphlet and newspaper after newspaper with her father bore fruit. Within months she was having lively discussions with her employer on all subjects political and, taking risk after risk for she was still only a maid, was never afraid to give her views. Timothy Worthington might have had a slow mind but he had survived in the political arena for some time, and was no fool. He realised that he had happened on a rare gem… an eloquent spokesperson for the lower classes, who was in touch with the mood of the countryside and who had many radical ideas which, of course, he took as his own.

After what seemed to be an obscenely short time she found herself leaving behind the mind-numbing drudgery of cleaning fireplaces at five in the morning, emptying piss-pots, and cleaning, and polishing silver and brass. Instead, she found herself acting as a 'sort of secretary', which involved her travelling to the capital where her employer spent the majority of his time.

Tongues could have wagged but it was common knowledge around Westminster that Timothy was not interested in female company, not in the slightest, certainly not since the Cathedral School.

She became his right-hand 'man' and, in secret, even helped in the writing of his speeches, and soon other members were listening to what he had to say. They had to admit that some of the ideas put forward in his speeches to the House, if not exactly policy altering, were novel. He began to get a name, to be noticed, and Lizzie felt that she was making a difference, could be instrumental in altering the lot of the poor and needy, maybe, very subtly, exert some influence.

But for all that, she was not content. She missed her parents and her brother and she missed the countryside. She was a real home girl at heart. The city was not for her. She missed the trees and the birds and the hedgerows and even, those most stupid of animals, the sheep. She wanted to go home.

When the letter arrived from her parents she packed immediately. Timothy Worthington had felt at times as though this remarkable young woman was teaching him his trade, but took her sudden departure in good grace for he was, amongst other things, a thoroughly 'nice' man, even though he knew deep down that she would not return. He was sorry to see her go but his sadness was tempered by the news that he had indeed been noticed and a promotion to a post in the government was being considered. He promised to do whatever he could to help and he was true to his word.

Within weeks Lizzie had written explaining that she would not be returning to her former employ and had written again several months later asking for a reference. Her work with John was almost finished: it was time to find work. A package duly arrived containing the reference and a new bonnet together with a personal letter to Lizzie wishing her and her family good health and hoping that she would except the bonnet and wear it to chapel the very next Sunday.

More important was the sealed letter also contained in the package. She was to present it to the General Manager of the timber company which Timothy's family had acquired from the estate of a gentleman from York who had recently died from a horrible foreign disease. She wore the new bonnet to the interview with the General Manager.

*

Lizzie's mother was sitting close to the window in the parlour to take advantage of the last of the daylight as she deftly threaded the needle through one of the final pieces of her embroidery; with her failing eyesight she needed good light. She was also studying her daughter as she got the meal ready. She was so proud of her that it made her heart ache. She knew that her daughter was happy at home, it was unmistakable, but to her mind a piece of life's jigsaw was missing.

Lizzie was the first to hear the footsteps on the garden path and looked out, expecting to see her father coming home. It was not her father but a much younger man.

The knock sounded on the door which was partially open. Lizzie wiped her hands and went to answer. Her mother heard the murmur of voices from the front of the house but could not make out what was being said. Lizzie came back into the room, looking more flushed than ever, followed by a young man.

'Mam, this is Mister... ah.' She was flustered. She turned to the man. 'I'm sorry, sir, but I did not ask your name.'

The man turned to the older woman and smiled, showing brilliant white teeth which showed up well in his deeply tanned face. He inclined his head, almost a small bow.

'I am George Porter, madam. I am glad to make your acquaintance. I have heard lots about you.'

Lizzie intervened.

'He has come to visit John, he says he is a friend from a long while ago.'

'How do you know my son? Did you meet him in the Navy? Did you serve together? Were you there when John got injured?'

The questions gushed out, one on another, until Lizzie shushed her mother quiet.

'Give Mister Porter a chance to answer, Mother, please.'

They had sat at the kitchen table, talking as the light outside slowly faded away. Lizzie offered Frenchie tea and as she passed the cup, from the best china set, their hands had touched, accidentally of course. The very same thing happened with the second cup.

Her father came home from the farm and the two men shook hands formally, sizing each other up. Frenchie must have measured up for he was instantly offered beer, not that 'woman's drink'.

Frenchie had left the house several hours later, promising to return the very next day. They had so many questions still to ask. Lizzie stood at the window and watched as he sauntered off down the lane. Her mother and father exchanged glances as they watched their daughter raise herself onto her toes to catch the last glimpse of the man who, they had learned, had been baptised Gaston Portier. The 'accidental' touching of hands as mugs and pots were passed, the surreptitious looks, the blushing cheeks and the wide smiles that had passed between the two during the course of the evening, had not gone unnoticed by her parents.

That night, for the first time in months, in fact not since the day John had returned home, Mother Harkin knelt at the foot of her bed and prayed. She prayed that, at last, the final piece of the jigsaw of her daughter's life had fallen into place.

PART II

WALK THROUGH THE VALLEY OF

THE SHADOW OF DEATH

CHAPTER 1

The Forest of Dean
Monday 10 May, 1822

It seemed that he had been travelling uphill ever since he had crossed the River Severn from Arlingham to the village of Newnham on the west bank. By his reckoning he had walked more than six miles and now, thankfully, up ahead he could see the brow of the hill and the signpost marking the fork in the path that he had been looking for, one arm of the post pointing straight on to Parkend and one pointing to the right indicating The Speech House. It had taken him more than four hours to come this far. He had known steeper climbs but the sheer remorseless length of this one had slowed his progress and his legs were aching badly, especially the left. He had not felt pain like this in his crippled leg for many a long year.

He had taken the ferry across the river on a whim, deviating from his usual route which, in all the years he had come this way, had always took him further north to Gloucester where he would either cross the river before turning north-west to head into Herefordshire or continue on into the counties of the industrial Midlands. He had never travelled this way before, although he had often wondered about the wild-looking, wooded hills which were clearly visible from the south side of the river. He was not so sure now that his decision to come this way was a good one, this was hard going. But he had come this far and it was probably easier to continue than to turn back, and as though in some kind of consolation, the scenery had been spectacular.

The sullen ferryman had been no help at all as the Limping Man had struggled with his load up the slipway onto the road, except to give him some directions as to the way to go. He had passed through the small village of Blakeney and had found the road to Parkend exactly where he had been told it would be. He had followed the rough track which wound for about a mile between piles of slag and scores of small iron-ore furnaces, all belching flames and filthy, acrid black coal-smoke which hung in the air of the small valley and made it difficult to breathe. A stream of black water flowed sluggishly along the valley floor. The sulphur fumes burned his lungs. But he struggled on with his cart and, rounding a sharp bend in the track, he suddenly emerged from all the noise and detritus into a sight which fairly took his breath away.

The hard-packed track stretched out before him, gradually climbing and dead-straight for as far as he could see, until it seemed to disappear amongst the trees. And it was flanked by the most magnificent stands of mature Beech, Sweet Chestnut and Oak which stood tall and straight, with their giant boughs arching out over the road forming the most magnificent avenue he had seen anywhere on his travels. And under the trees, hundreds of thousands of Bluebells made a carpet of the most vivid blue. He steered his cart to the side and stopped. This would be as good a place as any to take some food. He sat on a fallen tree trunk and stared about him, drinking it all in. He unwrapped his meagre bread and began to eat. He swilled the bread down with some water and packed everything away. He felt refreshed now and continued his uphill climb.

After what seemed like an age he reached the signpost and took the road to the right as he had been told. A few hundred yards further on he branched off to the left to follow a forest track which wound steeply down through the trees. He was becoming worried now. He looked up at the darkening skies not far off to the west. Earlier, as he had stood on the flat-bottomed ferry boat, he had seen the clouds that were gathering downriver over the Bristol Channel, promising to spoil what was a fine early May day. From his experience in the Navy he knew that they would bring rain, and lots of it.

The ferryman had assured him then that he had plenty of time to cover the distance to Coleford before the rains came, but progress had been slow and the clouds were closer now and the wind was strengthening. The air had turned much colder.

He pressed on, urgently now. He had no wish to be caught out in a storm with no cover. He thought he heard a clap of thunder from far off, but then realised that the sound had come from almost dead ahead. He recognised the sound. Someone, somewhere, was using blasting powder.

*

To Edwin Morgan the sounds of the explosions were surprisingly muted compared to the thunderous noise which followed as lumps of rock, shale and earth fell to the quarry floor. As the shockwave passed over him, he buried his head under the piece of sacking that he kept for the purpose and allowed the dust to swirl around him. There should have been three explosions and he was convinced that he had heard all three, but he was not one hundred per cent sure, the noises had been so close together.

When he thought that enough time had passed for the dust to have settled, he removed the sacking that covered his head and looked around. Other men were emerging from the cover they had sought and standing up to look at the newly exposed face of the quarry. But no-one approached the face for they all knew how dangerous this place could be and, after a shot-firing, it was the most dangerous time to be here.

The quarry floor directly beneath the newly exposed face was littered with a pile of dislodged rocks. They had been neatly split from the vertical surface and lay like a pack of discarded playing cards. Further up the face could be seen other huge slabs of rock which had been loosened by the blast but had not fallen. These would need to be prised free by the shot-firer and his team of labourers using long crowbars before it would be safe for the ground workers to start the work of moving and sorting those slabs that had already crashed down.

The shot-firer as always was the first onto the face, lowered down from above in a harness of leather strapping. He had set the charges and it was he who would face the danger of checking that the charges had all detonated as planned. He was quickly followed by his gang, armed with all manner of levers.

The work of clearing the face of loose rocks went on apace under the watchful eye of the quarry foreman. He was a hard taskmaster and constantly urged the shot-firer and his men to greater efforts, for the quarry owner could sell every ounce of stone they could dig out of the hillside and his wage at the end of the week depended on the amount of profit the quarry owner had banked. Times were good at the moment and there was good profit to be made and good wages to be had.

At long last the all-clear sounded in the quarry and the gang of ground-workers were able to get back to their work. They worked with gusto for they had been idle for longer than usual and were anxious to make up for the lost time. They swarmed over the pile of rocks and a cacophony of noise filled the confined space, echoing and reverberating off the quarry walls. The deep thuds of large hammers and the more rapid staccato sound of smaller hammers mixed with the sound of shovels and the shouts of the men as they encouraged their workmates to strike the chisels harder or put more energy into their work, and over by some dust-covered wooden buildings a steam engine puffed and wheezed as it struggled to drive the screens which graded the shale.

Edwin Morgan walked slowly over to the pile of freshly fallen stone slabs, taking particular care where he placed his boots. He was a frequent visitor to this particular quarry. The stone which the men extracted from Bixelton Quarry was special and was in great demand everywhere as quality building stone. The seismic upheavals which had taken place millions of years before gave the stone which the men extracted from this quarry the most amazing grains and textures. Stone this rare was too good for road-building.

The stonemason was looking for an unusual piece of stone and in his mind's eye he carried a picture of exactly the shape and texture he needed to complete the job. He had been commissioned to shape and carve a stone plaque which would have pride of place in the new church built in Coleford marketplace, and would be to honour Mr Poole, a local man who had almost bankrupted himself to provide the money for a new meeting house for the church that he served. Edwin Morgan knew that if he could not find the piece of stone here at Bixelton, then it probably did not exist anywhere.

As he searched his stomach gave a mighty rumble, reminding him that his young son Charlie would be joining him before long, bringing with him the leather satchel with his midday bait. He knew his son loved to accompany him to his work and he often 'forgot' to bring his dinner with him when he left the house in the morning, giving the boy the excuse he needed to join his dad. But today was the boy's birthday. Today he was ten years old and that morning, before leaving for work, his father had presented him with a jack-knife. It was second-hand, bought cheaply from an old matelot, but came complete with a lanyard, which he fastened around his son's neck.

'You're old enough now to have a knife of your own, butty,' he had told his proud son, 'but if I see you messing around and being silly with it I'll take it away again. Alright?'

Edwin had four children and, although trying to be a strict father, knew that at times he was too 'soft' with them, especially the girls. Charles was the oldest, followed by three daughters, Sarah eight and Rachel five, and then came Edwina, the baby at only one year old.

Charles wanted nothing more in life than to follow in his father's footsteps. He would sit for hours watching his father work and was fascinated by the way he could take a rough and broken piece of stone and, by the skill of his hands, change it into a thing of beauty.

Even at the tender age of ten, he had acquired some skills. His father had bought him his own set of hammers and stone-chisels after catching the boy hammering away at a piece of stone using some of his old tools, and had instructed the boy in their use. He had taken to the work like a duck to water and had mastered the basic skills easily. But what had impressed his father more was the boy's imagination and creativity. He was already producing work which Edwin himself had not been able to produce until well into his twenties. Edwin knew, beyond a shadow of a doubt, that his son would grow up to be a very skilful stonemason, probably better than he was himself. Edwin was very proud of his young son and had already determined to take him on, this very day, as his apprentice. He continued his search for the perfect piece of stone.

*

The young Charles was in a hurry to try his knife and had already left the small house in Staunton Lane that he called home, after his mother had made him finish his bread and dripping breakfast. He knew nothing of his father's plans to take him as his apprentice, but today he had plans of his own. He picked up a flat piece of stone and as he walked slowly along he honed the blade of his knife until it shone. He turned the knife in his hands and admired it from every angle. It really was a thing of beauty, he thought.

He turned into Spout Lane and cut a long, straight stick from the hedge. He ambled slowly along the shortcut, whittling away at the stick until, by the time he had reached the Poolway and had rejoined the main Gloucester Road, the stick had been cut away to virtually nothing. He threw what remained of the stick away, snapped the knife shut and stuffed it into his coat pocket.

He clambered over the toll-gate at the bottom of Bakers Hill where the road divided, and continued on up the road to the right. He felt in his pocket to check that the knife was still safely there. Although he could feel its weight pulling the jacket down, and the lanyard was still fastened about his neck, he needed to make sure. He loved his knife. It was the best birthday he had ever had and the best present he had ever had and he couldn't wait to try it out again. He cut another stick from the hedge and whistled tunelessly as he walked slowly on.

The weather had taken a turn for the worse by the time he crested the hill at the Broad Well, but he knew he didn't have far to go now, and it was all downhill from here. He left the road and followed a barely discernible footpath under the trees heading for the well-made and paved dram-road, built by the quarry owners and which, he knew, wound its way down through the woods linking all the quarries and coal-mines before joining the road which ran along the valley bottom and eventually went all the way to the docks at Lydney.

He cut yet another long, straight stick from a coppiced Hazel bush and, as he made his way along beneath the thick tree canopy, he fashioned a point on the thick end of his new Roman spear. The knife really did work a treat.

*

The Limping Man had crossed the stream at the stone-works in the valley bottom and was now eight or nine hundred yards up the steeply sloping, narrow dram-road, which was littered on both sides by disused workings, some no more than a scratching where a few pieces of stone had been removed, but others going back into the side of the hill for a hundred feet or more. Why they had been abandoned he had no idea, but guessed that the workers had met with rock that was too tough to extract.

And there were coal mines too. Eerie black holes that went back horizontally into the hillside with the usual pile of black spoil alongside, but these too were abandoned. He had passed the working quarry, which he knew to be the site of the explosion he had heard earlier, gouged into the hillside on his right maybe a quarter of a mile back and was passing yet another disused quarry, when he heard the sound of the approaching wagon. It was coming down the road towards him and he could hear the squealing as the driver applied the brakes to slow the wagon on the steep incline. He needed to clear the dram-road. He had to get out of the way if he wanted to avoid a collision. Descending wagons always had the right of passage. He pushed his cart into the entrance to the old quarry where the ground was soft, and waited.

The wagon rumbled by him, travelling very slowly. The driver was dressed all in black and wore a wide-brimmed felt hat pulled low over his eyes. A scarf was wound around his lower face against the rapidly cooling air, obscuring most of his face. He did not speak, seeming to concentrate on the job of controlling the wagon's descent. His right leg was braced rigidly against the brake lever and the huge horse out front was sitting back on its haunches as it fought the weight that tried to push them inexorably down the slope. Sparks flew from the horse's iron shoes as they slithered and slid on the smooth stones of the road.

The Limping Man pulled his cart further off the road and watched the wagon as it passed by and continued on its way. He turned to face the hill again and made to drag his cart back onto the road, but as he did so he felt the first spot of rain, a big spot that landed on his shoulder and sprayed smaller droplets onto his neck and face. It was quickly followed by another and then another. The rain had arrived and he needed some kind of shelter, quickly. He looked about him and subconsciously registered that the noise of the descending wagon had ceased.

He had no idea what was up ahead; how far he would have to travel to find some shelter. The rain was falling heavier now and he knew that his clothes would be saturated in very few minutes. He was growing desperate. He looked into the disused quarry and it was then that he registered the overhang where the face had been undercut to a depth of four or maybe five feet, enough to give him some shelter. He pushed his cart towards the overhang, the wheels of his cart and the soles of his boots sinking into the soft earth as he crossed a trickle of water that was running from among the undergrowth on the up-slope.

The overhang was larger than it looked and there was plenty of room under its cover for a man and a cart. There was a blackened patch of scorched earth on the right where a fire had been, and at the back of the space were a few logs and some kindling. Others had obviously used this place for the same purpose in the past. He took off his jacket and started a fire and, while he waited for it to burn up and become hot enough to boil some water, he stood and watched the rain. It was raining heavily now, huge drops falling vertically, and the sky was black above the trees. He thought it would be raining for a long while yet, maybe for the rest of the day. He prepared to make himself as comfortable as he could.

Several hundred yards further down the dram-road the man dressed in black had also pulled his wagon off the road as soon as he felt the first spot of rain. He was angry that the rain had come so quickly. He had hoped to get at least a few miles further down the road, maybe reach the other side of Parkend, before having to stop. But he could not afford to leave his load uncovered. No-one would want the black powder contained in the barrels that he was carrying, if there was any hint that it had become damp. He stretched a tarpaulin over the wagon. It was an old sail from a navy ship and was big enough to cover the entire wagon and reach to the ground all round, conveniently making a dry, warm space underneath, where he had slept on many a night. He covered the whole wagon but then carefully folded the cover back from the large box behind the driver's seat. He wanted to have access to the box later. He cursed loudly as he worked but eventually the job was done, and he crawled under the wagon and into the dry. He removed his damp coat and, lifting a section of the cover looked carefully around, taking stock of his surroundings. Maybe this wasn't such a bad place to stop after all.

He heard the sound of a wagon passing on the dram-road heading up the hill, and the voices of several men. He looked towards the road but the rain was so heavy now that he could only make out the vague shape of the wagon as it passed by the entrance to the quarry he was sheltering in. It continued on its way and disappeared from view. All was eerily quiet now, no sounds of birds or animals. There was just the sound of the falling rain.

CHAPTER 2

Mary Godwin

Clehonger, Herefordshire

The heavy rain that was falling so heavily on Gloucestershire, took less than an hour to spread north until it also covered most of the county of Herefordshire, turning the streams into rivers and the roads and lanes into quagmires. In the end Mary Godwin had to admit defeat and trudged disconsolately back to the cottage. As much as she hated to admit it her father had been right after all, she thought unhappily. It was useless her carrying on all alone.

As she kicked off her mud-caked boots and slipped out of her sodden outdoor clothes she pondered again on what could have been. It had never been like this in her dreams. In her dreams there had always been sunny days and laughter and love and a few children to care for, not this drudgery, not this miserable and lonely existence. But it had started out so well.

*

It had been when she went into service at Plainmoor House that the dream had started. She was only thirteen but even then she was a bright and headstrong girl, some said just like her father, the 'Irish Scotsman', James MacDonald. Definitely a chip off the old block, and proud of it. Plainmoor House was a happy place, a great place to work and Mister Jennings and his wife were wonderful employers, easy going and concerned for their employees. It was difficult to obtain a position at Plainmoor because no-one ever seemed to leave their jobs there. Mary realised just how lucky she had been.

The house wasn't that large and was easy to keep clean as everyone seemed to spend all their time outdoors. There was a nursery in the grounds but it wasn't for children, it was a nursery for trees and plants. The two Jennings boys were all grown up now and worked on the land alongside the fourteen gardeners who were also employed at the house. The nursery covered almost two acres of land and the glass-houses covered another eight. The whole property amounted to thirteen acres, counting the walled kitchen garden and with the lake included. Plainmoor House was a 'market garden' and the Jenningses sold all the produce they could grow in the markets in the seemingly insatiably hungry city of Hereford.

Mary thought that Plainmoor was wonderful. When she had finished her chores inside the house she would go out and work alongside the men in the gardens. Almost every day she could be seen among the plants. A diminutive figure with her long flame-coloured hair tied back and held in place with a ribbon and her white pinafore soil-stained.

No-one seemed to care that she was there, especially not Mister Jennings, who seemed to look upon her as more of a daughter than a servant. She was a quick learner and was not afraid to muck in and get her hands dirty and over the period of five years that she was employed at the house she learnt all about the seasons, and conditioning the soil and the balance between acid and alkali, and feeding plants, and seeds, and germination, and pollination, and transplanting, and grafting, and budding, and harvesting, and everything else that she heard from the men about growing healthy plants. She determined that she would marry and have a market-garden all of her own, and her husband and children would work alongside her and they would be as happy as the birds in the air. Just like the Jenningses.

But where was she to find a husband who would share her dream? The gardeners at Plainmoor were all much older than her. She was sure that some of them were so old they must be at least fifty years of age. Not one of them was eligible to be turned into a husband, and she needed a husband to help her fulfil her dream. No-one would take her seriously until she was wed. Then she met Henry Godwin.

Even at their first encounter she had thought that Henry Godwin was by far the most polite, gentlemanly and, dare she say it, cleanest man she had ever met, and quite the most handsome with his black, curly hair worn long and framing his face emphasising his pleasing regular features. He had come to the MacDonald house one weekend on cathedral business and she was furious with herself that she had blushed so badly when he had shaken her hand, and it was immediately obvious to her parents that she was smitten.

He became a regular visitor to the house and always, it seemed, when Mary was home for the day or the weekend from Plainmoor. They spent hours talking together and laughing and giggling and enjoyed each other's company. Henry had never worked on the land and had never considered the possibility of doing so, but gradually he got caught up in her dream. He was carried along by her enthusiasm and her excitement and, even though he could see the pitfalls more realistically than she could and had some reservations, he also began to believe that her dream could come true and it became part of him too. Together they could make such a venture work, but where to start?

It began with Henry calling formally on James MacDonald and asking for her hand in marriage. James had some nagging doubts, doubts which he could not articulate even to himself and kept the young man on tenterhooks whilst he went through the formalities. Eventually, to the young man's relief, he gave his blessing.

The nineteen months of the engagement seemed, to Mary, to take forever to pass, but gave them the time to save every penny they could. Henry worked all the hours possible and Mary sewed and crocheted and embroidered until her 'bottom drawer' was full to overflowing. It also gave them the chance to find the ideal property, a small cottage which a farmer had no further use for. James MacDonald, always a prudent man in every way especially with money, haggled with the farmer and was eventually able to buy it for a nominal sum. This was his wedding present to the couple. They also acquired with the cottage six acres of good, arable land, with a small sparkling river that bisected the land just behind the outbuildings.

Mary MacDonald and Henry Godwin were married in the chapel where her family had worshiped since their arrival from Ireland when she was only a baby, and that evening moved into the cottage which was to be their future together.

In the first months after the marriage, life was idyllic for the newlyweds. Mary worked at home, preparing the seeds and plants for the sowing season to come, whilst Henry continued with his work at the cathedral and brought home the necessary wage, as they had planned, and on Sundays they worked side by side on the land or on the buildings. At last they were ready to plant their first crops and Henry, with some regrets, left his employment.

But a life working on the land wasn't for Henry. The rigours of working outside in all winds and weathers were not for him. Working in the estates office at the cathedral had given him neither the stature, nor the stamina and physical strength required for such work. He had no notion of how exhausting continuous manual labour could be. Henry became permanently tired as the work took its toll on him and, as the seasons went by and autumn turned into winter and the weather turned wet and cold, his dream, or what he had thought of as his dream, turned into disillusionment, and the disillusionment turned into resentment and the unhappiness began.

Mary, however, was in her element and could not understand why Henry was not as happy as she was. She heard his voice but could not, or would not, listen to the message he was trying to give her. In the end he stopped trying and became sullen and argumentative and began to drink too much and stayed from the cottage as much as he reasonable could. He wasn't a bad man or a cruel man. He was just a man who now realised that he had made a terrible mistake and he felt trapped in a life he hated. Through all this, his affection for his wife continued, but it was not enough.

In early February he left the cottage for the last time. He took the coward's way out and sent her a long letter trying to explain; he had gone down to Bristol and there he would buy passage to America. He would not be back. That had been two years and three months ago.

*

Mary stood at the window and watched the rain and made her decision. She knew now that the work was too much for a person alone, and a woman at that. Everything was becoming dilapidated – the buildings, the machinery and even the soil itself. She knew about soil but she knew nothing of how to mend a leaking roof or repair a crumbling wall or how to straighten the bent blade of a plough. Some days she was so tired that she couldn't even eat and would just crawl wearily into her bed.

So now she would harvest the rest of the winter cabbage and the spring greens and then she would move back into her father and mother's house, as they had been urging her to do ever since Henry had left. She would sell everything, the cottage and everything in it and the land. She would relinquish the name of her husband, Godwin. She wanted nothing of what was left. There was nothing here for her except broken dreams and promises of what could have been.

She looked around the room that seemed, now that she had made up her mind to leave, to be growing colder with each minute that passed.

'I have given everything, I cannot give any more,' she said to no-one. The furniture stood silent, implacable. She slumped down onto one of the kitchen chairs. She knew now that she would be gone from this place within the week.

CHAPTER 3

The Forest of Dean

May 10, 1822

Whilst Mary Godwin, soon to be Mary MacDonald again, contemplated a bleak future in Hereford, the Limping Man moved closer to the small fire under the overhang and poured the boiling water into his enamel mug. The storm had blown through and the clouds were higher and lighter than they had been for several hours, but a miserable drizzle continued to fall. It wouldn't be long before it would begin to get dark again and spending the night under the overhang seemed to be the only sensible option.

He lit his small lantern with a spill from the fire and made himself as comfortable as he could on the hard ground. From inside his shirt he took a single news-sheet that he had found in the stable where he had spent the previous night. He unfolded it and, as he sipped the streaming tea, he began to read again the article that had prompted his decision to travel this way instead of following his normal route.

The news-sheet was ripped and dog-eared but the print was still legible between the folds. It was dated seven months earlier and told of a Cheltenham man who had visited the town of Coleford in the Forest of Dean to see his cousin, a Captain Richard Brookbanks, formerly of the Gloucestershire Regiment of Foot, but now a gentleman farmer and local Magistrate, on family business. It had been his first visit to the area and he wrote of his first impressions:

'the wildness of the countryside, the steep hills, the deep valleys and pity the poor traveller who has to travel on such poorly maintained roads, being deeply rutted with potholes and deep puddles, not at all fit for a carriage to make good time over. I despair at the feeling of poorness that pervades everything, in stark contrast to the natural beauty which is evident all around.'

On reaching the town he had been surprised and stunned by the obviously new building which had been erected in the marketplace in the centre. The new building was a church:

'innocent enough you would think, but the radical shape of the building, designed by Mr Poole the local benefactor who has reduced himself to near penury by providing the money for the enterprise, has proceeded to fragment the community. There were those, probably traditionalist-minded folk, who call the building an abomination and should be demolished forthwith, and there were others who welcome the building (the town has been without an adequate place of worship for almost two hundred years since the previous chapel was burnt down as a reprisal by the Royalists in the civil wars) as being of a fitting design 'to the Glory of God and Christian values'. As the argument rages on and on (the foundations of the church had been laid over ten years before) even individual members of the same family have taken opposing views.

Putting aside the arguments, as a student of fine architecture, I find the building fascinating. Built using local stone and roof beams cut from the mighty Oaks in the surrounding woods, all done with the finest of skill and precision, the church is (in my opinion) a joy to behold and a monument to the men who built her. For anyone who appreciates fine buildings which combine the best of workmanship with good design the church is well worth a visit'.

It was growing darker by the minute and the Limping Man folded the sheet of paper and put it back into his shirt. He drew himself closer to the fire and gathered his blanket around him, making himself as comfortable as he could on the stony ground. It would be a long night. He hoped that the visit to the church would be worth the trouble.

The loud banging on the studded Oak door roused Sergeant Watkins from his slumbers in the warm parlour of the house that served as both his home and the local jail. He was an unusually large man and, when he had pulled himself upright from the couch, he stood well over six feet tall. But despite his size he could be surprisingly fast on his feet as many a rowdy reveller in the town would testify. He had huge bony hands with scarred knuckles, a reminder of the time he had spent working the narrow underground coal-seams in his youth and the tough fist-fights he had been in since.

He reached out with his left hand and lifted the lantern as he made his way into the other room which served as the official part of the building. He didn't hurry, used to being roused at all hours in his capacity as law-keeper in the town, the town he thought of, not unreasonably, as being his to control. Hurrying never solved anything. He shouted loudly as he approached the door and the banging stopped. He turned the iron key, lifted the latch and swung the great door wide. His face registered surprise as he recognised the man standing on the doorstep.

'Edwin Morgan, what brings you here banging like that?' Then, seeing the man's face, he asked, 'What's amiss, man?'

He knew the man well, as he knew everyone in the town, and knew him to be a man of high morals and integrity.

'I need your help, Sergeant. My boy's gone missing, my boy Charlie. He ain't come home and he's been gone all day.'

*

'You, Edward Timpson, and you John Cookley, and you David Weaving.' The Sergeant pointed at the young men in the smoke-filled room. 'I need you to help us search for young Charlie Morgan who's gone missing.' He turned to go, brooking no argument. 'First thing in the morning then lads, up at the jail, and if he hasn't turned up by then, we'll have to search the woods up the Broad Well, so keep the ale out of you tonight.'

'But Sergeant, what about work?' The Sergeant turned back to face the men.

'Bugger your work,' he said angrily, 'this is a young boy we're talking about here. He could have fallen down a quarry or a pit and be lying there now. I need your help.' He turned away once again and made for the door. Two of the men followed him.

This was the eighth time he had had this conversation as he had visited the public houses grouped around the town centre. He and Edwin Morgan had returned from the toll-house at the bottom of Bakers Hill, where the old man had confirmed that Charlie Morgan had passed that way earlier and, no, he had not seen the boy coming back.

'There is nothing else we can do, in the dark.' Edwin Morgan had wanted to continue on but the sergeant had taken his arm. 'We'll search for him first thing tomorrow. I'll round up some men.'

As he left the bar-room he turned.

'We have to help each other, lads, it's only right.'

His voice much softer now. They nodded, they knew he was right.

'And by the way, Eddie lad, bring your dogs, we may have need of them.' The hubbub of conversation started up again as he stepped onto the street. He didn't need to guess what the topic of conversation would be.

CHAPTER 4

The Limping Man

Tuesday May 11, 1822

He had slept fitfully, kept from restful sleep by the cold, the hard ground and the sounds of scurrying animals and droplets of water falling gently from the trees. He had been awakened once by a shrill sound that reminded him of the scream of a small child. He had listened intently but the sound had not been repeated. Maybe he had been dreaming; he dreamed a lot these days. Or maybe it had been an animal. He had dozed again.

He opened his eyes, shifted onto his side and stirred the embers of his fire. There was no sign of life, but no matter. He recognised the intense blackness that is natural just before the dawn breaks and knew that he could be on his way before long. The rain had stopped and there was a freshness in the air. He lay back and offered up his usual prayer, asking God to keep his mother and father safe, and not forgetting Lizzie and Frenchie and their two small children.

He wondered what the day held in store for him; some dry, warm weather would be nice.

He left the confines of the quarry as the first sign of daylight had appeared above the trees, feeling his boots and the wheels of his cart sinking deeply into the patch of soft ground at the edge of the dram-road yet again. He had rejoined the hard surface and started his upward journey but within minutes he felt the cleat on the sole of his left boot come adrift. He sat at the side of the track and changed into his spare boots, knowing that if he didn't it would only be a short time before his left knee began to give him real pain.

Thankfully, he soon crested the hill at the Broad Well and walked into bright sunlight. He passed the public house there, closed up and well shuttered, and continued down towards the town and walked back into deep shadow. Three hundred yards down the track he came upon the big house and despite the early hour he heard voices in the yard. He turned his cart and went through the gate.

*

The men stood in a ragged group, wrapped up against the early morning chill. They numbered more than thirty and there was an assortment of dogs as well, mostly mongrels but some boisterous spaniels, a few border collies and one huge lurcher. The men shuffled their feet, as waiting men always do; some talked quietly amongst themselves, but most were lost in their own thoughts. One man coughed loudly and spat in the gutter.

The Sergeant and Edwin Morgan emerged from the studded door and faced the men. Edwin was dressed in his work clothes as usual but he looked rumpled and dishevelled and it was obvious by his tired eyes that he had not slept for a long while. The Sergeant wore a pair of old moleskin trousers that had seen better days and a pair of worn boots, but even without his uniform there was no mistaking who was in command. He faced the men and pulled himself up to his full height.

'Right then lads, heads up.' He never once thought of thanking them for coming. 'We are going out to look for Edwin's boy Charlie, who didn't come home yesterday afternoon. We,' he indicated Edwin, 'know that he went through the toll-gate at the bottom of Bakers Hill before dinner-time yesterday, so we'll start from there. We'll form a skirmish line and do a sweep up to the Broad Well and then down the dram-road. I want us to be thorough. I want every nook and cranny searched. I want every bush and coppice looked into.' He stared around at the group of silent men. 'The boy might be injured. He might not be able to shout for help. Remember, this could be one of yours out there.' He paused to let the thought sink in. 'Right, let's go. Quick as you like then, lads.'

*

The porridge with the honey and molasses had gone down a treat. He had offered to work for his breakfast but the cook, a charitable woman and a pushover for men with blue eyes, had taken pity on him when she had heard that he had spent the night on the hard, stony floor of the quarry. Now they were sat together on the back doorstep of the big house talking together quietly. After his meal she had offered him a clay pipe of tobacco but he had declined, preferring instead another mug of tea. She sucked steadily on her own pipe, taking advantage of the free time before the family rose from their beds, demanding her services.

They heard the sounds of a large group of men passing by on the road and the cook stood immediately.

'Sounds like something's going on,' she said, more to herself than to anyone else. 'I'd better go and have a looksee,' she smiled at him, 'me being a nosy beggar and all.'

He heard the men continue their way up the hill and the cook reappeared around the corner of the house.

'The Sergeant with some men, looking for a boy who's gone missing,' she replied to his inquisitive look. 'Never came home last night. Fell down a hole somewhere, I wouldn't be surprised.'

'I'd better get moving,' he said, rising to his feet, 'I've got miles to go before the end of the day. Thanks for the porridge and all.'

'Think nothing on it, it were the least I could do.' She looked again into his deep blue eyes. 'Make sure you get that boot mended in town, and tell Edgar I said he was not to overcharge you, or he will have me, Alice Comely, to deal with.'

*

He heard the barking of the dogs and the shouts of the men and he was instantly awake. He wondered why men were about in the pitch black until he realised that he was still under the wagon with the sail-cloth pulled down shutting out the light. He lifted the edge of the canvas and the light streamed in. It was full daylight, he had slept late. He knew exactly what the men and dogs were about. They were looking for the boy.

'Shit,' he cursed as the panic set in, 'fucking shit.'

He made himself listen to the sounds. They echoed and re-echoed from the walls of the quarry and he had no idea if they were coming down the slope or ascending from below. He had no idea of which way to make his escape.

He climbed from under the wagon and lifted the sail-cloth clear, exposing the naked body of the boy. He knew now he shouldn't have taken the chance. The boy was too old for his tastes; and too strong. It had been different and exciting to begin with and he had taken some pleasure from subduing the boy – or so he thought, for in the night the boy had suddenly erupted into action in the dim light of the lantern. Hitting and punching with his little fists, and kicking and screaming out and he had had to hit him with the piece of rock and, in his temper, he had taken the knife to the boy, cutting deeply into his abdomen and chest, silencing him forever.

He looked around wildly for a place to hide the body, but in the empty quarry there was nowhere that would defeat a determined search. He had often thought how it would all end, what it would be like to be caught by the mob, but he had never envisaged the blind panic that was engulfing him now. He had always thought that it would be a welcome relief and that he would face the end with calmness. But he was terrified and, now that it was near, the thought of the rope around his neck filled him with dread.

He dragged himself back from the edge of hysteria. He had to think straight. There had to be a way of disposing of the body and avoiding capture. He would have to look elsewhere. He gathered up the boy's clothes and tied them into a bundle. He was a strong man and it was easy for him to lift the body and the bundle and carry them to the entrance, paying no heed to the fact that he was still naked himself. He stepped cautiously out onto the dram-road and, now that he was out in the open, it was obvious that the sounds of the search were coming from up the hill. He scanned the road, expecting to see the men. There was no-one in sight and, not far up the road, he could see the entrance to another quarry.

The mixture of fear and adrenalin had given him strength and even with his burden he easily ran up the hill, ignoring the pain from the stones under his bare feet, and approached the entrance. He cautiously peered in, not knowing what to expect but immediately seeing that the space was empty and ideal for his purpose. Skirting around the patch of soft ground at the entrance which already bore the tracks of someone else, he carried the body inside.

Edward Timpson had found himself on the far right of the line as the men began their sweep down the hill from the Broad Well.. He knew this area well, having played here with his friends, as a boy, climbing among the rocks and searching for birds' eggs in the nests crammed into the nooks and crannies. He was nearly a hundred yards from the dram-road and his route would take him along the ridge above the quarries. His dogs were running free, treating the whole thing as a game, barking and running to and fro among the trees, but they were trained gundogs and he knew that they would soon let him know if they found something.

The going was easy and he was a young man. He had made good progress, managing to get well ahead of the men lower down in the valley. He had passed the first workings, known to the boys as Raven, and was nearing the quarry they knew as Jackdaw. He moved closer to the rim, taking care of where he put his feet and peered over the edge. From his vantage point high on the rim the body seemed small, and pale, and insignificant. And broken.

He tried to shout but no sound came out of his suddenly dry mouth. He licked his lips and tried again. At first he just croaked but then managed to shout. 'He's here. He's in Jackdaw.' And then he shouted again, but this time much louder, 'I can see him. He's in Jackdaw!' and the men making their way down the dram-road looked upwards before breaking into a run towards the entrance to the quarry.

*

He had soaked in the small tin bath until the water had become too cold for comfort and then used the water to wash his shirt and cotton 'union suit', before getting dressed in his clean shirt, and making his way across the street to the barber's shop. The bath had cost him four pence and the shave two but he considered it money well spent. He felt clean and refreshed and the stink of his body odour had disappeared along with the grey suds of the hard lye soap, and what better way was there to while away the hour that the cobbler had said the repairs to his boots would take?

From the barber's chair he had a fine view of the new church, and whilst the young barber's assistant had busied himself scraping away the fine blond stubble, he had studied the building with interest. It was indeed a fine-looking building, octagonal, and perfect in its geometric lines. He had walked fully around the exterior, appreciating the skill and craftsmanship that had gone into its making but not understanding why the building should have caused such controversy in the town. Entering by the main door he was surprised to see several, maybe as many as a dozen people already inside. The interior was bright and airy but cold and the people were dressed in outdoor clothes as they sat in the pews, which were arranged in a circle around a central altar. There was no service taking place but a man dressed in the black of the clergy moved among the people talking quietly. He looked up as the stranger entered and stood as though waiting for him to speak.

He would have liked to have stayed longer in the church. Perhaps he may have sat in one of the pews and thought about all that had happened to him. He liked churches. He found them restful and, mostly, uplifting and he always felt at peace after sitting quietly by himself with all the paraphernalia of religion around him, although he wouldn't have described himself as a religious man. No, certainly not a religious man. Not for a long time now.

But the Limping Man felt ill at ease under the scrutiny of the clergyman. Something was happening here, something that did not concern him. He nodded to the man, turned away and left the building. It was time he made his way back to the cobbler's shop. His boots should be ready now.

*

Sergeant Watkins bounded down the dram-road and came to a skidding halt in the entrance to Jackdaw. He turned to face the men as they gathered around and held out his arms just in time to prevent Edwin Morgan from rushing forward. Against his struggles he hugged the man powerfully to his chest.

'Steady Edwin, steady now,' he said quietly but firmly in his ear. 'Best I think if you let us go first. You never know what we will find in there. Stay here for a minute while we look.'

'But I need to see, my boy may need me. Let me go.' He struggled some more but he was no match for the big man.

Two men stepped forward and took hold of Edwin's arms,

preventing him from moving. The Sergeant moved forward, beckoning to the barber, who was there in his capacity as the town doctor, to follow. They moved off the road but before they had gone more than a few yards the Sergeant stopped, knelt down and studied the patch of soft ground.

'Someone's been here before today, these tracks are fresh.' He pointed to the deep footprints and then his fingers traced the tracks made by the narrow wheels. He stood and turned to the gathering of silent men.

'Right then,' he said loudly, 'I want no-one to walk on this patch of ground.' He pointed to the tracks. 'Some body has been here before us, today.' He didn't say they could be the tracks of a killer, but everyone knew what was implied, including Edwin, still struggling to break free.

The two men skirted around the patch of ground in question and passed through the narrow entrance. The barber suddenly realised that all was silent, no birds singing, no sound of the wind rustling through the new leaves on the trees. Even the dogs up on the rim had stopped barking and lay obediently at the feet of young Eddie Timpson.

*

He had run back to his lair as though all the devils of hell were after him, terrified that he may have been spotted. Squirming under his wagon he had pulled the sailcloth back into place, shutting out the light. His bare feet were cut and bruised from running over the broken stones and he clenched his fists against the pain. As he cowered there he could hear the dogs barking and the shouts of the men as they got closer and closer.

Just when it had seemed they were right on top of him all suddenly became silent. He lay under the wagon for what seemed like hours, hearing nothing, no voices, not even any dogs, until he could stand the uncertainty no longer and slowly lifted the covering. He prayed that the men hadn't crept up on him whilst he had been hiding, waiting silently for him to emerge, but he was alone still. He was almost physically sick with relief. The men must have discovered the body of the boy and ended their search in the quarry where he had thrown the corpse.

He hurriedly pulled on his clothes, all the while his ears alert to any sounds, before making his way towards the dram-road. He hunkered down amongst the rocks and, when he had gathered his nerve, he raised himself up and peered out. At first he could see nothing, but he crawled further forward until he was able to see up the slope. He was just in time to see the group of men disappearing over the brow of the hill. They were walking slowly, their heads down, not talking, and they were carrying something on a makeshift litter. Two men walked behind the others, slightly apart, and one man, the bigger of the two, had his arm on the other's shoulder.

He was about to rise, filled with relief and elation, when he heard the noise. He turned his head and there, not ten feet away, stood a large dog, showing its huge, yellow teeth as it made a rumbling noise deep in its throat. He lay still and tried not to lock eyes with the animal. He had heard somewhere that locking eyes with a vicious dog was to offer a challenge.

He barely registered the whistle that sounded from somewhere above, but the dog stiffened and in a flash was gone. Without realising it he had been holding his breath, and now it escaped with a whoosh, followed by a sob as he started to breathe again. He made to rise and as he gained his feet he realised that his trousers were wet. He had pissed himself in fright.

CHAPTER 5

Sergeant Watkins

Coleford
May 11, 1822

Sergeant Watkins crossed the street where it narrowed at the eastern end of the church and made for the alley between the blacksmith's shop and the Unicorn Tavern. The Blacksmith, standing close to the forge at the rear of the premises, watched him pass and they greeted each other with a wary nodding of heads. The Sergeant entered the tavern through the back door, something he would never do in uniform, but today he was still wearing the clothes he had worn on the search for the boy, even though it was now past five in the afternoon.

The back room was gloomy, having only one small window, caked in dirt, which looked out onto the alley down which he had just walked. He crossed to the plank which served as a counter. There was the murmur of male voices from the front of the building but he could not make out what they were saying. He rapped on the plank with a gnarled fist and the landlord appeared as though by magic through the connecting archway.

'Well speak of the devil, what can I do you for?'

'A jug of your best, and make it quick.' There was no love lost between the two men. Watkins had made plenty of enemies since his return to the town.

As usual he made no effort to pay for the drink and the landlord knew better than to ask. He had swallowed half the ale almost before the landlord had turned his back in disgust and returned to the front room. He smacked his lips at the bitter taste. He needed this drink badly and had quickly walked the mile or so from the Magistrate's house back to the town.

That tight bugger of a Magistrate had not offered him any refreshment, not even a drink of water, even though he had been in the house for what seemed like hours making his report. The Magistrate had wanted to know every detail of the search, the state of the body of young Charlie Morgan, how the Sergeant thought he had been killed, and the location in which it had been found. He questioned him closely. He knew that sometimes things were not what they appeared, but in this case both men agreed that all other possibilities could be ruled out. This was a murder, it couldn't possibly be anything else.

'You will apprehend the man who did this crime, won't you Sergeant?' It was more a statement of intent than a question. 'The people of the town are already unhappy with the petty thieving and all, and I am getting complaints from the townspeople nearly every day. The High Sheriff is also unhappy with the situation in the county as a whole, and this could be the last straw. If you don't catch him we may find ourselves out of a job, do you understand me?'

*

When the Sergeant had first taken charge in the town most common people possessed little of any value, consequently there had been very little to steal. It wasn't worth the bother. Mostly his duties consisted of patrolling the streets and breaking up the odd arguments and fistfights which flared up, usually outside the public drinking houses. But things were changing, rapidly. Now ordinary people, at least those in regular work, were becoming better off since the end of the wars and the cessation of the war-tax. They were finding that at the end of each week, they had a few coppers to spare to spend on 'luxuries'.

But these few 'luxuries' were attractive also to some of the people who had no money to spare at the end of the week. Unemployment had risen rapidly as peace was declared and whole armies were disbanded and the men sent home without any means of support.

The lack of money didn't prevent them from seeing the goods which others were buying from the shops and filling their houses with. In desperation, the only way for them to possess such things was to steal from others, and Sergeant Watkins couldn't cope with the new circumstances.

He knew that his position here in the town was in jeopardy of being taken from him, something that he couldn't contemplate. He would never stand the shame if he was demoted, his pride would not allow it. He knew he had to do something, and it had to be something major, to regain his reputation.

Sergeant Watkins lived alone in the damp and dismal building in Gloucester Road that doubled up as home and jail. He had never married and preferred it that way. That is not to say that he hadn't had opportunities with the ladies. When he was a lot younger he had been considered a 'good catch', but had resisted all attempts to get him to the altar.

He was a big man, shading six feet in his socks and broad in the shoulder. Strong, and reliable looking, although he knew within himself, that his forty-three-year-old body (by his reckoning) was starting to let him down. The hard physical work underground which his father had made him do when he had been no more than a mere lad, and all the fights and skirmishes, the broken bones, the knife wounds and the bumps and bruises he had suffered when he was with the Gloucester City Militia, were taking a toll.

But he had a good head of hair and most people, on first meeting him, usually considered him to be rather handsome with pleasing regular features. That is, until he smiled.

Not that he smiled that often. More often than not his face wore a frown or a scowl, expressions which matched his dour demeanour perfectly. But it hadn't always been so.

Sometime in the past, a change had come over Sergeant Watkins, a change in the way in which he viewed the world around him. Maybe it was the time during the 1819 Corn Riots in the city, when the government neglected to deliver on its promise of 'plenty for all', and Watkins had lost nearly all his own teeth to a blow from a half-starved rioter armed with a broken table leg. Watkins had been a private then. Young and impetuous, and he had not heeded the advice of his sergeant to bide his time before making the arrests. He had been laid low by the blow and it had taken a long while for him to recover enough, during which time the wooden teeth had been fitted into his mouth to replace his own, before he could take his place again in the company of Militia. Or maybe it was some other incident, but something had changed him.

In the years following the riots, his behaviour had increasingly become a real cause for concern for his Commanding Officer. It wasn't just the violent way in which he went about his duties, for he was in a business that often required extreme violence, but it was his argumentativeness and his stubbornness, stubbornness which bordered on the obsessive. Once he had made his mind up nothing was going to shake his belief that he was right.

His behaviour had become such an embarrassment that when the newly appointed Magistrate for the Coleford area, a certain Captain Brookbanks had come calling, asking for the help of a militiaman to keep the peace and 'man' the town gaol, the Colonel jumped at the chance to offload Watkins and he was duly transferred, much to the relief of his company.

The promotion to Sergeant had come with the transfer, and Watkins, in his mind if not in fact, returned to the town of his birth in triumph. He knew this town. He knew the people and he knew the Forest. He knew what made them tick but he hadn't taken into account the natural distrust and disdain that they held for anyone in authority. And his attitude had not helped him win the people over either, in fact the opposite. They had made him a pariah. They had kept him at arm's length and he was made to live on the edge of the close-knit society.

But in a grudging way, he was respected.

*

Sergeant Watkins leant heavily on the 'counter'. He felt weary to his very core and the throbbing headache was back again. He hated days like this, days that seemed to last forever and sapped his energy and left him feeling empty and impotent. He reached again for his mug and took another mouthful. He felt like getting drunk but knew that he would need to do it in the secrecy of his own home, such as it was. To be seen under the influence of strong drink in public was not acceptable.

His thoughts returned again to the words of the Magistrate and the implied threat to his position here. 'What does he expect me to do?' he fumed, suddenly angry. 'I'm not a sorcerer, I'm just a militiaman. Where do I start? The murderer could be anyone.' The bitterness swept over him. 'It's alright for him, sat in his big house and lauding it over me and everyone else. He doesn't have to live among these people. He doesn't have to face them every day and them knowing that if they break the law I will lock them up and me knowing that they hate me for it and, for my troubles, I have to live in that poxy jailhouse.'

He would have descended further into self-pity if he hadn't, at that moment, been disturbed by a shuffling sound from behind him. He spun round, ready to defend himself, always aware of the sneak attack which may come from behind. It wouldn't have been the first time he had been attacked from behind with no warning. He had thought he was alone in the dingy room but now, as he sought the origin of the noise he had heard, he could make out the shape of a man in the gloom next to the unlit fireplace.

'Good evening to you, Sergeant.' The Cobbler, a coward at heart, always thought it was best to stay courteous to anyone who could cause you strife. 'Bad business today,' he added.

'Aye, it's a bad business alright and no mistake.' Then, much to the surprise of the man sitting in the shadows, 'I doubt if Edwin Morgan or me will get much sleep tonight.'

He turned and picked up his mug again, only to place it back on the 'counter' without taking a drink as a thought struck him. He lifted the shove-ha'penny tallyboard and the tiny piece of chalk from its place on the counter and crossed to the Cobbler, cleaning the board with his sleeve as he walked. He sat next to the man and, using the piece of chalk, drew a fair likeness of the distinctive shoeprints he had seen at the entrance to the quarry that morning. The Cobbler watched, fascinated, and when the drawing was finished the Sergeant thrust it forcefully in front of him.

'Ever seen anything like that, then? What kind of shoe would make a print like that?'

The cobbler took his time studying the drawing before reaching for his mug and, pointedly, looking inside. It was empty.

'What do you want to know for?'

'Never you no mind what I want to know for, just tell me what you think.' The Sergeant was in no mood for delaying tactics. The Cobbler looked into his mug again.

'Well, I might know something and I might not. But my brain works better if it's well lubricated.'

For several seconds Sergeant Watkins seriously thought about giving the man a clout around the head from one of his massive fists, but he hadn't the energy in him and it wouldn't have helped anyway. Instead he rose, went to the 'counter' and drained his own mug before using it to rap loudly on the plank.

'Two mugs of best, landlord.' And he fished in his pocket and held out some coins. 'How much?' he asked.

The landlord was so taken aback by the offer of payment that he could only stammer, 'N-n-nothing, nothing to you, Sergeant. It's on the house.' He would wish later, when he had had time to think, that he had taken the coins from the man. The Sergeant pocketed the coins again and took the mugs back to the table.

'Well? What do you make of it? Any ideas?'

'It's a boot, not a shoe.' The Cobbler was in his element now, and it was time to show off a little. 'A boot made from the finest leather,' he spoke quickly now, 'with the most superb stitching. It could have been made in London, but I would say, it's more likely it was made abroad, probably in France, but maybe in Spain.'

'How do you know that?'

'That's for me to know,' he answered and rubbed the side of his nose with his index finger. 'The deep, curved indentation you see is caused by a cleat which has been added to the sole in order to hold the sole of the wearer's foot at a particular angle, saving the wearer excruciating pain, and allowing him to walk without the aid of crutches or a stick.' He reached for his mug and took a deep draught. 'Very clever.' He was in full flow now.

'How do you know all this?' the Sergeant asked again.

The Cobbler looked at the Sergeant with a look of superiority on his face.

'The boot is worn by a man of more than usual height, of slim build and with a terrible limp.'

Once again he reached for his mug and poured more ale down his throat. He was enjoying himself. And at last the Sergeant put two and two together.

'You've seen this man, haven't you? You know who he is.'

'No, I have no idea who he is. I'd never seen him before today. He just walked into town, pushing a handcart with a whetstone on it. He's just another tinker as far as I can tell and yes, I did mend his boot this morning, the self-same boot that made the print that you have drawn. I would stake my reputation on it.'

The Sergeant leapt up from the table.

'And where's this stranger now? Where's he staying in town?' The questions came thick and fast but the Cobbler sat back unperturbed until, eventually, he also put two and two together and guessed why the Sergeant was so anxious to know more.

'This has something to do with the murder, hasn't it?' he asked excitedly. 'Are you looking for this man for the killing of young Charlie?' The Cobbler looked aghast as realisation dawned. 'The killer was in my shop and I let him go. I showed him the way out of town. I even gave him directions.' He lowered his head and said quietly, almost as though he was speaking to himself, 'He has already left town, he has already gone.'

'Gone! Gone where? Which way did he go?'

'He said he was heading for Ross, to cross the river there. I showed him the way, up Sparrow Hill.'

'How long ago? How much start has he got?'

'He left as I was closing up for dinner.'

'Bloody hell, even walking he could be miles away by now. What time is it now?'

'It must be nearly six; I heard the church clock strike five before you came in. There's still a few hours of light left if you go after him, you might catch up to him if you're lucky.'

'Aye, I might at that, if I hurry. What did he look like, this stranger?'

'Taller than me, but not as tall as you I reckon, and slim, dressed in a black coat, no hat.'

'That could fit half the people in England, I bet. I couldn't be sure to recognise him from that.'

'Oh you'll recognise him alright; he couldn't be mistaken for anyone else. He has fair hair, bleached by the sun and worn long, he ties it back with a braid as sailors used to do in the time of Nelson so that it hangs down his back, and he walks with a bad limp. And if that isn't enough to recognise him by, when you see his eyes, you'll know. He has the biggest and deepest blue eyes this side of Christendom.' Then, thinking he could be in on the action, feeling brave after a few pints of strong ale and thinking maybe he could become a bit of a hero in the town, he added, 'Want me to come with you? I could point him out to you.'

'No, you stay here,' the Sergeant said, not even trying to hide the contempt in his voice, 'I reckon I can travel faster without any hindrances such as you.'

And he was gone.

*

At about the same time that the Sergeant had entered the Magistrate's house to give his report, the Limping Man had reached The Gorse at the top of Sparrow Hill. Here the ground formed a sort of plateau and the track levelled out for several miles before beginning the long descent down to the River Wye at Lydbrook.

The afternoon had become hot and humid as the sun evaporated the moisture that had fallen during the previous day and he was sweating heavily from his exertions, even though he had removed his coat as soon as he had begun the climb. He paused to catch his breath and held his arms aloft to allow the slight breeze, which was blowing gently across the fields, to dry him.

He turned to face the way he had come and was afforded a magnificent view over the town with its religious centrepiece glowing in the sunshine. From this distance the town looked orderly and peaceful, but a mile or more beyond, a column of dirty, black smoke hung over the brilliant green of the trees, spoiling the tranquil picture. He shrugged in dismay and turned to resume his journey, wanting to get on now. It was already the middle of the afternoon by his reckoning and he knew would need to hurry if he was to make Ross by nightfall. Up ahead a coach pulled by four horses crossed directly across his path, travelling fast from right to left. He watched its progress until it disappeared from sight down a slight incline but he could still hear the sound of their iron-shod hooves, until eventually even that faded away to silence.

He reached the point where the road he was on crossed the main Gloucester/Monmouth road. There was a signpost there which informed travellers that Monmouth was to the left and was four miles distant. Suddenly, on the same kind of impulse which had brought him to the area in the first place, he turned to the left instead of crossing the road and following the sign for English Bicknor, on the Ross road. Ross was still more than seven miles away, but he could make Monmouth easily by the time it began to get dark. He had never been to the town before but it was on a main route, and he knew there must be a bridge over the river there.

He walked on and descended the incline following the route taken by the speeding coach.

CHAPTER 6

Sergeant Watkins

Wednesday 12 May, 1822

Sergeant Watkins climbed his weary way up the hill out of town following the road that would take him to the Magistrate's house. He was not looking forward to making his report, but it had to be done and sooner now than later. He had no good news to impart.

The Magistrate seemed to be in an affable mood but still did not offer any refreshment to the Sergeant.

'What news have you of the tinker? Good news I hope.' He had already received a missive from the Sheriff of Gloucester stressing the urgency of the investigation and the need for a speedy arrest.

'Good news, sir, no. I am afraid not.' He knew he had done his best to apprehend the man but all his efforts had been in vain. After his conversation with the Cobbler he had ridden the road that the man would have taken in order to reach Ross, out through Bicknor and down to the river at Lydbrook and then on to Kerne Bridge, the first available crossing place. The Sergeant gave his report, and added, 'I have called at every farm and large house between here and there. I have questioned farmers, field-hands, servants, cooks and everyone I met on the road, but no-one has set eyes on such a man. Not even the old woman who keeps the toll on the bridge has seen him and she sees everything, and more. It is as though the man has disappeared into thin air,' he concluded.

'He can't have done. Such a feat is impossible, he must be somewhere.' The Magistrate showed his displeasure.

'Aye, but where? The trail has gone cold and I don't know where else to look.'

'Well you'll have to think of somewhere. We have to act with all speed. The Sheriff has a Judge standing by to attend immediately we make an arrest. I need to think this through, I need to consider our positions in this matter.'

*

An hour later he was in the back room of the Unicorn Inn with a flea in his ear. He had been torn off a strip and once again had been warned of the threat to his job. He was angry and needed a drink.

Two men were seated in the gloom watching him. He recognised the Cobbler straight away but could not recall the other man. The Cobbler spoke.

'I take it that you haven't caught the tinker yet then?' He had noticed the scowl on the face of the man stood at the bar.

'No, not yet,' he growled back, 'but it's only a matter of time.' He tried to put a brave face on it.

'Who's this then?' the other man enquired. 'Have I missed something while I've been away?' There was a definite Welsh lilt to the way he spoke.

The Cobbler turned to the other man. He had not realised that the man didn't know about the murder of young Charlie, and was now eager to be the bearer of bad news. It didn't take long to bring the man up to date.

'So,' said the Sergeant, assuming the lead again, 'we're looking for a tinker who passed this way. A tall man with blond hair and deep blue eyes and walking with a limp. He would be pushing a hand cart.'

'I think I know the man you mean. Yesterday, we were making our way home from Abergavenny Market, my brother and me, and we stopped off for a pint at the pub at the bottom of the hill this side of Monmouth. A man answering your description was working there, out in the yard. He had a handcart with a wet wheel on it and was sharpening some tools.'

'That sounds like our man. Where did he go from there?'

I don't know. We left before he did. He could still be there, for all I know.'

The Sergeant wasted no time but was too late, the man had left the inn and moved on. No-one knew where he was heading. Once across the river he could have gone in any direction. He had all of Wales before him, the bastard.

CHAPTER 7

The Limping Man

Friday 14 May, 1822

It had taken him two days to reach the village of Wormelow after leaving Coleford. He had crossed the bridge at Monmouth and entered the town. He disliked towns, too many people and too much noise and bustle for his tastes, but sometimes needs must. He bought a few meagre provisions and, after considering his next move, took the road out of town which would take him all the way to Hereford.

The road was one of those he would have described as 'lumpy'. Hardly any flat but plenty of uphill and downhill. Hard going for a man with a cart to push. Not too steep but tiring, for holding back on the down slopes was as bad for him as pushing on the up slopes and on this road there was no respite from either, and his legs were beginning to give him pain with each step. He knew that he would have to rest or pay the consequences for days to come.

Now he was faced with a dilemma for here the road divided into two equally rutted tracks. A signpost informed him that the track to the right would take him to Hereford but as he followed the line of the route the track took he could see that it rose steeply for at least a mile or more before crossing the ridgeline. What lay beyond he could only guess at but he doubted if his leg could cope with the initial uphill stretch. Another hour or more of strenuous pushing was the last thing he needed at this moment.

The other track was posted as the road to Hay-on-Wye, and in smaller lettering on the same pointer was printed Clehonger. In stark contrast to the other route this way seemed to follow a level course which meandered between the trees which grew on either side of the hard surface.

There was a small hostilerie off to the side of the road and John entered the dark interior, which seemed to be empty. It would be several hours before the light faded and the field workers would fill the place with noise before making their way home to their families.

Two hours later John was still sitting comfortably in the settle by the unlit fire. He had eaten well for only a few pennies and had drank more beer than he should have but as he had rested the muscles in his legs had stiffened and he no longer had the urge to carry on that night. The road would still be there in the morning.

A nice, clean, comfortable bed would have been good but he decided to save his money and settled for a free stay in the straw in the barn instead.

During his time in the inn, he had received much in the way of advice on which route to take to Hereford, but most of the locals preferred the road to Hay over the climb up the ridge, and when he reached Clehonger, if he had the mind to bear right, the road would take him to Hereford anyway, maybe a mile further but in the long run, consensus had it that it would take him less time, and it would be much easier on his sore legs.

With the effects of the beer and a full belly he slept well. He awoke just after dawn and, after a small and very basic breakfast, which was all he could afford, got off to an early start.

CHAPTER 8

Coleford
Saturday 15 May, 1822

It seemed as though the whole town had turned out for the burial of Charlie Morgan. Hundreds of the townspeople formed a straggling procession that stretched back behind the wooden box that enclosed the small body. They had climbed the steep hill and had reached the Scowles as they followed the burial path from the church in the marketplace to the graveyard at Newland. The bearers sweated freely in the heat of the afternoon and thankfully handed their burden over to others who would carry the coffin for what was left of the very last journey of the murdered boy. Luckily for the new men, from here it was all downhill and the going was easier.

The last three days had dragged by slowly for Edwin Morgan, as one day followed interminably after another, and all the while his son's body lay in the front parlour, a reminder of what had happened on what should have been a joyous birthday. As though he needed any reminder. But now the time had arrived and he was laying his son to rest. Maybe things would get better now. Eventually he and his wife would smile again. Everyone kept telling them so, but it would take a very long time.

The preacher, who now led the procession reciting passages from the Psalms and the Book of Prayer, had spoken of the tragedy that had befallen Edwin Morgan and his whole family, a tragedy that had affected the whole town also. He had practised his sermon time and time again and spoke with all the piety that he could muster, for seldom did he get the chance to address a congregation as large, or as angry, as this one.

He had spoken of the senselessness of the boy's death. A young lad, not even a man yet, but with everything to look forward to. A young lad who had been dearly loved by his parents and who had been liked by everyone who knew him. A lad who had been cut down before his life had hardly began. He had spoken of the Lord's will and the mysterious way in which He worked. The boy would be with the Lord now and could feel no more pain or have any earthly worries. He would be happy in Heaven.

Finally he spoke about forgiveness. The Christian way, he said, was to forgive those who hurt us or harmed us. Didn't the good book teach us, he asked, to turn the other cheek? Everyone, even the murderer, he said, would receive their reward in Heaven or in Hell.

But there was no forgiveness in the hearts of the people who trudged the burial path up the long hill. Not one iota. Their collective hearts were full of hatred for the man who had killed the boy and a burning desire to avenge his death. They all wanted nothing more than to see the man die. Especially Edwin Morgan.

Only a few days ago he had such dreams for him and his boy; they would work together, be friends and partners. They would work hard and enjoy a jar on the way home at night, and the boy would grow into a fine young man, respected, liked, and then he would marry a nice girl and give him grandchildren and he would love them as much as he loved his boy. But now all those dreams had been swept away by one callous act. It was too soon but already he was saying goodbye to his son for the last time, and it was so hard and the dreams that he had nurtured for the future made saying goodbye harder still. And in her hours of need he was unable to give his wife the love and comfort she so badly needed. And the other children, they were so afraid and bewildered, at what had happened. One day Charlie was there and the next day he wasn't. They needed him to be strong and to be their guardian and he should be helping them to understand what had happened to the family, but he couldn't. He was in danger of being consumed by the anger that burned so fiercely in his heart.

Now, as he walked alone behind the coffin, he thought of the preacher's words. Bugger forgiveness, bugger receiving your rewards in Heaven. He thought of other words from the Bible, 'an eye for an eye', and even more relevant, 'vengeance is mine, sayeth the Lord'. And he knew that he would have vengeance of a sort. He didn't know how or when or where, but he knew it would happen.

Like everyone else in the town, he wanted the Limping Man caught and brought back to the town. He wanted to meet the man, face to face. He wanted to look into the man's eyes, see what kind of a man could kill a young boy, and he wanted to be looking into the man's eyes as he died. If he had half a chance he would kill the man himself, with his bare hands if needs be, without a second thought. Sadly, his every waking thought had come down to this, and in future his dreams would be of revenge.

CHAPTER 9

Clehonger
1822

Mary Godwin rose from her bed not long after first light. Within minutes of finishing her meagre breakfast, she was in the yard hitching the pony to the already laden cart. She was thinking this was the last time that she would need to do this, take produce to market. *This is the last of any crop I will ever grow here,* she thought with sadness. *So much for dreams.*

The cart was old and rickety, badly needing some repairs and maintenance, but there was no time for that. It would have to get her through this last journey. After that it could fall apart completely for all she cared, and the cottage as well, but please, just last a few more hours. But even as the thought entered her head she knew she didn't mean it and a tear shone in the corner of her eye.

She loved this place, the cottage, the land and the river that had been clear and fresh ever since the day she had moved in. If she had any choice she would stay here forever but there was no choice. It was impossible.

She led the pony out through the space where the gate should have been and on to the rutted track which would take her the short distance to Beech Tree Cross and the main Hereford road. Behind the horse the cart gave out a cacophony of squeals from the worn wheel bearings as they began to turn but there was nothing for it but to press on, and she knew that once on the main road the going would be smoother, thank goodness, for she was unsure how much of a battering the old cart could take. She was about to find out as one of the rear wheels got caught in a particularly deep rut, gave out a louder than usual squeal and collapsed in upon itself. The cart lurched sideways and, as the bed of the cart hit the ground, deposited its load of carefully collected produce all over the track and into the ditch.

During her time working alongside the gardeners at Plainmoor she had heard some ripe comments and choice swearwords, things she would never hear at home, but which she knew the meaning of. Now, in her frustration and anger, that had been building for months, they came freely from her mouth.

'Bugger, bugger, bugger.' With each word she aimed a kick at the cabbages strewn over the track.

Mary had a temper to match her red hair, a few strands of which had come loose from her ribbons and had escaped from her cap.

'You bloody useless piece of dung.' This time the kick which accompanied the swearing was aimed at the rim of the broken wheel.

She was crying now in her anger and tears rolled down her tanned cheeks.

'Where is a bloody husband when you need one?' Another kick at the wheel. 'Gone fucking walkabout, that's where.' The bitterness of her failed marriage rose to the fore. 'The useless bastard. And as for you,' another kick at the wheel, 'I ought to set fire to you and burn you to a bloody crisp.'

She suddenly realised that she was shouting at the top of her voice, and such words she was using too. She quickly looked around to see if anyone was in earshot and could have heard her.

Her heart missed a beat. Not twenty feet away stood a man. A blond-haired man with, she noticed, the most startling blue eyes in an olive tanned face. He must have heard her but just seemed to be amused at her tantrum. He was wearing a broad grin.

'You look like you could do with some help,' he said. He spoke slowly with a strangely soft accent.

He walked towards her and straight away she noticed that he walked with a pronounced limp, but all that was immaterial as her heart missed another beat. She thought he was the most good-looking, even gorgeous man she had ever seen.

*

She watched him work and marvelled at how effortless everything seemed. In no time at all he had shaped new spokes for the broken wheel and with the tools he carried in his own cart he fitted everything together into what seemed like a new wheel.

While he had worked on the wheel she had shifted the cabbages and whatever else she could salvage and put it all aside, out of the way, as he had told her to. He explained that he needed space to rig up some lifting gear, although, how he intended to lift such a heavy cart all on his own was beyond her, but he spoke with confidence and found that she didn't doubt him for one minute, even though she had no inkling of his knowledge of lifting gear and levers he had learnt in the Navy.

He went off into the yard and scouting around looking here and there, searching for something. He eventually returned to the cart carrying a long baulk of timber that had been bought to repair a roof truss, before her husband had gone away. It had lain in the barn ever since.

He gave her precise instructions. He would do the lifting and, using flat stones from the dry-stone wall, she would build a pillar each side of the cart, to support the timber. He slid the timber under the cart, took the strain and Mary slid the first stone into place. Little by little, inch by inch, they raised the body of the cart until it was high enough for him to slide the repaired wheel over the already well-greased axle. He spun the wheel on its axis and it turned easily with only a slight rumble.

'I might as well grease the other wheel before I lower the cart,' he said more to himself than to anyone else.

When he was done he took the strain again and Mary removed the stones one by one. When the cart was back on firm ground he hitched up the horse again and tentatively moved the cart forward. It moved easily and the squeals had almost disappeared. Mary skipped over to John with a loud whoop of joy.

'We did it. We did it,' and in her excitement threw her arms around his neck and kissed his cheek, before backing off again, her face blushing bright red as she realised what she had just done. She had embarrassed herself but the man was grinning at her again.

'After that, I think I had better tell you my name. They call me John Harkin,' he gave a small bow, 'and I am at your service.'

He had no idea how to address her, whether she was married, or widowed or what, but from what he had heard and the dilapidated state of the cottage and outbuildings he surmised that she lived alone. This interested him more than anything else, for he too had been smitten with her from the very first second he had laid eyes on her.

She was up and about earlier than usual the following morning and went about stoking up the fire and putting the kettle to boil. She resisted the urge to go to the back window and look for the man.

The day before, after what to her seemed like a miracle with the cart-wheel, he had washed in hot water in a bucket out in the yard and when he was clean they sat at the table and ate heartily from the crock-pot. Her fascinated her. Even the way he chewed his food was of great interest to her.

Fixing the wheel had taken longer than any of them had realised and when they had finished and reloaded the cart, it was too late for her to go to market or for him to move on. He had stayed overnight, bedding down in the barn. After she had made ready for bed and had blown out all the candles except one, she could not resist the urge to look out of the bedroom window, which overlooked the barn. A faint light was glowing down there but she was disappointed that she could not see him.

*

Eventually she could wait no longer and went to the back door of the cottage and looked out. All was still. *He ought to be out of bed by now,* she thought. She crossed the yard to the barn and felt her heart nose-dive into her boots. Neither him nor his cart was anywhere to be seen. She looked around, bewildered, and realised that for some reason she was almost in tears. Why had he gone? Why had he gone in the middle of the night and not even taken the trouble to say goodbye?

'You are behaving just like a lovesick girl.' she scolded herself. 'What did you expect? He's a travelling man, a tinker. Travelling men do not put down roots, they have no depth. They take advantage and then they leave, that's the way it is.'

But he had not taken advantage of her, if anything she had been the one to take advantage. He had not even taken any payment, if you discounted a measly bowl of stew.

'But I did so want him to stay, even if only for a short while,' she said forlornly.

She turned on her heel and almost stumbled into him. She had not heard him approach. He was wearing that big, bold grin again.

'Talking to yourself, now then?' he teased and she realised that she had been talking out loud and he had probably heard every word. 'How long might a short time be, in this part of the world?' She looked down at the ground and absently moved some hay about with her shoe.

'Sneaking up on people you will never hear anything good about yourself,' she said to the piece of hay. 'You can leave right now if you want to, see if I care.' Immediately she regretted what she had said and hoped desperately that he wouldn't take her at her word and simply walk away. She needn't had worried. When she looked up the grin was still plastered all over his face.

'I was hoping to stay for a few days or so. You know, get my strength back and all. Do a few jobs about the place to pay for my keep. Or maybe a week or two if that's agreeable. The place needs a bit of work doing to it. I can fix it up a bit, will that pay for a bed in the barn and my supper?'

She pretended to consider what he had just said but they both knew that it was only for show. Her heart was singing.

'It's a deal. Shake on it?' She held out her hand towards him and he stepped forward and took it in his.

'Done. It's a deal.'

He kept hold of her hand much longer than was needed which kept them close, close enough to exchange kisses, she thought. Why wasn't he kissing her? Could he not see that she wanted him to kiss her?

How could she be so brazen? She had only known the man for less than a day, but she couldn't help her thoughts, couldn't control them at all.

The moment passed. He turned and disappeared around the side of the barn. She watched him go and sighed.

'You need to pull yourself together, girl. No man wants a simpering, useless female around him.'

She went back to the kitchen to prepare breakfast. She realised that she was singing.

They worked together all day around the yard and by suppertime the transformation was staggering, even though she had spent half her time watching him work, and not being as much help as she could have been.

Sometimes, for no reason at all, she would get close enough to reach out and touch him, and she found herself smiling at him, even when his back was to her.

They shared supper and not long after he had eaten he returned to the barn. She blew out the candles and stood at the window looking down into the barn hoping to catch the last glimpse of him before he settled down to sleep. It was like a sickness, she couldn't stop herself.

The third day that John was at the small-holding it began to rain in the early afternoon and the wind got up. He and Mary stood together in the open door of the barn and watched the rain falling until it became obvious to them that the rain was in for the rest of the day and probably the night too. Once again she stood close to him, almost willing him to reach out and touch her. John resisted the temptation although he was not quite sure why.

In the dismal afternoon, darkness began to close in early and Mary went into the kitchen, stoked up the fire and put the evening meal to cook. She then took the kettle of gently simmering water up to her bedroom to wash. She then put on her best dress and went to the back door to call John in to supper. He too, had taken care to wash thoroughly, and had donned a clean, starched shirt. They didn't talk much while they ate. Mary cleared away the dishes and put them to soak.

'I have a spare room. It's not much but at least it's dry and not draughty like the barn. You're welcome to sleep there tonight, if you want.' She spoke quietly, hesitantly, not daring to turn to look at him, to see his reaction.

'Thank you,' he answered. She needn't have worried. 'That would be most welcome. The wet weather plays me up these days, and a bed sounds much better than a blanket in the hay.'

He had never been a heavy sleeper, even in a bed, and after years of sleeping rough with all the dangers that go with it, his senses had been honed to listen for any sounds in the night. He heard her moving about during the night and heard her pass his bedroom door several times.

She had been down to the kitchen again. She had never intended to go downstairs but her nerve had deserted her at the very last minute, right outside his door. She had decided that he was not going to do anything without being given a shove, but part of her queried if he would appreciate being pushed. After all, she wasn't the prettiest woman in the world or a good catch if it came to that. Another part of her brain wondered why he had not at least kissed her when she had made it so obvious that she would not have minded, even would have welcomed it. But it had been a long time since she had thought about men. Perhaps she was giving out the wrong signals. Maybe she needed to be bolder, but did she have the nerve to grab the bull by the horns?

She climbed the stairs again, very slowly and purposely. She paused outside his door yet again but this time she took a deep breath, reached for the handle and pushed the door open. The room was in semi-darkness, the stub of candle not able to illuminate the room fully, but it did give enough light for her to see that he lay in bed with his back to the door, fast asleep. She pulled back the eiderdown and slid into what little space was left in the bed. He didn't stir.

The bed was only a truckle-bed with little more than enough room for one and she had to snuggle up against his back. *Just like two spoons,* she thought.

John was wide awake but lay still. He could feel the softness of her against his back. She was cool but he felt his temperature rising. Then, tentatively, he felt her arm slip around him and her hand began to caress him. He could stay still no longer and turned to face her. He felt her breath on his face in the darkness, and then their lips met, softy at first, but then with growing urgency until they were clinging to each other frantically.

He rolled over, on top of her, and she opened her legs and raised them as she felt him pushing against her. She used her hand to guide him and then he entered her.

The following day not much in the way of work was done at all, but there were lots of kisses and cuddles and giggles and banter.

The day had dawned dry and bright, the kind of brightness with clear air that you get after a storm. They decided to take what was left of the produce into the market in town. Even sitting on the cart, in full view of all and sundry, they could not resist kissing and touching each other, which drew some curious stares from all quarters as they passed by. But they were oblivious to it all.

They sold most of what they had brought and, not wishing to carry what was left back home, gave the rest away. They were in a hurry to get back to the cottage but Mary, who had taken up the reins, stopped close to the cathedral.

'Come on, I want to show you something.' And she took him by the hand and led him into the precinct.

She had been there many times before and she led him own aisles and through doors until a man appeared. He stopped dead in his tracks and then enveloped Mary in a huge hug, picking her up and swinging her around like a small child. John, taken completely by surprise by the turn of events just stood and watched, not knowing what to do, but he could tell that Mary was enjoying the whole experience. Eventually, she broke away from the man and turned towards John.

'Dad, I want you to meet John Harkin. He is helping me around the farm, getting things fixed up and that.' She didn't go into detail about exactly what he was fixing.

James Macdonald was no fool. If he was not mistaken, and knowing his daughter as well as he did, he knew there had to be more to this than met the eye. He studied his daughter whilst he considered his reaction to the man, and realised that he had not seen her look like this, or show so much vitality in a long, long time. He turned his attention to her companion. There was nothing fancy about the man, but he did have an air of confidence, of inner strength and the way he gazed back at James spoke volumes. It must be serious, he thought, for his daughter to bring the man into his workplace, almost like she couldn't wait for them to meet. After what seemed like an age to John while he was being scrutinised, but what was in fact only seconds, Mary's father held out his hand.

'Good to meet you, John. I hope you are taking good care of my little girl. It would be nice if you could stay and take supper with us. Give you a chance to meet Mother.'

John made some feeble excuse about getting Mary home before it grew dark but he did not fool anyone. The encounter had taken him by surprise.

They rode back to the cottage in virtual silence but when he had stabled the horse and returned to the kitchen, John looked at her with a look of mock seriousness on his face.

'That was pretty devious introducing me to your dad without any warning. I think you should pay a forfeit.'

'Have you any idea as to what that forfeit should be?' she asked. 'Have you anything in mind?'

Within minutes they were in bed.

CHAPTER 10

Kerne Bridge

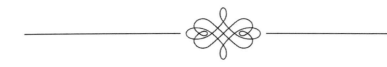

1822
Three Months Later

They had got away early and had made good time all day, surprised how easy it was to manage the cart with two pairs of hands and their combined energy. They could now see the Kerne Bridge and the curve of the River Wye from where they stood on the ridge that was Goodrich.

They were a good team and had worked in unison except when they got to close to each other and neither could resist the urge to kiss and cuddle, but they didn't care, they had all the time in the world. John studied his companion as they followed the track down the hill to the river and detected the beginnings of the strain that she was starting to feel. He was well used to walking all day, covering mile after mile, but it was all new to her.

He had taken everything off the cart that he did not need, lightening the load for the journey south, but the space that he had made had been filled with a huge carpet-bag full of clothes and 'stuff' which Mary did not want to leave behind. Everything else had been given to family or friends and, although not one of them liked to see her go, they all wished her and her new man the best of luck and the very best of good health, for John had become popular with everyone in his short stay at the farm.

Through their tears her parents said goodbye to their daughter, but knew that she and John were doing what they wanted and needed to do. James was reminded of the time he had taken his family from Ireland and had crossed the Irish Sea searching for a better life in England. He knew it was for the best. There were promises made to return and visit and then they were gone.

The old woman at the bridge toll-gate offered them refreshment, hoping that they would stay a while and their company would brighten her day. If John had been travelling alone he would not have bothered but this time he accepted to give Mary a rest. The kettle was already on the hearth and took no time to boil, and while the old woman made tea they made themselves comfortable on the step leading up to the door of the toll-house and giving good views of the fish leaping in the river.

'So, where are you two youngsters off to then?' the old woman asked as she poured the first mugs of tea.

'We're going to my home in Devon. I'm taking my lovely girl to meet my parents and they are going to love her, but not as much as I do.'

He looked at Mary and the love that he felt radiated from him. He loved her so much that sometimes it hurt, really hurt.

'When we get down to Lydney we'll take a boat across to Sharpness and from there it's all on foot from there to home. We may come back to Hereford or, if Mary settles there we'll make a home and have a family, and the girls will have red hair like Mary and the boys will have hair like me.'

The old woman looked at the pair. They still looked, to her, like children themselves. She could remember being like that herself but that was years ago now.

'Aye, I thought your accent was from down that way in the west country, but,' she turned to Mary, 'you sound like you're from Hereford but there is something odd about the way you sound, when you speak quickly. Are you from Hereford or further afield?'

'My father has Scottish grandparents and my mother was from Southern Ireland, so I am a mix of both. They left Ireland during the

Troubles and brought me, when I was just a baby, to England. We ended up in Hereford and have lived there ever since. Dad found work at the cathedral, so I have been brought up speaking Irish and English. I wanted to work the land and I own, or did own, a small-holding at Clehonger, on the Hay-on-Wye road.'

'And now he,' she indicated John, 'has made you walk all the way from there today? I hope he is not expecting you to walk all the way to Devon.' She had never been further than Ross but had a vague feeling that Devon was a lot further away than that. Maybe as far as forty miles probably, she guessed.

'I enjoy walking with him,' she linked arms with her man and then said, 'and I may walk all the way back again, too. It's been John's life for a long time now, travelling the countryside earning his living doing whatever work he can find, and then moving on.'

Something in the back of the old woman's mind began to trouble her, something about his boys having the same colour hair as him, but she couldn't quite put her finger on what it was.

'Have you been this way before then?' she asked.

'Only once, and I never came this way. I went through Coleford and on down to Monmouth to cross the river. I wish I had come this way though, the going would have been a lot easier.'

'When was this? Was it this year by any chance?'

'About three months ago, back in the middle of May.'

There it was, and the old woman knew what it was that had been troubling her. It was as though she had suddenly woken up. The description, the blond hair, the blue eyes and the limp and the timing all fit together. This was undoubtedly the man that the Sergeant from Coleford had been searching for and had questioned her so closely about. Wasn't it all to do with the murder of that young boy? The one in the quarry? How could she have been so blind? The thing that had thrown her off the scent was the woman. There had been no mention of a woman so she hadn't put two and two together until now. What to do about it? Then she remembered mention of a reward and realised that she had to stop them moving on at all costs. She went back into the toll-house supposedly to refill the teapot. She needed time to think.

By the time she came back with the fresh tea she had a plan. She wasn't going to let them out of her sight if she could help it.

'You look all in, deary. Shame on him for making you walk so far.' She turned to John. 'It wouldn't do to wear her out on the very first leg of your journey, now would it?' He felt suddenly guilty and nodded his head in agreement.

'I have plenty of room here and I could soon make you up a nice comfy bed for the night, and, I've got a nice plump chicken roasting slowly in the oven for supper. It won't cost you anything. I'm glad of the company.'

While they settled into the room, the old woman left the toll-house and headed off down the road to the bridge owner's house. She left the toll-gate open. She wanted nothing to spook the couple or anyone else poking their noses in. She wanted everything to be calm, at least until the Sergeant arrived.

CHAPTER 11

Kerne Bridge

1822

The messenger from the toll keeper found the Sergeant in the back room of The Unicorn, already downing his second pint of the day. He seemed to spend quite a lot of his time leaning on the bar in the back room or just sat morosely staring into whatever drink he happened to have in front of him at the time.

He listened to what the boy was saying, not really listening to what was being said until he heard the words 'limping man'.

'What did you just say? Did I hear you say limping man?'

He made the boy repeat the message all over again and then leapt to his feet and disappeared out the door as though all the demons in hell were after him. He ran to the gaol and roused his two constables.

'Get three horses from the stables in Spout Lane, quick as you can,' he ordered one of the men, 'and make sure they are the best horses they've got.'

The men did not yet know what was happening but while one went for the horses, the other gathered together swords and muskets.

They were on the road in a matter of minutes, and a little while later had turned off the main Gloucester road and headed down the dram-road towards Lydbrook. They travelled at a fast canter, ignoring the dangers from potholes and overhead branches.

When they arrived at the toll-house the horses were blowing hard and sweat dripped from their flanks. The old lady was waiting anxiously for them and lead them immediately around to the back of the cottage, and the Sergeant saw the man he had been seeking for the first time.

John had left Mary to rest in the room above the kitchen and had gone for a walk along the river's edge. As he returned he saw the small group of men galloping along the track to Ross and wondered what would be so urgent as to make people take such risks. The sound of the horses died away and the three men turned the corner of the cottage accompanied by the old woman. They were pointing their weapons at him, and his blood ran cold. He knew this could not be good.

Within two hours the enlarged party were descending Bakers Hill on the way back into Coleford. Word had spread that something was happening and a few curious people were gathered around the gaol. John was taken into the building, shuffling as fast as the shackles around his ankles would allow.

When the Sergeant was satisfied that he was locked up good and proper, he left the building and headed to the Magistrate's house.

For the first time in a long time, he would enjoy making his report.

CHAPTER 12

Newnham
1822

He had got to know his wife all over again and had discovered why he had loved her so much when he had married her all those years ago. He also loved the house, as big as it was. He loved the village with its views out over the River Severn, part of the reason why he had purchased the house in the first place.

He loved his children, all grown up now, he loved his dogs and he loved the freedom of being able to go anywhere, do anything at any time, without having to answer to anyone.

So, what was wrong? Why then was John White, Capt: R.N. (Ret), not the happiest man on earth? The cause of his apparent lethargy after several years of retirement, was simply boredom. He lacked direction, targets, objectives and challenges. His life on the high seas had been one of action and adventure, always seeing new things. Now he felt like he was just drifting, rudderless, through life.

When he had first left the Royal Navy behind he felt liberated, free. He was his own man, at last, and thanks to many years of service to the crown he had been awarded a substantial pension that came with the rank of Captain and this, together with all the prize-money he had been awarded, he could afford to do virtually anything. The question was, what to do?

What in civilian life could compensate for the thrill of the chase and the eventual capture of an enemy ship? What in civilian life could replace the danger and the risk-taking that made him a successful leader? Where was the excitement?

His wife could see that he was restless, having trouble settling back into the humdrum routine of life, he had been a military man for such a long time and that could not be worked out of a man's system quickly, it would take a while.

Being more sociable than her husband, she had taken to life in the tiny community quickly and easily. She had made new friends and rarely did a day pass without someone calling by for tea or lunch or just to discuss the latest purchase on their trip into Gloucester.

But for John White life was very different. He felt that he was living his life on the periphery, on the edge of society. He had soon realised that he had visited places and seen things that the ordinary man could not even imagine and he could have talked for hours of his experiences, but no-one seemed interested in what HE had done. All they seemed to want to talk about were the merits of a good horse and the upcoming hunt, a practice that filled him with disgust. The problem was he found it impossible to hide his disgust and that did not endear him to the local 'gentry'.

But this morning a tingle had ran down his spine. The adrenalin had flowed again almost as it had done in the past. He had walked the dogs and was sitting down to breakfast, pouring tea with one hand while pulling the paper towards him with the other. He ran his eye over the front page. The lead headline took his attention and with interest he read the article which followed:

Child Murderer Arrested

It was announced yesterday morning, that a man who had been sought for three months or more in relation to the murder of a ten year old boy had been apprehended. The boy, a certain Charles Morgan, of Coleford in The Forest of Dean, died of knife wounds and his body had been secreted in a disused quarry outside the town.

The local Magistrate, Captain Brookbanks, said that the man had been questioned by the local militia-man, a Sergeant Watkins, and the man had given his name as John Harkin.

It is understood that the said John Harkin is a native of Exton, a village in the County of Devon, and an ex Royal Navy rating.

It is also understood that the man now earns his living as an itinerant worker.

Captain Brookbanks later confirmed that the High Sherriff of Gloucester had been informed and he had dispatched a Circuit Court Judge to Coleford to convene a trial in the town as soon as possible, as everyone was anxious to see a speedy resolution of the business.

We understand that the Judge will travel to Coleford today.

Could this be the same young man who had served with him in the West Indies on board *Relentless*? The rating who had joined his ship as nothing but a mere boy and whom he had had to put ashore after the successful action against the French ship, which had taken refuge in the bay of one of the remote islands. Is this what had become of him? Was he now a child killer? Surely not. It didn't sound like the John Harkin that he had known. The man he knew had served with honour and had been lucky to survive. If it was him, and it sounded like too much of a coincidence not to be, then it sounded as though he needed some help.

He folded the paper neatly and laid it back on the breakfast table, all thoughts of eating forgotten.

'I have to go to Coleford, I think I may be needed there,' he spoke urgently to his wife sitting opposite him. She didn't even think to ask why. She had seen him like this many times in the past, alive, brimming with nervous energy, and, as in the past, and in the fullness of time, she was sure everything would become clear. He noticed the questioning look on her face.

'Someone I knew a long time ago may need my help.' That was all the explanation she needed. In a way she was glad that, at last, something had shaken him from the doldrums. He always kept his sea-chest ready out of habit and she only had to add clean shirts and underwear. Twenty minutes later he was ready to leave and they said goodbye.

'How long will you be gone?' she asked as she gave him a final hug.

'Not more than a few days, I would think, but I'll let you know if it looks like I shall be away longer.'

With that he boarded the trap and was gone, eager to be on his way. He turned to wave just before he disappeared from view around the bend on the track to Littledean.

At almost the exact same time as John White left home another coach crossed the bridge out of Gloucester on its way westward. This coach carried Circuit Court Judge Fletcher, also bound for Coleford.

CHAPTER 13

Coleford
1822

Considering that this was usually the front bar-room, overnight the landlord had made a passable effort of turning it into a courtroom. With great difficulty he had removed all the heavy tables except two of his best, one for the use of the Judge set against the rear wall and facing the huge bow-windows that gave out into the market square, and one for the use of the Magistrate who was to be the prosecutor. Both tables were bare except for a jug of water and some glasses set in the centre.

Twelve hard chairs had been placed against the side wall to the left of the Judge's table, set in a double row with another chair placed between the Judge and the Jury, but in full view of the spectators, for the use of witnesses. The rest of the chairs and benches, augmented by many more that he had borrowed from other drinking houses in the town, were in orderly lines between the Magistrates table and the windows. The windows were already wide open allowing people who could not get into the room space to lean into the room from the street to listen to proceedings.

A single chair, directly in front of the Judge, was for John Harkin, the accused.

At precisely ten o'clock, as the town clock struck, the door from the street was opened and the townspeople filed in, in good order, under the watchful eye of the Sergeant. The early ones were lucky. They were able to find seats and when these were all filled, more people squeezed into the room and stood against the walls, until the room was crammed full and the Sergeant ordered the doors closed against the crush. Immediately, the unlucky ones out in the street, fought for a good position around the windows, until there were as many leaning in the windows as there were inside the room. It soon became apparent that opening the windows had made good sense as the temperature inside the room rose and the bodies crammed together began to sweat. Thank God it wasn't raining.

This was the largest room in the entire town except for the church, but still there were more people outside than in. All the shops in the town were shut for the day, as were all the other businesses. It seemed that everyone wanted to attend, to hear what had happened on that day three months before when Charlie had been killed, and to hear the outcome. Emotions were running high.

It was unusual for a trial such as this to take place in the town in which the crime had been committed. Normally, a crime of this type would have been tried in the Crown Court in Gloucester Prison, but for political expediency and on the pretext of allowing the population to witness justice in action, it had been decided to hold the trial as soon as possible in Coleford. Concerns about a fair trial were conveniently forgotten. Just get the job done, was the order to the Judge.

The door at the back of the room opened and the Magistrate entered, crossed to his table and, in what seemed like a well-rehearsed move, deposited a bundle of important-looking documents bound in red ribbon, and a box, onto the flat surface. He undid the ribbon with a flourish and spread the papers over the table-top, just as the door at the back opened once again. The Court Usher called for everyone to stand and the Judge entered the room, dressed in all his regalia. After the Judge had taken his seat the Usher stated that the Court was in session and ordered everyone to sit. Those that had a seat did so. The rest just laughed.

The Judge surveyed the 'courtroom' and scowled at the standing crowd.

'If you want me to clear the room, carry on laughing,' he threatened. The room became quiet.

'Bring in the Jury,' he ordered.

The rear door opened yet again and into the room trooped twelve local men who had been chosen at random the night before by the Magistrate. The door had been left open and as soon as the Jury had taken their places John Harkin was brought in, escorted by two young militiamen, to be met with hoots and boos and general shouts and swearing, as he was led to his chair and shackled.

'Quiet, quiet. I'll not have such unruly behaviour in my court.' The Judge was angrily banging the table with a gavel which had appeared in his hand as though by magic and much to the consternation of the landlord who was worried about damage to the table-top. 'This may be the way you behave out here in the Badl... eh, countryside, but in Gloucester we do things in a much more civilised and gentlemanly way.'

The Judge was still smarting from the fact that he had had to stay in the Temperance Hotel, having been turned away from all the other hotels in town, which were full of people here for the trial. The Judge was fond of a drink and his lodgings were not to his satisfaction at all. He had had to use the bar of the Unicorn Inn for his liquid sustenance, just like all the common people.

There was a pause and the Usher, not to be denied his moment stepped forward into the middle of the room.

'This court has been convened under the direction of His Honour Judge Fletcher, County Court Judge, appointed by The Lord High Chancellor of all England.' He liked to use such words, he thought it made him sound important. 'We are here to try the accused for the murder of a young boy, christened Charles Morgan, and living in the town of Coleford in the county of Gloucestershire.'

He paused for effect before turning to John Harkin.

'Do you understand the charge?' he asked. John nodded.

'How do you plead? Guilty or not guilty.'

'Not guilty, I haven't murdered any boy...'

The rest of what he said was drowned out by shouts of 'killer' and 'liar' which filled the room and the Judge leapt into action once again with the gavel.

'I will not tolerate this behaviour. I have warned you once already. If you persist I will have the court cleared and you can all stand in the street. Which is it to be?' he asked.

The room quieted down until not a murmur could be heard.

'That's better, now, let's continue. The plea of not guilty will be entered.' He turned to the Magistrate.

'Mr Brookbanks, sir. It is my understanding that you are acting as the prosecutor in this case.' Brookbanks nodded. 'Good, Would you like to present your evidence and call your witnesses?'

Brookbanks had been waiting for the signal and rose to his feet and faced the Jury.

'We are gathered here today to...' He was cut short by a shout from outside the window.

'You sound like a vicar, get on with it. We want to hang the bugger not marry him.'

Even the Judge had to suppress a smile at this outburst and did nothing. He was relaxed now that the trial had started. It wouldn't be long before he would be back in Gloucester. He had seen all the evidence, spoken to the Magistrate at length and had questioned the Sergeant. He knew what they were going to say. This was an open-and-shut case if ever he had seen one, especially as there was no-one to speak up for the accused or defend him in any way. All the evidence pointed one way.

'As I was saying. We are here to try this man,' he indicated the accused, 'for the brutal murder of a young boy. A boy we all knew, a boy who was the apple of his mum's eye. A boy who showed great promise in the trades, a boy with skill in his young hands.' He paused for effect.

'A boy killed on his birthday, no less. On a day that should have been a joyous day, a day full of laughter. On the very day that his father, Edwin, was to take him on as an apprentice, something he had been wanting for a long time. This is what we have to remember when we consider the evidence.' He looked down at the table and shuffled a few papers.

'My first witness is Sergeant Watkins.'

The Sergeant came forward and took his place by the witness chair. He preferred to stand.

'Do you swear on the Bible that you will tell the truth, before the court?'

'Yes, of course.'

'Sergeant, tell us the whole story, beginning with the evening before the day you found the body.'

'That day back in May, the twenty-third I think it was, I had had my supper and was settling for the night when there was a banging on the door of the gaol. I wondered who it could be, out on such a filthy night. If you remember it was the day that we had the worst thunderstorm in living memory. The caller was Edwin Morgan and he was soaking wet and in a bit of a state. He told me that young Charlie had gone missing. Charlie had gone out before dinner-time to take some food to his dad down at the quarry where he was working that day. He had never reached the quarry and had not come home. I put on my boots and together we searched up Spout Lane, which is the route we thought the boy would have taken. We searched, as well as the light would allow us to, the stream and the banks thinking he may have fallen in, but there was no sign of him. We searched up the back of Poolway as far as the toll-gate at the bottom of Bakers Hill. I knocked up the gatekeeper's wife,' he blushed red as laughter echoed round the room, 'who told us that she had seen the boy late that morning heading on up towards the Broad Well. Edwin wanted to carry on but it was too dark to search anymore and I told him he was to go home and wait there. I went back to town and organised a search party for first thing the following morning.'

'What happened on the following day?'

'We started out just after dawn. There was getting on for two dozen of us and Eddie Timpson had brought his dogs. We searched from the toll-gate up to the Broad Well but found nothing. We organised ourselves into a skirmish line and began to make our way carefully down towards Bixelton. As you know, that place is full of disused quarries, coal levels and holes of all kinds, all overgrown and treacherous. We were being thorough, not wanting to miss a thing and progress was slow. Eddie had taken his dogs up onto the ridge above the dram-road and had gotten quite a way in front of us. We had just checked out Raven Quarry when we heard Eddie shouting. From above he had spotted a body in Jackdaw and we all rushed down to the entrance.'

He paused as though the memories were painful for him.

'It was obvious to me that someone had recently been in the quarry, I could still smell the embers of a fire and there were fresh footprints in the mud at the side of the track. I stopped the men from getting too close and me and the Barber went in, carefully skirting the footprints. Inside we found Charlie. He was dead.'

'Was there anything unusual about Charlie when you found him?'

'Other than him being dead, you mean? Well, he was as naked as the day he was born.'

'And where were his clothes?'

'In a bundle among the rocks.'

'Stay there, Sergeant. Where is the Barber?' The Barber joined the Sergeant by the witness chair.

'In your opinion, how did Charlie die?'

'He had two different types of injury, either of which could have been fatal. He had a deep wound to his skull, probably caused by a blow with a piece of rock. His skull was fractured. But he also had stab wounds to his chest.'

'Have you any thoughts on the type or size of the knife used to stab poor Charlie?'

'Well it must have been a big 'un to have gone through the chest like that, and it must have been as sharp as a razor.' He looked around the room, enjoying the free advertising. 'I know about such things and how hard it is to get a blade that sharp. Oh, and the blade was double-edged.'

'You can go back to your place now.' He turned again to the Sergeant. 'Sergeant, tell the court about the footprints, was there anything special about them?'

'I had never seen footprints like those before so I took special notice, and as soon as I got back to the gaol I made a drawing so that I wouldn't forget. After I had reported to you, sir, I made my normal rounds of the pubs in the town, and as luck would have it, I met the

Shoemaker who was enjoying a quiet pint. I showed him the drawing and he immediately said that he knew of a boot that would leave a print exactly like the one I had drawn.'

'Right, let's hear from the Shoemaker.'

'I had just opened the shop and was making a brew when this man came in. He was a stranger to me, I had never seen him before. He was limping something terrible and he asked me if I could mend his boot. He showed it to me and I had never seen anything like it before in all my born days. He told me that a Shoemaker in Devon had altered the boot so that it would support his foot better and allow him to walk with hardly any limp. There was a cleat built into the sole so that all the weight of the wearer would be pushed towards the instep. And the boot itself was different to any you will find in England, anywhere. It was of the finest quality and when I asked him how he had acquired such a boot he just told me that he had got it from a Frenchman. I had not seen stitching like it before.'

'Spare us the technical bits and tell us what happened next.'

'Well, I could see immediately what needed doing but, because he was a stranger, I asked for three pennies on account like, in case he didn't come back. He said he couldn't afford three pennies, and as he knew Alice Comely, I settled for two.'

'But you still had the boot. Surely that would have covered the cost of any repairs.'

'Aye, that's true as long as you know someone with one leg as needs a limp sorting.' A swell of laughter filled the room again.

'Let's move on,' the Magistrate directed when order had been restored.

'Well, he did come back several hours later, all washed and shaved and smelling as sweet as you like. He told me that he had been up to the church for a looksee, that being the real reason why he was in the town at all. He then asked the way to Ross where he intended to cross the river and travel on into Hereford. I directed him up Sparrow Hill and he went on his way. I've not seen him since.'

'Good. Have you finished? Is there anything else we need to know?'

'That's about it, I reckon.'

'Just one more thing. Do you see that man here today?'

'That's him there.' He pointed towards John Harkin.

'Right, go and sit down.' The Magistrate turned to the Sergeant. 'After you spoke to the Shoemaker in the Unicorn and heard what he had to say, what did you do next?'

'There was still a few hours of daylight left so I cadged a horse from the Blacksmith and went after him.' He indicated the accused. 'I managed to get up through Christchurch, down into Bicknor and then on down to the river at Lybrook before the light began to give out, but there wasn't any sign. I decided that I would return to Coleford and take up the search again next morning.'

'What happened next morning?'

'I started out early and this time made a more thorough search. I asked at every house and farm all the way to Kerne Bridge. I called at every pub and inn,' this drew sniggers from the bystanders, 'I questioned people I met on the road and people working in the fields, but no-one had seen hide nor hair of any limping man with a handcart. When the old woman at the toll-gate at Kerne Bridge had not had any sighting of him either, I knew that I had lost him. She sees everything that passes that way. She has got better eyesight than most even though she is, by her own admission, blind.'

'So you gave up the search?'

'I didn't know what else to do. Where was he? Where had he gone? He could have been anywhere. Have you any idea how far a man can travel in two days, even on foot?' The Sergeant felt the anger building up in him. It was typical of the Magistrate to try to push the blame his way after all he had done to find the man. 'Anyway, it came good in the end didn't it?'

'More by luck than judgement.' Praise was not a thing the Magistrate gave willingly to the Sergeant.

'No sir, not by luck at all.' Sergeant Watkins was not the kind of man to hide his light. 'I had told everyone to report directly to me if they saw or heard of such a man. I mentioned the possibility of a reward, which always makes people take notice. The old woman at the toll-gate at Kerne recognised the man straight away and was determined not to share the reward with anyone so kept him there on the pretence of giving him and his companion free board and lodging for the night. I arrested him there and brought him back.'

'So what about the murder weapon? Did he have a knife on him?'

'No, not on him, but he did have a knife, more of a dagger I would call it, among his possessions. When I showed it to the Barber he said it matched the wounds on young Charlie.'

The Magistrate produced a knife from the box on the table and held it aloft for all to see. It was larger than the kind of knife usually kept in a man's pocket, double edged and sharply pointed.

'Is this the knife you found being carried by the accused?'

'It looks like it. If it is the same one it should have an X marked on the handle.'

The Magistrate studied the knife as though he had never seen it before although, of course, it had been in his possession for the last day or so. He held it in full view and pointed triumphantly to a mark clearly visible on the hilt.

The Magistrate turned to face the Judge and was disconcerted to see that he had his eyes closed. Was he asleep? The Magistrate cleared his throat loudly.

'Your Honour, that concludes the case against the prisoner.'

'And very well presented too, if I may say, sir. Thank you.' He hadn't been asleep at all, just thinking about lunch. Ham off the bone, potatoes and a honey sauce was the offering for lunch at the Temperence. A lamb stew with fresh crusty bread at the Angel. Which to choose? Probably the lamb stew, but only because he could down several pints of good beer as well.

But first things first. It had gone well. Almost word for word just as they had rehearsed it. The Judge knew that the evidence was all circumstantial, weak to the point of being flimsy, but enough to convince a Jury such as he had before him The looked over to study the twelve men. They looked relaxed, nothing to worry about there, he thought, but he had to follow the protocol. Justice must give the accused every chance to challenge the evidence.

'Is there anyone here who would speak on behalf of the accused? Anyone who would offer up another version of events? Is there anyone who could cast doubt on any of the evidence?' He looked around at the crowd of faces before him. 'Anyone at all?'

He had expected no response. The man had no friends in the town that he could call on but he did have plenty of people against him though.

'I would like to speak, Your Honour, if I may,' a voice sounded from among the crowd.

CHAPTER 14

Coleford
1822

This was a turn of events and no mistake. The crowd in the room parted to let a man through who had been standing back against the wall. He walked slowly to the centre of the room. There were whispers around the room. People looked questioningly at each other. Who was he? Nobody knew but he seemed perfectly at home, as though used to speaking before a crowd and used to being listened to. He was not a huge man but appeared bigger than he actually was, as he stood confidently facing the Judge. Most people would, if asked, put his age at about fifty but they would be wrong, fooled by his upright stance and the aura of vitality that he exuded. In fact, he was nearer sixty.

His black frock coat was of fine material and fitted him to perfection. He cut a fine figure.

'And who might you be, sir?' The Judge was nonplussed by the appearance of the man. This was not supposed to happen. The accused was in no state to defend himself and he had been assured that no-one in these parts knew the prisoner, leave alone wanting to speak for him.

'My name is John White and I would like to address the court. I know of this man.' He indicated John Harkin.

The Judge, whilst wanting no delay to the proceedings had asked the question, and now had to live with it. The man had to be allowed to speak.

'Very well, you may have your say, but I warn you not to waste the Court's time. We only need to hear what is relevant.'

The man, John White, gave a slight bow to the Judge and turned to the Jury. He took several paces towards them, stroking his chin as though collecting his thoughts. He was looking for anything that he could build upon, any sign in any of the faces that he could work with. He turned away and surveyed the onlookers. They were silent waiting for him to begin, intrigued as to who he was and what he had to say about the murder. He began to speak, slowly and quietly, but loud enough that everyone could hear every word. His demeanour demanded their attention.

'I have listened, as you all have, to the evidence offered to this Court by the Magistrate.' He paused and looked around the room again to make sure that he had their full attention. He need not have worried.

'There is no doubt in my mind that the Sergeant, the Barber and the Shoemaker are worthy people and would only state the facts as they know them. I am sure that they would not even consider lying to the Court.' He turned to the Sergeant who was still standing next to the Judge's table. He looked him squarely in the eye. The Sergeant stared dolefully back.

'Am I correct, Sergeant?'

'Yes sir, that is correct.'

John White paused again until the silence was broken by the sound of the town clock striking twelve.

'However, I have heard nothing here this morning that suggests or proves that the accused killed the young boy Charlie Morgan. For sure, a footprint matching those that would have been made by the boot worn by the accused was found at the entrance to the quarry. He does not deny that the footprint was made by him. He does not deny that he took shelter in a disused quarry when the rain began on the day the boy went missing. He does not deny that he was in the town the following morning and that he had the Shoemaker mend his boot.' He picked up the boot and held it up. He studied the boot as though checking the work that the Shoemaker had carried out.

'A very distinctive boot, I think you will agree, not one that would be forgotten in a hurry. The accused then went and had a bath and a shave and walked around your fine new church. He took his time, having a good look around town. Ask yourselves this. What man would have been so stupid as to hang around town all morning if he had just committed a murder? A stranger. A man easily recognisable by his obvious limp, and how could he hide that blond hair? If you had just killed someone what would you have done? I would suggest that you would have put as much distance as possible between yourself and the scene of the crime.' He was pleased to see several Jurors nodding, following the logic of the argument.

Around the room there were whispers and he heard someone say, 'Makes sense.'

'Get to the point. We know....' The Magistrate was cut short by a withering look. He also had heard the whispers and did not like the way that this was going. He fell silent.

'The Barber said that the boy was hit with a rock and had stab wounds and stated that either of the injuries could have been fatal.' He turned to the Magistrate. 'You then produced this knife which the Sergeant had taken from the prisoner and you claimed it was the murder weapon.' He turned to the bystanders.

'How many of you men carry a knife? How many of you have a knife with you at this very moment?' Several men looked around sheepishly and others suddenly found something very interesting on the floor. 'I would guess that there are at least a dozen, maybe more of you who are carrying a knife of some sort. Maybe several of the Jury as well.' He turned to face the Jury.

'Does it make you a murderer just because you carry a knife? No, of course not. I understand that carrying a knife is natural in the countryside, am I right?' There were nods all round the room.

The Judge was sat upright in his seat. He did not like the way that things were going. This was not good, not good at all. He wished he could turn the clock back. He wished he had never asked the question. He knew the prosecution was losing the Jury. He could see the doubts in their eyes. But he could not stop John White without a very good reason. John White was already addressing the room again.

'The prisoner was arrested at the toll-house at the Kerne on a route that would have taken him to within several hundred yards of the spot where young Charlie was found. I ask you if that is that the action of a guilty man. No. He was taking the shortest route home. And why was he in such a hurry to get home that he did not take the easy route through Gloucester? It's because he had with him his new love, his beautiful bride-to-be who he was taking home to proudly introduce to his parents. He wanted to show her off the whole village.' He paused. 'Or was it stupidity again, like staying in town for half a day after killing someone? I don't think so.' He suddenly changed tack.

'How many of you men here have seen military service? How many have served King and Country?' He waited for a response. Several men raised their hands in the air including the Magistrate. John White addressed the man by his name.

'Mr Brookbanks, sir. You served in the army of the Duke of Wellington did you not?' Brookbanks nodded. 'Down in Spain and Portugal? Were you wounded?' Again a nod. 'When you were wounded, what happened?'

'We were by a river bridge somewhere in Spain, the whole regiment held up by an artillery battery that held some high ground.' In his mind, the Magistrate was back there on that fateful day. 'My company were ordered forward to clear the way. We crossed the river and advanced meeting hardly any resistance, but the French had a surprise for us. When we were well out in the open we were ambushed by a regiment of cavalry and lancers. We were cut to ribbons. Foot soldiers cannot match the cavalry in such open ground. I took a sabre through my left side. When enough damage had been inflicted on us, the French commander recalled his men and we were allowed to pick up our dead and wounded.' He was near to tears as he pictured the killing ground again. 'Of my one hundred and fifty men who advanced only twenty-seven of us lived, and each of us had scars to carry for life.'

The room was deathly quiet. Only a few knew what it was like to be in a war and no-one knew what the Magistrate had been through. He had not spoken of those days until now.

'Me and my men were discharged then, as fast as they could get us on a ship to England.' He looked up at John White. 'We were no longer any use to them, you see, and it is not good for morale for men coming into the line to see the dead and wounded.'

'What did you feel when you arrived back in England?'

'Somehow I made my way back to Coleford, thinking I was coming home, but things had changed. In the nine years I had been away I had changed and the town had too, but in a different way. I felt lost and abandoned. I had no friends here anymore. Do you know what it is like to have not a single friend in the whole world? I feel ashamed to admit that many times I contemplated taking my life, and probably would have done if I had been brave enough and if my cousin Amelia Lambert had not come to my aid.' John White moved the questioning along, not wishing to dwell on the man's obvious distress.

'How did you feel about the military?'

'I was bitter about the way they had treated me and my men. I still feel bitter to this very day, bitter about the impunity with which orders were banded about, without any thought for the men or the consequences for those men. But I feel honoured to have served with, and to have fought alongside, the men in my company. Good men all.' It was obvious that he had come to the end of his story.

'Just one more question, if I may? You are trained in the use of deadly weapons. Could you kill anyone now?'

'After what I have seen and been through, never. I could never again lift my arm against another man.'

John White let the words of the Magistrate hang in the air, for long seconds before he continued.

'This man,' he pointed at John Harkin, 'is just like Mr Brookbanks here. He is not stupid, just innocent. He is no murderer, just a man trying to find his rightful place.' He strode to the centre of the room again.

'Let me tell you about the man sitting here accused of murder. His name in John Harkin. A man of Devon. Born and bred in a small village called Exton. He was born a country boy not unlike yourselves, coming from a hard-working family. But for the young John Harkin, country life held no attractions, it was not exciting enough and at the age of fourteen he left home to join the Royal Navy to fight the French and to see the world. He lied about his age. He was probably no older than this young boy.' He pointed to a young face pressed against the window. A woman, sitting in the courtroom waved at the boy with a beaming smile, and his face turned bright red under the unwanted attention. 'Imagine him as he left home, not knowing if he would ever see home again or his parents or his sister, but determined to go. He joined my ship days later.'

'Your ship, sir. You say "your ship".'

'As I have already stated, my name is John White, promoted to Captain in the Royal Navy by none other than Admiral Lord Nelson himself.' It never hurt to name drop when it suited the purpose. 'I commanded H.M.S. *Relentless* on patrol in the West Indies, tasked with the capture or destruction of any French or Spanish ship we could apprehend. For this young boy,' he looked at the prisoner, 'the change in his way of life must have been astonishing. I am sure that there must have been times when he would have been terrified of what he was required to do, but never once did he shirk his duty, not once. He learnt the ropes and the drills and had to get used to the chaos which is war aboard ship, especially when the big guns fire and the heat and smoke is enough to make grown men quake. He was a good sailor and was marked down in my book for promotion, but first he had to grow physically into a man and to learn how to lead. That is, until the day he received his injuries.' He paused and crossed to the Judge's table, poured himself a glass of water and as he drank he studied the townspeople and the Jury and fancied he could detect a change in their demeanour. They seemed intrigued.

'We had been on station in the Indies for many years and thought we knew all there was to know. We were stalking a French three-decker which we had intercepted earlier in the day. We were outgunned and needed to be especially careful and alert. We could have been blown to smithereens before we could close up enough to use our own guns. No, this needed stealth, not brute force, and we were determined that we would have the better of the French. We tracked the ship all day, waiting for darkness, our only hope of getting close enough to engage, but as dusk approached our quarry disappeared from our sight. We closed up and a small island came into view. The French had made landfall. At first light I decided to send a small landing party ashore to ascertain the position and capabilities of the French ship, without revealing our presence. My

First Lieutenant chose to take John Harkin and a signaller and they went ashore to scale a headland that was between us and the enemy to observe and to signal back to us on board if an attack was possible. The signaller returned to the beach to signal that the French ship was in the next bay and had half its crew ashore. They appeared to be replenishing their fresh water before attempting the long voyage home. I sent a squad of marines to the beach to assist the landing party. On board we went to action stations and sailed around the headland. As we entered the bay we heard musket fire from up on the headland but we were committed and opened fire with our forward cannon. The French Captain surrendered his ship. She was a sitting duck with half the crew ashore and the water not deep enough for him to manoeuvre. The ship was ours. But the French Captain had posted lookouts up on the headland, an officer and two sailors armed with muskets. The French officer killed my First Lieutenant and would have killed this man if he had not been sharp about and got the better of the man. The Frenchman was badly wounded with his own dagger.' He left out the more distressing details. 'The man you see here tried to tend to the man, and the Frenchman, knowing that he was dying, asked John to pray with him and made him promise that, if ever he was in France, he would let his wife know that he had died honourably. He then forgave John for killing him. The two French sailors, who were shirking, had heard the commotion and came upon the scene. They immediately discharged their weapons and the accused was shot twice, in the back.'

John White walked over to the accused.

'Could you remove your shirt, John?'

John Harkin stood and took off his shirt. There were gasps around the room at the sight of the huge, white scar that was his shoulder, easily discernible against the tan of his skin. John White addressed the Jury.

'The second shot was much more deadly. Unlike the shot to the shoulder, which passed straight through and left a clean hole, this one hit him in the buttock, smashed its way down through the thigh and became lodged in the back of the knee. Within days this wound had started to turn rotten and the only way to save his life was to cut away all the putrid flesh and dig for the ball. It fell to the Navigator to perform the cutting without knowledge of what damage he was doing.

It saved his life but left him crippled.' He emptied the glass of water.

'Like the Army, the Royal Navy has no use for cripples. We gave him time to heal but it became obvious that he would never walk again without crutches. What was more relevant was that he confessed to me that, just like your Mr Brookbanks, he doubted he could raise his hands against any man ever again, after the experience of killing the Frenchman and having him bleed to death in his arms. There was nothing for it but to put him on the first ship home. The knife displayed here as the murder weapon is the very same dagger that killed the Frenchman. He wanted John to have it so that he would never forget what had happened. The accused has carried that dagger on his travels ever since, not to kill people but as an aid to remember by. I swear, and my life on it, this man is no killer of children.'

John White, Capt: R.N. (Ret) returned to his place against the wall amid utter silence. He was exhausted but elated. He had seen the looks on the faces of the townspeople. He had done his duty and had presented the case in the way that the people would understand. No frills, just common sense. He had won. He felt it all over the room.

Suddenly, as though coming to life again there was noise among the people. Almost a collective sigh of relief and a babble of conversation. The Judge banged his gavel again and called for silence but without much enthusiasm. He knew he had lost the case. He had seen the men of the Jury following the arguments and had seen the change happening. The prosecution had been too lax, too arrogant. Expecting to lead the jury to a guilty verdict on a tide of emotion and the flimsiest of evidence. He should have known better. He worried for his future. Some one's head would roll for this. Someone would have to pay.

Eventually the room became quiet again and all faces were turned towards the Judge expectantly.

'Has anyone else anything to say? Has anyone else anything to add?'

The Sergeant could also see what had happened. He drew himself up to his full height and took a deep breath.

'There is the matter of the confession,' he said.

*

On the other side of the Market Square and opposite the Angel Hotel stood a large haberdashery shop, closed today for the trial, but normally a hubbub of activity. The shop owner, Amelia Lambert, lived in the comfortably furnished apartments above. Amelia had decided not to attend the trial, something telling her to stay away, and instead she was sitting at her writing desk answering a letter from her dead husband's mother and father. She had received a formal invitation to the wedding of their daughter, but it meant she would have the arduous journey to London to attend. After thinking long and hard she had decided to go. It had been over a year since she had travelled up to the capital. She needed to make an effort.

The high windows overlooking the Square were partly open to allow in some of the warm fresh air, and sometimes she would catch part of a conversation as people passed by below.

She heard the shout go up from across the road, and heard it repeated by the bystanders, as the news travelled around the square like a ripple in a pond. 'He's confessed. He's confessed.' Momentarily she thought of the family of the boy Charlie and what they must be going through. She wondered if the man accused of the murder had any family and what they must be thinking. It was a sad time for everyone and no mistake. She sat and stared out of the window, studying the blue sky for a few more seconds before sighing and returning to her letter.

*

The lamb stew had gone down a treat, accompanied by the two large glasses of celebratory porter. He still had a few minutes before he would reconvene the court. His thoughts ran over the case again. Thank God for the Sergeant, he thought. Saved at the last hour. The verdict would go the prosecution's way now, without a doubt.

He had asked the Sergeant why he had not mentioned the confession in the first place, and the Sergeant stated that he thought there was enough evidence without it, and he had been afraid to introduce it because it was his word against the word of the accused. There had been no other witnesses to the confession. A lame excuse if ever he had heard one, but never mind. The Sergeant had stuck to his guns and delivered his new information in a compelling way. It had been more than enough to sway the Jury, and that was the main thing. The Judge cared not if the man was lying.

He entered the court and brought it to order. The Jury gave the verdict that he knew they would. During the long lunch he had already conferred with a local builder as to the erection of the gallows. The price and the timescale had soon been agreed. Without any more ado he sentenced John Harkin to death by hanging, the sentence to be carried out at twelve o'clock, midday, on the following day.

CHAPTER 15

Coleford
1822

Even at this early hour there were small knots of people scattered around the marketplace, eager to claim the places that would give the best view of the hanging.

Amelia Lambert surveyed the scene from between the half-closed curtains of her sitting room. She was able to see, for the first time, the scaffold that had been erected on the Tump, not many yards from the entrance to the church. Even to her uneducated eyes it looked like a well-built piece of work, consisting of a platform, raised about four feet above ground level, with a single upright on each side supporting a beam which, precisely over the centre of the platform, crossed from one side to the other. Directly under the beam was what appeared to be a trapdoor. A man stood on the platform coiling some ropes.

The Ropeman liked an audience when he worked and so far in his 'career' had not been disappointed. Everywhere he went there were always some people who were fascinated by the paraphernalia of his trade. His audience had grown larger as he worked and by way of greeting he kicked at the lever once again. He watched with satisfaction as the trapdoor fell smoothly away leaving a four-foot hole in its place. That's six out of six successful trials now. Good enough.

He had been told to give the expected crowd a good show. They should all go away after today knowing that justice was being meted out by the Judiciary, no quarter given. Part deterrent, part reassurance. With his knowledge of the hanging business he was confident that the town would not forget this day, ever.

He sensed someone standing on the platform behind him and turned to see the vicar, in full robes of office, hovering near the steps that led up to the platform. He glanced up at the town clock sixty feet above him and was surprised to see that it was well gone half-past eleven. Where had the morning gone to? Not long to go now, he thought. Soon the crowd swelled as people made their way from the various pubs after enjoying some early refreshment until the square was filled with onlookers. Some sections of the crowd were boisterous, especially near the doors to The Angel, whilst others waited with something approaching trepidation. No-one in the town had ever been present at a public hanging before. No-one knew what to expect.

The Sergeant had improvised and had used a haycart to transport the prisoner the short distance from the gaol to the place of execution. John White and a pretty young woman with red hair walked alongside, ignoring the shouts of abuse which grew in volume as they stopped at the foot of the scaffold steps.

The shackled and manacled prisoner was helped down from the cart by the two militiamen who had ridden with him. He stumbled as he mounted the steps and John White stepped forward and set him back on his feet.

'Steady man, steady. Remember what we talked about this morning. Look them straight in the eyes. Do not allow them to take your pride as well as your life.'

The vicar stepped forward but was waved away. The prisoner had already made his peace with his God. The Ropeman positioned him at the very centre of the trapdoor. Usually he would have chained weights to the feet of the condemned man to accelerate the drop and to ensure the neck was broken immediately but these he neglected to use, neither did he use the traditional hangman's knot but a variant which would slowly tighten and cut off the air supply. The black hood was also dispensed with. He had been ordered to make this a show and a show was what he was going to give the townspeople. He placed the thick rope around the prisoner's neck. There was a shout which could be heard even above the hubbub of the crowd encouraging the Ropeman to stretch the bugger's neck good and proper.

The Magistrate took centre stage at the front of the crowd and asked, 'Have you anything to say? Any last words?'

'My name is John Harkin. A man of Devon and an Englishman.' He made a final effort and drew himself up. He surveyed the crowd and found what he was looking for.

'I swear I did not kill your boy,' he said, locking eyes with Edwin Morgan who was stood in the front of the crowd. 'I swear it.'

Above their heads the town clock began to toll twelve, and suddenly the memories of Sundays in Devon filled John's mind. Memories of dressing up for Chapel and walking to the village arm in arm as a family. Days when the sun always seemed to shine, and the air was full of the smell of roasting meat, and people took their time about things and laughed a lot, for Sundays were days of rest. He remembered things he had been taught in Sunday school and his favourite words filled his head. He found himself reciting by heart:

'The Lord's my Shepherd; I shall not want.

He maketh me to lie down in green pastures;

He leadeth me beside the still waters.

He restoreth my soul; he leadeth me in the

paths of righteousness for his names sake.

Yea, though I walk through the valley of the

shadow of death; I will fear no evil for thou

art with me, thy...'

The clock struck for the final time and the Ropeman stepped forward.

'Aye, I've heard it all before,' he said, and gave the lever a mighty kick. The trapdoor swung open with a crash and John Harkin dropped through into the void until halted by the rope around his neck.

As the noose slowly tightened, his body began the fight for life, gasping for the life-giving air that his heart craved. His body thrashed and convulsed within the confines of the opening into which he had fallen, his legs kicking against the platform. His face reddened and his tongue protruded from between the lips that were already beginning to turn blue. His eyes bulged until it seemed impossible that they could stay within their sockets. He made no sound other than the sounds of his shin-bones bones cracking as he kicked against the platform.

Those people at the very front of the crowd heard the sound of water as his bladder lost control and urine soaked his trousers and trickled off the toe-ends of his boots.

'He's pissed himself,' someone shouted. 'He's gone and pissed himself.' The shout could be heard plainly as the crowd fell silent and a hush slowly descended on the market place. No-one had expected this. This was not justice, this was the worst form of vengeance. The man may have deserved to die but not like this, not in this way. A shocked woman near the platform began to cry and her sobs could be heard all around. Then a single voice was heard. 'Shame, shame on us,' and the cry was repeated by others.

The Ropeman knew that he had overestimated the feelings among the crowd. These were honest folk who worked hard and played hard but they were not as callous as city crowds he had dealt with in the past. The hanging had gone badly wrong. The mood had changed. He was now aware that he should be concerned for his own safety. This could really get ugly for him.

The Sergeant, sensing the animosity from the people toward the Ropeman, stepped forward and held up his arms.

'Stay back,' he ordered, 'stay back and let the man do his job.'

'No-one deserves to die like that, we're not savages.'

But it was too late to retrieve the situation, and the hanging took its course until John Harkin's heart stopped and his body stilled and there was no sound now except the creaking of the sisal rope as the body swung gently in the faint breeze. It had taken but a few minutes to take his life.

Under orders from the Sergeant, the Ropeman and the Militiamen quickly retrieved the body and placed it in a box waiting in the haycart, before it was hastily driven away in the direction of the gaol.

The Ropeman made a hasty escape as the attention of the crowd was on the haycart, creeping into the church and out the other door. He crossed the street and entered the Temperence Hotel. Only then did he give a sigh of relief.

On the other side of the square Amelia Lambert sat in her favourite chair staring at nothing in particular. She was upset and stunned by what had occurred below her windows. She had closed the curtains until the room was in semi-darkness but she could still hear the people out in the Square who had not already made their way elsewhere. No-one would forget what had occurred on this day.

CHAPTER 16

Exton, Devon
1822

'I think this must be the place.' The driver brought the horse and trap to a halt alongside a gateway into a well-kept cottage garden. He had never been this far out of Exeter before but had followed the given instructions explicitly. He turned around to look at his passengers. 'What do you think?'

'You're probably right,' the man said, but made no move to alight. He wasn't looking forward to delivering the news. He glanced at his companion but she was staring at the cottage, ashen faced.

'Do you want me to go and ask?' the driver enquired.

'No, but thank you,' the man answered, 'this is something we need to do ourselves. I would appreciate it though if you would wait out here for us. We are on the kind of business which needs no interruptions.'

With a heartfelt sigh he stepped down from the trap and turned to assist his companion to descend. They walked with little enthusiasm to the front door and he gently knocked. The door was opened almost immediately by a woman who could not possibly be the one he sought.

'I am sorry to bother you,' he said softly, but I am looking for a Mr and Mrs Harkin, 'I have news for them.'

'That would be my mum and dad you would want.' For the first time he heard the low hum of conversation from within. It sounded like two men. 'You say you have news for them. May I ask what the news is about?'

'It's about their son John.'

'News about my brother, now that is a rarity. Please come in, Mum and Dad are in the kitchen.' She turned to lead the way, took a step and then suddenly turned to face them again. She studied their faces in silence. 'It is not good news that you bring, is it?'

'Not good news, no. In fact the worst.'

'Please. Please don't tell me that he is dead. Please not that.' The man averted his gaze, not ready yet to face what he knew was coming. A man's voice called from the inner room.

'Lizzie, who are you talking to?'

Lizzie couldn't answer and then there was the sound of a chair scraping on a stone floor and a man appeared at the end of the tiny hallway, filling the doorway to the kitchen.

'What is it, Lizzie? What is going on?' Gaston Portier did not immediately recognise his former commanding officer but John White knew him straight away.

'George Porter, as I live and breathe. I often wondered what had...' He paused, remembering why he was here. 'I have news of John Harkin. Bad news, I am afraid.' He and Mary MacDonald were ushered into the kitchen, a bright, homely room which smelt of fresh bread.

*

They had drank the teapot dry several times during the telling of the story of the trial and the subsequent hanging of their son and brother. As the details emerged there were sobs and tears from the women and muted swearing from the men. Mary told everyone of how she had met John and their instant attraction and their plans for the future which brought more tears and hugs.

Leaving the women to make even more tea the three men took a turn around the back garden, each lost in his own thoughts. They came upon a settle, placed so that it gave a good view of the surrounding fields. They took a seat and James Harkin took to absent-mindedly filling his pipe. After a while he turned to John White.

'Do you think that my John killed the boy?'

'In all honesty, no. I spoke to John before the trial and he told me all he knew. I believed him then and I still believe his story now.'

'Then why did he confess?'

'After the trial I spent a long time with John, in fact most of the night, and he assured me that the confession was a lie, and the confession as told by the Sergeant did not ring true with me either. I think he made up the confession because he knew the Jury were wavering. Furthermore, I think the Magistrate and the Judge also knew he was lying but they let the story stand and it was entered as evidence. Between them they led the Jury up the garden path. They desperately needed a conviction, a scapegoat, and your John was it.'

'And did he die bravely, was he in pain at the end?'

John White cast his mind back to the hanging. It seemed like an eternity ago but was less than a week and a half. He looked James Harkin in the eyes.

'You knew your son better than I. He died with all the dignity that he showed in life, and I don't believe he was in pain at the end, no,' John White lied, but held the man's eyes as long as he could before he was forced to look away as he remembered the manner of the death throes of this man's son. 'The night before the death of your son we spent time talking about things. John told me that through his dark days after being shot and discharged from the Navy, he had come to understand himself fully. He thought that he had been searching for something all his life without knowing exactly what it was he sought, but when he met Mary he knew he had found it. She made him happy as he had never been before and she made him, somehow, feel complete for the first time ever. He was looking forward to marrying her and raising a family and growing old together, but sitting in that cell he knew that his dream was shattered and he found that difficult to comprehend and deal with. In the final hours of his life, I think he was a broken man in heart and soul.' James Harkin stifled a sob.

'One last question before we go inside. Where is my boy buried? Has he a grave? Did they at least give him a Christian burial?'

This time there could be no lies.

'There was no funeral or service of any religious nature and as far as I know, no-one had the opportunity of saying a prayer over him. I am not aware of the exact location of your son's grave,' he paused, 'but I do know that he is buried in unconsecrated ground, probably in the yard at the gaol.'

James Harkin took John White's hand.

'I would like to thank you, sir, for all that you did for my son throughout his ordeal. You have proved to be a true friend to him and us. You are welcome in my house at anytime.' He turned and walked slowly away. Frenchie made to follow him but John White held him back.

'You have not said much, George, but I know you. What are you thinking?'

'I think it is good that you cannot read my thoughts. As to what I intend to do, I have no more idea than you have. I need to consider things.'

'Can I say one thing to you? Whatever you decide to do please consider everyone around you who loves you. You have a wife and children to consider. Please, I beg of you, don't bring any more heartbreak and misery down on these good people. They have had enough. Can you let the matter rest?'

'I hear what you say and I shall remember your advice. Come, enough. Let's go inside.'

*

Lizzie forced herself to prepare some food but then found that no-one had any appetite. George broke open a few flagons of cider, of which the driver of the coach had had his fair share along with the leftover bread and cheese. Eventually the conversation came to a stuttering end and everyone was left with their own thoughts, to be disturbed by the driver, who, being worried about the lateness of the hour and the gathering dusk, knocked at the door and, not knowing the nature of the visit, asked if they would be much longer.

The Harkins tried to persuade Mary to stay over for a while.

'After all,' said Lizzie, 'if such a terrible thing had not happened you would now be part of our family, and I would like to get to know you better.'

Mary took Lizzie's hands in hers.

'I would love to get to know you better as well. Already I think of you as a friend, but I miss my mum and dad and I feel the need to be at home, in familiar surroundings. But I will write to you and maybe, in the future I could come back and stay with you for a while. Would that be possible?'

'It would be such a pleasure to have you visit. I am heartbroken because it took such a tragedy for us to meet. Please write to us, tell us how you are at least.' They held each other's hands and knew that they would have to wait to see what the future held for them.

They climbed aboard the trap and, amid much waving and shouts of goodbye, they were gone as the driver urged his horse into a fast pace in the gloom.

PART III

REDEMPTION

CHAPTER 1

London
1823

Mister Henry Goldsmith strode confidently into the breakfast room of the hotel and surveyed the scene. There did not appear to be a spare seat anywhere. Immediately, he was aware of a waiter in a starched white jacket alongside him.

'I am sorry, sir,' he said, 'it may take a few minutes to find you a table. The hotel is fully booked for the race meeting and it seems that all of the guests have slept late and want breakfast at exactly the same moment.' He made to walk away but was stopped by an arm placed on his.

'That table there.' Henry Goldsmith pointed to a table set against the broad windows. 'I would like to sit there if I may.'

The waiter looked dismayed. The table he had indicated was already occupied by a lady sitting alone and gazing contentedly at the view.

'But sir, the table is already occupied.'

'Would you at least try for me?' The waiter walked away, weaving his way between the tables, giving Goldsmith the chance to study some of the guests. He was back in moments.

'If you would follow me please, sir.' He retraced his steps between the tables until they reached a table with a good view of the street through the picture windows. A woman was about to vacate the table even though it was obvious to Goldsmith that she had not finished eating. He studied her face. It looked thunderous, if it was possible for such a strikingly handsome face to be so.

'Excuse me, madam, it seems that you are still in the middle of breakfast. Is there something wrong?' he asked.

She studied him before answering.

'Only if you call being told to change tables in the middle of a meal because you happen to be sitting at a table that is reserved, even though there does not seem to be any visible sign that in fact this table is taken. I am being moved to a table over there,' she indicated with her hand the far corner, 'next to the kitchen door.' She waited for his reaction, which wasn't slow in coming.

'I agree with you entirely,' he said, 'it hardly seems fair. I will take the table by the kitchen. Please, carry on with your breakfast.' He beckoned the waiter, who had retreated several yards whilst this conversation went on, closer.

'I will take the other table, this lady should remain here. Or...' He suddenly had a thought and turned back to the woman. 'Are you expecting anyone to join you for breakfast?' She shook her head. 'I too am eating alone. Perhaps we could share this table, I hate eating alone. My name, by the way, is Henry Goldsmith, recently returned from the Americas.'

'Well, Mister Henry Goldsmith, perhaps you had better sit down and we can get on and eat.' She held out her hand to him. 'Amelia Lambert, recently arrived in London from my home in Gloucestershire.' She softly squeezed his fingers, and he gave her a smile which was so broad it lit up his entire face.

The waiter was hovering, wringing his hands.

'Sir. Is everything to your satisfaction now?'

'Very much so, thank you.' He had noticed the gold band that the woman wore on her right hand, not the left. Probably a widow, he thought.

'Are you ready to order then, sir?'

'Eggs Benedict I think, with coffee and toast, and take Mrs Lambert's food away and bring a fresh plate.'

Mr Henry Goldsmith, not the name he had been born with but a name he had adopted on his return, had sailed from Liverpool bound for a new life in America already a fairly rich man. This was back in 1810, he was middle aged, and relished the challenges that a new country would throw at him. He found that everything about his new country was huge, geographically, socially and economically. The population was expanding at an enormous rate and, for anyone with the imagination, the opportunities were huge also. In the decade that he lived and worked there he prospered and his fortune multiplied at a staggering rate without, it seemed, having to do much more than he had been doing in England.

Life was good but despite that he always felt that something was missing, and the pull of the old country, some would call it homesickness, was dragging him back. When he returned he brought with him a wealth of experience and a solid trunk full of gold. Both he and his friend and employee, who had sailed to America with him, returned much changed from when they had left.

When the food arrived he busied himself buttering toast and dipping it into his eggs. He seemed to be famished and savoured every bite. She watched him with a smile on her face.

'Are you enjoying your breakfast, sir?' she asked, between mouthfuls of her own food.

'Best meal of the day,' he stated, 'especially when returning from a brisk walk around the park.'

'Is that something you do often, then?'

'It's a habit I picked up in America, where they seem to lead a more active life than is the norm in England, especially, it seems, in London.'

They chatted on as the time slipped by and the breakfast room emptied of guests. He told her he had been in America for almost a dozen years but had grown weary of the hustle and bustle of the excolony and, dare he say it, he was homesick for England, but now that he was back he had learned that he could be just as lonely anywhere. She described the wedding that had brought her to London, the wedding of a much younger sister of her dead husband who had been killed serving in Spain. She told him that she now lived a pleasant but rather dull life in a small market town in the west of Gloucestershire, where she had good friends and some family around her.

'Family is important and good friends too. I learned many years ago from a good friend of mine, that if you use your wealth to help others then the rewards are enormous, but I still find it very difficult to make friends. I find some people tiresome in the extreme but that is probably my failing rather than theirs.'

She was warming to him, found him easy to talk to. She asked mischievously, 'And am I included in that category?'

'That's a very leading question,' he answered. He pretended to think hard, rubbing his chin with his hand. 'No, I don't think that you are in that category at all.' In truth he found her fascinating and was already wondering how he could see more of her. His ruse to share a breakfast table with her had worked to perfection.

'Have you anything planned for the rest of the day?' he asked innocently.

'I thought I would take advantage of my time here and do some shopping. See the latest trends. I am afraid that fashion in my little town is months, if not years, behind London. Not that I am bothered all that much, I prefer to dress for comfort these days. What about you? Have you plans for today?'

'Do you know London well, then?'

'Well I know my way around if that is what you mean. My late husband and I lived here for several years when he was attached to the peacetime garrison here. Why do you ask?'

'I find the city much too big and much too confusing. Yesterday, I had planned to visit The Tower of London and Tower Bridge, which I have been told are well worth a visit, but I am afraid I became hopelessly lost and even had to take a cab to get back here, I'm ashamed to say. I suppose that I'm still just a small-town man at heart despite all the travelling I have done.' He looked suitably crestfallen.

'Don't feel bad about yourself,' she smiled and reached out her hand to touch his arm, 'it is so easy to lose your way in these narrow streets.'

'I beg of you though, please don't tell anyone else.'

'Of course not. May I make a suggestion? What if I show you around? We could take in the sights.'

'What about your shopping?'

'There is nothing I really need. I was only filling in time until the coach for home leaves tomorrow morning.'

A man dressed for the outdoors approached their table but stopped several yards away until Henry Goldsmith beckoned him nearer.

'What news?' he enquired.

'I thought you would be interested in this article.' He laid a copy of the *Financial Times* on the table. It had been opened and folded to reveal an article on one of the inner pages. Amelia, reading upside down was only able to make sense of the heading.

'So far so good. What has happened in the markets?'

'The shares are already down eleven per cent. My guess is that they will fall a few more points before stabilising.'

'Sell ten thousand, then. Wait until you think the time is right and then buy fifteen. I leave it in your hands, for now.'

The man left without a word, heading for the door to the street. Amelia was curious.

'Would you mind if I asked what that was all about?'

'A bit of a game really. A newspaper editor who owes me a great deal, was kind enough to print this story.' He passed the paper across the table. She read the few lines.

'But it says here that Alabama Cotton Company is on the verge of going under and yet you instructed that man to buy more shares, if I am not mistaken.'

'The man to whom you refer is my trusted employee and friend Richard, probably the only friend I have got in England at the moment, and as for the newspaper story, it is all a fantasy but the market reacted in exactly the way that it always does. People are afraid to lose money.'

'And you're not, I suppose?'

'I never gamble with money I cannot afford to lose, and beside which, I have promised that any profit made from this little escapade will go to a very good cause.' He looked at her and recognised the scepticism in her expression.

'And what good cause might that be?' she asked.

'I can see that you are doubting me,' he said.

'We are talking about a lot of money here,' she countered. 'I happen to know of that company and each share is worth sixteen shillings.'

'As my friend taught me, the only way to enjoy great wealth is to share your wealth with others. The rewards are worth all the money in the world. I have no doubt that he has passed on by now for he was very ill the last time I met with him, but I shall never forget his words. It was at a time of great upheaval in both our lives and the last words I heard him say were 'it's too late. All too bloody late.' I hope that he did not die thinking such thoughts.'

'So what are you intending to do with the profits, if there are any?'

'Without any doubt there will be profit and plenty of it, enough to fund my new project.'

'I am intrigued to know what this project is.'

'I could show you.'

For a man who professed to getting lost he seemed to know his way around quite well. They reached a part of the city where the squalid streets narrowed, where the buildings almost touched at the upper levels and daylight merely served to light the way between the filth and effluent that moved sluggishly down the centre channel of the cobbled lanes. Suddenly they entered an area where the decrepit houses and shops had been demolished, leaving a broad square which was littered with rubble and building materials. The place was a hubbub of activity. Men rushing here and there, carrying heavy loads or pushing barrows but all intent on what they were doing.

'This is my project,' he said, holding both arms aloft to encompass the whole area. Amelia was perplexed.

'But what is actually happening here?' she queried.

'An effort on my part to give local people some hope.'

'I can see something is going on but what?'

'Over there,' he pointed to where a gang of men were laying bricks, 'will be the school,' he said, 'and all around will be new houses. Well-built houses that do not let in water and which will be warm and have sanitation, and there will be shops and a doctor.'

'Are you telling me that you are paying for all this?'

'Yes, but not just me. Unknowingly the rich people of London are paying as well, and the workers are paying with the only thing they have to offer, their labour.'

'So you will become a landlord, then, and charge rent and become richer than you already are.' She was disappointed. She had expected something other than this. 'I think I would like to return to the hotel.' The tone of the conversation had suddenly turned icy. He studied her face, not really understanding what had gone wrong.

'As you wish,' he said, his tone as icy as hers. They did not speak to each other until they reached their destination and then it was only to say goodbye.

CHAPTER 2

London
1823

Amelia Lambert approached the front desk and was greeted with a huge smile from the man stationed behind it. She tried to return his smile but found it impossible, smiling was the last thing on her mind. She had slept very little but that was not the cause of her bad mood. She felt badly misled and more than a little foolish. How naive she had been the previous day. She had always been the same, always thinking and looking for the best in people but, despite all the disappointments and the many times she had been let down, she still kept her faith in humanity.

'Could you prepare my account, please? I will be leaving on the midday coach for Oxford.'

'We will be sorry to see you go, Mrs Lambert. I hope you have enjoyed your stay with us.'

'I would say it is the most comfortable and friendly hotel I have had the pleasure to stay in, but it is a shame about some of your customers. I am going into breakfast, I will not be long.'

Fifteen minutes later she was back at the desk to be met with the same beaming smile but no bill.

'There is no charge to you, Mrs Lambert. The hotel will not charge friends or guests of Mr Goldsmith.'

'I am no friend of Mr Goldsmith,' she bristled, 'I insist on paying my own way.'

'But I cannot charge you, Mrs Lambert, it is company policy.' The smile had faded ever so slightly.

'I am afraid that I must insist. May I speak to the owner, or at least the manager, about this matter?'

'Certainly, madam,' but he made no move to fetch anyone.

'Well, are we to stand here all day smiling at each other?'

'You are speaking to the owner, or at least one of them,' he said.

'But you are a...' She stopped herself just in time. She had been on the very verge of insulting the man. She was flustered and it showed. 'I am sorry.'

'No need to worry, if you have a minute I will explain everything.' He gestured for her to follow him. He led the way to the seating area and indicated that she should take a seat. He sat opposite.

'A little while ago,' he began, 'the hotel got into terrible trouble due to mismanagement. All the staff were given notice. However, we were saved by a gentleman, who having stayed here knew of our dilemma. He bought the hotel.'

'You are speaking of Mr Goldsmith?'

'Yes.'

'Then Mr Goldsmith owns the hotel?'

'In a manner of speaking, yes. But in another way, no.'

'How can that be?'

'Mr Goldsmith called us all together, from the cleaners to the handymen, the cooks and the maids and the front of house. Almost four hundred of us in total. He told us that we were to run the hotel for ourselves and we would sink or swim by our own efforts. He told us that he was convinced that we could make a go of it, maybe even make it into the best hotel in London. He had put the hotel in a kind of trust and issued ten thousand shares. Each year we would all receive five shares until they had all been distributed and then between us we would own the hotel outright.'

'Are you telling me that he has nothing to do with the running of the hotel? That he takes none of the profits or a salary of any kind?'

'That's exactly what I am telling you, yes. As a group we set the levels of wages paid and all the profits will be re-invested in the business. Mr Goldsmith takes nothing, but we insisted that he and any guests he has will never pay a penny to stay here. It is the least we can do for a man who has been our benefactor and saviour.'

Like the solving of a complex puzzle, it was all making sense to Amelia now. She could now see why the staff all seemed so happy in their work, why there were smiles everywhere, why nothing was too much trouble, why they were so courteous to the guests and each other. They were working for themselves. The man was still talking.

'I understand that Mr Goldsmith has turned his attention to doing something similar down by the east-end docks but this time it involves housing. I understand that the people there are building their own community, houses and schools and medical care all at Mr Goldsmith's expense.'

Amelia lowered her head. She was in turmoil and the thoughts swirled around in her head. How could she have been so stupid? Why did she not give the man a chance to explain fully? She had jumped to the conclusions and had labelled him wrongly. It was not the first time she had been guilty of this. She was much too headstrong for her own good, and look where it had got her this time. He would probably label her as a stupid woman and would want nothing more to do with her, and, now that the truth of the matter was out, she did so want to see him again even if it was just to apologise.

CHAPTER 3

Mr Henry Goldsmith

London
1823

He returned to the hotel just before two o'clock and made his way directly to the dining room. He hoped he had not missed lunch for it had been a long morning. First the meeting with the other trustees of his east-end project, followed by a protracted visit to the site to monitor progress. But for the first time ever his heart had not been in it. Everyone could see that his mind was elsewhere.

He took a seat in the corner furthest from the dining-room door and ate his lunch alone. Each mouthful may as well have been cardboard for the enjoyment he took from the food as he methodically chewed and swallowed.

He finished his food and went out to the foyer where the sign for the bar-room took his attention. He altered course. A pint or two would wash his lunch down nicely now, and hopefully help him forget the last day or two.

His thoughts were interrupted by the sound of his name being called from the front desk.

'A letter for you, Mr Goldsmith, sir.' The man took a letter from the pigeon holes behind him and handed it over.

He found a seat in the bar-room and was settled behind a frothy pint before he opened the envelope. His heart missed a beat as he saw that it was signed by Amelia Lambert. He read the letter quickly and then read it again, more slowly this time, although his heart was now racing away inside his chest.

Dear Mr Goldsmith,

I hope that you will not think it too forward of me

to write to you in this manner but I felt I had to,

before I left the city and made my way home.

I owe you my profoundest apologies, sir, for

behaving in such a despicable manner towards you.

This morning I was informed of the truth of the

matter both with regard to the hotel and your

project in the east-end and I was ashamed of myself

when the truth was revealed, but relieved also

that my first instincts about you, which were all

favourable, were right all along.

I can understand if you are angry with me as you

have every right to be. It has always been a

failing of mine that I am quick to judge. Too quick

at times as I have now found.

I would have liked to have got to know you better

but I am afraid that because of my actions, that

may now never happen. However, if it were ever

to come about that you find yourself in the

vicinity of Coleford in Gloucestershire, you will find

a warm welcome in my home.

I would have apologised to you in person and I

waited as long as possible but the coach to Oxford

leaves at exactly midday. I could not let it leave
without me as it is imperative for me to be back
in Coleford in three days from now, as I too have
a project in hand.
Even if we never meet again my best wishes and
my deepest admiration for what you are
attempting to achieve go with you.

Yours Sincerely
Amelia Lambert.

Henry Goldsmith laid the letter down on the table and stared into space for a few minutes before picking it up and reading it again. He wanted to memorise every word.

Half an hour later he was aware that his friend Richard had placed another foaming glass before him and taken a seat directly across the table. Richard took a long swallow from his own glass and smacked his lips.

'Penny for them,' he said.

Henry pushed the letter across the table towards his friend.

'What do you make of that?' he asked as his friend finished reading.

'What should I make of it?'

'If you were me what would you do about it?' The two men studied each other. After a while Richard spoke.

'If I were you and you were me then I would not be sat where you are now.'

'Where would you be?'

'I **would** be halfway to Oxford. I saw you with her yesterday and I have seen you today without her and I cannot, for the life of me, understand why you let her go. It is obvious to everyone that you are smitten, and she as well.'

'Right, that's it then. Will you go with me or would you rather stay here in London?'

'Gloucestershire is a place I have not visited or ever thought I would visit, but I understand they make good sausages there and a very flavoursome cheese. You know that I am partial to both so the answer to your question is, when are we leaving?'

CHAPTER 4

Forest of Dean
1823

'Where are you gents heading then?' the man enquired.

Henry Goldsmith couldn't tell if the landlord was truly interested or just making small-talk.

'Why do you ask?'

'We don't get all that many travellers passing this way. The coaches pass by but very rarely stop. I suppose we are a bit off the beaten track.'

Henry decided that the man was just being friendly.

'We are heading for Coleford. I need to be there as soon as possible, preferably by eight o'clock tomorrow morning.'

'Will you be needing an early breakfast then, before you head on up into bandit country?'

'Bandit country? Why do you call it that? Are there still bandits around here?' At the end of the war with France gangs of out of work military men roamed the countryside robbing the rich and unwary but Henry was under the impression that they had all been caught and dealt with. The landlord's voice took on a conspiratorial tone.

'No, not really, but it is a myth that the Foresters like to persist with. They think it tends to keep strangers and the law away and, in a way, they could be right. But I have always found the people hereabouts to be kind to a fault and loyal to their friends, but they make very bad enemies.'

Henry and his friend Richard had caught the first available coach out of London heading west. They had made good time to Oxford and the following day had reached the city of Gloucester. Here the difficulties began. Coaches out of town heading into the Forest of Dean were infrequent to say the least. The next coach which could take them to their chosen destination would not be leaving for another two days. There was a coach, with seats available heading out to Hereford, but they would need to leave the coach at Huntley and take the lesser used road west. Not wishing to lose any time hanging about in Gloucester, they boarded the Hereford-bound coach and arrived in the small village of Huntley. For what seemed like an exorbitant amount of money they managed to purchase two half-decent horses and began the last leg of their journey. Making reasonable time they reached Mitcheldean as it began to get dark, and found shelter in the George Inn.

It was on the verge of dawn when they left the inn and headed up the hill away from the town. Henry had allowed plenty of time to travel the rest of the way. They had enjoyed a hearty breakfast of bacon and sausage and being well fortified, they were in good spirits.

The hill climbed for nearly a mile and before the summit the horses were blowing. They dismounted and walked to the top before mounting again. From there it was downhill and, if they believed the directions given to them by the landlord, the road would continue like this for another mile before levelling off for a way before another downhill stretch would take them into the hamlet of Brierley, which had been described as the halfway point of the journey. Through the hamlet the road dropped away again until they would be confronted with a climb that would require more walking. Half a mile of walking would see them on another piece of level track until they would eventually drop the final mile into Coleford.

Reaching the bottom of the gradient they dismounted. Here two roads crossed at right angles and a finger-post stood at the left edge of the road they were on. Lydbrook to the right, Parkend to the left and Coleford straight ahead. In the valley they were still in deep shadow but there was still enough starlight to make out the lettering. Up ahead they could see the treeline against a rapidly lightening sky, the tops of the trees already bathed in sunlight. It promised to be a fine day.

They walked in silence, saving their breath for the climb, Henry deep in thought of what he would say to Amelia when they met. Now that he was this close he was getting nervous. What would his reception be like? How would she react to seeing him again? They allowed the horses to walk on the very edge of the road where there was enough young grass to make the going softer. Their steel-clad hooves made hardly a sound. Suddenly Richard stopped dead in his tracks.

'Did you hear that?' he asked nervously. He found being out in the open like this without any sign of habitation slightly off-putting.

'Hear what?'

'That. There it is again.'

Henry stood and listened intently. He could hear nothing except the rustling of the new leaves and a few birds.

'There. It's coming from over there.' His companion indicated an overgrown and obviously little-used cross track that disappeared between the trees off to the left. 'Can't you hear it? It sounds like a child.'

At last the sound reached Henry.

'Probably a small animal of some kind.' He had been told that the woods hereabouts were full of deer and wild boar. Both men stood still waiting for the sound to repeat again, but when the sound came it was not the one they had been expecting but the unmistakable sound of a man and, by the sound of it, an angry man at that. Both men looked at each other in the gloom. Something was not right here.

'Let's take a looksee.' Henry led the way after leaving the horses with reins dangling.

They made their way gingerly along the track avoiding the brambles that tried to snag them, until they were some forty yards in. There was a flash of light up ahead, rapidly extinguished but it had been enough to pinpoint the source of the noises they had heard. Henry turned to his friend and whispered, 'I think it's a wagon of some kind and there's someone underneath it.'

A man suddenly emerged from under the wagon dragging a small girl after him. He stopped dead when he saw the two men. It would have been difficult to decide who was the most shocked. The girl was naked and the man wore only a pair of skivvies, but he was carrying a vicious-looking knife which he pointed at Henry.

'Fuck off,' he growled, 'keep your noses out of what doesn't concern you.' The girl tried to pull away and he turned and landed a punch to the side of her head that sent her flying, but only as far as the rope tied around her ankle would allow. He turned his attention back to Henry.

'Right, then,' he said. 'Which one of you wants it first?' Henry turned to his companion.

'It seems that we have a situation here,' he said.

'Aye. Nothing I can't handle though.' As though by magic a billy-club appeared in his right hand and he stepped forward confidently. He had been in many a skirmish and he had studied knife fighting with the experts. He feinted left then right, tempting his opponent to come for him and make the first move, and when the move came he was ready. He turned his body away from the knife thrust and it slipped harmlessly by, but the billy-club did not miss its target. With a resounding thud and the unmistakable sound of breaking bone he brought the club down on the arm of his assailant, who screamed in agony, dropped the knife from his suddenly lifeless hand and fell to his knees. Richard stepped forward quickly, picked the knife up and passed it to Henry, at the same time giving the knifeman a hefty shove which pushed him all the way to the ground. He knelt down beside the man.

'Who are you?'

'Bollocks, mind your own business. Look what you've done to me arm. I'll have the law on you, see if I don't.' The man was still defiant.

'Tell me or I might have to hurt you a bit more.' He grasped the man's injured arm and gave it a twist which brought another scream of agony from the man. 'I could go on doing this all day but I don't think you would like that much. Now, is the girl yours? Is she a relative?' He gripped the man's arm again ready to give it another twist.

'Course not. She's just a little piece of fun I picked up on my travels.' Richard glanced at Henry who was now kneeling by the girl.

'I think we had better take them into town and get this sorted properly.'

They found the girl's scraps of clothing under the wagon and she slipped on her dress herself, all the while keeping a wary eye on the three men. It was obvious that she was terrified and in shock and didn't trust any of them to come too close to her.

The man was loaded aboard the wagon and secured with his own rope. He was no longer in any state to resist and sat morosely staring at his boots, the only piece of clothing they had allowed him to have. The girl sat up front with Richard, staying as far from him as possible and looking like she would run away at the slightest provocation.

They enquired of the first person they saw on the way down into town and received directions to the gaol.

CHAPTER 5

Coleford
1823

Sergeant Watkins was out of town but the Constable who had been left in charge of the gaol, being a bright young man, quickly sized up the situation and took charge. The wagoner was transferred to a cell until he could be questioned and, seeing that the young girl was in a distressed and poorly state, took himself across the Gloucester road to the house of Mrs Thomas. She would be just the person to comfort the girl, being a mother to eight children herself, all under the age of fifteen. She arrived at the gaol with a young child on her hip and another clinging to her skirts.

The constable had also sent one of her older children for the barber with a message that there was a man in custody needing medical attention.

'You poor little mite,' she cooed to the girl and gathered her up in a huge hug. The girl clung to her as though her life depended on it and buried her face in the woman's embrace. 'Whatever have they done to you? Come with me, my dear, I have some breakfast on the table. Are you hungry?' she was heard to say as they disappeared out the door.

The wagoner was brought from the cells and while they waited for the barber to arrive they began to question the man but without any success. He was refusing to say a word. The barber came ambling up to the gaol with a dour expression on his face. One of these days he would get paid for all the time he spent patching up people who had been 'chastised' by the Sergeant, but he was surprised to learn that the Sergeant was away and wondered who had broken the man's arm. To him it had obviously been inflicted by a blow from a blunt instrument. Without a word he began to re-set the prisoner's arm. There was the sounds of bones grinding on each other and stifled moans of pain. Henry and Richard went out to the yard at the side of the building.

'Something is bothering me about this wagon,' Henry said, pointing to the heavy vehicle, 'it doesn't look right somehow. We're missing something.'

'Looks alright to me. It's just a wagon.'

'Let's see what's under that cover, maybe that'll give us a clue as to who he is and what he is doing in these parts.'

They untied a corner of the sheeting and threw it back to reveal some crates and barrels. There were no markings to indicate what the barrels contained, but the crates were stencilled as belonging to a steam engine company in Birmingham.

'There's only one thing to do. Let's go and ask him what's in the barrels.'

They were about to re-enter the gaol when Mrs Thomas hurried across the street to intercept them. She still had the toddler on her hip but the skirt-clinging child was nowhere to be seen.

'How is the girl?'

'Playing in the backyard with the others, right as nine-pence, just as though nothing had happened to her. Tough little bugger if you ask me. Had a bit of breakfast and couldn't wait to get out to play.'

'Has she said anything, where she lives or who she is?'

'Comes from Lydney, she says, name of Truelove off Primrose Hill. She says she is eight, but she seems to be small for her age. The man took her away yesterday, she thinks, and hurt her, if you understand what I am saying. The bastard needs to be strung up if you ask me.' She was quiet for several long seconds. 'I've sent a message to Mrs Lambert asking for help. She'll know what to do. She'll get a message to the Trueloves and get them up here.' She turned on her heel and hurried back across the road as there came the sound of crying from her house. She passed through the open door and the crying stopped immediately. The two men continued into the gaol but Henry was preoccupied, he had forgotten all about Amelia. He needed to get a move on.

'Black powder,' the wagoner said when asked, 'enough black powder to blow half the town to smithereens.' He laughed at the looks they exchanged at this information. 'Don't worry. It won't go bang unless you set fire to it or you introduce it to a detonator. I've been carrying powder for years and I'm still here.'

He refused to answer any more questions until he had had something to drink. The Constable went off to fetch some strong beer, hoping that it might loosen the man's tongue.

Henry also left and headed for the town centre. He asked after Mrs Lambert and was directed to the apartment above the haberdashers. He approached the street-door and rang the bell. He heard the sound of approaching footsteps from within. His heart was beating furiously and for some reason he had trouble getting his breath. The door opened but not by Amelia Lambert. A woman of about thirty stood before him.

'Good morning, sir. Can I help you?'

'Good morning to you also. I would like to speak with Mrs Lambert if I may?'

'I am sorry, sir, but you have just missed her, she left but minutes ago. Can I give her a message when she returns?'

'I don't think a message would suffice, thank you. I will return later. Have you any idea of when she will be back?'

'I wish I had. Sometimes the meetings go on for a long time, but my guess is that she will certainly be back before lunch.'

'Then I'll come back later this morning. Thank you.' Henry was disappointed and relieved all at the same time. *What is wrong with me?* he thought as he turned away and made his way thoughtfully back to the Gloucester road.

The questioning had not gone well and they were no further forward.

'Give me a few minutes alone with him,' whispered Richard. 'I'll make the bastard sing.' Henry brought his mind back to the present. They were sat around the bare scrubbed table in the station house, and something, not just Amelia Lambert, was troubling him. A feeling of familiarity was creeping over him, and it wasn't pleasant. He had a growing feeling that he knew the prisoner, but how could that be? He had been back in the country for less than a year and certainly had had no dealings with wagoners. But the feeling persisted, growing stronger as the minutes passed. At last he could bare it no longer.

'Do I know you? You seem very familiar, but I cannot for the life of me think how that could be.' He asked the question casually, as though it had no importance to him. There was a moment's silence before the prisoner spoke, the first words he had uttered for a good while, almost as though he was only willing to talk to the man who sat opposite him.

'Aye. You know me alright and I know you, and your bastard of a henchman.' He pointed at Richard. 'Nobbler Knowles, the bully and the man who enjoyed beating women. I've known you for a long time, before you put up this front of respectability and your 'holier than thou' attitude. I wonder what the people who know you now would make of the truth?' The answer hit Henry deep in the pit of his stomach. The mention of the name Knowles proved the truth. This man knew them both. Henry searched his mind for a new question, something to shed light on the man's identity.

'I still don't know you,' he said lamely.

'You're not very good at this, are you? In fact you seem to me to be a bit on the slow side. Try using your eyes and your ears and maybe the right questions to ask me will come to you.' The remarks were delivered in a derisory fashion.

The Constable took charge as the questioning staggered into silence.

'Tell us where you live, where you come from.'

'The whole country is where I live. I haven't slept in a bed since God knows when. As for where I came from, why don't you ask him?'

They looked at Henry who could only shake his head. This man was in his memory somewhere, everything about him was trying to tell him something, but he could not drag it out of the recesses of his brain.

'I need some fresh air,' was all he could muster in reply.

CHAPTER 6

Amelia Lambert

Coleford
1823

Amelia arrived home from her meeting to be met at the street-door by her maid in a high state of consternation.

'Something's going on,' she said without preamble. 'I had a message from Mrs Thomas in Gloucester road, you know the one, has all those kids around her, she needs your help urgently. There is a story going around that she has a little girl up there who was kidnapped yesterday from Lydney. I don't know how true that is but it came from Dora who is rarely wrong about these things.'

Amelia knocked at the open door and listened to the sounds of children from within. Mrs Thomas emerged from the scullery and shushed the younger children to be quiet. She spotted Amelia standing at the door and beckoned her in.

'A fine pickle and no mistake,' she said as she began to explain the situation. The children fell silent at the vision of the lady in the fine dress but Mrs Thomas seemed not to notice anything out of the ordinary and put the kettle on to boil as she spoke. 'We need to get a message to the Trueloves and, if you don't mind me saying so, I've got enough to do,' she indicated the children all around her, 'so someone will need to take the girl and look after her until her mum and dad arrive.'

'I'll take the girl with me when I leave, Martha can look after her for a few hours. She can take her shopping. Looks like the girl could do with some new clothes and it will take her mind off what has happened to her. James can borrow the Blacksmith's horse and get down to Lydney as quick as possible. Primrose Hill, you say?'

As she left the modest house with the girl clutching her hand she spotted the man on the other side of the road. He had emerged from the gaol and had his head down, deep in thought. Her heart missed a beat. Mr Goldsmith. What was he doing here? He had not noticed Amelia and stood studying a wagon that was parked in the yard. She took the girl back into the house, asked Mrs Thomas to oblige for a few more minutes then walked slowly across the road, approaching him from the rear. She stood and watched him for a few seconds, she had no idea what to say, her brain seemed to have stopped working. Eventually she spoke.

'A penny for them.'

He spun around and his jaw dropped before he regained some composure.

'Amelia. I didn't hear you approach. You scared me half to death.'

'I hope not. Scared you half to death, I mean.'

They stared at each other for what seemed like an eternity, each trying to gauge how the other might be feeling. The silence began to get awkward for both of them.

'What are you doing here?' It seemed like an inane question but it was all she could think of to say.

'I read the letter you left for me at the hotel.' The words came out swiftly, like a dam bursting. 'I was so sorry that I missed you and had no chance to say goodbye and that you misunderstood me, so I caught the next available coach to Oxford and then Gloucester but then we were stuck and had to buy some horses to get here. We arrived this morning. We would have been earlier but we got held up by a bit of an incident and I have been to your house but I'd missed you, I was going to call again later.'

He had to stop, he was breathless. Amelia took a step forward and gave him a kiss on the cheek. She was smiling now.

'What an adventure,' she said. 'Welcome to Coleford.'

CHAPTER 7

Henry Goldsmith

1823

Henry was staring at the wagon when Knowles found him.

'I've just seen Amelia. She seemed pleased to see me.'

'I can tell that by the look on your face. You have that expression that young children have when you give them sweets.' He looked around. 'Where is she now? I would like to say hello.'

'She has taken the girl back to her apartments. I have arranged to see her later, as soon as we can get this mess cleared up.'

'Well at least you look happier now. You've not really been with us these last few hours.'

'Well I was worried. I kept asking myself, would she still feel the same when she arrived back in her real life or would she feel differently?'

'You know the answer to that question now. Shall we go back inside or are you going to stay out here staring at that wagon? You are in danger of becoming obsessed.'

'There is still something that bothers me about it. It is almost as though it is trying to tell me something.' He walked around the wagon again. 'Let's get that cover all the way off. Have a good look at it.'

They untied all the ropes that kept the cover in place and dragged it back until it fell to the ground.

'Oh my god,' gasped Henry. 'Do you see what I see?'

'I sure do. What a turn up.'

The removal of the cover had revealed writing down each side.

J. DESCHAMPS
GENERAL HAULIER

'We had better get back inside. We have something to work with now.' They were about to go back inside when Henry spun on his heel and went back to the wagon. 'There, I knew something wasn't right. Now that the cover is off I can see it clearly. The proportions are all wrong. Something has been added to the body behind the seat. There, look. Don't you see it?'

His companion had to admit that something was amiss but couldn't quite make out why. Henry walked slowly around the wagon once again.

'There it is, as plain as a pikestaff. That,' he pointed at the tool box, 'does not belong, it's much too big for a wagon of this size.'

He jumped aboard and pulled at the lid of the box. It was securely locked.

'Fetch me a nail-bar or a hammer from the stable. We'll soon see what's inside.'

They prised the lid open and were met with a fetid smell from within. Inside there was another box which they also had to prise open. This time the smell was terrible.

'This must be how he hid the girl as he travelled around. See, it's padded to make it soundproof.'

Richard bent and took a small box from inside.

'What's this then? The box wasn't secured in any way and they opened it to reveal what appeared to be a mish-mash of jumble. They rummaged about in the box but could make no sense of its contents. Perhaps the prisoner would explain what the contents meant. They carried the box back inside the building.

Richard used the last of the second jug of beer to refill the pots. The Constable, as ever, refused a drink but the prisoner had a taste for it. He had already finished a flagon and a half, just as they had hoped.

'What's all this stuff in this box?'

'Just a few mementos, nothing much.'

'Mementos of what?'

'They remind me off all the boys and girls I have known over the years. Some I liked more than others but they were all my friends.'

He picked up an embroidered button.

'She was a sweet little thing. One of my oldest friends, I was sorry to see her go. And this one.' He picked up a petticoat. 'She's still around here, not many miles away.'

'And what about this one?' Henry had picked up a folding knife from among the pile. 'Was it a boy or a girl who carried this?'

'A boy and a tough little bugger at that. Fought me all the way. I couldn't have that, could I? I had to bash him about a bit and use my own knife on him.'

The Constable, who had been watching and listening intently to the exchange between the two men, stepped forward and took the knife from Henry.

'Tell me about this knife. Where were you when you took it from the boy?'

'Round and about. You know how it is.'

The Constable went to the door and beckoned Henry outside. His face was ashen like he had just received bad news.

'God help me I hope I am wrong, but I think I know this knife. See it has the initials C.M. engraved into the handle.' Henry could clearly see the letters scratched deep into the metal. 'A young boy by the name of Charlie Morgan went missing from the town on his tenth birthday. His father had given him a knife like this as a present. He had scratched his sons initials into the handle himself.'

'You think this is the knife and you think we have caught the killer?'

'Worse than that. The Sergeant was convinced that the murderer was a man who had passed through the town on that day. He pursued him and three or four months later he was apprehended making his way back through the area on his way to his home in Devon.' Henry began to get a bad feeling in the pit of his stomach.

'What happened to the man?'

'Despite maintaining that he was innocent he was put on trial right here in the town. Feelings were running high at the time and the Magistrate wanted the people of the town to see justice in action. He was found guilty as charged and sentenced to death. He was hanged right in the centre of town, on the Tump. He didn't die easily. Most of the people will not even speak of that day. I think we hung the wrong man.'

'The first thing we need to do is get to the young boy's father and see if he can identify the knife. If he does, I don't know what can be done to put things right. We need to cross that bridge when we come to it.'

CHAPTER 8

Edwin Morgan

Coleford
1823

Edwin Morgan arrived at the gaol within the hour. He had been working on the new ironworks and had come as quickly as he could. The summons from the Constable meant that something important must have happened in town; something which could not be ignored.

The four men were sitting around the table when he entered the room. The Constable and three strangers. One of the men appeared to be injured and looked dejected.

'Good of you to come, Edwin.' He was greeted by the Constable who seemed to have taken charge. 'We need you to look at something and see if you recognise it.' Edwin was intrigued.

The Constable crossed to a small side-table on which sat a wooden box. He took an object from the box and handed it to Edwin. Edwin gasped and almost dropped the knife as though it was red-hot. The others were watching him intently.

'Where did you find it?' he blurted. 'Where has it come from?'

'You recognise it then?'

'Of course I do, it's the knife I gave Charlie for his birthday. See,' he indicated the initials in the handle, 'those are his initials, I scratched them in myself. How have you got hold of it?'

The Constable looked crestfallen.

'It's a long story. The trouble is I think we've done something awful.'

Henry left the gaol and headed for town again as the others sat to rehash the events of the morning for Edwin. He was hungry, it seemed such a long time since he had eaten breakfast, but he also hoped that he would see Amelia, their meeting earlier had been all too brief. By the time he had eaten a fresh meat pie and returned Edwin had been told everything.

In the silence that had followed Edwin had addressed the prisoner.

'Did you kill my boy?' He did not expect to get an answer but had to ask the question.

The man stared back at him and then, much to their surprise, he said, 'They are going to hang me anyway so I may as well come clean. Yes, I was the one who killed him. You hanged the wrong man in your haste to blame someone, anyone, and to get your revenge. The moment I snatched your boy it was always in my mind that I would have to dispose of him, but it all happened so quickly. He was a fighter, your boy. Your search party almost caught me the following morning, I thought it was all up. If you had gone a few more yards down the track you would have seen me, but once you found the body you thought that was it and retraced your steps. I got out of there as quickly as possible and made my way down to Lydney docks. I never thought any more about it until this morning when these two bastards happened upon me.'

Edwin and the Constable exchanged looks. It was obvious that the man was telling the truth. His story tallied exactly with the events that had occurred. He could not have made it up. Edwin got up from the table.

'What a bloody mess. All that we went through last year and all the time we had the wrong man. What about his family? Look what we put them through. How can we try to put things right? I have to get home and tell my wife, she needs to know before the story gets around town. I don't know how she will take it. Last year she just wanted it all to go away and now here we are going through it again, and her being about to give birth and all.

'What shall I do in the meantime? I can't just sit here.'

'I suggest you get over to the Magistrate and give him a full account. He needs to know.'

'I'll send a message, get him over here, I can't leave the prisoner alone.'

CHAPTER 9

Joshua Deschamps

1823

'Did you know a Louisa Deschamps?' Henry tried to make the question sound as innocuous as he could.

'You know very well that I do. Been to have another look at my wagon, have you? Bet that name came as a bit of a shock, eh?'

'I recall that she had a young boy of her own. Was that you?'

'I hate to admit it, but yes.'

'Do you know that Louisa has passed away these many years?'

'Aye, and good bloody riddance if you ask me. She was never a good mother, she had no idea how to be caring and loving unless, of course, it was to her advantage. But I suppose it wasn't all her fault, someone drove her to be like she was.' He stared Henry straight in the eye. 'I went back to Dover many times over the years, just to see how things were. I was even there when you put her in the ground, but you didn't see me. No sir, Harry-no-Home, that's me, left to fend for himself, no family, no home, not a lot of anything really, but I got by and now it's all over, well and truly.'

'Are you using that as an excuse for what you have become?'

'I make excuses for nothing. I know what I am and don't pretend to be anything other. In the early years I blamed her for everything but as time has passed my feelings have changed. It was never her fault entirely.'

'Who was to blame then?' Henry asked the question but knew the answer before it came.

'She was driven to it, manipulated. She was easily led and was naive enough to believe all the promises. You knew what you were doing when you chose her, didn't you? I bet you and your friends sniggered about her behind her back. You broke her first, got her into a state where she would do anything and then you used her, just to make more money, and what about Dorcas Teague? You ruined her husband and then took everything that they possessed, even their children. I saw it all. All of this is your fault. You robbed and stripped the dignity from all the poor people you came in contact with. My mother was not to blame, you are. You are the evil one here. You are the spawn of the devil.'

Henry was stunned by the outpouring, surprised that the man knew so much. He had had no idea. The Constable was first to speak. He addressed the prisoner.

'You seem to know a lot about this man, how can that be?'

'I have known him since I was a small boy in Dover. My mother was in service and was sent home to have me. She was only a child herself. I was brought up by my grandparents and everything was good until they died and my mother had to return to care for me. This man, this bastard here, was the Money Lender. Times were hard; the war with France was bleeding the country dry and many people turned to him for help. This other bastard was his henchman, his enforcer, and God help you if you fell behind with your repayments. He would take every spare penny and, if the debtor happened to be a woman, much more besides. He carried a club that he used on the men. Many a man suffered a cruel beating from him.'

He paused while he collected his thoughts and then continued.

'My mother was weak and he took the house and everything she owned until she had nothing. He turned her into a whore, a plaything for his rich friends and he pocketed the money she earned. He owned lots of houses in Dover, houses that he had taken from other unfortunates. He lodged my mother in the best one. A house he had taken from a respectable family which had fallen on hard times. The word was that he killed the husband, although his body was never found, took the wife for his own and turned the young girls into whores to work with my mother. They look respectable now, don't they, all done up in their fancy clothes, but I intend that the whole world will know about them before you string me up, as you surely will now.'

The room was filled with a terrible silence.

CHAPTER 10

Coleford
1823

He had reached a decision. Amelia needed to be told before the story reached her through the town gossips. There was no way that he could stop the story spreading, the Constable had heard every word. No doubt he would repeat the story word for word to the Magistrate and to anyone else who would listen and there would be plenty of those.

He had no idea how the woman would react but he knew he needed to put his side of the story first, limit the impact. He had a feeling that all the charm in the world would not help him today.

He approached the street-door of the apartment with leaden feet. He was dreading the next minutes. The bell rang inside and he heard the sound of approaching steps. The door was opened by Amelia herself.

Martha had taken the girl shopping, leaving Amelia alone. Despite herself she spent half her time looking out of the tall windows, craning her neck this way and that to catch a glimpse of the man who had travelled all the way from London to see her. At last she had seen him pass by and then heard the doorbell ringing down below. She raced down the stairs.

'Henry, welcome. Come along in.' She shut the door and turned to face him. He pulled her into his arms and kissed her slowly and gently, fully on the lips. She did not resist but stood on the tips of her toes, raised her arms and wrapped them around his neck. His kiss was sweet and she wanted it to go on and on. Eventually he pulled away but she didn't let him go. She pulled him back to her and this time she kissed him. His arms were around her holding her tightly and with a slight shock she felt the beginnings of his erection pressing against her belly.

Flustered, she pulled away and, pretending that she had not noticed his arousal, led him up the surprisingly ornate stairs to the sitting-room above.

They sat opposite each other in two chairs placed either side of the main window and giving views over the marketplace. A small table laden with tea cups was nearby.

'I need to speak to you on a matter of some importance,' he started the conversation.

'Would you like a cup of tea first?' She had regained some of her composure and her manners.

'I am afraid that I have no appetite for tea.'

This was not how she had envisioned things would be. She understood that the events of the morning had been unusual to say the least but she could see that something else was troubling the man. The encounter in the downstairs hall was all but forgotten now.

'Should I be worried about what we are about to discuss?'

'I can only tell the story. I have no idea what your reaction will be.'

'So, what is it that can be so bad that it has got you in such a state?'

Henry told her about the prisoner and about how he had recognised him from his time in the port of Dover. He told the story as dispassionately as he could, missing out some of the details, but no matter how he dressed the story up it did not sound good. Amelia listened intently but by the time he had finished she was staring out of the window, seemingly miles away. She had heard such stories before in other towns and cities and had no doubt at all that the story was true.

'And is this story true, you don't deny it? You knew each other in Dover?'

Henry could say nothing. He nodded his head in the affirmative.

'All the money that you are spending in London, did you come by it in the same way?' His silence confirmed what she thought.

'This has come as a great shock. I don't know what to say. I was so looking forward to seeing you again and now this. I need time to think. Perhaps it would be best if you went now.' He hesitated but then stood and held out his hand to her. She did not move.

The prisoner was securely locked away and the Magistrate had been and gone. The Constable made his way down to the town to begin his rounds.

Mr and Mrs Truelove had collected their daughter from Martha with promises of payment for the new clothes, settled at a bag of runner beans now and another bag of cooking apples in the autumn, and were on their way tearfully back home.

The sun was setting fast and the story of the day's events were spreading throughout the town quicker that the lengthening shadows.

The church was fully lit and the doors were wide open, it had been a warm day. Amelia stood at her window and watched as, in dribs and drabs, people entered the church. She made up her mind, put on a warmer coat and went out to join them.

The vicar had no sermon or words of comfort prepared and he was not good at speaking verbatim and he stood at the altar not knowing what to do or say. He was a stunned as everyone else at the day's news. Even though the church was reasonably full it was silent except for a few whispered greetings. A man, sat near the back, got to his feet and in a rich tenor began to quietly sing the only hymn he knew:

Abide with me; fast falls the eventide;
The darkness deepens; Lord with me abide;

Others joined him and their voices soared until the church was filled with sound and it spilled out into the square, causing people to stop and look at the church in wonder.

A note was waiting for Henry Goldsmith when he descended for breakfast the following morning.

The story you told me yesterday came as a great
surprise and I feel badly let down and disappointed
in you. I don't know if I can forgive you.
I can see no future in any kind of relationship
between us and therefore I think it would be better
if we did not meet again.
Mrs A. Lambert

The Money Lender ate breakfast in silence then went back to his room and collected his things together. He and Knowles quietly left town unseen by anyone except the Constable who watched them pass by the gaol on the Gloucester road. Four hours later he and his colleague Knowles were entering the city of Gloucester. They did not stay but immediately boarded a coach bound for Oxford.

*

The townspeople wasted no time before they swung into action. The re-burial was the priority and Edwin Morgan insisted that he should be the one to lead the group of men who went to the gaol and exhumed the body of John Harkin.

The vicar had written a fine sermon, the best he had ever written, full of emotion and feeling and he delivered it to packed church before the new coffin was carried shoulder high to the cemetery in the grounds of Newland Church.

It seemed the whole town was there except for one notable exception. Edwin Morgan was at home tending to his wife. Her waters had burst and she was deep into her labour.

When the people returned from Newland they were greeted by the news that she had given birth to a beautiful son. A few weeks later he was baptised Charles Edwin Morgan, for even though he was the youngest child in the Morgan household he was still the eldest son.

CHAPTER 11

Coleford
1823

As the horse clattered to a halt in the enclosed yard of the Angel Hotel a boy sprinted forward from the darkness of the stables and took the reins. The tall man in the long, black top-coat dismounted easily and untied the leather satchel from its place behind the saddle.

'Take good care of him, he is a good friend to me, but I have worked him hard today. He needs a good rub down and some of your best oats. Only the best, mind you. If you do a good job for us then this will be yours.' He showed the boy a shining new shilling piece.

'Don't you worry, sir. I'll make sure that he gets only the best.' He led the horse away, looking tiny alongside such a huge beast.

The man booked a room for one night only and after a light lunch of bread and cheese exited the hotel and proceeded to wander around the town getting his bearings. He felt that he knew the town already. It was exactly as it had been described.

He returned to the hotel and after booking a wake-up call for eight o'clock that evening he went to his room, stretched out fully clothed on the bed and was asleep in minutes.

*

Something had disturbed the Sergeant and brought him back from a deep sleep. He lay still in the darkness and listened for the sound to

357

be repeated. There it was again. It sounded as though someone had left a gate open somewhere and it was swinging to and fro in the breeze. He would never get back to sleep unless he did something about it. He sat up in bed, fully awake.

The sound came again. It sounded like it was the gate into the prison yard, maybe the Constable had forgotten to latch it properly. He got up and went to the window. The downstairs windows were barred but up at this level they could be opened wide. He leaned out and looked up and down the road. There was not a soul in sight. The noise came again and now he was certain that it came from the yard at the side of the gaol.

Grumpily he shoved his feet into his boots and felt his way downstairs. When he went outside the lantern he carried threw dark shadows all around but gave enough light for him to see the gate swinging slowly before contacting the gatepost once again.

He pulled the gate closed but at that precise moment he heard a different sound emanating from within the stable. Someone was in there.

He approached the stable. It was pitch black inside and he became aware of his vulnerability wearing only his skivvies and his boots.

'Who's there?' he shouted. 'Show yourself.' There was no movement from within.

'Come on, show yourself. If I have to come in there and get you it will be the worse for you.' He waited but there was no response. He was about to turn away when he heard the sound again, way at the back of the stalls.

Holding the lantern out in front he advanced.

'I warned you. I'll give you a bloody good hiding when I get my hands on you.' He took two steps into the gloom and something hit him on the back of the head. Hard.

He felt himself being lifted as though by a giant hand until he was dangling in mid-air. Even in his semi-conscious state he felt something being shoved under his booted feet and he was lowered until he was able to take his weight. The rope that had been used to lift him was removed to be replaced by a similar rope placed around his neck and tightened until it took some of his weight. His hands were tied behind his back and a foul-tasting gag had been pushed into his mouth. He tried to shout out but all that penetrated the gag was a low moan.

'So, you're awake are you?' The voice came from behind him and carried an accent that the Sergeant did not immediately recognise.

A tall man dressed in a long top-coat came and stood in front of him. He watched the Sergeant silently as he struggled against his bonds, testing for any weakness. He found none.

'I am going to ask you some questions. You will answer me truthfully and fully. If I suspect that you are holding something back from me I will kick this bucket out from under you.' The man nudged it with the toe of his boot and the Sergeant felt it move. Wobbling frantically, he felt the noose around his neck take up even more of his weight but he managed to keep his balance, just.

'I am going to remove the gag. If you try to shout or make any noise which could be heard outside these walls, then you know what will happen. Do you understand me? Blink your eyes for yes.' The Sergeant blinked his eyes frantically. He was beginning to realise that he was at the mercy of this stranger and wanted to do nothing to anger him. The man reached up and removed the filthy rag which he had found lying on the floor in the stable.

'Who are you? What do you want with me?' he croaked. His throat was dry and the rope was tight.

'Do you believe in ghosts? Do you believe that some people die but never leave this earth until a wrong has been put right?' the man answered. 'You do not know me but I know you. You could say that I am your conscience.' He paused. 'I have been wanting to meet you for a long, long time.' It was quiet in the stable. The Sergeant's nerve gave first.

'Why are you doing this? What do you mean put a wrong right? What have I ever done to you?'

'Oh, you have not wronged me in any way, directly, but you have done terrible things in your life and I am here to call you to account.' He paused. 'We need to get on, your time is ebbing away. Let's talk about John Harkin, you remember John Harkin?'

The Sergeant forgot himself and nodded, almost toppling himself off the bucket.

'You hanged the man here, right in the centre of town.'

'It wasn't just me,' he whined, 'the whole town were in on it, and the Magistrate and the Judge.'

'The Magistrate killed himself late last night. A single gunshot through the mouth. He will no doubt be found where I left him, later this morning. The Judge will suffer a huge heart attack later today after accidentally swallowing a large amount of Belladonna, as will the Ropeman. So, that just leaves you.'

The Sergeant knew now what his fate was to be. The man had given him too much information for him to be allowed to live.

'Did you lie at the trial of John Harkin? Did you lie about a confession he so-say made to you about the killing of young Charlie Morgan?'

'What if I did?' The Sergeant decided to be defiant now that he knew how his life was about to end.

'Your bravado is misplaced. All it has done is deny you the time to make your peace with whatever god drives you. Goodbye, Sergeant, may you rot in hell.'

The bucket bounced off the stall where the man in black had kicked it. The Sergeant dropped the few inches which extended the rope to its full extent and began to writhe in agony.

The man left the stable and returned to the Angel Hotel just in time for breakfast. He did not feel like eating anything but knew that there was still a long day ahead of him so he forced the bacon and sausage down. The stable-lad was well pleased with the shilling that the man gave him. He put it between his teeth and bit down on it just as he had seen the men do and then placed it in his deep pocket. The man left the stable-yard and turned in the direction of Gloucester. By the time he passed the gaol a small crowd had gathered around the gate. He tipped his hat and rode on.

CHAPTER 12

Exton, Devon
1823

The children rushed to the gate when Frenchie arrived home four days later. They were full of questions about where he had been and what he had done there and why he had gone in the early morning without saying goodbye. He waved their questions away and they soon went back to playing hide and seek around the gardens.

After he had downed his first glass of weak beer and had taken a refill, he sat in the garden with his father-in-law on the very same seat that they had sat on when they had talked to John White about John's death.

'Have you news for me?'

'Aye, everything is settled. John now lies in a proper grave in hallowed ground. He can rest in peace now.'

'And the rest, the people who put him to death?'

'You will hear no more about them, they no longer exist in this world. The Judge, the Magistrate or the Sergeant.'

'And the town?'

'The town and its people are much like any other, a pretty place and good people. They have tried to make amends, to make up for the way in which they allowed themselves to be duped so easily. To a man I think they are genuinely sorry for what happened.'

'We can get on with our lives now, then?'

'I think that would be best.'

The old man rose from his seat and wandered off to his favourite place at the very end of the garden where the cultivated land changed to meadowland. He whispered to the faint breeze, 'Goodbye John, goodbye my son.'

CHAPTER 13

Coleford
Eighteen Years Later

Charlie Morgan had grown into a fine young man. Already several inches taller than his dad and well-muscled. He may have been on the first steps of manhood but still retained enough of the mischievous boy about him to make him a real handful for his mum.

The Morgan household had not done well though, through what had turned out to be a long and freezing cold winter. Work had dried up for Edwin and Charlie, who normally worked with his father, sometimes with enthusiasm and sometimes without. Charlie had not the skill in his hands or the imagination to become a top-class stonemason, but it could never be said that he was lazy or idle.

The church had long been completed and the ironworks was in production. No new buildings were being started so that left only minor repair work, which did not carry the rewards of new build.

In these hard times, Charlie would do any kind of work to earn a few shillings to help with the family budget. Today Charlie had heard that Tom Jenkins, the long-time driver for the Corn Exchange, had cried off sick. Charlie rushed down to the town to offer his services.

He was loading the wagon with a dozen sacks of flour bound for the baker in Newland, from the stack inside the Exchange. His next stop would be the Brewery in the Wine Vaults to collect two barrels of best to deliver to the Ostrich Public House, also in Newland. He paused in his work as he heard the rumble of the coach from Monmouth approaching. He wiped the moisture from his face with the red neckerchief he wore loosely tied around his throat. The weather had certainly picked up in this the last week in May, and today was a scorcher.

The coach passed by, slowing as it entered the town. It appeared to Charlie that there was only one passenger, not really unusual because Coleford was only a stop on the way to somewhere else, but this passenger held his attention. She was a girl about his own age and very pretty too. Charlie was always interested in pretty girls whether his age or not.

As the coach passed him their eyes met and to his surprise she held his gaze until the coach passed into the yard at the Angel Hotel.

Charlie finished loading the flour and moved on to collect the beer. He tied the load securely and arranged several gardening implements around the load. With the loading complete it was time for some refreshment and Charlie tarried over the glass of ale that the Master Brewer had offered, making his break as long as possible.

Charlie had travelled less than a mile down the Newland road when he spotted the girl up in front sitting on a low wall. Even from the back it was obvious that it was the girl from the Monmouth coach. She was dressed in a light, floral cotton dress that reached to halfway between her knees and the ground, showing off her slender ankles. Her head was covered with a straw hat decorated with wild flowers and holding her hair in place. At her side rested a bag that was bulging at the seams and over her arm she carried a shawl of some kind. As he drew level he could see that her face had reddened in the heat and she was perspiring.

When he drew level with the girl the horse stopped without being told and bent its head to the grassy verge. She had watched him approach but now her eyes were on her dainty shoes.

'It's a lovely day for a stroll but you look like you are ready to take a lift. Going far, are we?'

'We? What we? I'm perfectly capable of making my own way to where I'm going without your help, thank you very much.'

'Where are you going then?' Charlie had decided to try again, she would be worth winning over.

'That's for me to know and you to find out.'

'Why do you speak so funny?' Charlie wished he had never asked as soon as the words left his lips.

'How have you got the nerve to say I speak funny? Have you never listened to yourself?'

'Look, I'm sorry. We have got off on the wrong foot. Can we start again?'

'No.'

'Alright, I know when I am beaten. I'll bid you good day and hope that you enjoy the rest of your walk.' He flipped the reins and the horse took the strain. As he moved away the girl's eyes lifted and followed his progress. He was rather good looking, she was thinking, despite his accent.

Within ten minutes the horse and cart reached Newland and Charlie began to unload at the Baker's shop.

The landlord of the Ostrich Inn offered Charlie a glass as he did to all his deliverymen, but Charlie declined; even at his young age Charlie knew that it was a bit early in the day for too much strong drink. Instead he made his way across the road to the lychgate that gave access to the church grounds and the cemetery.

He had taken a scythe and a gardening fork from the back of the wagon and these he carried slung over one shoulder, as he made his way to the south-east corner of the grounds. Here the graves were in a sorry state having been neglected over the winter, and now with the mild weather, the weeds had taken over, except for a small patch that contained two graves. Here the grass and weeds were well under control and on each of the graves had been placed a bunch of bluebells, sadly wilted now and in need of changing. Lovingly he brushed the headstones with his hand before laying the fork and scythe aside.

A gentle cough sounded to his right and he turned to face the noise. The girl he had passed on the road stood not many yards away watching him.

Charlie was in two minds whether to speak or not after their previous encounter, but he took the bull by the horns anyway.

'Can I help you?' Then in a placatory tone, 'It can be difficult finding a grave if you are not used to the layout, especially with it being so overgrown and such.'

The girl had spent what seemed like ages wandering around the graveyard but, she had to admit she had not found what she was looking for and at this rate it could take all day.

'I am looking for a grave,' she said lamely.

'Well you've come to right place.' Charlie smiled at her to take the edge off the words. He wondered why he felt compelled to act so stupidly, and to say such stupid things, in front of this girl. 'If you give me a name, perhaps I can help.' *That's better,* he thought, at least he had said something civil.

'It's the grave of my father and I have been told it's here somewhere. His name was John Harkin.'

Charlie was staggered. It was the last name he had expected to hear. All he could do was stand gaping with his mouth open.

'What name did you say?' His voice came out as a croak.

'My father's name was John Harkin.' She said it slowly and clearly. 'Are you deaf as well as stupid?' Her emotions had taken over. She had been planning this trip for many years, filled with a feeling of dread but knowing that she had to see the place where her father rested. She had envisaged many scenarios but they were all forgotten. Instead she now faced the truth.

'Do you know the grave? I won't be messed about.'

Without a word, Charlie stepped aside so that she could see the graves behind him, and held out his hand. He had no idea what to say. The girl approached, staring at the two graves now exposed to her. Her eyes were fastened on the headstones, one in particular.

Here Lie The Mortal Remains Of

JOHN HARKIN

1700 - 1822

A True Man Of Devon

Wrongly Accused

She stood for many long minutes and then slowly turned full circle to take in the scene.

'But I don't understand.' No-one heard her. Charlie had backed away several yards and the words had been spoken very quietly. Eventually she turned to look at Charlie face to face and repeated herself.

'I don't understand. Who has been tending his grave? I expected it to be…' Her eyes were filling with tears. 'Oh, I don't know what I expected. Who around here cares enough for my father to tend his grave in this way? And look at this headstone, who paid for that?' Her head was swimming with questions.

'We all do, care that is. My dad, my mum and the rest of the town, and the headstone cost not one penny.' The girl was crying openly now, the tears rolling down her cheeks and a dripper appeared on the end of her pretty little nose.

Charlie offered her his red neckerchief but she was already pulling a tiny, lacy square of material from her sleeve. She blew her nose loudly and that somehow broke the spell. Another thought struck her.

'Did you come here today to work on his grave?'

'That and my brother's grave, aye.' He pointed to the smaller of the two graves. 'Thought I might as well being as I was coming down here anyway. Most of the townspeople cast their eyes in this way if they are down this way and do a spot of tidying up an' that.'

'Oh my god. But isn't that the boy that my father was accused of killing? They are side by side.'

'That's the grave of my big brother. They are at rest together. It's a long story and I'm not sure that I know all of it, but look, let's sit over there and I'll tell you what I do know, that is if you have the time.'

It was a long story and took ages to tell. They made themselves comfortable on a bench. The girl took off her hat and her blonde hair cascaded down over her shoulders. At that moment Charlie thought that she was the most beautiful girl he had ever seen in all his life, ever.

She had been told about her father by her mother, but listening to this stranger, who had introduced himself as Charlie, telling the same story was a revelation to her. There was no bitterness, no animosity, and she gained a feeling of true remorse and contrition from the town even though Charlie told the story in a simple way unique to young people.

The afternoon passed and the couple found themselves sitting in shadow as the sun crossed the heavens. Only as she felt the chill did they realise how time had flown by. She leapt up from the bench.

'I'll miss the coach back to Monmouth, it'll leave without me.'

Charlie threw the tools into the back of the wagon and they set off in a hurry. Charlie appeared to be chivvying the horse along at its best pace but in reality was holding back on the reins, he wanted this afternoon to go on and on. Rachel Harkin, her own introduction, sat alongside him and was not fooled for one moment, she had been brought up around animals in Hereford and knew when a horse was having an easy time of it.

They eventually reached the town and, as hoped for by Charlie, the coach had just left. She tried to be angry but her heart wasn't in it.

'What shall I do now? I have a few shillings. Is there anywhere around here that can put me up? A boarding house, perhaps?'

'I know just the place. The best boarding house in town. Clean, good food, comfy beds and friendly people.' They began the walk out of town onto Staunton Lane.

'Where are you taking me?'

'To meet my mum and dad.'

CHAPTER 14

Coleford
1844

To the town it seemed that absolution day had arrived at last, and a fine excuse for a party if any were needed. Late June, balmy evenings and bunting hanging from every spare hook, tree, rope or railing. Even the vicar had entered the spirit of the occasion and the church looked a picture, perched on a Tump that was to be the venue for the dancing that would come later. But first there were formalities to go through.

The marriage ceremony, a small family affair, had taken place in the church at Clehonger. It was a beautifully simple affair and the bride and groom had spoken their wedding vows in good clear voices as they had been told to do by anxious parents. Charlie, his mum and dad and his sisters had travelled to Clehonger and planned to return to Coleford with the bride and her mother to celebrate the wedding with all their friends, after a blessing at the church on the Tump. They did not expect the whole town to want to be involved.

As they reaffirmed their love an almost audible sigh went around the church. Charles Morgan and Rachel Harkin were pronounced man and wife for the second time in as many days.

As the celebrations began around the square, Rachel and Charlie slipped away unnoticed. The pony and trap were waiting as the Blacksmith had promised and they made their way down to the churchyard at Newland. Rachel gently placed the posy of flowers that she had carried to her wedding on the grave of her father. She said a prayer whilst Charlie watched. When she turned to face him, he said, 'I do so love you, Mrs Morgan-Harkin,' and he took her in his arms and kissed her. It made no matter to Charlie that Rachel had insisted she retained the name of a father she had never met. To him, one name was as good as any other.

By the time they returned to Coleford the party was in full swing and they joined in with the dancing. It turned out to be a wonderful day as the collective guilt that had been felt by the townspeople was expurgated. Frenchie and Eliza watched the couple as they waltzed around the square. They smiled at each other, happy in the thought that this was history in the making.

EPILOGUE

Forest of Dean
2017

David Harkin increased his pace slightly and pushed on along the well-worn forest track that he used as a training circuit for his long-distance runs. He was well into 'the zone' and was deep in thought. He had felt as though his head was full of cotton wool as he had left the Gloucester Records Office earlier that afternoon and as soon as he had arrived home he had changed into his running gear and was into the woods within minutes.

Running helped him think more clearly, he found, not that tracing his father's family tree needed much thought. He had found it all straight forward but there was a niggling thought at the back of his mind that he had missed something important.

He was an only child. His father had died in a work accident when he was four years old. As far as he could remember his mother had never mentioned his father in his presence. Now his mother had passed away and it was too late to ask the questions that were constantly in his mind.

The County Records showed that his father was also an only child. This was surprising at a time when large families were encouraged and families as large as ten were not uncommon.

When the records indicated that his grandfather was also an only child he thought that he was misreading the records somehow and sought the help of the helpful young lady who had shown him around on his first visit. She however, confirmed what he was seeing. None of them had any siblings.

David thought of the book, *The Last of The Mohicans*, and knew exactly how Uncas would have felt. He was indeed the last of his family line.

ABOUT THE AUTHOR

Michael J Martin, after leaving the Royal Navy, where he served as an engineer settled in the Forest of Dean with his wife, and has two grown up daughters. *The Outcast* is his debut novel.

Unfortunately he did not live to see it published, but at his request his family arranged to continue with this publication as his legacy.

Michael sadly lost his battle with cancer in September 2018.

Printed in Great Britain
by Amazon